Runic Awakening

Books by Clayton Taylor Wood:

The Runic Series
Runic Awakening

Runic Revelation

Runic Vengeance

Runic Revolt

The Fate of Legends Series
Hunter of Legends

Seeker of Legends

Destroyer of Legends

Magic of Havenwood Series
The Magic Collector

The Lost Gemini

The Magic Redeemer

The Magic of Magic Series
Inappropriate Magic

Runic Awakening

Book I of the Runic Series

Clayton Taylor Wood

Published by Clayton T. Wood.

ISBN: 978-0-9980818-1-6

Cover designed by James T. Egan, Bookfly Design, LLC

Printed in the United States of America.

Special thanks to my brothers, my father, and my wife for their invaluable advice. And to my son, for whom this book was written.

Table of Contents

Runic Awakening

Prologue

"Daddy!"

Ampir leans back in his chair, watching as his four-year-old son Junior sprints from the sandy shore of the Great River toward him, a huge grin on the boy's face. Grandpa trails behind, hardly able to keep up. Junior rushes up to Ampir, nearly bursting with joy.

"I did it!" he gushes. "I skipped a stone!"

"Good job buddy," Ampir replies, leaning forward and tousling Junior's hair affectionately. Grandpa walks up from behind the boy, shaking his head ruefully.

"Nothing like kids," he pants, "...to make you feel goddamn old."

"I'm already feeling it," Ampir admits. Grandpa snorts.

"Bull," he gasps, "...shit!"

Ampir chuckles, then hears footsteps behind him. He twists around to see his wife Vera walking up to them.

"Time for bed Junior," she announces, kneeling down. "Give me a hug!" Junior runs up to Vera, giving her a big bear hug. Then he turns to Ampir, giving him a hug too. Ampir kisses the boy on the forehead, holding him close for a moment.

"Sweet dreams kiddo," he murmurs. "Love you."

"Love you too daddy."

"All right Junior," Grandpa interjects, picking Junior up and holding him at his hip. "Grandpa's gonna tuck you in tonight!"

"Mommy?" Junior asks. "What's bull-shit?"

"The fact that Grandpa keeps using bad words around you," Vera answers, giving her father a look.

"Sorry honey," Grandpa grumbles.

"Goodnight Dad," Vera says, kissing Grandpa on the cheek. "Don't teach Junior any more new words."

"If I do, they'll be good ones," Grandpa promises with another grin. "Come on, kiddo! Grandpa's going to tell you a hell of a story tonight!"

Ampir watches them make their way across the backyard to the house in the distance, then sighs, turning to face the Great River. Over two miles wide, the river flows slowly westward, flecks of orange light glinting from its dark waters. The setting sun sends a splash of orange-red across thick, angry-looking clouds. Beyond the river lies Stridon, the capitol of the Empire.

"See something you like?" Vera inquires.

He turns, seeing his wife sitting down in a chair across from him, her legs crossed in front of her. Her shimmering white nightgown clings to her slender body, making it quite clear that it is all she is wearing. Vera's auburn hair flows in gentle waves to the small of her back, her face strikingly...no, *painfully* beautiful. He finds his gaze lingering, and realizes that she's smirking at him.

"I do now," he replies with a grin.

Vera's eyes twinkle, and she stands, dragging her chair until it is beside him, then sitting back down. She wraps her slender arm around him, leaning her head on his shoulder. The faint musk of her perfume tantalizes him – the same perfume she'd worn the day they'd met. The day they'd first kissed.

"You okay?" she asks, stroking the nape of his neck. Ampir sighs, shifting in his chair. He fingers the ring hanging from the necklace around his neck. The engagement ring Vera had proposed to *him* with.

"I don't know," he admits. He glances back over the Great River, at the cityscape of Stridon miles away. Tall buildings rise up from the opposite shore as far as the eye can see, all of them dwarfed by the massive Great Tower. Over forty stories tall, its crystalline peak glitters like a jewel in the night sky. And above this stands the massive translucent dome of the Gate Shield, a four-mile-wide energy field protecting the Tower and its campus.

"You're sure you want to resign from the Council tomorrow?" she asks, her tone gentle. Ampir turns away from the Great Tower, gazing into Vera's beautiful brown eyes.

"I'm sure."

"The Council won't be happy," Vera warns. Ampir snorts.

"Good."

"You're still the greatest warrior in the Empire," she presses. "And you're in line for the throne. They're going to wonder why you're quitting."

"Let them."

Vera hesitates.

"They're afraid of you," she warns. Ampir smirks at her.

"They should be."

Vera falls silent. They sit there, the fire slowly dying before them. The dark clouds above roll slowly toward the city, blocking out the stars. Ampir feels Vera's other hand rest on his upper thigh, and turns to face her. The front of her nightgown clings to her every curve, and he finds himself staring again. His heart thumps in his chest, and he glances up, finding her gazing back at him, her eyes twinkling mischievously.

"Junior will be asleep soon," she informs, her hand sliding up his thigh.

Ampir turns his head, glancing back at their house…at the second story window of their son's bedroom. Four years old already, and Ampir had barely gotten to spend time with Junior, working day and night for the Council. Four long years, wasted on the Empire. That will change tomorrow.

"Have you decided what you're going to do with all your free time?" Vera asks, leaning close, her lips inches from his. Her hand slides further upward, making his breath catch in his throat.

"I have a few ideas," he replies, intoxicated by her closeness. Five years they've been married, and she is still as bewitching as she'd ever been. He leans in to kiss her, and she pulls away just before their lips touch.

"Oh really?" she murmurs, putting a warm hand on his cheek. "Do tell."

"You always did want a girl."

"Is *that* how you plan on staying busy?" she inquires playfully.

"Yep."

"Can't you wait until tomorrow?" she presses, leaning in again.

"I doubt it."

Vera kisses him then, her lips warm and soft on his. He kisses her back, relishing the experience. She pulls away then, standing up and turning back toward the house. A strong breeze blows against her nightgown, flattening it fetchingly against her curves.

"Well then," she says, offering a hand. He takes it, letting himself be pulled to his feet. "...I think it's time you started enjoying your retirement."

She pulls him back toward the house, giving him a radiant smile. He grins back, allowing himself to be led. Their home is a mansion sitting on some of the most prized land in the city. But compared to the other Councilmen's estates, it is relatively modest.

"I knew there was a reason I married you," Ampir quips. Vera laughs, reaching the rear door and pulling it open. She pulls him inside, toward the stairs leading to the second floor. Ampir's boots *clunk* on the wooden steps.

"Shhh," Vera warns, giggling under her breath.

Ampir reaches down and pulls off his boots, leaving them on the stairs. Vera arches an eyebrow, and Ampir bends down, gathering her in his arms and lifting her up. She stifles a squeal, and he continues up the stairs. Halfway up, he notices something in the periphery of his vision...blue light rising from his arms toward the ceiling. He pauses, and Vera frowns at him.

"What's..."

The windows shatter.

Glass bursts into the living room, and then the living room wall explodes inward, plaster and wood flying at them. A shockwave slams into Ampir, hurtling him backward into the stone wall behind him. His head bounces off of the stone, pain lancing through his skull. He feels himself falling down the stairs, the world spinning madly around him.

Then his head smashes into the floor at the bottom of the stairs, stars exploding in the periphery of his vision.

Time slows to a crawl.

Ampir hears Vera screaming, feels her land on top of him, her auburn hair spilling over his chest.

"Ampir!" she shouts.

Ampir reacts reflexively, pulling cords of power into his mind's eye, twisting them around each other to form a throbbing knot in the center. He shoves the knot outward, and a translucent blue sphere appears around them...just as a second explosion hits. The living room disintegrates, debris hurtling at them at deadly speed. It ricochets off of the translucent blue sphere surrounding them, pieces of glass, stone, and wood scattering across the floor and stairs.

"Junior!" Vera cries in horror, pushing herself up from Ampir and pressing her hands against the inside of the blue sphere. "He's up there!"

Ampir grunts, pushing himself up from the floor. Rays of blue light rise from his body, the blue sphere surrounding them fading, then vanishing.

The hell?

Vera scrambles up the stairs, and Ampir follows after her, feeling a wave of nausea as he does so. His right temple throbs terribly, and he feels something wet trickling down his neck. The blue light leaking from his arms grows fainter...his power is being drained. Fast.

"Come on!" Vera urges, grabbing his hand and yanking him forward. Ampir spots movement to his right, sees dark shapes spilling into the massive hole in their living room wall.

Ampir rushes up the stairs after his wife, pushing through the pain. He reaches the top, turning left down the hallway toward his son's room. His imagines his son's room in shambles, his lifeless body splayed across his bed.

Oh god oh god please no...

The door to Junior's room bursts open, and Grandpa rushes out, Junior clutched in his arms.

"Mommy!" the boy cries. He slides down from Grandpa's arms, running up to Vera.

"My baby!" she replies, picking him up and squeezing him tightly to her bosom. Ampir feels relief course through him, and walks up to his son, kissing him on the back on the head.

"What's going on?" Grandpa asks.

"We're under attack," Ampir answers. "They're draining our magic. We need to leave. *Now.*"

Footsteps echo from the bottom of the stairwell.

"What do you mean they're..."

"Come on!" Ampir orders. He sprints down the hallway, struggling to pull more threads of power into his mind's eye...but nothing comes. Something is draining it. Something close.

He passes the stairwell, spotting a half-dozen men in black armor rushing up the stairs toward them.

"Go, go!" he urges, rushing down the hallway, Vera right at his heels, Grandpa at the rear. They reach the end of the hallway, then turn left down another, this one lined with windows on the right.

Footsteps follow them, closing in fast. Ampir glances back, seeing the armored men turning the corner behind them. Starlight reflects off of the daggers in their hands.

"Ampir!" Vera warns.

A man smashes through the window to Ampir's right, slamming into Ampir's side and shoving him against the wall. Ampir pushes back, sees a flash from the man's dagger as it thrusts toward his belly. Ampir twists to the side, feeling a sharp pain in his flank as the blade grazes him. He grabs onto the man's wrist, forcing the blade back.

"Ampir!" Grandpa shouts, rushing up behind the man and grabbing his arm. The man twists around, jerking his wrist free and slashing at Grandpa's throat.

Grandpa's neck gapes open, blood spurting out of the wound.

"Daddy!" Vera screams.

Grandpa clutches at his own throat, his eyes widening. He stumbles backward, slumping against the wall and sliding down onto his buttocks. Blood sprays out from between his fingers, pouring down his neck and chest. Vera rushes to his side, pressing on his neck.

Their attacker spins around, his knife arm whipping down at Ampir in a deadly arc. Ampir grabs the man's wrist, stopping the blade's tip inches from his own chest. He hears footsteps, sees a half-dozen more black-clad men rushing toward them. He *rips* magic into his mind's eye, ignoring the searing pain in his skull. He weaves it into a tight knot, shoving it outward.

A shockwave bursts forward, sending the knife-wielding man hurtling down the hallway. Windows shatter, paintings flying from the walls. The half-dozen armed men are thrown backward, landing in a pile on the floor at the far end of the hallway.

"Go!" Ampir shouts at Vera, grabbing her arm and pulling her away from grandpa, toward the door at the other end of the hall. Vera resists, clutching her father tightly. The old man's eyes are wide and glassy, his skin pale and slick with sweat. Blood streams between his and Vera's fingers. He coughs, more blood spilling from his mouth.

"Daddy!" Vera cries, tears pouring down her cheeks.

"He's gone," Ampir states, his tone sharp and cold. He reaches down, wrapping his arms around her waist and pulling her bodily away. She wails, digging her heels into the floor.

"No," she yells. "No!"

Ampir ignores her, freeing one hand to grab Junior, and dragging both of them down the hallway toward the door. The door to their master bedroom.

And my armor.

Ampir reaches the door, shoving it open and pulling the two inside. He closes the door, rushing to the nearby dresser and pulling it to barricade the door shut.

"Help me!" he shouts at Vera, but she just stares at him, her eyes blank, her pale arms spattered with her father's blood. He grunts, shoving the dresser up against the door. He turns then, spotting the safe at the far end of the room, as tall as he is. Something slams into the bedroom door from beyond, pushing the dresser back an inch. "Hold that door!" he shouts, sprinting to the safe and opening it. Its power drained, the magic lock securing it is useless. The safe opens, revealing a full set of midnight-black armor, countless tiny runes etched on its surface. Unlike the safe, his armor cannot be drained so easily. It is possessed of incredible power, the power to make him nearly invincible.

The power to make him a god.

He hears a *crack* behind him, turns to see the bedroom door being shoved open another few inches. A black-clad arm appears through the doorway.

Damn it!

Ampir turns back to the safe, grabbing a black, metallic gauntlet from within. He pulls it on, knowing that with his magic nearly drained, it will take a few moments to recognize him, for its runes to activate.

He hears a grunt behind him, then hears Vera scream. He turns back toward the door, seeing men pushing through the gap in the doorway, streaming into the bedroom, their daggers gleaming in the starlight. One of the men sprints up to Vera, shoving her onto her belly on the floor.

"No!" Ampir shouts. He runs toward her, but another black-clad man rushes at him, slashing at him with his dagger. Ampir raises his armored fist, the blade bouncing off of it. The man rams Ampir, shoving him backward. Ampir stumbles, twisting his ankle, pain shooting up his leg. He barely keeps his balance, swinging his armored fist at the man's face. The black gauntlet connects with the man's cheek with a terrible *crack*.

The man drops like a stone.

"Ampir!" he hears Vera scream.

He sees her crawling on her belly toward him, her eyes wide with fear. A man grabs her legs from behind, dragging her backward. The man straddles Vera's legs, raising his hands above his head, a dagger clutched between them, blade down.

"Vera!" Ampir shouts, lunging forward. His ankle gives out in a burst of pain, making him fall forward onto his hands and knees.

The man straddling Vera swings his arms downward in a vicious arc, burying his dagger to the hilt in Vera's lower back.

No!

Ampir struggles to his feet, feeling his gauntlet finally reacting, tightening around his hand and forearm. Its tiny runes flare to life, glowing a faint blue.

The man on top of Vera yanks the dagger out of her back, reaching forward to grab her hair, yanking her head backward to expose her neck. He leans over her, bringing the cruel edge of his blade to her throat.

"Mommy!" Junior screams.

Ampir shoves his armored hand outward, a burst of blinding white light searing his eyes.

Chapter 1

Kyle bolted upright in bed, yelling out as bright light seared his eyeballs. He threw his arms in front of his face, turning away from the deadly glare…then cracked an eye open, realizing that he was being attacked by gentle rays of sunlight peeking between the blinds of his bedroom window. He sighed in relief.

What a nightmare!

He flopped back onto his pillow, wincing as he landed on cool, wet sheets. He looked down, horror seizing him. A huge wet circle stained the sheets.

No, no, no!

He pulled the sheet up to his nose, but didn't smell anything. It was just sweat, thank god! He'd wet the bed so many times recently that his mom had threatened to take him to the doctor for it, and in response he'd threatened to take a swan dive out of his bedroom window. It was why he never went to sleep-overs; the thought of kids at school discovering his terrible secret made him want to curl up and die.

School!

Kyle shot upright, glancing at the alarm clock on his nightstand. To his relief, it was only 6:30…his nightmare had woken him up early. He'd been having similar nightmares for weeks now. Unlike normal dreams, they were incredibly vivid, almost *real*, and he always remembered them, even days later. They were usually unpleasant, but this one had been the worst yet. He'd seriously considered asking his mom if he could sleep with her last night – something he hadn't done in years – but she and Steve had gone out to an early dinner, leaving him with his aunt. They'd told him they needed some "us" time, whatever that meant.

He sighed, rolling out of bed and walking over to his dresser, changing into clean, dry clothes. He walked to the bathroom, wetting his hair under the sink, then emptying his bladder in the proper place – for once. That done, he sprinted down the stairs, slowing down for the last few steps. His mom hated it when he ran down the stairs. She was a doctor – like his real dad – and she relished telling him stories about people who fell down the stairs, cracked their skulls, and turned into drooling vegetables. He walked to the kitchen, where Mom was already up, pouring him a bowl of cereal.

"Hey mom," he mumbled, plopping down on one of the stools at the center island.

"Morning honey," she greeted, handing him the bowl of cereal. "Eat up," she added, "…or you'll be late to school again." Kyle nodded, chowing down. "Slow down!" she scolded. "You'll choke." Kyle rolled his eyes, but obeyed. That was the problem with having doctors for parents…they were always telling him that whatever he was doing could kill him.

"Hey guys!"

Kyle looked up to see his stepfather walking into the kitchen, already dressed for work. Mom went to kiss him, and handed her new husband a bowl of cereal. They were both in a really good mood today…they usually were after having a night of "us time." He didn't want to think about it.

"Hey Steve," Kyle mumbled. He refused to call his stepfather "dad," even though his mom had married again a few months ago. His real dad had left over a decade ago, and his parents had gotten a divorce soon after. Kyle had always wondered why they'd split up, but mom didn't like to talk about it, and he'd never mustered the courage to ask his dad.

"What's wrong Kyle?" Steve asked between gulps of cereal, wiping his mouth with the back of his hand. "You have another nightmare?"

"Nah," Kyle lied.

"Didn't your dad get really bad dreams when he was a kid?" Steve pressed. Kyle nodded, but didn't say anything. It was weird to talk to Steve about his dad. "Well, I used to get nightmares too," Steve offered. "I dream a lot less now that I'm old." Mom glared at Steve, putting her hands on her hips.

"If you're old, what does that make *me?*" she retorted. Steve hid a smirk with one hand, then focused on his bowl of cereal as if it were the most fascinating thing he'd ever seen. Kyle ignored them, slurping up the last of his breakfast, then hopping down from his stool. Mom was already putting Kyle's lunch into his backpack by the door. He threw on his backpack, tolerating a quick peck on the cheek from his mom.

"Bye sweetie," she said. "Have a good day at school."

"Bye Kyle," Steve called out.

Mom inspected Kyle's shirt collar, then gave him a tight smile. "Your father's going to pick you up from school today."

"I know," Kyle replied, unable to stop himself from grinning. His dad had been working a string of overnights at the hospital, and Kyle hadn't seen him for nearly a week. "Love you mom."

Kyle waved goodbye, then turned to run out the door toward the bus stop. It was only a few blocks away, but the bus driver was notorious for being early – and not bothering to wait around – so most of the kids were already lined up there on the sidewalk. Sure enough, the bus came barreling down the street, passing Kyle and stopping before the line of kids. Kyle ran as fast as he could, his backpack bouncing up and down painfully on his lower back. He barely made it, reaching the doors just as they started to close. The old, frumpy-looking bus driver scowled at Kyle as he got on – as if the bus being two minutes early were *his* fault – and pulled the lever to shut the double-doors behind him.

"Kyle!" he heard a voice shout, and turned to see a familiar face; it was Ben, Kyle's best friend. Ben was sitting halfway down the aisle, and he'd saved Kyle a seat. Kyle grinned, walking down the aisle and plopping himself down next to his friend.

"Hey, check it out," Ben urged. He reached inside his backpack and pulled out a handful of various candies. "Want one?" Kyle nodded, taking one and unwrapping it. His dad rarely let him eat candy, no doubt because it could kill him somehow, at least eventually. He plopped the candy in his mouth, sucking vigorously. Ben was always sneaking Kyle candy, and in return, Kyle let Ben play in his backyard when Ben's parents were fighting. They'd been arguing a lot recently, to the point where Ben was convinced they were going to get a divorce. If that happened, Ben might move away, and then Kyle would lose his best friend. They didn't talk about it much, but Kyle could tell it was always on Ben's mind.

That was probably why Ben was always getting into trouble at school…which only made things worse at home.

The bus lurched forward, the driver guiding the bus slowly across town, stopping a few times to pick kids up. The seats filled up rapidly, and soon the bus reached its last stop…and the best part of Kyle's day.

The bus came to a halt, and a blond-haired girl in a blue dress stepped inside. She had crystal-blue eyes, pale, flawless skin, and curves that made him have to put his backpack on his lap to avoid making a scene. Kyle tried not to stare; her name was Desiree, and she was Kyle's first great love…not that she knew it. She'd never noticed or talked to him, not in the four years they'd been in school together. Probably because he'd never had the guts to talk to *her*. He'd always been useless around girls, terrified that he'd say something stupid, or get rejected. Desiree probably didn't even know he existed.

Ben elbowed him in the side.

"Aren't you going to say hi to your *girlfriend?*" he teased. Kyle shot him a baleful glare.

"Shut up," he hissed, elbowing Ben back. "She'll hear you, idiot!" Ben laughed, making loud, wet kissing sounds and thrusting his chest outward provocatively. Kyle slithered down in his seat, mortified that Desiree might spot Ben's little performance. Thankfully she didn't appear to notice.

The bus slowed down suddenly, pulling up to the curb and coming to a stop in front of the school. The bus driver pulled a lever, and the doors opened.

"Everyone out!" the driver barked. Kyle followed the other students out of the bus, stepping down to the sidewalk and walking to the school entrance.

* * *

Kyle's first class was American Literature, with the usual dry, boring "classics" that were never enjoyable to read. Supposedly designed to make you think, all they made Kyle think of was closing each book and never reading them again. Then came Pre-Algebra, which he strongly suspected he would never end up using in real life. Then gym class, which was reliably sadistic. Finally — mercifully — there was lunch break. Kyle ran to his locker to get the lunch Mom had packed him. Ben had already beaten him there, and was offloading books into his own locker. They traded horror stories about the morning's classes, then turned to walk down the hall toward the cafeteria.

"Hey shrimp, what'd you bring me for lunch?" a voice called out from behind. Kyle turned around, seeing a tall, husky kid with a crew cut looming over him. Kyle's guts squirmed in his belly; it was Big Joe, one of the least academically gifted students at their school. He more than made up for it with his physical gifts, which he used to smack around anyone smaller than he was. Which was everybody.

Before Kyle could answer, Big Joe tore Kyle's lunch bag out of his hands. The oaf peered inside, pulling out a banana and a sandwich. He snorted, making an obscene gesture with the banana and tossing it over his shoulder.

"Thanks for the sandwich, Chinkerbell," he jeered, offering Kyle his lunch bag back. Kyle reached for it, but Joe pulled the bag away at the last minute, dropping it on the floor. Then he laughed, shoving Kyle to the side and heading off to the cafeteria. Ben yelled out at Joe, running after the big brute, but Kyle grabbed the back of Ben's shirt to stop him. Ben spun around to glare at Kyle.

"You're really gonna let that moron get away with that?" he accused.

"Who cares," Kyle muttered. "I'm not that hungry anyway," he lied. He was heartened that Ben wanted to stand up for him, but he hardly wanted to see Joe give his best friend a beating. And the last thing Ben needed was to get suspended again.

"Bet he feels real tough picking on a scrawny shrimp," Ben grumbled.

"Thanks for that," Kyle muttered. Ben shrugged, clapping Kyle on the back.

"Hey, you're short," Ben replied good-naturedly. "Nothing wrong with that." Kyle ignored him, retrieving his bruised banana and lunch bag from the floor. He hated the nickname Big Joe had given him: Chinkerbell. His real dad was white, and his mom was Vietnamese. He wasn't even Chinese, but it hardly mattered; almost everyone called him Chinkerbell now, when they knew the teachers couldn't hear.

The two walked silently to the dining hall, sitting at one of the empty tables and digging in to their meals.

"You shouldn't let Joe pick on you like that," Ben advised.

"What can I do, fight him?" Kyle shot back. "He'd murder me!"

"He doesn't pick on *me*," Ben retorted.

"Because you're a psycho," Kyle muttered. A few months ago, Big Joe had shoved Ben, and Ben had come right back at the brute, swinging his fists like a madman. Joe had beaten Ben up pretty badly, but Ben had gotten a few good punches in too. They'd both been suspended for a week...and that was the last time Joe had ever picked on Ben.

"Exactly," Ben stated proudly, crossing his arms over his chest. "Bullies are all the same. Stand up to 'em, they beat you once. Chicken out, they beat you over and over." Kyle sighed.

"I can't get suspended," he complained. "My dad would kill me."

"My dad's a piece of shit," Ben muttered. "I don't care what he thinks."

"Well I *like* my dad," Kyle countered. "My real dad, I mean."

"That's because he's not a douchebag," Ben retorted. Kyle lowered his gaze, not sure how to respond. "Hey, when you hanging with your dad next?"

"Tonight," Kyle answered. "I haven't seen him in a week. He's been working late."

"My dad stays late too," Ben replied. "...to work on his secretary."

Kyle burst out laughing, milk spewing out of his nose and mouth. Ben jerked out of the way just in time, dodging the spray, and Kyle fell into a fit of coughing, tears coming to his eyes. His nose burned, and he wiped it with a napkin.

"Sorry," Kyle mumbled. Ben grinned.

"That was *awesome*," he gushed. He grabbed an apple from his lunch bag, offering it to Kyle. "Hey, want this?"

Kyle nodded, taking the apple and chowing down. Thankfully, they changed the subject, spending the rest of the meal making fun of Big Joe in between bites of food. Despite Ben's apple, Kyle's stomach still growled a bit after he'd finished eating. The sandwich Joe stole had been the bulk of his meal, after all. And his parents always wondered why he pigged out so much when he got home.

After lunch, Kyle and Ben parted ways, walking to their respective classes. After suffering through history and art, Kyle's final class was science, easily his favorite. Mostly because Mr. Potts, the teacher, was younger and cooler than the other teachers. Today he was lecturing about black holes.

"Black holes," Mr. Potts explained, showing a picture of a giant black sphere on the projector screen, "...are *massive*. They're so massive that they generate an enormous amount of gravity. Anyone know why they're called 'black holes?'"

The girl sitting immediately behind Kyle – Sally Druthers, the class suck-up and know-it-all – raised her hand so fast Kyle was amazed she didn't dislocate her shoulder. Mr. Potts nodded at her.

"Because not even light can escape a black hole's gravitational pull," she answered with a smug smile. Mr. Potts, apparently not realizing that Sally was pure evil, smiled back.

"That's right," he replied. "Nothing can escape a black hole's gravitational field." He then went on to explain about how scientists had discovered black holes, but Kyle was too sleepy from weeks of nightmares to pay much attention. His eyelids grew heavy, and he stifled a yawn. A hand shoved him from behind.

"Wake up!" Sally hissed. Kyle scowled. Sally was the quintessential teacher's pet. She got straight "A's," and made sure everyone knew it. He hated sitting in front of her. He imagined being married to her, and stifled a shudder. Apparently her mother was just like her; frankly, he didn't know how her father put up with it.

Then he thought of Desiree, looking across the room to find her. She was sitting perfectly in her chair, drawing doodles on her notebook. Kyle sighed, wishing he could sit next to her instead of Sally. Not that it would matter; he was too chicken to ever talk to Desiree, and he was short, scrawny, and awkward...the exact opposite of someone a blond bombshell like her would be interested in.

In the end, Sally's efforts to reform Kyle were in vain, as he found himself studying the clock – and Desiree – more than the seemingly endless parade of celestial bodies presented. After an eternity, the bell rang, and class was over. Everyone stood up, and Kyle followed the rest of the students out of the classroom, walking to his locker to pick up his books. Ben, who had once again gotten to his locker before Kyle, observed with amazement that each of his classes managed to suck worse than the one before it.

"Let's go," Ben said after they'd gathered their things. "You wanna hang out at your place?"

"I can't," Kyle replied, throwing his overstuffed backpack over one shoulder. "I'm with my dad today, remember?"

"Oh, right," Ben replied. "Maybe tomorrow?"

"Yeah, I'm with my mom then," Kyle agreed.

"Cool."

They walked side-by-side down the hallway, reaching the double-doors at the entrance to the school. Throngs of fellow students were already pouring through them, and Kyle and Ben joined them, stepping out into the hot summer sun. Ben said goodbye, then made his way toward the waiting school bus while Kyle scanned the parking lot for his dad's car. He spotted it almost instantly...and saw his dad getting out of the car. Kyle broke into a run to meet him.

"Hey big guy," Dad called out. His father always called him "big guy," even though he was the second-shortest kid in his grade. Dad tousled Kyle's hair, then started walking back toward the parking lot. "How was school?"

"Boring."

"You ask Desiree out yet?" Dad pressed. Kyle's cheeks flushed, and he shook his head. His dad was the only person – other than Ben – that knew how he felt about Desiree.

"Nah," he mumbled.

"She'll just reject you anyway, right?" Dad guessed. Kyle nodded. "Yeah, you're probably right."

"Gee, thanks," Kyle muttered. Dad grinned, patting him on the shoulder. They both got in the car, and Dad started the engine, pulling out of his parking space.

"How was work?" Kyle asked, eager to change the subject.

"Boring," Dad answered. "Any nightmares recently?"

"Yeah," Kyle admitted. He'd told his dad about his nightmares, although not in detail. Just that he'd been getting them for the last three weeks. Dad used to get nightmares too when he was a kid – about that, Steve had been right.

"Bummer," Dad replied. "I still get them sometimes," he added. "Used to get them every night after I woke up from my coma."

Kyle nodded absently, having heard the story many times before. His dad had been found lying unconscious in the middle of the street as a young boy, his face all bruised and swollen. A passer-by had called an ambulance, and he'd been rushed to the hospital. The doctors there had discovered that his father had bled around his brain, and that both of his lungs had collapsed. And there'd been a bleeding stump where his left big toe should have been. He'd laid in a coma for a few days before coming to, and the injuries to his brain had all but wiped out his memories. He had no idea who his real parents were, and no one had come to claim him; a nice middle-aged woman – a widow – had heard about Kyle's father on the news, and ended up adopting him.

"Ah, home sweet home," Dad declared, turning into the driveway that led to his house. He parked in the garage, then turned to face Kyle. "Rejection isn't so bad," he stated suddenly, putting a hand on Kyle's knee. "Sometimes you have to take a big risk to get a big reward."

"Huh?"

"Desiree," Dad clarified. He grinned ruefully. "Take it from a really, *really* late bloomer. You'd be amazed what can happen if you take a chance."

"Sure," Kyle mumbled. They got out of the car, walking into the mud room. Kyle deposited his backpack and shoes there, and they both walked over to the couch in the living room, plopping down on the comfy cushions with tandem sighs. Dad laughed.

"Long day, huh?" he asked.

"Yeah."

"Things any better with Steve?" he pressed. Kyle shrugged.

"Not really."

"What's wrong?" Dad asked.

"He's nice and all," Kyle admitted, "...but he's not you."

Dad leaned forward, propping his elbows on his knees.

"That's true," he conceded.

"Mom wants me to call him my stepdad," Kyle muttered.

"And you don't want to?" Dad asked. Kyle shook his head.

"He's not my dad."

"You're right," Dad replied. "He isn't." He paused then, rubbing his hands together. "But just because he isn't your father doesn't mean he can't be a father-*figure* to you." He smiled then. "I've had a lot of father-figures in my life."

"Really?"

"Yup," Dad confirmed. "Some better than others. But I learned from all of them. Some taught me what to do," he continued, "...and others what *not* to do." He tousled Kyle's hair, shooting him another smile. "Anyway, it sounds like Steve is really trying," he said. "Maybe you can try too."

Kyle kept his eyes on his lap, saying nothing.

"How's Ben doing?" Dad inquired. Kyle had told his father about Ben's parents, and how they might get a divorce. It'd been awkward to talk about, for obvious reasons.

"Okay I guess."

"Probably not," Dad countered gently. "He's probably really hurting." He leaned forward, propping his elbows on his knees, and glanced sidelong at Kyle. "Divorce hurts everyone."

Kyle said nothing, staring straight forward, afraid to meet his dad's gaze. He was seized by the sudden, mad urge to ask about his own parents' divorce. To finally figure out what had happened...what had *really* happened...once and for all. But fear got the better of him, and he said nothing. Dad sighed, leaning back into the couch.

"You look beat," he observed. "You get any sleep last night?"

"Not really," Kyle confessed. Three weeks of nightmares had taken their toll.

"Why don't you take a nap?" Dad suggested. Kyle frowned; he hadn't seen his dad in nearly a week. He hardly wanted to waste their time together sleeping. But Dad was insistent. "I need a nap too," he confessed. "These overnights have been kicking my butt. We'll hang out after."

Kyle nodded, walking toward the staircase. He trudged up the stairs, then went into his room, flopping unceremoniously onto his bed. Something hard jabbed into his back, and he sat up, spying a small ring on the bed. He picked it up; the band was shiny and silver-colored, with a large yellow gemstone set on top. The yellow turned to a pale blue color at the edges...it was actually pretty cool looking. Intricate symbols were carved in the band, with tiny bluish crystals dotting the sides.

It was his father's ring, or at least it had been until a few weeks ago. Dad had given it to Kyle for his birthday. Of course, what Kyle had really wanted was a paintball gun like his uncles had, but Mom had refused, saying something about losing an eye. Instead, his dad had given him this ring. Kyle frowned at it; he could've sworn he'd left it on his dresser, but with his recent insomnia, his memory wasn't what it used to be.

Kyle stared at the ring, rolling it between his fingers. It'd been clutched in his father's hand when he'd been found beaten and bloodied on the street as a boy. Dad had kept it all these years, insisting that it had been his father's, although he had no real memory of who his father was. He'd given it to Kyle on his birthday three weeks ago, much to Kyle's disappointment. There was no way he'd be caught wearing the thing, after all. Luckily he'd gotten some money from his grandparents, so he could buy himself a *real* gift. He glanced at his left wrist, where he wore the new watch he'd bought. It was an outdoor survival watch...equal parts waterproof, shock-resistant, and awesome.

He laid back down on his bed, holding his ring out in front of him; it didn't really fit on any finger other than his thumb. He slid it onto his left thumb, staring at the center gemstone. His eyelids grew heavy, and he closed them, feeling his mind wander.

He jerked awake suddenly, opening his eyes and looking upward.

A ripple appeared in the center of the ceiling, spreading outward.

Kyle froze.

Another ripple appeared, as if the ceiling were the surface of a lake, and a pebble had been thrown in.

What the...

Suddenly the ceiling ripped open, revealing a black hole that grew rapidly, engulfing the entire ceiling. The blackness spread down around the walls, tiny pinpoints of light appearing, then streaking outward in all directions. The pinpoints grew painfully bright, coalescing into a single, blinding white light.

Then a force slammed into Kyle, shoving him against his bed. Agonizing pain shot through his chest, ripping upward into his jaw and down his left arm.

He tried to scream, but no sound came out.

Kyle clutched his chest, his vision blackening. Pain lanced through his ears, his skull feeling as if it would explode. The bed dropped out underneath him, and suddenly he was falling. He flailed his arms, screaming silently.

And then the blackness took him.

Chapter 2

Ampir shouts, a beam of white-hot light shooting out of his armored palm. It slams into the man straddling Vera, taking his head clean off of his shoulders. He falls forward onto Vera's back, a charred stump all that is left of his neck. The dagger he'd held against Vera's throat falls to the floor with a clatter.

The other men in the room freeze, staring wide-eyed at Ampir. Then they burst toward him, daggers gleaming.

Ampir sweeps his armored hand from left to right, another beam of light shooting outward from his palm. It annihilates everything it touches, burning through his enemies' flesh at their mid-sections. Their upper bodies topple from their waists, falling to the floor in a smoldering heap.

"Vera!" Ampir calls out, limping up to her. She tries to get up, then stops, grimacing in pain. The back of her nightgown is stained with blood.

"Are they...?" Vera begins.

"They're dead," Ampir confirms.

"Mommy!" Junior cries, rushing to Vera's side. Ampir lifts her nightgown up, exposing her lower back. Blood wells up from a narrow gash to one side of her spine, trickling down her side. He'd seen wounds like this before, in the military. Small wounds that hid devastating internal injuries. He had to get her to a surgeon...fast.

"Grandpa," Vera says, grimacing as she pushes herself up to a sitting position. "He's still out there!"

"He's gone baby," Ampir replies, but Vera shakes her head, rising unsteadily to her feet. She pulls him toward the bedroom door and into the hallway. There, propped up against the wall, is Grandpa.

"Daddy!" Vera gasps, rushing forward. They reach the old man's side, and Vera kneels before him. Grandpa's eyes are open, but they see nothing.

"No Daddy, no!" Vera cries, tears streaming down her cheeks. She hugs her father, pressing her cheek against his.

"Honey," Ampir begins, then stops himself. He waits, though he knows that more enemies will be coming. No one would be stupid enough to try to kill him and fail. "We need to go," he says at last, putting a hand on her shoulder. She pulls away from his touch, turning on him.

"You let him die out here!" she accuses. "You..."

"*You're* going to die," Ampir interrupts, his tone sharp. "You *and* Junior, if we don't leave. Now."

She stares at him silently, her eyes filled with rage. He grabs her under one arm, lifting her up, and she lets him. But he can feel something different between them now, something that had never been there before. A wound that might never heal. The thought terrifies him.

"Come on," he urges, guiding her back into the bedroom. Junior is still there by the doorway, his face deathly pale. The boy says nothing, but Ampir can tell he'd heard everything.

I let his Grandfather die.

He walks past Junior, gently setting Vera on the bed, then stepping up to the safe. He puts on his armor, until he is covered from neck to toe in black metal, runes pulsing blue in random, shifting patterns on its surface. He grabs a silver visor from the safe, pulling it over his eyes. The room instantly brightens, the visor sharpening every detail.

Before, he was mortal. A man. Now he is a god.

They were going after my armor, he realizes. It's the only explanation for why they hadn't simply bombed his home into oblivion. They must have been afraid they'd destroy his armor.

The fools.

Still, they'd almost succeeded. And whatever had drained his magic earlier was still out there, close by. While he has little to fear with his armor on, Vera and Junior are still vulnerable.

He turns to Vera and Junior, both sitting on the edge of the bed.

"We're going," he tells her, "...to get you to a surgeon."

Vera says nothing, pushing herself up from the bed, wincing

with the effort. Ampir steps forward, slipping one hand under her legs, the other around her shoulders, and lifts her up. With the power of his armor, she seems to weigh next to nothing.

"Junior," he calls out. "Get on my back." Junior hesitates, still standing by the doorway, his eyes wide with fear. Ampir takes a step toward the boy, then feels a vibration in his skull. Something big punches through the ceiling above their heads, slamming through the floor beside them, leaving a gaping hole there. A large metal cylinder.

A *bomb*.

"Junior!" Ampir yells, bolting toward Junior. He *yanks* strands of power into his mind's eye, weaving them frantically into a tight knot and shoving it outward.

* * *

Kyle's back slammed into something...*hard.*

The air burst from his lungs, making him see stars. He gasped for air, clutching at his chest, the pressure and pain there excruciating.

And then, as quickly as it had come, the pain vanished.

Kyle laid there for a moment, taking deep, gulping breaths. The blackness in his vision faded, revealing dozens of stars glittering in an inky black sky far above.

Kyle grimaced, propping himself up on his elbows. A bed of dirt and dry, dead leaves lay beneath him, small stones poking his buttocks and the backs of his legs. All around him were tall trees with gnarled branches, their leaves lined with a faint blue glow.

Kyle froze, staring at the trees. His heart began to hammer in his chest, a cold sweat trickling from his armpits down to his flanks.

Where am I?

He hesitated, then pushed himself off of the ground, rising to his feet. He spun around in a slow circle, seeing forest all around him.

Okay, he thought, fighting down a rising panic. He took a deep breath in, and let it out slowly. *I was just in bed. I fell asleep.*

And then the ceiling had ripped open, and he'd fallen...and now he was here.

I must be dreaming.

If so, it was by far the most vivid dream he'd ever had. He could *feel* the hard dirt and tiny twigs under his feet, poking into his socks. But there was no other explanation. He'd fallen asleep, and then started dreaming about all of...this.

"Well then," he mumbled. He looked at the tree nearest him, spotting crescent-shaped fungi clinging to the base of the trunk, a faint orange glow pulsing from their underbellies. He took a step closer, putting a hand on the tree's rough bark. He spotted something crawling on its trunk – a small, caterpillar-like insect with glowing red spots on its back. It was crawling right toward his hand; he withdrew it quickly, and the insect froze, the spots on its back flashing bright red. Kyle took a step backward.

The caterpillar split in half, falling to the ground.

Kyle stared at the fallen insect, then squatted down, grabbing a small stick. He poked at one of the caterpillar halves with it, but it didn't move.

Maybe it's playing dead, he reasoned. If so, splitting in half sure made for a convincing act!

He stood, spotting something to his right...a tree much larger than the others, about fifty feet away. It was as good a destination as any; he stepped gingerly toward it, suddenly wishing that he was wearing shoes. The tree was huge, and thick green vines spiraled up the massive trunk and branches. Some of the vines hung down from the branches, extending all the way to the forest floor, where they lay in long, tangled loops. Small, white, root-like appendages lined the sides of each vine, each one digging into the smooth bark.

Kyle walked up to one of the vines on the ground, squatting before it. He poked at it with his stick. Nothing happened. He wedged the stick under the vine, lifting it upward. There was a glowing yellow stripe on its underside, and some sort of slimy goo. He grimaced, dropping the stick and standing up.

Suddenly his legs shot out from under him, a sharp pain lancing through his left calf. He fell flat onto his back. Something tightened around his leg, and he reached down, feeling something cool and slimy there...a vine wrapped around his calf! Little white root-things sprang out from the sides of the vine, poking into his skin. Kyle screamed, kicking his leg. He grabbed the vine with his hands, trying to pull it off, but the vine tightened its grip, squeezing his leg so hard that it turned purple. Kyle screamed again, flipping onto his stomach and trying to crawl away. The vine coiled up his leg like a snake, its slimy underbelly wrapping around his knee and lower thigh. Its grip tightened, his foot starting to go numb.

Then the vine went slack.

Kyle scrambled forward on his hands and knees, feeling the slick vine slip off his leg. He sprang to his feet, backing away from the vine quickly. But to his relief, it didn't move. Kyle followed its length with his eyes, then did a double-take.

The vine had been severed, thick, yellow fluid oozing from each end. The glowing stripe on its underside had faded.

What the...?

He glanced down at his left leg, seeing a spiraling double-row of tiny red dots marking his skin there. He imagined them burrowing into his flesh and sucking on his blood. A chill ran down his spine. His dream had nearly turned into a nightmare!

The wind picked up, howling through the forest, making the vines on the huge silver tree swing on their branches. Kyle shivered, then turned away from the tree, walking back the way he'd come. The forest seemed darker now, the soft orange glow of the mushrooms on the tree trunks the only indication of the trees ahead. He stepped carefully through the darkness, wincing as a rock jabbed into the sole of his foot.

He heard a *snap* behind him.

Kyle froze, goosebumps rising on his arms. He turned slowly, peering into the darkness...and froze. There, not fifty feet from where he stood, two iridescent eyes stared back at him from deep within the shadows.

Kyle blinked, half-expecting the eyes to vanish, but they didn't. They floated there in the darkness, staring silently at him. Kyle took a step backward, swallowing in a suddenly dry throat.

Okay Kyle, he told himself. *Dream's over. Time to wake up now.*

The eyes moved, seeming to grow as they weaved sinuously through the shadows. Kyle took another step back, his heart racing. The disembodied eyes moved...right toward him.

Time to wake up Kyle!

He made out a dark form around the glowing eyes, thick tufts of black fur sprouting from a long, arched back. Two cropped ears standing erect above a large, wolf-like head. He heard a low growl, saw a row of razor-sharp teeth shimmering in the starlight. Silver cords of slimy drool hung from the beast's mouth.

It stopped, staring at him. Lowered itself to the ground slowly, crouching, now only some forty feet away.

Then it lunged forward!

Kyle cried out, breaking into a mad dash away from the beast. He heard a *thump* behind him, followed by rhythmic grunting.

Oh god oh god oh god…

Kyle ran as fast as he could, leaping over a fallen log and nearly crashing into another tree. He glanced back, spotting the beast bounding toward him with frightening speed, its teeth bared in a vicious snarl, ears flat against the back of its head.

Then his left shoulder slammed into a tree…hard.

He spun around, tripping over his legs and falling forward, landing on his right shoulder. Pain shot through his arm, and he cried out, scrambling to his feet. The beast lunged at him, slamming into his back and knocking him onto his belly on the ground. He felt something sharp rip down the center of his back.

Kyle screamed.

He twisted around frantically, seeing the nightmarish creature looming over him, thick cords of saliva dripping from its razor-sharp teeth. It snapped at Kyle's face, and he threw his hands in front of him, feeling its teeth slash at his forearms. Blood poured down his arms, dripping into his eyes. He cried out, frantically beating at the beast's head with his fists.

The beast drew back, then lunged for his face again, twisting its head sideways, its jaws clamping down on his temples. Kyle felt its teeth sink into his flesh, clamping on his skull. He shrieked, grabbing at the creature's head blindly, trying futilely to push it away. His right thumb sank into something soft.

The beast yelped, releasing Kyle's head and backpedaling, pawing at its left eye.

Kyle scrambled to his feet, stumbling away from the horrible creature. He gained speed, weaving around the trees, pumping his legs as fast as he could. He heard the beast's rhythmic grunting behind him.

No no no!

He saw a gap in the forest ahead…the edge of a cliff dropping to a river some twenty feet below. He sprinted toward it, hearing the beast's grunting getting louder as it gained on him. He neared the edge of the cliff, seeing the sheer drop to the dark waters below. He hesitated for a split second, fear twisting his guts.

The beast slammed into him from behind, shoving him off of the cliff. He screamed, his stomach lurching as he entered into free-fall. He felt the sudden shock of icy wetness enveloping him, soaking instantly through his clothes. He swam upward, bursting through the surface of the river and taking a deep, gasping breath. He looked back, spotting the wolf-like creature standing at the edge of the cliff twenty feet above, its iridescent eyes following him as the river carried him slowly away from it. The creature stared at Kyle for a moment longer, then turned away from the cliff.

Thank god, Kyle thought, staring at the terrible beast. *Oh thank you god!*

Then the beast turned back toward the river, running and leaping off the edge of the cliff, plummeting to the river behind Kyle.

Shit!

Kyle kicked his legs madly, swimming downstream away from the creature. His heart pounded in his chest, his breath coming in short gasps.

It can't swim that fast, he hoped. *It can't possibly...*

He felt something clamp down on his leg, pain lancing through his calf. There was a sharp tug, and suddenly he was underwater, icy blackness enveloping him.

Kyle kicked his legs, clawing his way frantically upward, but it was no use. He felt another tug on his leg, pulling him deeper into the water. His lungs started to burn, specks of light appearing at the edges of his vision. He grit his teeth, kicking violently, raking his hands through the black water...to no avail. His lungs were on fire now, the urge to breathe overwhelming.

Then his body betrayed him, his lips opening of their own accord, his lungs pulling fluid into his mouth and down his throat. He coughed violently, bubbles spewing from his nose. He took another breath in, water coursing down his windpipe and into his lungs, burning it as went. He flailed his legs uselessly, the world beginning to fade around him, his body going numb.

And then the tugging at his leg stopped, the weight there vanishing.

Kyle scrambled upward, his head bursting through the surface of the river. He coughed violently, water shooting out of his mouth and nose. He gasped for air, feeling more water trickle down his windpipe, and coughed again. Then he took another breath in, feeling air – sweet air! – rushing in.

Yes!

He took deep, gulping breaths, feeling life seep back into his limbs. The stars in the periphery of his vision faded, the burning in his chest subsiding. He stared up at the night sky above, just treading water and breathing.

I'm alive.

A giddiness came over him, a mad joy, and he laughed, his voice echoing in the cool night air.

I'm alive!

He felt a sudden bolt of fear, remembering the horrifying beast. He spun around in the water, his eyes darting across the rippling surface of the river, but saw nothing. It was gone...or was it?

Get out of the water, he told himself.

Kyle spotted the shore some thirty feet to his left, and swam toward it, the current pulling him further downstream. His toes scraped against mud and rocks below, and after a few more strokes he was able to get his feet under him. He stood, trudging slowly toward the shore. His legs wobbled as he made it out of the water, and he lowered himself onto his belly, resting his temple on the rough sand. He felt suddenly exhausted, the mere thought of continuing onward overwhelming.

It was then that the pain in his back returned, going from a mild burning to a sharp, throbbing pain. Kyle groaned, reaching around and feeling the center of his back. His fingertips dipped into a deep, moist crevice there, his pain suddenly worsening. He jerked his hand away, staring at his fingers.

They were covered in blood.

Kyle's heart pounded in his chest, a wave of nausea coming over him. He felt suddenly dizzy, his lips and fingertips tingling. He stared at his forearms, seeing the deep gashes in them, blood pouring from the wounds and staining the sand. His temples throbbed terribly, and he touched them, feeling slick blood trickling down his face.

Oh god oh god...

He clenched his teeth against the rising pain, his breath hissing in and out.

How can I be hurt? This is a dream!

Kyle reached around, pinching his own forearm...hard. The pain was sharp, and immediate. He felt a surge of panic, his pulse pounding in his ears.

This wasn't a dream...it was real!

***

Kyle lay there on the sandy shore of the river, his breath coming in short gasps. He dug his fingertips into the sand, gritting his teeth.

Don't panic, he ordered himself. That's what his Dad had told him to remember if he ever got hurt. *Breathe*.

He laid there, forcing himself to take slow, deep breaths.

Get up, he told himself.

Kyle slid his hands underneath him, pushing himself up onto his knees, then rising slowly to his feet. He staggered to one side, a wave of nausea coming over him. He caught himself, then took one step away from the river, and another. Ahead of him, the sandy banks of the river gave way to dense forest, the leaves on the trees no longer glowing as brightly against the steadily brightening sky. He continued forward, ignoring the twigs and small stones jabbing into the bottoms of his feet.

The ground on either side rose steeply, forming two rocky cliffs. A narrow dirt path snaked between them, and Kyle followed it. He felt something trickling down the back of his legs, and reached down, feeling slippery wetness there. When he withdrew his hand, it was covered in blood.

He stared at his soaked palm, feeling woozy.

He focused ahead, pushing forward through the narrow path, the cliffs on either side throwing cool shadows over him. The path widened over time, the cliff sides giving way to a field of tall, golden grass. Each blade was as broad as his palm, and easily a few feet taller than him. The grass grew so densely that it was impossible to see beyond it, forming a veritable wall in either direction as far as the eye could see. Kyle stopped before it, his head swimming. He licked his lips, having a sudden, desperate craving for ice-cold water. He imagined himself holding a tall glass, bringing it to his lips and feeling cool liquid pouring down his parched throat.

Focus.

Kyle pushed through the grass, parting it with his hands, leaving streaks of blood on the broad blades. He continued forward blindly; after a few minutes, the tall grass ended abruptly, opening up to reveal a broad dirt road, beyond which another line of tall golden grass waved in the wind. Kyle stepped onto the road, looking left, then right; it cut a swath through the grass on either side as far as the eye could see. He stood there, swaying a little, feeling as if his head were rising from his body.

Which way?

He looked up and down the road, his mind wandering. He shook his head, digging his fingernails into his arms.

Come on, he scolded himself. *Think!*

There was no sign of anyone on the road, and no buildings in the distance. No way to know which way was the right way to go to find help. But if he didn't choose soon...

He paused, then turned right, walking down the road. The sun rose behind him, sending a long shadow out in front of him. He shivered despite the warmth of its rays on his bare skin, feeling strangely disconnected from his body. He looked down, concentrating on putting one foot in front of the other.

*One, two, three, four...*he counted his steps, building a rhythm. *Five, six, seven, eight...*

His left knee gave out suddenly, and he stumbled forward, landing face-first onto the dirt, his head bouncing off of the ground. Pain exploded from the center of his forehead, and a wave of nausea overtook him, bile pooling in his mouth. He swallowed it back with a shudder, pushing himself up from the packed dirt with his hands, then rising shakily to his feet.

He took a deep breath in, swaying slightly. Then he continued forward, putting one foot forward, then another.

His mind began to wander, and this time he let it. The pain in his back was gone now; he felt numb, as if his body belonged to someone else. Onward he shuffled, watching as the tall fields of sun-kissed grass on either side swayed majestically in the breeze, like waves in a golden sea. He closed his eyes, feeling that warm breeze glide over his bare skin, bringing a light, sweet scent to his nose.

After a few more minutes, his legs started to wobble, and he felt himself falling, his knees slamming into the ground, then his face. There was no pain this time. He felt nothing at all. He opened his eyes, turning his head to the side and staring at the long blades of grass dancing in the wind, sunlight glittering through them. It was hard to think now, hard to concentrate on anything.

I'm dying, he realized.

He closed his eyes, feeling himself drifting away. There was no fear, only exhaustion; an exhaustion so complete that he yearned for sleep. He gave into it, feeling his life slipping away.

Something cold and wet pressed onto his back, and then the world went black.

Chapter 3

Kyle opened his eyes, seeing a plain white ceiling above.

He yawned, rubbing the sleep out of his eyes. Then he stiffened. How long had he slept for? He turned his head to glance at his alarm clock on his nightstand, but neither the clock nor the nightstand were there. He blinked, turning his head the other way. Still no clock...and no nightstand.

Kyle frowned, then sat up...or tried to. Pain shot up his spine, and he cried out, falling back onto the bed. He froze, gasping for breath.

What the...

He waited for the pain to subside, then rolled carefully onto one side, reaching around to feel his back. His fingers slid over something soft, like gauze. He pressed down on it, feeling immediate pain. Suddenly it came back to him; the wolf-like creature that had chased him. The pain as it had mauled him, slashing his arms and head with its deadly jaws.

It wasn't a dream!

A chill ran through him, goosebumps rising on his arms. He looked down, seeing bandages wrapped around his forearms...and his right calf. He turned his head slowly, scanning the room. It was all wrong. The walls were painted a faint yellow; his room at his dad's house was white. Fine paintings hung on the walls, an elegant wooden desk sitting in one corner. A glass of pale green liquid stood on the top of the desk, along with a few books.

Where am I?

Kyle pushed himself up into a sitting position carefully,

swinging his legs over the side of the bed. The movement sent stabbing pains through his back, which quickly turned into a gnawing ache. He sat there for a long moment, waiting for the pain to subside. He realized that he was wearing bright white pants, and that a neatly folded white shirt was laying on the edge of the bed. He reached for it gingerly, pulling the shirt on, wincing with every movement. Then he stood up.

More pain.

He breathed through it, clenching and unclenching his fists. Again the pain subsided. A window by the bed caught his eye, and he shuffled over to it. Sunlight poured through, making his eyes ache. Maybe twenty feet below, a huge green lawn extended far out into the distance, bordered by a white fence.

Where the heck am I?

Kyle turned away from the window, struck with the sudden urge to lay back down, to close his eyes and rest. He felt terribly weak, his mouth dry. He resisted the urge, spotting a partially open door opposite the bed. He paused, then walked up to it, cracking it open a bit more and peering out. There was a hallway beyond, with a closed door directly opposite his. The walls were a faint yellow, the same as his room, and the wooden floor was polished to a mirror shine. Kyle opened the door wider, glancing up and down the long hallway.

It was deserted.

He hesitated, then stepped into the hall. To his left was another closed door; to his right was a broad staircase. He walked to the edge of the stairs; they spiraled downward, a golden railing on either side.

Gathering his courage, he grabbed the railing with one hand, then went down the stairs until he'd reached the bottom of the stairwell. Beyond was another long hallway; rows of closed doors were on either wall, with a door at the end of the hallway some forty feet away. Unlike the others, this door was slightly open…but not enough that he could see past it. Kyle paused at the foot of the stairs, staring at the door, then turning to look back up the stairwell.

Without warning, the door at the end of the hallway burst open!

A man strode through the doorway into the hallway, then stopped abruptly, his eyes locking on Kyle. Kyle backpedaled, catching his heel on the stair behind him, and fell onto his butt. Pain shot up his spine, and he cried out, freezing in place.

The man continued to stare at Kyle. Kyle stared back, petrified; the man was dressed in a simple black shirt and black pants, with black boots polished to a mirror shine. He was older, with thick white hair in a crew cut, and an equally white goatee. He was strikingly handsome despite his age, and quite fit, his toned muscles showing through his clothes. He moved toward Kyle suddenly, striding down the hallway with surprising swiftness. Kyle barely had time to stand before the man was nearly upon him; the stranger stopped a few feet from Kyle, looking down at him with sharp brown eyes.

"Flarg maneli wizi?" the man asked.

Kyle blinked, then swallowed in a dry throat, his heart pounding in his chest. He tried to say something, but the words caught in his throat. The man's eyes narrowed, seeming to stare right through Kyle.

"Marpisi saduri?"

Kyle shook his head, shrugging his shoulders helplessly. The man frowned, then stepped forward, reaching out at Kyle with one hand. Kyle shrank backward, but the older man merely held his hand out, palm up. He gestured for Kyle to take it.

Kyle stared at that hand; it was wrinkled, with thick callouses at the base of each finger. The man in black smiled, bringing his outstretched hand a bit closer. The stranger's smile was surprisingly warm, and despite Kyle's better judgement, he found himself reaching out to grab the man's hand.

The stranger gripped Kyle's hand firmly, then turned around, striding back down the hallway toward the open door he'd come from. Kyle followed behind and to one side; the man let go of Kyle's hand as they passed through the doorway, entering the room beyond. It was a large room, tastefully but sparsely decorated, with a long, rectangular table in the center. The table was made of dark, polished wood, and was easily two dozen feet long. Intricate symbols had been carved into its thick, sturdy legs, with glittering gemstones imbedded in colorful patterns at the tabletop's edges. Huge paintings hung on the walls, flanked by life-size marble statues.

Kyle's gaze returned to the table. There were chairs lining its length; in one of them sat a man dressed entirely in golden armor. This man had short, dark brown hair and startlingly blue eyes. He looked to be in his thirties, but it was difficult to tell for sure. The man stared back at Kyle, his expression utterly flat.

The man in black walked up to the chair to the right of the golden-armored man, motioning for Kyle to sit down.

"Noxa sans ibis," he urged.

Kyle hesitated, then obeyed, walking up to the chair and sitting down carefully. The man in black sat down in the seat next to Kyle's, reaching into his breast pocket and retrieving something small and yellow. He leaned forward then, reaching toward Kyle's right ear. Kyle jerked away reflexively, feeling immediate pain in his back as he did so.

Suddenly a cold, metallic arm wrapped around his neck from behind!

Kyle cried out, lurching forward, but the arm around his neck tightened, and something gripped the back of his head with terrible force, locking it in place. Kyle reached up with both hands, prying at the arm around his neck, but it was no use.

The man in black reached forward again, grabbing Kyle's right ear with one hand and pressing the yellow object into his earlobe with the other. Kyle felt a sudden, sharp pain there, and cried out again, reaching up to bat away the older man's hands. But he was too late; the man in black leaned back, resting one elbow on the tabletop and staring at Kyle with those intense brown eyes. A slight smirk curled his lips.

"Well then," he stated. "That should do it. My name is Kalibar. What's yours?"

* * *

The arm around Kyle's neck slipped away, along with the hand on the back of his head. He swallowed, then raised a hand to his right earlobe. He felt something small and hard there. It throbbed slightly, and felt wet; when he looked at his fingertips, he saw they were smudged with blood.

Kyle returned his gaze to the older man – Kalibar – and saw that the man was still staring at him. Kyle blinked, realizing that he'd been asked a question, but unable to remember what it was.

"Sorry?" he managed, his voice cracking.

"What's your name, son?" Kalibar asked. His tone was patient, but his fingertips drummed on the tabletop. Kyle cleared his throat.

"Uh, Kyle" he replied, rubbing his bloody fingers on his pants.

Kalibar's eyes darted down to the red streaks on Kyle's otherwise perfectly white pants, but his expression didn't change.

"Welcome to my home, Uh, Kyle," he greeted.

"Um...my name is Kyle, not Uh, Kyle," Kyle corrected, his cheeks flushing even more. Kalibar smirked ever-so-slightly.

"I know," he replied. "I was making a joke at your expense." Kyle smiled at Kalibar automatically, then realized that this wasn't a good thing.

"Do you know what that is?" Kalibar asked, pointing to Kyle's right ear. Kyle frowned, bringing his hand back up to his earlobe. It felt like there was a small earring there.

"An earring?" he ventured. The corner of Kalibar's mouth twitched.

"Think of it as a...universal translator," he corrected. "It understands the meaning behind spoken words, and that is what your ear registers." Kalibar paused, seeing Kyle's blank stare, then added "So you can understand what anyone is saying, even if they don't speak the same language."

Kyle stared at Kalibar mutely.

"The earring also allows me to understand what *you're* saying," Kalibar continued. "Now that we understand each other, tell me...where are you from?"

"Um," Kyle answered, "...Massachusetts."

Kalibar stared at him blankly.

"You know, in the United States," Kyle continued. "...of America."

Another blank stare.

"...on Earth?" Kyle added weakly. Kalibar frowned.

"I know the names and locations of every country in the known world," he replied authoritatively, "...but I've never heard of these places. Tell me, where is Urth?"

Kyle stared at Kalibar for a long moment. Then he realized that his mouth was hanging open, and he shut it with a *click*. The younger man wearing the golden armor stirred.

"Maybe he hit his head," the man offered dryly. Kalibar glanced at the man.

"Kyle, this is Darius," he introduced. Kyle turned to look at Darius, and saw the man staring back at him with those striking blue eyes. "He's one of my bodyguards," Kalibar explained. "If it weren't for him, you wouldn't be alive right now."

Kyle turned back to Darius, nodding slightly in thanks. The man just stared at him, not so much as blinking. Kyle squirmed in his seat, lowering his gaze to his lap.

"A farmer found you lying in the road three miles from here, as near to death as he'd ever seen," Kalibar continued. "He brought you here, to Bellingham, and Darius brought you to me." He frowned, leaning back in his chair. "And now I need to decide what I should do with you."

"Uh," Kyle mumbled. "...where am I?"

"You're in my home," Kalibar answered. "In a small town called Bellingham, east of Stridon."

Kyle stared blankly at Kalibar.

"Stridon, the capitol of the Empire," Kalibar continued. When Kyle's expression didn't change, Kalibar's brow furrowed. "On Doma," he added. Kyle just shrugged helplessly. Kalibar's eyes narrowed. "Interesting," he murmured.

"Maybe he's slow," Darius offered.

"I'm not slow," Kyle protested, blushing furiously. Darius hardly appeared convinced.

"Yes, well," Kalibar interjected. "We'll have time to decide that later. I have an important matter to attend to." He stood up then, nodding at Darius. "Darius, please escort Kyle back to his room."

Darius rose from his chair in one fluid motion, then grabbed Kyle's arm, yanking him up out of his chair. The motion sent pain shooting down Kyle's back; he cried out, and tried to pull his arm free. But Darius's grip was incredibly strong, and resisting only made the pain in Kyle's back worse. He glared at the bodyguard, feeling a red-hot flash of anger at the brute. Darius ignored the look, pulling Kyle out of the room and back down the hallway, then up the stairs to the bedroom.

"Sit," Darius commanded, shoving Kyle toward the bed. Kyle grit his teeth, but walked up to the bed and sat down gingerly. "Stay," Darius ordered, and walked out of the room, slamming the door behind him. Kyle glared at the closed door, seething with indignation.

I'm not a dog, you jerk!

He sat there for a long moment, the throbbing pain in his back fading slowly. Then he sighed, scooting up the bed carefully, then laying on his side. It felt surprisingly good to lie down; the short visit downstairs had taken more out of him than he'd realized. He laid there, thinking back to what Kalibar had said.

How could he not know where Earth *was?*

Kyle glanced down, spotting something glittering on his left thumb. It was his ring, he realized; the ring his father had given him. He wondered if Dad was looking for him back home. Dad *had* to be looking for him...a whole day had passed already. Dad had probably reported him missing. The police had to be scouring his neighborhood right now, searching for him. Worrying that he'd been kidnapped...or worse.

Kyle felt a lump in his throat, and clutched his left thumb to his chest, feeling his heart thumping there.

There was a knock at the door, and Kyle flinched, sitting up with some difficulty.

"Come in," he called out.

The door opened, and Kalibar walked through, closing the door behind him. He pulled a chair out from the desk nearby, sitting down across from Kyle.

"How are you feeling, Kyle?" he asked. Kyle stared back at the man mutely, not sure quite how to answer the question. Kalibar regarded Kyle wordlessly, a kind smile on his face. The silence stretched on for some time, making Kyle more and more uneasy.

"Lost," he answered at last.

"I can only image how you must feel," Kalibar replied. "Waking up in a strange place, in pain." He gestured at Kyle. "How are your wounds?"

"They hurt," Kyle admitted.

"Here," Kalibar stated, turning about to grab a glass of pale green liquid from the desk. He leaned over to hand it to Kyle. "Drink this."

"What is it?" Kyle asked, sniffing it. It smelled faintly sweet.

"Tea," Kalibar replied. "It'll help with the pain." When Kyle hesitated, Kalibar smirked. "It's not poison," he reassured. "I wouldn't go through all the trouble of saving your life just to kill you."

Kyle had to smile at that, and he took a small sip of the tea. It was quite delicious, with a hint of apple. He took a big gulp, the cool liquid soothing his parched throat. He was about to take a second gulp when Kalibar lunged forward to stop him, snatching the glass out of his hand.

"Careful," he warned. "It's...potent medicine."

"Sorry," Kyle mumbled. "Just thirsty I guess."

"You've lost a lot of blood," Kalibar explained. He set the glass back on the desk, then turned to Kyle. "What happened to you?" Kyle paused, then shrugged.

"I was attacked by something," he answered. He was about to say more, but Kalibar put up one hand.

"Tell me from the very beginning," he requested.

"The beginning?"

"Yes," Kalibar confirmed. "Start with how you got…lost."

Kyle frowned, unsure of how to proceed. Kalibar clearly had never heard of Earth, and the trees Kyle had seen in the forest earlier…there were no trees like that anywhere back home. But if he so much as hinted that he might be from another planet, Kalibar would think he was crazy.

Maybe I am crazy, he thought.

"I'm not sure," Kyle answered at last. "I was at my Dad's house," he continued. "…and I fell asleep for a nap." He described waking up to find himself hurtling through space, then landing on the forest floor. The words kept spilling out, and once they did, Kyle found that he couldn't stop. He told Kalibar everything, all the way up to the point where he'd woken up in this very room. When he'd finished, Kalibar turned to stare out of the bedroom window. At length, he sighed.

"That," he murmured, "…is an interesting story."

"It's not a story," Kyle countered, feeling a flash of righteous indignation. "It really happened!"

"Yes, well," Kalibar stated. "If so, how you managed to live through all of that is beyond me."

"What do you mean?"

"Well for starters, the vines you described are called 'rip-vines,'" Kalibar answered. "Once touched, they wrap themselves around their prey, sinking their roots into the flesh, slowly digesting their victims."

The blood drained from Kyle's face. He glanced at his left calf, remembering the little white things burrowing into his skin.

"And they don't have a habit of spontaneously dying," Kalibar continued dryly. "Because dying is the only thing that would ever stop a rip-vine. The same for the Ulfar – the animal that chased you." Kalibar gestured at Kyle. "Your wounds were hardly fatal, but Ulfars' saliva prevents blood from clotting…that's why you almost bled to death."

"Oh."

"You're lucky there was only one," Kalibar continued. "They usually hunt in packs."

"So you believe me?" Kyle asked, daring to hope. Kalibar nodded.

"I think I do."

Kyle felt a wave of relief, and couldn't help breaking out into a smile. He felt almost giddy, in fact. For some reason, Kalibar smirked.

"How is your pain now?" he asked. Kyle twisted his back slowly, and to his surprise there was only a faint twinge.

"Much better."

"The tea is working," Kalibar observed. Kyle glanced at the glass of tea on the desk. He was a bit woozy, but in an indescribably good way. He realized that he was still grinning rather stupidly, and tried to compose himself.

"Now," Kalibar stated, "...where was it you said you were from again?"

"Earth," Kyle replied.

"Ah yes," Kalibar murmured. "And what is Urth, exactly?"

Kyle tried not to laugh, and failed miserably, a loud snort blowing through his nostrils. He covered his nose and mouth with his hands, staring at Kalibar in horror. But the look of confusion on the old man's face was priceless, and despite himself, Kyle burst out laughing again.

"What's so funny?" Kalibar asked, his voice oddly calm. Kyle shook his head, trying desperately to control himself. At length he succeeded.

"It's a planet," Kyle answered, rubbing an itch out of his nose. Kalibar's eyebrow rose.

"A planet," he echoed.

"Yeah," Kyle insisted, as if it were the most obvious thing in the world. Which it was.

"And the...united states?" Kalibar asked.

"Of America," Kyle stated. "It's a country. The most powerful country in the world," he added rather proudly. Kalibar raised both eyebrows at that.

"Oh really," he murmured.

"Yup."

"And what continent is your country in?" Kalibar pressed.

"North America," Kyle answered. Kalibar's eyes narrowed.

"Kyle, how many continents are there?"

"Um," Kyle replied, "...seven."

Kalibar leaned back in his chair, cradling his chin in one hand and staring off into space. Then he blinked, settling his gaze back on Kyle.

"Well, thank you for your honesty," he said at last, leaning forward and patting Kyle on the knee. Kyle smiled back; Kalibar had listened to him...*truly* listened, without always interrupting, like adults tended to do. He felt a sudden affection for the man.

"Kyle, you deserve *my* honesty," Kalibar admitted, rubbing his palms together in front of him. "When Darius found you, I was more interested – at first – in your ring than I was in you."

"My ring?" Kyle asked, glancing down at his left thumb. "Why?"

"It is a...most unique runic device, as you must know. The tech..." He paused then, noting Kyle's blank stare. "You *do* know what a runic device is, don't you?"

"Um, no," Kyle admitted. Kalibar arched one eyebrow.

"Do you know what magic is?" he asked.

"Yeah, sure."

"Well, a runic device is an object that is infused with magic. This magic allows it to perform a particular function," Kalibar explained. "Take your earring for example...its magic is very complicated. In fact, it is so complicated that no one has been able to make one for over two thousand years."

Kyle stared silently at Kalibar, unable to keep a straight face. Magical earrings? How gullible did the old man think Kyle was? He'd stopped believing in magic and fairy tales years ago, after all. His stepfather had once said that magic was just a word people used to explain things they didn't understand. Then he'd added "...like reli-" and Mom had hit him so hard and so fast, he'd never finished the sentence. Kyle remembered them arguing for a long time afterward. Steve had never brought it up again.

"Why are you smirking?" Kalibar asked. He looked slightly perturbed. Kyle shook his head.

"Sorry, I just...well, I'm old enough to know that magic isn't real," he confessed. Kalibar blinked.

"What do you mean?" he retorted. "Of course magic is real!"

"No it isn't," Kyle insisted.

"It most certainly *is*," Kalibar stated heatedly. He stood from his chair then. "Come," he continued, standing up and offering one hand to Kyle. "Perhaps you need a demonstration!"

Chapter 4

The sun was at its peak in the sky, blazing brightly atop the trees outside Kalibar's massive mansion, its warm rays gently baking the earth. Kalibar had led Kyle downstairs and out of the house, walking across the huge backyard beyond. They'd passed dozens of people in the process; a maid busily mopping the floor, a pair of guards standing rigidly at the rear door of the property, and many more patrolling outside. More men worked the endless acres of farmland behind the mansion. If Kalibar really owned this mansion – and by the way everyone, including the armed guards, behaved around Kalibar, he most certainly did – then he was obviously filthy rich.

"So you own this whole place?" Kyle asked, glancing back at the mansion behind them. Two stories tall in some places, and up to four stories in others, the massive building was big enough to house a hundred people.

"I do," Kalibar replied. "I was…a man of some importance before I retired here, in Bellingham. I came here to get away from the distractions of the city, so that I could concentrate on my research."

"Your research?" Kyle pressed. Kalibar nodded.

"On the void mineral," he clarified. "It's complicated," he added, noticing Kyle's confused look. "In any case, I chose Bellingham because its people value privacy, and they respect mine." He sighed. "For me, that is a rare luxury."

Kalibar fell silent then, and they continued down the dirt path past the seemingly endless fields of crops on either side. Eventually these gave way to the towering edge of the tree line beyond. The dirt path continued into this forest; tall trees lined the path as it curved this way and that, and in the distance Kyle could hear the gurgling of running water.

"I've lived here for almost six years," Kalibar said, breaking the silence. "Rather uneventfully...until recently. When Darius brought you here..."

Kyle's expression immediately soured, and Kalibar smirked.

"I understand Darius is a bit...rough," he stated. "But he came to me with the highest of recommendations." His smirk faded. "I hired him after someone tried to assassinate me." Kyle stopped in his tracks, and Kalibar did so as well.

"Wait, someone tried...?"

"...to assassinate me, yes," Kalibar confirmed. "About three weeks ago. They didn't do a very good job of it, obviously." He began walking again, and Kyle followed beside him. The path led to a small bridge that arched over a stream some ten feet wide. The stream was quite shallow, cutting through the forest with a merry, gushing, gurgling sound. Kyle spotted colorful rounded pebbles on the stream bed, with silver fish darting through the clear water. Kalibar turned to Kyle, gesturing at the stream.

"This is a tributary that feeds the Great River – the one you nearly drowned in this morning," he stated. Then he pointed with his other hand, toward a mountain far in the distance. "It, in turn, is fed by rainwater from that mountain." Kalibar paused for a moment, then spread his arms wide.

"Streams," he continued, "flow downhill toward rivers, and rivers flow downhill toward the sea." He paused then, staring intently at Kyle. "This is the way of things; the stream obeys the laws of nature."

Kyle nodded; he'd heard it all before in school, of course.

"And nature, in turn," Kalibar continued, his voice suddenly grim and powerful, "...obeys *me*."

Without warning, the waters of the stream rose upward above the smooth pebbles of the stream-bed, lifting slowly into the air. The water flowed through the air in a wide fan, tiny droplets flying outward from the main stream in all directions. The sun's rays shimmered through the water, sparkling brilliantly; small silver shapes darted through the hovering water, tiny fish swimming in their newly airborne channel. A faint blue glow surrounded the levitating stream, growing brighter as it rose higher and higher into the air.

Kyle gasped, staring in disbelief.

Suddenly, pebbles lifted up from the ground all around him, dead leaves and dirt following suit. Within seconds, a layer of forest floor debris was hovering at waist-level all around them. Kyle turned to the right, spotting a half-decayed log hovering a few feet above the ground next to him, rotating slowly in mid-air. Then he felt a sickening lurch, and his feet lifted off of the ground. He cried out, flailing his arms and legs wildly, but this only caused him to somersault forward in mid-air, until he was hovering upside-down. He looked down – or rather *up* – at his feet, and saw an endless expanse of blue beyond them. He screamed, terrified that that he would soar upward into that infinite abyss.

He continued to rotate until he was right-side-up, and moments later he descended back to terra firma. The levitating sea of leaves, dirt, and rocks around him descended as well, returning to their rightful place on the ground. Even the stream lowered itself to rest upon its bed once more, flowing merrily through its narrow channel as if nothing had happened.

"I assure you," Kalibar stated authoritatively, staring down at Kyle from where he stood a few feet away, "…that magic is *quite* real." A slight smirk played on the old man's lips.

"Whoa," Kyle breathed. Sweat trickled into his eyes, and he wiped it away, his hand trembling with the motion. Kalibar's eyes twinkled.

"Whoa indeed."

Kalibar turned toward the small bridge arching over the stream, stepping across it and gesturing for Kyle to follow alongside. Kyle did so, staring up at the man wordlessly. If Kalibar noticed, he didn't show it; he kept his eyes forward, on the path beyond the stream.

"So, we've established that magic is real," Kalibar stated casually, as if nothing unusual had happened. "As I was saying earlier, your earring is powered by magic. Objects powered by magic are called runic devices, or runics," he added. "Your earring is actually over two thousand years old. They were very common in Ancient times."

"Uh huh," Kyle mumbled. He glanced back to look at the stream behind them, unable to believe what he'd just witnessed. It was impossible – magic didn't exist – but he'd *seen* it. He put a hand to his lips then; had Kalibar drugged him with that glass of tea, making him hallucinate?

"The Ancients last lived over two thousand years ago," Kalibar continued. "They had formed a remarkable civilization that had endured for thousands of years. Their runic technology was far more advanced than it is today. Your earring is a relic of that time. It is relatively simple by Ancient standards, but today it is considered impossibly complex, and no one knows how it works."

Kyle frowned, reaching up to feel the earring with one hand. It was impossible to deny that the earring did as Kalibar suggested. Kalibar's lips moved as if he were speaking a foreign language, but what came out was English. It was as if Kyle was living in a dubbed movie.

"Anyone trained in the use of magic can sense magic in other people, and objects," Kalibar lectured. "We can detect the strength and complexity of a runic device in this way. When I met you, I felt the presence of such a device." With that, Kalibar pointed to Kyle's ring. It was still on Kyle's thumb, sparkling slightly in the sunlight. Kyle frowned.

"Wait, what?"

"Your ring," Kalibar explained. "It's magical."

"It can't be," Kyle countered, drawing his hand to his chest protectively. "My dad gave it to me." Whatever strange forces existed here, there was no magic on Earth…that was a scientific fact.

"I assure you," Kalibar retorted, "…it is." He stopped walking then, facing Kyle. "Your ring is very special, Kyle. It's extraordinarily sophisticated…beyond anything I've ever seen."

"What do you mean?"

"Well, in terms of complexity, if a typical runic device were a spark," Kalibar began…and suddenly a tiny white light appeared, floating in mid-air between Kyle and Kalibar. "…and if your earring were a flame," Kalibar continued. A small flame flickered gently in the air next to the spark. "Then your ring…"

"What?" Kyle asked. Kalibar said nothing for a moment, instead turning his gaze upward, to the heavens.

"Well," Kalibar answered. "Your ring would be the sun."

* * *

"I find it fascinating that there's no magic where you come from," Kalibar said as they walked back into the large room they'd been in earlier. Kalibar sat down where he had before, and motioned for Kyle to sit on the seat next to him. Kyle did so, rubbing his nose again. It still itched something fierce; he wondered if he'd suddenly developed allergies. Kalibar had spent much of the walk back to the mansion asking Kyle about Earth. The old man seemed quite perturbed that he'd never heard of Kyle's homeland.

"You're sure you're not from Verhan?" Kalibar asked, not for the first time. Kyle nodded.

"I'm sure," he answered. Kalibar frowned, tapping his chin with one finger. There was a sudden knock on the door, and it opened shortly thereafter. To Kyle's dismay, Darius walked through, sitting down on the chair to Kyle's left. Kyle ignored the man, keeping his eyes on Kalibar.

"Well, most living things use magic here," Kalibar stated. "Plants, animals, birds, insects…almost everything possesses magic that enhances their survival capabilities."

Kyle nodded, although he hardly believed what he was hearing. Despite Kalibar's impressive demonstration, he still had a hard time believing that magic really existed.

"People can use magic too – or at least some of them can," Kalibar continued. "The gift runs in families, it seems. Most people can't make magic at all."

"Wait," Kyle said, rubbing his nose again. "So how *do* people make magic?" Kalibar shrugged.

"We don't know," the old man admitted. "Magic is made by the brain, that much we do know. But flesh is actually a poor storage substance for magic, and so magic tends to leak from it. This 'leak' can be detected by other magic users," Kalibar continued. "In fact, this is how we determine who can be trained to use magic, and who can't."

"Wait, so you can tell if someone makes lots of magic?" Kyle asked. Kalibar nodded.

"Or whether they make any at all," he replied. "Like I said, most people can't make magic. Those who can usually do so by puberty. I can tell if someone makes magic by simply standing near them, and sensing the amount of magic leaking from their mind." Kalibar paused for a moment, then pointed at Kyle's ring.

"This 'leak' of magic also allows us to detect runic devices," he added. "The magic of your ring is mostly stored in the crystal. Minerals are far better at storing magic than flesh…I believe it has something to do with the geometry of the crystalline matrix, but no one knows for sure."

Kyle nodded. So crystals were like batteries for magic...simple enough. He glanced at his ring, flexing his thumb. He still couldn't understand how his ring could be magical. There was no magic on Earth, after all. It was only special because his father had given it to him...it was the one tangible reminder he had of home. A reminder of where he'd come from...and where he belonged.

"What's bothering you, Kyle?" Kalibar inquired. Kyle glanced up at Kalibar.

"Nothing..." he lied. Then he shook his head. "I mean, it's just that...my parents don't know where I am." He turned away from Kalibar and stared at the floor, taking a deep breath in, then letting it out.

"Hmm," Kalibar murmured. Kyle glanced up at Kalibar; the old man was staring at him, an odd expression on his face.

"What?" Kyle asked.

"You said that Urth was a...planet," Kalibar stated. Kyle half-expected the man to smirk, but he didn't.

"It sounds crazy, I know," Kyle muttered.

"It does," Kalibar agreed.

"Magic sounds just as crazy to me," Kyle protested, crossing his arms over his chest. Kalibar arched an eyebrow.

"I gave you proof of magic's existence," he countered. Kyle said nothing, recalling the demonstration earlier. There was nothing to say...Kalibar was right, of course. Kyle sighed, slumping back in his chair.

"I just want to go home," he muttered.

"I can't help you with that, I'm afraid," Kalibar admitted, leaning back in his chair and tapping his chin with one finger. "I have no idea how you got here...and no idea how to get you back to your home, wherever that is." He frowned. "The Ancients once dreamed of visiting other planets," he added. "But their dreams died with them long ago."

Kyle nodded, slumping over. He glanced at his father's ring, its yellow gemstone glittering dully on his thumb. If this *was* a different planet than Earth – which he still had a hard time believing – then he wasn't going back home.

Ever.

"Kyle," Kalibar said, snapping Kyle out of his thoughts. The old man leaned forward, putting a hand on Kyle's forearm. "I'm sorry."

Kyle nodded silently, swallowing past a sudden lump in his throat, turning away from Kalibar and staring at the floor. He felt Kalibar squeeze his forearm gently.

"There's no loss more painful than losing one's family," he stated gently. Kyle glanced up at Kalibar, and saw him staring off into the distance. A moment later, he snapped out of it, focusing on Kyle. "Hmm?"

"Uh…"

"Anyway," Kalibar stated, "…trust that I am eager to solve the mystery of where you're from, how you got here, and most importantly, *why* you're here."

"Why?" Kyle asked.

"See it from my perspective," Kalibar answered. "A young boy appears from a place I've never heard of, speaking a language I've never encountered, wearing a mysterious ring more sophisticated than any runic item in the known world." He leaned forward. "It raises so many questions! How did you get here? Does it have anything to do with your ring? What saved you from the rip-vines and the Ulfar?"

Kyle considered this, saying nothing.

"I also have to consider what would happen if anyone else found out about your ring," Kalibar added. "Or about…you. As much as I hate to admit it, most people here are not as principled as I am. Your ring might be the most valuable runic commodity in the known world. Many would kill – or worse – to possess it."

Kyle felt a pang of fear, and clutched his ring to his belly. People would *kill* him just for his ring? He shrank into his chair, glancing at Darius. The man was staring back at him. Kyle turned away quickly, facing Kalibar again.

"But you don't even know what my ring does," Kyle protested.

"True," Kalibar agreed. "…but I know someone who may have better luck figuring it out. His name is Erasmus."

"Erasmus?"

"A close and trusted friend, and one of the finest Runic scholars I know," Kalibar replied. "If anyone can deduce the functions of your ring, he can."

"Can we show it to him?" Kyle asked, perking up. If this Erasmus could figure out how his ring worked, he might be able to get back home.

"It's not quite that simple," Kalibar admitted, leaning back in his chair and sighing. "Travel may not be as...safe as it used to be."

"What do you mean?" Kyle pressed. Kalibar waved away the question.

"If we *did* go," the old man stated, "...it would be a three-day carriage ride from here. Erasmus lives in the capital of the Empire – a city called Stridon. He works at the Secula Magna."

"The Secula what?"

"The Secula Magna," Kalibar repeated. "The school of magic. It's the most powerful magical institution in the known world," he added. "...and the political center of the Empire."

"Could he figure out how to get me home?" Kyle asked, daring to hope. Kalibar shrugged.

"I'm not certain that your ring played a role in your coming here," Kalibar replied. "Nevertheless, the possibility is worth the risk. I'll take you to Erasmus, and we will see."

"Thanks," Kyle said, feeling relieved.

"You're welcome," Kalibar replied. He stood from his chair then. "The trip will require careful planning. We'll leave tomorrow evening."

"Thanks," Kyle said again. He hadn't expected things to move so quickly, but he wasn't about to complain!

"Wait here," Kalibar ordered. "My staff will provide you with lunch." He walked toward the door. "I suggest you get plenty of rest."

With that, Kalibar left, Darius following close behind, leaving Kyle alone in the room. Kyle sighed, putting his palms down on the tabletop. He stared at his ring, thinking back to what Kalibar had said.

How could it be magical?

He flexed his thumb, making the gemstone's facets glitter. If his ring *was* magical, then it had to be what had brought him here...there was no other explanation. And if it brought him here, then maybe it could send him back.

Or maybe not, he thought darkly.

He sighed, lowering his head and resting his cheek on the table. There was only one way to know for sure. Maybe, just maybe, this Erasmus would be able to figure it out.

Chapter 5

Ampir rushes toward Junior, leaping over the hole in the bedroom floor left by the massive bomb that had punched through the ceiling only seconds earlier.

Junior!

He weaves magic within his mind's eye, throwing out a pulsing knot of power at his son...just as the bomb detonates.

No!

The floor explodes, debris shooting upward all around them. The shockwave shoves him forward, catapulting him into the disintegrating hallway.

Vera screams.

Ampir hurtles forward, clutching onto Vera. He careens through the collapsing floor, the world spinning around him madly. Thick black smoke billows upward around them, flaming chunks of wood and stone ricocheting off of the magical shield surrounding them.

He feels a jolt as his feet slam into the ground, hears Vera cry out in pain.

Debris rains down around them, clattering on the surface of Ampir's translucent blue shield. Fine ash falls from the sky, the black smoke surrounding them making it nearly impossible to see. Ampir stands up, finding himself in a shallow, charred crater that is all that remains of their home. Vera twists in his arms.

"Junior," Vera says, her voice rising in panic. "Where is he?"

Ampir peers through the wall of smoke and ash surrounding them, turning in a slow circle. He sees a pile of rubble nearby, spots a faint blue light shining from between slabs of stone and ash. Ampir rushes up to it, lifting the rubble and tossing it to the side, revealing a shimmering blue sphere beneath. And within that sphere is Junior, curled up in a ball on the ground, staring up at Ampir with wide, terrified eyes.

"My baby!" Vera cries, struggling against Ampir. He sets her down, the blue sphere around his son vanishing. Vera rushes to Junior's side, embracing him. Ampir puts a hand on her shoulder, then feels a faint vibration in his skull. He glances upward, peering through the thick smoke. There, hovering above the ruins of their home, is a huge silver airship. Rays of blue rise from the ground toward it, converging on a large white crystal on its underbelly.

That's what bombed us, he realizes.

"Get down," Ampir urges, kneeling and pulling Vera down with him.

"What is it?" Vera asks, looking upward. But of course she can't see the ship; it is invisible through the blanket of smoke. Ampir can see it only through the power of his visor.

"Don't move."

The ship hovers there for another minute, then moves away from the house toward the Great River, picking up speed rapidly. It flies over the river toward the heart of the city.

Ampir scoops Vera up in his arms, then turns to Junior.

"Get on my back," he orders. Junior obeys silently, climbing onto his father's armored back. Ampir trudges through the rubble, until he stands on the scorched remains of their backyard. Beyond lies the Great River, and the cityscape of Stridon, capitol of the Empire. The Great Tower stands above all, its crystalline peak glittering in the starlight. Thick, angry clouds hang low in the sky above the city, illuminated by countless street lights.

"What's happening?" Vera asks. "Why are we being attacked?"

"I don't know," Ampir admits.

"Who were those men?"

"Don't know," Ampir repeats. "But I'm going to find out." He looks down at her. "First we need to get you help. The Royal surgeon is in the Tower…I knew him in the military. He's the best there is."

"What's that?" Junior asks, pointing at something ahead. Ampir looks up, spotting a huge, faintly glowing green light coming from deep within the clouds above the city. As he watches, the light grows brighter.

"I don't…"

Then something falls through the clouds. Something *huge.* Two black metallic feet, followed by massive legs, each as tall as a five-story building. A metal torso, and then a massive, dome-shaped head. The behemoth falls through the sky toward the city below, wisps of cloud trailing from its limbs.

What the...

The monstrosity descends toward the translucent blue dome of the Gate Shield, falling toward it with incredible speed.

The Gate Shield flickers, then vanishes.

"Ampir!" Vera shouts.

The behemoth's feet slam into the courtyard near the Great Tower, sending plumes of dirt high into the air. Its domed head turns, revealing a single diamond-shaped eye in the center, glowing an eerie, hazy green through the cloud of dust.

"What the *hell* is that?" Vera asks.

The thing – the Behemoth – stands perfectly still for a moment. Then its lone eye flashes. A beam of brilliant green light shoots outward from that eye, striking a building miles away. The building explodes, sending debris flying in all directions.

Holy...

The Behemoth's head spins 360 degrees, its ungodly beam slicing through the buildings surrounding the campus of the Great Tower. Entire city blocks disintegrate, debris flying high into the air over the city. The beam fades away, the Behemoth becoming still for a long moment.

Then its head turns, its lone eye pointing right at the Tower.

"It's going to attack the Tower!" Vera exclaims in horror.

"Hold on," Ampir warns. "We're going up."

With a thought, he feels himself become weightless, his metallic boots lifting off of the grass. He flies upward and forward, gaining speed gradually. The shoreline passes underneath them, the river's dark waters rippling below. He feels Vera stiffen.

"What's wrong?"

"It's starting to hurt," she confesses, putting a hand on her belly. "Bad."

"Almost there baby," Ampir murmurs, increasing his speed. The wind howls around them, becoming higher-pitched as they accelerate toward the Tower...and the Behemoth in the distance. The monstrosity faces the Tower, the city burning all around it. Ampir clenches his jaw, the wind screaming around him as he blasts across the river toward the city. He's still too far away to attack the

Behemoth…and the best surgeon in the city is in the Tower.

Come on, he urges himself, pushing his armor to the limit.

The Behemoth's diamond-shaped eye flashes.

* * *

Kyle yawned, rolling onto his side in bed, and immediately regretted it. Pain shot up his spine, and he nearly yelled, freezing in place. He opened his eyes, squinting against the bright rays of sunlight splayed across his bed. It took him a moment to remember where he was…and where he wasn't.

It wasn't a dream, he thought, his heart sinking.

He sighed, turning away from the window slowly. There was a fresh glass of tea on the dresser opposite the bed; he shimmied over to the edge of the bed, then swung his legs over, walking to the dresser and picking up the glass. He took one gulp – Kalibar had warned him against taking more – and set the glass back on the table. He barely recalled falling asleep the night before; he'd had a gulp of the tea right beforehand. Surprisingly, he hadn't wet the bed…and for that, he was immensely grateful.

He yawned again, then gingerly made his way out of his room, walking down the spiral staircase to the hallway below. He'd been instructed by one of Kalibar's attendants to come down here for breakfast. He opened the door at the end of the hallway and entered the large room he'd met Kalibar in the day before…then froze.

The room was *packed* with people. The long table was surrounded by men and women, the polished tabletop covered in plates of steaming food. More people stood around the room, holding their plates of food while they ate and talked to one another. Some of them were clearly guards, but most were not. Kyle recognized a few of the farmers he'd seen during his walk with Kalibar yesterday.

Kyle stood in the doorway, gripped by the sudden urge to go back to bed.

"Hey kid," a voice said from his right. Kyle turned, spotting a tall man in silver armor leaning against the wall. The man's armor was smeared with dirt, but his face and hair were clean. He was quite handsome, and looked like he knew it. The man grinned at Kyle, putting a hand on his shoulder.

"I'm Fintan," he greeted.

"Hey," Kyle mumbled. "Uh, I'm Kyle."

"You're that kid they found on the road," Fintan observed. He stepped away from the wall. "You holding the door for someone?"

Kyle blinked, then realized he was still in the doorway.

"Get in," Fintan urged, pulling Kyle into the room. He made a face, looking Kyle up and down. "Geez, when's the last time you ate, a week ago?"

"Uh…"

"What's the matter kid, you slow?" Fintan pressed. Kyle was about to reply, but Fintan clapped him on the back. Kyle bit back a scream, his spine exploding with pain. "Hey, relax, will ya?" Fintan admonished. "I'm just fooling with you." He walked toward the table in the center of the room, pulling Kyle with him. They maneuvered through the crowd until they reached the table, stopping before two women that were sitting and eating. Fintan let go of Kyle, putting a hand on each of the ladies' shoulders. "Good morning ladies," he greeted. They turned to look up at him, their expressions instantly souring.

"We're eating," one of them protested.

"Somewhere else," the other grumbled. She got up from her chair, taking her plate and glaring at Fintan before walking away. Fintan sat down, turning to the remaining woman and grinning devilishly. She pointedly ignored him. He gestured at Kyle.

"This is…what's your name again, kid?" he asked.

"Kyle."

"Right," Fintan agreed. "This is Kyle. He's a little slow," he added, making Kyle blush. The woman arched an eyebrow.

"And you're a little quick, as I remember," she shot back. Fintan grimaced, turning to an elderly man wearing a black vest and white shirt, who was carrying a large serving platter.

"Hey Faisel!" he called out, pointing at the man. "Two plates!" The woman next to Fintan pushed her own plate away, rising to her feet.

"Suddenly I've lost my appetite," she muttered.

"That's a first," Fintan replied with another grin, shamelessly ogling her rear as she left. Then he turned to Kyle. "Sit down, kid." Kyle did so, and moments later Faisel returned with two plates, setting them before Fintan and Kyle. It looked like eggs and some sort of meat, and the smell of it made Kyle's mouth water. Fintan dug in immediately, eating the meat with his bare hands. Then he paused, turning to Kyle.

"Dig in," he urged. Kyle obeyed, grabbing a hunk of meat with his bare hands, then nibbling on a corner of it. To his surprise, it was pretty good. He took a bite, chewing on it greedily.

"Where you from, kid?" Fintan asked between bites.

"Earth."

"Never heard of it," Fintan replied, taking a swig of liquid from a half-empty glass beside him. The owner of said bottle – a young woman with red, curly hair – glared at him.

"You're not going to even ask me for it?" she declared angrily.

"I just assumed you'd give it to me," he replied smoothly. "You know, like you…"

"Get lost," she interrupted, standing up quickly and walking away. Fintan turned back to Kyle.

"Is it cold in here or is it just me?" he asked.

"Uh," Kyle began, but Fintan wasn't even looking at him anymore.

"Hey Nash," he called out. An older guard sitting opposite them turned to look at them. "When's the sparring start?"

"Five minutes ago," the man answered.

"Damn it," Fintan swore. He turned to Kyle, who was stuffing the last of his meat into his mouth. "Come on," he urged, standing up from his chair. He grabbed Kyle's elbow, lifting him from the chair and pulling him toward a door on the other end of the room. Kyle followed behind mutely, his mouth still full. They weaved through the crowd, making it to the door and leaving the room. Fintan led him through a veritable maze of corridors until they found themselves outside. Kyle swallowed his food, squinting in the sunlight.

"Where are we going?" he asked.

"The sparring ring," Fintan answered. "I have a lot of money to win back." He picked up his pace, pulling Kyle toward a large dirt field a hundred or so feet away. A few dozen guards stood in a loose ring around the field, all facing inward. "I've got bets on a few of the fights," he added eagerly. Moments later, they reached the ring of guards, joining them. In the center of the field were two men; they stood facing each other, crouched low to the ground. Each was carrying a thin wooden stick in one hand and a shield in the other.

"You're betting on them?" Kyle asked.

"Not these jokers," Fintan snorted. "See that guy?" he added, pointing to the man on the left. "He'll be on the ground in a minute." As Kyle watched, the man on the right lunged forward at the other guard, stopping suddenly and drawing back. His opponent flinched backward, ducking behind his shield.

"How do you know?"

The guard on the right lunged forward again, but this time he didn't stop, slamming his shield against the other guard's body instead. The other guard stumbled backward, and soon found himself on his back on the dirt, a wooden stick jabbing into his armored chest.

"Typical," Fintan observed. "New recruits always dodge straight back. Good way to die. We beat that outta them real quick." He frowned then, shaking his head. "Not sure why we're training townspeople to replace all the guards we lost," he added. "Shoulda gotten experienced soldiers from Stridon by now."

"Good morning, Kyle," a smooth voice called out from behind. Kyle nearly jumped, spinning about...and saw Kalibar standing before him. Fintan turned as well, and stiffened, raising his arm in salute. Within moments, every man on the field – including the men sparring – had turned to face Kalibar, saluting sharply.

"At ease," Kalibar ordered, his voice easily carrying across the dirt field. His tone – one of effortless command – was far different than it had been a moment ago. The guards relaxed somewhat, but still stood facing Kalibar. Kalibar gestured for them to continue. "Please, as you were gentlemen," he insisted. Then he turned to Kyle.

"I trust you had some breakfast?" the old man asked. Kyle nodded, finding himself standing rigidly before Kalibar, as the guards had been.

"Yes sir," he replied. "Fintan helped me," he added, gesturing at the young guard.

"Thank you Fintan," Kalibar said, nodding at the guard. "I'm sure Kyle will want to watch for a bit longer," he added. "See that he returns to my office in twenty minutes."

"Yes your Excellency," Fintan answered crisply.

"Carry on," Kalibar stated, then turned about, walking back toward the mansion. Kyle noticed a man in golden armor – Darius – walking toward Kalibar as he neared the mansion. Darius leaned in to whisper something in Kalibar's ear, then walked with the old man into the house. Kyle turned, and noticed Fintan glaring at Darius's back.

"What?" Kyle asked. Fintan glanced at Kyle, then shook his head.

"That bastard is what," the young guard replied, leaning over to spit on the ground. "Frankly, I don't know why the Master puts up with him."

"The Master?" Kyle asked. "You mean Kalibar?" Fintan's expression hardened.

"Don't ever call him by his first name," Fintan scolded. Then his expression softened. "Anyway, none of us can stand Darius," he continued. "For one, he acts like he owns the place. He does whatever he wants, treats us guards like we're dumb kids pretending to be soldiers – no offense," he added hastily. "Thing is, he's never once agreed to spar any of us," he added. "And it ain't for lack of being challenged. If you ask me, he's scared."

"Why did Kal...er, the Master hire him then?" Kyle pressed.

"Beats me," Fintan answered. "Couple weeks ago, a group of assassins tried to kill the Master. Watched a lot of friends die that night," he added darkly. "The Master was asleep, and one of our men managed to wake him up before the enemy could get to his room."

"What happened?"

"The Master took care of things," Fintan answered, shaking his head. "Never seen anything like it," he added. For the first time since Kyle had met him, Fintan seemed subdued. "The legends about him...they're all true."

"What legends?

"You don't know?" Fintan asked incredulously.

"Uh, no."

"Oh, you'll learn soon enough," Fintan promised. "Anyway, after the attack, we shoulda gotten more soldiers and elite guards from Stridon. Instead, golden-boy over there came by a week or so later, ignoring everyone, acting all high-and-mighty. Heard he charges a pretty penny for standing around being useless, too. That's why he's scared, I bet; if he spars, and loses, he'll be found out." He shook his head. "No one knows why the Master hired the guy," he added. "Master Kalibar's *nobody's* fool."

Fintan paused, then turned back to the center of the field. Two new guards had entered the ring with their wooden shields and sticks. One of them took out a dark bottle, leaning down to drink from it. Then he turned the bottle upside-down – without anything spilling from it – then corked the bottle, turning it right-side-up again and handing it to his opponent. His opponent did the same, handing it back to the first guard.

"Watch this," Fintan said. "I've got a hundred on the guy on the left." Kyle complied, watching as the two guards crouched down low, eyeing each other. They circled each other slowly, making feints at each other.

"Come on ladies," the guard standing next to Kyle shouted. "Quit dancing and start fighting!"

Without warning, the opponent on the right lunged forward, swinging at the other guard. The other guard leaped forward and upward, flying high into the air – over twenty feet! – and landed gently near the other edge of the ring, turning about to grin at his enemy. Kyle gasped, his eyes wide.

"Did you see that?" he exclaimed.

"Pfft, that's nothing," Fintan countered with a grin. "Wait till the feathergrass extract *really* kicks in." Kyle stared blankly at Fintan, making the guard frown. "You never heard of feathergrass?" he asked incredulously. Kyle shook his head.

"I'm not from around here."

"Where you from, another planet?" Fintan pressed. Kyle's breath stopped in his throat, and he almost choked on his own spit. "Makes people light as a feather," Fintan continued obliviously. "Got feathergrass fibers lining my armor," he stated, patting his breastplate. "This weighs forty pounds without the lining – but it feels like five." Fintan gestured toward two women walking past the sparring ring, carrying huge baskets of vegetables above their heads. "See them?"

"Yeah."

"Those baskets have feathergrass fibers in 'em," Fintan explained. "That's why those girls can carry all that weight." He eyed the women. "They use it in their bras too," he added, grinning from ear to ear. "Gives them a nice little lift."

Kyle frowned, glancing furtively at one of the women, and realized that Fintan was right; there was a definite buoyant quality to her top. He tore his gaze away quite reluctantly, not wanting to get caught staring, and turned back toward the sparring ring. The opponents were circling again.

"Damn, this is taking too long," Fintan muttered. "I'd better get you back inside," he added, patting Kyle on the shoulder. "The Master hates to wait."

They both turned away from the sparring match, leaving the rest of the guards behind and returning to the mansion. Fintan navigated expertly through the corridors, climbing a few flights of stairs before eventually stopping at a door at the end of a long hallway. The guard knocked on the door twice, then took a few steps backward, motioning for Kyle to do the same. The door swung open, seemingly of its own accord. Beyond, Kyle saw Kalibar sitting at a large wooden desk, a rather hefty-looking book open in front of him. The old man looked up from the massive tome, gesturing for Kyle to come in. Kyle did so, leaving Fintan behind. The door closed behind Kyle, again of its own accord, leaving the two alone.

"Sit," Kalibar ordered, closing his book. A chair at one end of the room slid sideways across the floor, stopping right in front of Kalibar's desk, by Kyle's side. Kyle paused, then sat down, folding his arms on his lap. Kalibar's office was large – twice as big as Kyle's living room on Earth, and over two stories high. Massive bookshelves lined the walls, reaching all the way up to the ceiling. As Kyle watched, Kalibar's book flew up from the desk, soaring through the air until it placed itself into an empty spot on a shelf some ten feet up.

"I trust you enjoyed your time with the guards?" Kalibar asked.

"Yes sir," Kyle answered. "Fintan taught me about feathergrass."

"I know," Kalibar stated. "I saw how much you appreciated the plant's more...intriguing uses," he added with a wink. Kyle looked away, blushing fiercely. Kalibar chuckled.

"Oh, relax," he said, glancing out of a large window at one end of his office. "You'll never grow out of that particular fascination, so you might as well get used to enjoying it." He leaned back in his chair. "On a more serious note, there's been a slight...complication in our plan. Darius notified me of a series of attacks on carriages attempting to leave Bellingham."

"What happened?"

"The carriages were attacked at the edge of town," Kalibar replied grimly. "There were no survivors."

"Why were they attacked?"

"Indeed," Kalibar answered. "Why?"

Kyle thought about it for a moment.

"Could it have anything to do with the attack a few weeks ago?" he asked. Kalibar nodded.

"Almost certainly," he agreed. "Whoever ordered my assassination must know that they've failed." He brought a finger up to his chin, tapping it thoughtfully. "The attempt was surprisingly well-orchestrated. I never would have survived if the protective wards in my bedroom hadn't woken me in time."

"Wait, Fintan said one of your guards woke you," Kyle countered.

"A necessary deceit, for their morale," Kalibar explained. "Most of my wards had been deactivated by the enemy, but luckily they missed one, and it woke me." He smiled grimly then. "Taking me in my sleep was their only chance."

"You killed them?" Kyle asked.

"Oh yes."

Kyle swallowed, remembering Kalibar's demonstration earlier…and what Fintan had said.

"In any case," Kalibar continued, "…after the attack, I sent a letter to Stridon with the details of the attack, and a request for more soldiers and Battle-Weavers to replace those I'd lost. They were magically sealed and protected letters," he added. "So far I've had no response…even after sending several more letters." He peered through the window again. "Whoever planned the attack is cutting off my supply line."

"What does this have to do with the attacks on the carriages?" Kyle asked.

"The entire town knows about the assassination attempt," Kalibar answered. "Anyone leaving town could potentially bring that news to Stridon."

"So they're killing everyone who tries to leave?" Kyle pressed. Kalibar nodded, leaning forward in his chair.

"Correct."

"So we can't leave," Kyle concluded. But Kalibar shook his head.

"We can and we will," he retorted.

"But won't they attack us?"

"Perhaps," Kalibar replied. "But if we stay here, we'll be letting them cut off my resources one by one. I have few wards left, so the next attempt to take me in my sleep may be successful. Or they'll set fire to Bellingham's crops, cutting off my food supply. Even with my magic, there's no way I could constantly protect such a large area. Then they'll wait us out, starve us until we get desperate and make a mistake." He gave Kyle a grim smile. "I may be powerful, but even I need to eat."

"What can we do?" Kyle asked.

"We're going to leave town tonight," Kalibar answered. "We'll be traveling in an older carriage, one the enemy won't associate with being mine. I'll send a few guards ahead of us in my personal carriage as bait. If the enemy takes the bait and reveals themselves, I can ambush them. If they don't – or they don't notice us passing in the night – then we'll have avoided the problem altogether."

"What if they attack *you*?" Kyle pressed. Kalibar smiled grimly.

"Well then," the old man replied, leaning back in his chair. "I doubt they'll live to regret it."

* * *

Kyle spent the rest of the day trying to forget about the approaching trip, with little success. After his meeting with Kalibar, his back had started to hurt again, and he'd been led back to his room by one of the maids. Once there, he'd taken another gulp of the tea, then laid down on his bed. Despite having just slept, he'd found himself exhausted, and had fallen into a fitful sleep. He'd awoken to find his room plunged into darkness, and had gone downstairs to find dinner waiting for him. By the time Kyle had finished his dinner, Kalibar's plentiful staff had almost finished packing a carriage for the trip to the Secula Magna – the school of magic.

Kyle yawned, standing up from his chair at the dinner table and stretching his back carefully. One of Kalibar's staff – a short, quiet man wearing glasses and a light gray suit – gestured for Kyle to follow him. They exited the room, making their way to the front lobby of the mansion. They walked through the large double-doors leading outside, stepping into the cool night air. Stars twinkled in the sky above, a gentle breeze blowing through Kyle's hair. There, parked on the broad street in front of Kalibar's mansion, was a carriage. The thing was larger than Kyle had expected – larger than his dad's SUV – and two burly-looking black horses stood proudly in front of it. Kalibar and Darius were busy lifting large leather packs into the trunk of the carriage; when Kalibar noticed Kyle standing there, he stopped what he was doing, walking up to Kyle.

"Ah, thank you Reo," Kalibar stated, nodding at the short man in the gray suit beside Kyle. Reo gave a quick bow. Kalibar turned to Kyle. "I'll be back in a moment," he stated. Then he and Reo walked back inside the mansion, leaving Kyle alone with Darius.

Kyle yawned, glancing back at the horses. Then he did a double-take; how could there be *horses* here? If this was really a different planet from Earth, having horses evolve to be the exact same on both planets made no sense at all. Neither did having *humans* on both planets, now that he thought about it. He didn't have long to ponder this mystery, however. Darius, with thousands of shimmering stars reflecting off of his polished golden armor, grabbed a pack from the ground with one hand, walking right up to Kyle.

"Make yourself useful," Darius growled, shoving the pack at Kyle's chest. Kyle grabbed it, then fell forward immediately, dropping the pack on the ground and landing on top of it. Pain tore through his back, and he cried out, stiffening immediately. He lifted himself up slowly, glaring up at Darius. But if the bodyguard noticed the look, he certainly didn't show it.

Jerk, Kyle muttered silently.

He grabbed the pack again, trying to lift it, with no success. He glanced up at Darius, who was watching him silently, his armored arms crossed over his chest. Kyle grit his teeth, then pulled on the straps of the pack, dragging it across the ground toward the back of the carriage. Then he left it there, crossing his arms and standing beside it. Darius walked up beside him, lifting the pack with one hand and tossing it easily into the back of the carriage.

"On second thought, stay useless," the bodyguard grumbled, "…you're really good at it."

Kyle glared at the bodyguard, but before he could reply, he heard the rhythmic clopping of horses' hooves. He turned to see another carriage approaching. Unlike Kalibar's carriage, this carriage had no wheels; it levitated a few feet from the ground, a soft blue glow between the underside of the carriage and the road. One of Kalibar's guards sat in the driver's seat, behind the two horses that were pulling it along.

Kyle heard footsteps coming from behind, and turned to see

Kalibar striding toward them, carrying a long metal staff. It was nearly as tall as Kalibar, with small symbols etched into its surface, revealing crystals of various colors underneath. A large pack levitated at Kalibar's other side, following him as he strode to the back of the carriage. The pack dropped itself into the trunk; Kalibar opened the pack, revealing a large number of books within...probably from Kalibar's office. They certainly weren't Darius's; Kyle doubted the bodyguard even knew how to read, the dumb brute.

Kalibar rummaged through the pack, then nodded to himself, apparently satisfied. He closed the trunk, then opened the side door of the carriage, motioning for Kyle to hop in. Kyle stepped up into the carriage, marveling at the interior. It was tastefully ornate, with polished wood and soft, comfortable leather cushions. He sat down, looking around for a seat belt...and finding none. Moments later, Kalibar opened the door on the other side, sitting down beside Kyle. He laid the long metal staff down on the carriage floor beneath the seats, then leaned back. Darius closed Kalibar's door, walking to the second carriage.

"Where's he going?" Kyle asked.

"He's signaling the other carriage to leave first," Kalibar explained.

"Wait," Kyle said, feeling suddenly uneasy. "The other carriage is the bait?"

"Don't worry," Kalibar reassured. "Their carriage is equipped with advanced runic defenses. My guards will be as safe as they can be."

Kyle looked out of the side window, catching a glimpse of Darius walking back to the front of their carriage. The bodyguard hopped up into the small driver's seat in the front, grabbing the two pairs of reins there. He snapped them sharply, prompting the two horses to trot forward, pulling the carriage along with them.

Kyle sat back in his seat, ignoring the slight burning in his spine. He noticed a large glass panel in the front of the carriage; it looked out to the driver's seat, and he could see Darius's back through it.

"We'll follow a few hundred feet behind the other carriage," Kalibar stated. "All of the attacks on the other carriages occurred near the town limits, twenty minutes from here." He eyed Kyle then. "How are you feeling?"

"Nervous," Kyle admitted. Kalibar smiled.

"Don't be," he reassured. "I have a great deal of experience with these kind of things."

"What kind of things?"

"Combat," the old man clarified. "I spent much of my life in the military as a Battle-Weaver," he added. "And Erasmus – the man we're going to show your ring to – worked with me as a military Runic."

"Wait, what's a Weaver?" Kyle asked.

"Ah, I forgot," Kalibar replied. "Of course you wouldn't know. A Weaver is someone who uses magic to make an immediate change in the world around them," he said. "Like lifting a stream from its bed."

"So you're a Weaver?"

"Yes," Kalibar replied. "A Runic, on the other hand, creates objects that have magical properties," he continued. "Like your earring…and your ring."

"And the other carriage," Kyle added. Kalibar nodded.

"We call magical objects 'runics,'" he explained.

"Wait," Kyle stated, "…if you can control gravity, couldn't we just fly to the Secula Magna?"

"I already thought of that," Kalibar answered. "For one, the enemy will undoubtedly anticipate that I might choose to fly. It could prove enormously dangerous to fly you and Darius, much less our cargo, while at the same time fighting an airborne battle with multiple enemies. The carriage is easier to defend."

"Couldn't you just fly there alone with the ring, and then fly back?" Kyle pressed. He had no desire to part with his ring, but he had even less desire to meet up with Kalibar's enemies. Kalibar chuckled.

"I could," he admitted. "But it would still be extremely dangerous…and I have other plans."

Kalibar fell silent then, staring out of the window on his side. Kyle suppressed the urge to ask more questions, staring out of his own window. They'd already left the grounds of Kalibar's mansion, reaching a wide dirt road. They passed the occasional house on either side, but mostly there was just farmland…endless fields of various crops. Beyond the crops, fields of tall golden grass grew. It looked familiar.

"Is this the road I was found on?" Kyle asked.

"Yes, this is the road," Kalibar confirmed. "You were found

lying on your belly on the dirt a few miles from here. You had no clothes on but your underwear." Kalibar paused. "I nearly forgot...they found the sap of a balm-tree in your wound."

"A balm-tree?"

"A tree with sap that, when placed in a wound, contracts slowly, bringing the wound edges together tightly," Kalibar explained. "The body slowly absorbs the sap, leaving only the thinnest film behind to hold the wound together until it heals."

Kyle nodded; it was a lot like the stitches that his Dad used to sew people up in the emergency room. Only better, because there weren't any needles involved.

"Now that I think of it, it's strange that the sap was found in your wound," Kalibar continued, tapping his chin with one finger. "You obviously couldn't have put it there...so who did?"

"I don't know," Kyle admitted. Kalibar frowned for a long moment, then sighed.

"So many unknowns," he murmured.

There was a sudden flash of blood-red light, followed by an ear-splitting *boom* that rattled the carriage windows. Kyle flinched, covering his ears with his hands, his heart hammering in his chest.

What the...!

He saw Darius yank back on the reins, then leap down from his seat, sprinting forward into the darkness. Kalibar swore, reaching down under his seat and grabbing his staff. He reached into his breast pocket, retrieving a pair of sunglasses and putting them on.

"Stay inside!" Kalibar commanded. He threw open his door, leaping out into the night. The door slammed shut on its own, leaving Kyle alone.

A shrill scream pierced the night air.

Kyle slid over to the Kalibar's side of the carriage, staring out of the side window. Utter darkness greeted him. He turned to look out of the sliding front window, but only saw the back of the horses' heads. One of the horses reared up, kicking its forelegs in the air. Then it bolted forward, throwing Kyle back into his seat. He cried out, pain lancing through his spine. The carriage veered to the left abruptly, throwing Kyle against the rightmost door.

A flash of eye-searing light exploded all around him.

Kyle cried out again, throwing his arms in front of his face and squeezing his eyes shut. He heard one of the horses scream, and the carriage began bouncing erratically. It veered sharply to the

right, throwing Kyle onto his side on the seat. The carriage began
to tip over, making him slide across the seat. His head struck the
left carriage door sharply, stars exploding across his vision.

Boom!

The carriage tipped all the way over onto its side, flipping Kyle
onto his back on top of the door. He screamed, curling into a ball,
his spine on fire.

The carriage lurched forward once, then again, scraping loudly
on the ground below. Kyle braced himself on the carriage door
below, gritting his teeth against the pain. Something warm and wet
dripped down his back.

A short, high-pitched scream echoed through the air, followed
by muffled shouting.

Kyle twisted around onto his belly, getting his hands and knees
underneath him. He stood up, leaning against the ceiling; the
carriage had tipped over onto its left side, and the rightmost
carriage door was up above him. He reached up for the door
handle, his fingers stopping mere inches from it. He got up onto
his tip-toes, stretching himself as far as he could. His fingertips
brushed up against the cool brass of the door handle. He hopped
and grabbed it, pulling it downward as he fell, but the door didn't
open.

Kyle cursed; of course the door wouldn't open inward...it could
only open *outward*.

He stared up at the door, his mind racing. Then he had an idea;
he braced one foot on the front of the carriage, and wedged the
other between the creases in the leather seat backing, pushing up
with his legs. This gave him the extra height to easily reach the door
handle. He grabbed it, pulling downward, then pushing up on the
carriage door. The door lifted upward partway, cool air rushing
inward. Kyle grabbed the front edge of the doorway, kicking his
legs to push himself upward, wedging his body in the doorway. He
ignored the pain as the door scraped against his back, lifting
himself up onto the side of the carriage.

Suddenly Kyle felt his head jerk involuntarily to the right, then
heard a loud thump an inch from his left ear. He turned, and saw a
metal bolt sticking out of the open carriage door right where his
head had been.

Kyle cried out, sliding backward into the carriage and landing
feet-first onto the carriage door below. The door above slammed

shut…then opened again.

A dark, red-hooded head peered below at Kyle, the face beyond lost in shadow.

The figure froze for a moment, then pulled the hood back over his head, revealing a long black beard and dark eyes. The stranger stared at Kyle for a moment, then turned around, swinging his legs down into the carriage. Kyle backed up, wedging himself in the corner as the stranger fell down toward him, landing beside him on the carriage door. The man grabbed the front of Kyle's shirt, shoving him hard against the carriage ceiling behind. Kyle's breath caught in his throat, his back exploding in pain.

The stranger held Kyle with one hand, reaching for something at his waist with the other. A knife.

Kyle screamed, dropping to his knees and trying to yank free of the man's grasp. The stranger lifted him back up easily, slamming him against the wall again. He raised the knife up into the air, then plunged its cruel tip downward, right at Kyle's chest!

Kyle didn't even have time to scream.

He squeezed his eyes shut as the blade slammed into his chest, trying futilely to twist away at the last minute. He felt a horrible pain in his chest, felt the stranger let go of him. There was a loud grunt, and then there was silence.

Kyle took deep, gulping breaths, sinking to his knees and clutching at his chest. Against his better judgment, he looked down, expecting to see blood spurting out from between his fingers. But there was nothing…not even a wound.

What the…

He heard a *thump*, and looked up, spotting a pair of black boots vanishing through the open carriage door above. There was a muffled scream, followed by a sickening *crack*. Kyle heard another loud *thump*…and then a man's head appeared through the open door above, blue eyes staring down at Kyle.

"Darius!" Kyle cried.

"Stay here," the bodyguard ordered gruffly, grabbing the carriage door and pulling it closed. A warm flood of relief coursed through Kyle, and he looked down, seeing another warm flood spreading across the front of his pants. He crouched low, covering his groin with his hands, his cheeks hot with shame. The carriage jolted, then lifted upward off of the ground, rolling back onto its wheels. Kyle fell onto the soft leather seats, then pulled himself back into a seated position. The left carriage door opened, a familiar face peering through.

"Are you all right?" Kalibar asked, climbing quickly into the carriage and patting Kyle's shoulders and arms. Kyle curled his legs up, terrified that Kalibar would discover his urine-soaked pants. Darius appeared behind Kalibar, peering over the old man's shoulder.

"He's fine," Darius answered matter-of-factly. Then he paused. "Can't say the same for his pants." Kyle and Kalibar both looked down at Kyle's pants, noting the large wet spot in the middle. Kyle's face flushed a deep crimson, and he clutched his knees to his chest, wanting nothing more than to curl up and die.

"We need to deal with the survivors," Kalibar stated, mercifully ignoring Darius's comment. He pulled his sunglasses and placed them in his breast pocket, then exited the carriage, motioning for Darius to follow him.

"He should see this," the bodyguard said. Kalibar frowned, glancing at Kyle, then back at Darius. He paused for a moment, then nodded.

"Very well," he replied. He gestured for Kyle to exit the carriage. Kyle did as he was told, following Darius and Kalibar to the side of the road. He glanced down the road, spotting debris strewn across it some fifty feet ahead…and something else.

Bodies.

"Stop," Kalibar ordered, putting a hand out in front of Kyle. Kyle froze in place, turning forward. There, just beyond the side of the road, were three dark shapes silhouetted by the faint glimmer of the stars. As his eyes adjusted, Kyle saw that they were men dressed in red uniforms – simple pants and shirts, with a hood to cover their heads. Each had a black sash around their waists, with a green diamond-shaped symbol woven in the center. The air shimmered around them like hot air over a parking lot. In front of the three men, Kyle saw Kalibar's staff standing upright, floating a few inches above the ground. Tiny symbols glowed a faint blue all the way up the length of the staff, and a large blue crystal glowed faintly at the staff's tip.

Kalibar stopped before the three men, his arms folded in front of him.

"Good evening gentlemen," he stated, his tone ice-cold. "You know who I am." It was a statement of fact, not a question. "Pay attention," he advised. "The next few minutes will be the most important in your life."

The first man drew his head back, then spat at Kalibar. The saliva flew toward Kalibar, then turned about in midair, flying right back into the man's face. Kalibar didn't even blink.

"You're a dead man," the second man – the one in the middle – growled.

"We're all dead men," Kalibar replied coolly. "If you tell me who ordered this attack, you will die well."

"Go to hell," the man spat. Then he gasped as a faint blue sphere surrounded him, lifting him up into the air a foot or two. His red robes suddenly crushed inward, pressing tightly against his body. His eyes widened, and he gasped again, his chest heaving with great difficulty as he struggled to breath.

"Who?" Kalibar pressed, staring impassively at the levitating man. The first man yelled out, and a burst of light flew from his body toward Kalibar. Kalibar's staff shimmered, the symbols carved into its surface flashing blue. The light curved sharply in midair, arcing back toward its creator. The man screamed as it slammed into him, hurtling him backward through the air. His chest burst into flames, and he landed with a *thump* on the grassy field beyond. The flames licked at his clothes, burning higher and brighter, and he screamed again, flailing his arms and legs wildly. Within moments, his entire body was engulfed.

Kyle turned away, his stomach lurching. He felt Darius's hand on his shoulder. The bodyguard forced him to face the burning man, who was lying on the ground, no longer moving.

Kalibar turned his gaze back to the second man, the one levitating in the air before him. The man was sweating profusely, his hair matted to his skull. His breath came in short gasps.

"Who?" Kalibar repeated.

"Our master…will…kill…you," the man promised. Darius, standing behind Kalibar, knelt down to pick something up off of the ground. He lifted it up, presenting it to the levitating man. Kyle's stomach lurched; it was a man's head, severed at the neck. There was a deep hole in the center of the dead man's forehead.

"Only if we trip over him," Darius retorted. Then he casually tossed the head over his shoulder. The two remaining men turned very pale.

"Impossible!" the man standing on the ground exclaimed in

disbelief, the blood draining from his face. "How?" Darius smirked.

"Easily," he answered.

"Talk, or join your leader," Kalibar commanded.

"It was Orik!" the third man blurted out. "He…"

"Shut up!" the levitating man hissed. "You traitor!"

"He killed the master!" the third man retorted.

Kalibar stared at the two men for a long moment, his face expressionless.

"Orik ordered my assassination?" Kalibar asked, his eyes on the third man.

"He did," the man confirmed.

"You're a goddamn fool," the second man spat.

"Who cares if they know?" the third man retorted. "Xanos will destroy them!"

Kalibar turned away from the prisoners, rubbing his goatee with one hand. He glanced at Darius.

"If Orik is behind this, I'll need their testimony," he muttered. "We can't just kill them…and they're too dangerous to leave as is." He turned back to face the captives. "I have every right to take your lives," he stated, staring coldly at the two men. "Consider it a gift that I will only take your eyes."

Suddenly the shimmering field imprisoning the second man vanished, and he leapt at his companion, a ball of light appearing in his hand.

"For Xanos!" he cried, slamming the ball of light into the other man. The light *exploded*, sending a shockwave outward, a burst of hot air slamming into Kyle. He stumbled backward, landing on his butt on the dirt on the side of the road, momentarily blinded.

"Kalibar!" he shouted.

He felt hands under his armpits, felt himself being hauled up onto his feet. He blinked rapidly, staring at the spot where the two men had been standing. There was nothing left of them…other than a puddle of blood and hunks of burning flesh splattered across the dirt.

"Damn!" Kalibar swore, staring at the remains of the two men. His jawline rippled, his fists clenching, then unclenching. At length, he turned away, walking back toward the carriage. "Let's go," he muttered. Kyle stole a glance at Darius, but the bodyguard said nothing, following his employer. Kyle trailed close behind, glancing back at the blood on the side of the road, feeling nauseous.

Darius stopped before the horses, inspecting them; both were spooked, but seemed otherwise unharmed. The bodyguard stepped up into the driver's chair, grabbing the reins. Kyle and Kalibar got back into the carriage, and within moments Darius was steering them back onto the road, avoiding the flaming debris scattered across it.

"What's all that?" Kyle asked.

"The other carriage," Kalibar answered. Kyle stared at the wreckage, feeling a sudden pang of dread.

"Wait, where are your guards?" he pressed. Kalibar took a deep breath in, then let it out.

"They should have been safe," Kalibar muttered, staring down at his own lap. "The wards on my carriage should have protected them."

Kyle said nothing, turning away and looking out of his window. The last of the debris passed by, and he turned away, feeling strangely numb. He closed his eyes, remembering the guard he'd seen driving the carriage. It was impossible to believe that the man, who he'd just seen alive earlier that evening, was now dead. He opened his eyes, glancing at Kalibar. The man was busy staring at his staff, clenching it so hard that his knuckles turned white.

They rode in silence.

A light rain began to fall around the carriage, pattering gently on the roof. The carriage picked up speed, the *clip, clop* of the horses' hooves sounding on the road below. Kyle turned back to his window, staring out of it absently.

"It makes sense now," Kalibar stated suddenly. Kyle frowned.

"What?"

"It must be Orik behind all of this," Kalibar explained. "It all fits."

"Who's Orik?" Kyle asked.

"A man with plenty of reasons to want me dead," Kalibar answered. He ran a hand through his short white hair. "If he's behind all of this, then I'm in more trouble than I thought."

"Who is he?"

"A powerful man," Kalibar replied. "Soon to be the most powerful man in the Empire." He sighed again. "He's a politician, like I was. We go way back, him and I...it's a long story, I'm afraid."

"Oh," Kyle mumbled. Kalibar put a hand on his shoulder.

"You did well back there," he stated approvingly. Then he

grimaced. "It's my fault that the man who attacked you was able to make it inside the carriage," he added. "I just can't understand how the carriage's defensive runics were neutralized so quickly..."

"It's okay," Kyle replied. "Darius saved me."

Kalibar nodded, saying nothing more. The rain fell heavily now, pounding on the roof of the carriage. Kyle leaned forward in his seat slightly, taking the pressure off of his aching back. After a few minutes, Kalibar opened the sliding window at the front of the carriage, and leaned forward to speak through it.

"Let's make camp," he shouted over the rain. Darius cocked his head, then nodded. The carriage veered to the right, bouncing as its wheels went off-road, making Kyle wish that he had a seat belt. He braced his palms on the ceiling, feeling the carriage slow, then stop. Darius jumped off of his perch, walking over to Kalibar's door and opening it. Kalibar got out, and Kyle opened his own door, knowing full well that Darius wouldn't extend him the same courtesy. He hopped down into the mud, his boots sinking in a few inches. All three squished their way to a clearing in the tall grass around them. Kalibar looked around, then nodded at Darius, who walked back to the carriage to grab a few packs. Kyle looked around, spotting the road far in the distance.

"Are we safe here?" he asked.

"As safe as we were in the carriage," Kalibar replied. "But at least we'll be able to lay down and sleep out here."

Kyle stared at the mud around them, rain dripping down his soaked hair and clothes. He gave Kalibar a skeptical look. Darius returned carrying a heavy pack in each hand, his golden boots squelching in the mud. Kalibar took the packs from Darius, handling their enormous weight with surprising ease. It took Kyle a moment to realize why; the packs were actually hovering a few feet above the muddy ground...more of Kalibar's magic, no doubt. The old man rummaged through one of the packs, pulling out three sleeping bags. Darius took one of them, throwing it down. To Kyle's surprise, it too hovered a few feet above the mud.

"Are you doing that?" Kyle asked, looking up at Kalibar.

"They're magical," Kalibar replied. "They do it automatically." Darius laid down on his sleeping bag, and it held the bodyguard's weight without sinking. Kalibar walked back to the carriage, opening the side door and retrieving his staff from it, and what looked like a large stick. Then he made his way back to Kyle and

Darius. Kyle threw down his own sleeping bag, half-expecting it to sink into the mud, but it didn't. He paused, then sat on it. The sleeping bag didn't budge. He pulled off his muddy boots, then lay on top of it, pulling the covers over himself. It was quite comfortable, with soft, plush material on the inside.

Kyle turned to watch Kalibar, spotting the man standing in the mud nearby. First Kalibar jammed the large stick into the mud; it immediately started to glow a faint green color. Then he jammed his staff into the mud, then stepped back. A few symbols on the staff's surface flashed blue, and suddenly a faint, translucent blue dome appeared around them. Easily twenty feet in diameter and ten feet tall, the rain poured down its sides, leaving them dry.

"What is that?" Kyle asked. The old man sat down on his own sleeping bag, pulling off his black boots.

"I made a magical shield around the camp," Kalibar answered.

"So it won't rain on us," Kyle reasoned. Practical magic, indeed!

"So no one kills us in our sleep," Darius grumbled back.

Chapter 6

The wind whips through Ampir's hair as he flies over the wide expanse of the Great River, Vera clutched in his arms. He feels his son on his back, the boy's arms locked in a death grip around his neck. In the distance, miles from the fast-approaching shore ahead, the Behemoth stands in front of the Great Tower, nearly a third of the 42-story building's height.

The Behemoth's eye flashes.

A deadly green beam shoots outward from that eye, slamming into the mid-shaft of the Tower. Countless runes carved into the Tower's walls flare bright blue, the Behemoth's beam repelled by their power. Eventually the Behemoth's beam fades away, the Tower unharmed.

Then the monstrosity raises one metal fist, opening its fingers to reveal a huge white sphere imbedded in the center of its palm. The sphere pulses, and rays of blue light pull from the Tower toward the Behemoth's hand, converging on the white sphere.

What the...?

The Tower's runes fade, then go black.

"The Tower!" Vera cries. "Ampir, do something!"

Ampir says nothing, watching as the Behemoth's hand drops to its side, its eye focusing on the mid-shaft of the Tower once again. He's too far away to attack the Behemoth effectively now, and he knows nothing about its defenses. If he attacks, the Behemoth will know his position...and the enemy will realize he is still alive. He has no fear for his own life, not with his armor. But Vera and Junior's lives will be at risk.

The Behemoth's eye flashes.

A beam of deadly green light shoots outward from it, slamming into the side of the Great Tower. Without its protective runes, the Tower walls glow red-hot, streams of molten stone dripping down them. The beam cuts through the massive building rapidly, slicing it in half.

Ampir watches in stunned silence as the top half of the Tower begins to tilt toward the Behemoth. The monstrous machine steps to the side, and the upper Tower falls, breaking away from the lower half and slamming into the ground. A cloud of dirt and debris explodes upward from the impact, the glittering crystalline peak of the Tower shattering.

Seconds later, the shockwave reaches them, a tremendous *boom* that echoes in the night air.

Ampir stares at the remaining half of the Great Tower, watches as it crumbles, its foundation destroyed by the impact. In less than a minute, the Tower – the heart of the Empire, and his home for over half his life – has been destroyed.

He looks down, sees Vera staring wide-eyed at the devastation, tears dripping down her pale cheeks. He feels numb, unable to process what has just happened.

Dozens of dark shapes plunge through the thick clouds above the city, ships identical to the one that had bombed Ampir's home. They fly over the city at incredible speed, clusters of bombs dropping from their underbellies. Countless explosions rock the skyline in rapid succession, skyscrapers collapsing in plumes of fire and smoke.

Vera clutches onto Ampir, burying her face in his chest. He holds her close, watching as their city...their home...burns.

* * *

Kyle opened his eyes, squinting in the waning sunlight streaming through the windows of Kalibar's carriage. He stretched his legs, wincing as he did so. His back was stiff after three days of being cooped up in the carriage, and it was still awfully sore where the Ulfar had slashed him. Kalibar had checked Kyle's wounds a few times during the trip, changing the dressings periodically. After traveling together for so long, Kyle and Kalibar had settled into a comfortable silence; the old man had spent most of that time with his books. Darius, having nothing to say to either of them, did just that.

Kyle looked out of his window, watching the fields of tall golden grass beyond the road pass by. The sun was a few hours from setting, hovering over the hills in the distance. He thought of the guards who'd died during the attack earlier, feeling a familiar glumness fall over him. He glanced at Kalibar, hoping for a distraction, but the old man was thoroughly engrossed in a book.

Kyle sighed, turning back to the window. In between reading his books, Kalibar had taught Kyle a great deal during the trip. He'd learned all about feathergrass extract – the stuff that Fintan had introduced him to earlier. A short, tough grass, it generated an anti-gravity field that prevented feet and hooves from crushing it. More importantly, most bugs that tried to eat it ended up floating away before they could take a bite. Savvier bugs with sticky legs could latch on and feed, however. The more grass they ate, the lighter they got…until they pooped, of course. That poop would float upward, high into the sky. Swarms of insects sometimes created huge clouds of excrement that flew up into the atmosphere. When the magic of the feathergrass eventually faded, the poop would fall to the ground in an unfortunate downpour. Kyle had heard his dad talk about poop-storms before, usually when talking about work…although his dad had used a more colorful word.

In any case, farmers grew the grass, then harvested it, cutting very carefully from the edge of the lawn inward. Careless harvesters had been known to have their blades fly up and lop off bits of their faces. Then, as Fintan had said, the feathergrass could be woven into clothes and armor, making them extremely light. Or it could be ground up and pressed, making a juice that, when swallowed, would make a man weigh a fraction of his normal heft. Feathergrass wasn't the only magical plant, of course. There were countless others…and animals used magic as well. Alchemists used extracts of plants and animals to create a wide variety of potions.

All in all, despite the soreness of his body, Kyle had found the trip rather refreshing. He couldn't remember ever having spent three full days doing nothing but talking to someone, much less an adult. Kalibar didn't seem to mind their conversations, and appeared truly interested in teaching Kyle…and hearing what Kyle had to say. The old man shifted from talking to reading to resting without any frustration whatsoever, and seemed to enjoy all three whenever they occurred.

It was…different.

Kyle glanced out of the window again. The road here was wider, made of flat, interlocking stones instead of dirt. The tall golden grass became sparser as the carriage moved ever forward, giving way in the distance to a truly massive river...maybe the widest he had ever seen. In the distance, the road led to a huge bridge that formed a long arch over that river.

"That," Kalibar stated suddenly, making Kyle jump, "...is the Great River."

Kyle nodded. On the other side of the river was the skyline of a large city – nearly as large as Boston back home. There were no real skyscrapers, although several of the buildings were quite tall. One of them stood head and shoulders above the rest...a tall, stately stone tower in the center of the city. It looked to be at least forty or fifty stories high, and was topped by what appeared to be a glass pyramid. Its facets glittered in the sunlight like a massive diamond.

"That," Kalibar said, pointing to the tower, "is the Great Tower of the Secula Magna." The carriage angled upward slightly as it passed onto the bridge. Kyle turned to look out of Kalibar's window on the left, spotting carriages traveling in the other direction. A few of them were like the carriage Kalibar's late guards had ridden a few days ago, in that they didn't have wheels.

"They're becoming more common every year," Kalibar informed him. "A young Runic named Banar reinvented them a few years ago." He stretched his arms, his book falling to his lap. "We're having a renaissance in runic technology now. Archaeologists discovered artifacts in Ancient ruins on a small island to the west a few years ago. Some of them contained detailed descriptions of advanced runic technology. We've managed to recreate a few of them, but we've got a long way to go before we match the sophistication of the Ancients."

They rode over the remainder of the bridge in silence, and Kyle turned to look out of his own window. Beyond the bridge were crowded city streets; throngs of people traveled on the sidewalks, stopping at various shops. Peddlers stood over bins of brightly-color fruit by the side of the road, while butchers laid out cuts of meat for passers-by to purchase. It was like a scene out of a movie, riding in a horse-drawn carriage, with people in strange clothes milling about in the streets. And while Kyle could understand everything people were saying, the writing on signs by the shops was gibberish to him. The magical earring had its limits, he supposed. He wondered if there were magical glasses that would allow him to read foreign languages.

"This is Stridon, the capitol city of the Empire," Kalibar explained as they went. "The campus of the Secula Magna is in the center of the city. It's surrounded and protected by a magical dome." Kyle nodded absently, only half-listening as he took in the scenery. He noticed a few men standing at the edge of the roof of one of the buildings, three stories up. Suddenly, right before his very eyes, one of the men jumped!

Kyle yelled out, tugging on Kalibar's shirt. The old man started, then chuckled as the roof-jumper sailed slowly and gracefully downward and forward, crossing the busy street in mid-air and landing on a red square tile on the sidewalk on the other side.

"How did he *do* that?" Kyle asked.

"He's wearing a jumpsuit," Kalibar replied. "Densely woven with feathergrass fibers. The red squares are where he can land; the other pedestrians know to walk around the squares." Kyle looked, and realized it was true; the pedestrians avoided the red square expertly. Then he looked around, noticing lots of other red and blue squares on the walkways. "The red squares are for jumping down to, and the blue squares are for jumping up to," Kalibar continued. "There are squares on balconies, and rooftops," he added. "With a jumpsuit or feathergrass extract, you can get around most of the city without setting foot on the street."

Kyle's mouth fell open. To be able to jump fifty feet down without being hurt...he suddenly wanted very much to get a jumpsuit for himself! Kalibar must have noticed his expression.

"I'll get you some feathergrass extract so you can try it out," he promised.

At length, they left the roadside shops behind. The buildings became larger and taller, most built of stone, some up to eight stories high. They passed a massive building on the left, with wide stone steps leading up to a set of enormous double-doors. Huge columns on either side held up a stone overhang some twenty feet above. The building looked quite imposing, the few windows it had armed with rows of vertical bars.

"What's that?" Kyle asked.

"Stridon Penitentiary," Kalibar answered. "A prison for Weavers and Runics. Some of the most dangerous men in the Empire are held there."

"Right in the middle of the city?" Kyle inquired. "Isn't that dangerous?"

"It's the most advanced prison in the Empire," Kalibar replied. "It's quite secure…and we've found that making prisons visible makes people less likely to end up in them."

They passed the massive structure, the buildings becoming fewer and farther between as the carriage rolled along. After a few more minutes, they reached a tall fence. Its thick black bars rose three stories high, each terminating in a viciously sharp spike. Countless runes were carved into the surface of the bars, some glowing faintly blue. The fence extended to either side as far as the eye could see, curving backward in a huge circle. Directly in front of the carriage, two massive, stately doors wrought of the same black iron bars formed a closed gate. Just beyond the fence, the air shimmered ever-so-slightly, with a faint blue tint. Kyle's eyes drew upward, and his breath caught in his throat.

"That," Kalibar explained, "…is the Gate shield." A shimmering blue dome that rose hundreds of feet above the fence, the Gate shield entirely covered the territory beyond the fence…like the dome of an indoor football stadium, but miles wide. Its size was beyond comprehension, larger than anything Kyle had ever seen.

"Whoa," Kyle breathed.

Darius stopped the carriage before the double-doors of the gate, and Kyle stared out of his window, spotting two small guard shacks, one on either side. Men in jet-black armor stood by these shacks, their faces and heads covered with intricate – and incredibly cool-looking – helmets. One of these men strode forward quickly, stopping about a dozen feet from the left side of the carriage. He turned to face Darius, his eyes invisible behind the black translucent visor forming the front of his helmet.

"Identify yourselves," the guard ordered brusquely. Darius, being Darius, didn't so much as turn to look at the guard. Instead, he pulled out a piece of fruit from a sack sitting beside him and bit into it, juice spilling down his chin.

The guard's lips drew into a tight line, his gauntleted hands balling into fists. He took a step back from the carriage.

"Identify yourselves," he repeated, "…*now*." He brought a finger up to the side of his helmet, and the visor snapped back up inside of it, revealing scowling brown eyes. Darius continued to ignore the guard, taking another bite out of the fruit. Kyle's heart skipped a beat; what was Darius *doing*? He slouched down in his seat, half-hoping the guard would have Darius arrested for his insolence. After a complimentary beating, of course.

"Step down from the vehicle!" the guard commanded angrily, a faint blue sphere appearing around him. Kyle's heart skipped a beat; was the guard talking to all of them, or just Darius? Before he could find out, Kalibar opened his door, stepping down to the ground below.

"Good morning, officer," he stated calmly. The guard turned his baleful glare on Kalibar, then jerked backward as if he'd been slapped. His face turned very pale, and he dropped to one knee before Kalibar, lowering his eyes to the ground. The blue sphere surrounding him vanished.

"Forgive me, your Excellency," the guard blurted. Kalibar walked up to the man, putting a hand on his shoulder.

"You've done nothing needing forgiveness," Kalibar replied. "Rise," he added, and the guard instantly obeyed. Kalibar turned to regard Darius with a cold glare. "I have a high tolerance for many behaviors," he told the bodyguard. "But insolence is not among them."

Darius stopped in mid-bite, staring back at Kalibar silently. He gave a slight nod, then went back to eating his fruit. Kalibar turned back to the black-armored guard.

"As you were."

"Your Excellency," the officer murmured, bowing sharply. Then he turned and jogged back to the guard shack, waving and shouting excitedly at his fellow guards. The huge gate doors swung inward slowly, compelled by an invisible force. Kalibar stepped back into the carriage, sitting down beside Kyle and closing the door behind him. Darius snapped the reigns, and the horses took the carriage forward through the open gate. Kyle peered out of the rear window, seeing the gates closing behind them. Then he stole a glance at Kalibar.

"What was that all about?" he asked.

"You'll see soon enough," Kalibar replied wearily. He fell silent then, staring out of his window at the scenery beyond. Kyle did the same, seeing huge areas of well-manicured lawns decorated with bushes and shrubs, with the occasional tree here and there. He spotted a large red-brick building in the distance, six stories high. People walked to and fro from the building, some dressed all in black, like the guards. Others were dressed entirely in white.

"Those are students," Kalibar said before Kyle could ask. "The ones in white are Runic students, the ones in black, Weaver students. The officers at the gate were Battle-Weavers, members of the elite guard." Kyle nodded. It made sense, after all...who better to guard a gate than a Weaver? That explained why the guard hadn't been carrying any weapons.

The carriage led them on a winding path forward, and they passed more dormitories along the way. Then Kyle saw their destination – a tall tower in the distance, the same one he'd seen when they'd gone over the bridge. The one Kalibar had called the Great Tower. It was monstrous up close, its stone walls decorated with countless intricate carvings. The road led them straight toward massive double-doors at the Tower's entrance; above these doors was carved a three-story high relief of the Tower itself, a large, superficial crack cutting horizontally through the middle of the carving.

Throngs of people in black and white uniforms spilled out of the double-doors of the Tower, flanking the road on either side of Kalibar's carriage. They pushed their way toward the carriage, each craning their necks for a view. A group of black-armored guards ran out of the double-doors, pushing the crowd back from the road, leaving it unobstructed. One guard walked up to Kalibar's door, opening it slowly. A collective gasp arose from the crowd, then a hush. Kalibar stepped out, turning to the crowd and waving.

The crowd erupted into thunderous applause.

Kalibar turned around, motioning for Kyle to come out of the carriage. Kyle froze, staring out into the crowd. There were hundreds of people out there now, some still screaming Kalibar's name. But Kalibar leaned into the carriage, extending his hand toward Kyle. Kyle hesitated, then took it, allowing himself to be pulled out of the carriage and onto the cobblestone road below. Kalibar put a hand on the small of his back, leading him forward toward the double-doors ahead. Though he kept his gaze glued on the road below, Kyle could still feel countless eyes watching him; he clung to Kalibar's side, feeling incredibly ill-at-ease. A half dozen guards in black armor formed a loose ring around them, escorting them through the double-doors and into the Tower. The doors closed behind them, leaving the crowd behind, and Kyle let a breath go that he hadn't realized he'd been holding.

Then he lifted his gaze from the floor, and his jaw went slack.

The room they'd entered was enormous, with granite walls rising three stories up to the ceiling above. Massive paintings hung on the walls, and thick stone columns rose from the polished granite floor to the ceiling. A large reception area stood before them, in the middle of the huge room, with impeccably-dressed men and women standing behind a long, semi-circular granite counter. Kalibar did not go to this; instead, he turned to one of the half-dozen guards still surrounding them.

"I'd like to speak with Erasmus," he stated. The guard nodded briskly, saluting, then sprinting away. Kyle watched him go, then turned to look up at Kalibar. The old man glanced at Kyle and smiled, putting an arm around Kyle's shoulders and holding him close. Kyle wrinkled his nose; after three days of travel, the old man smelled strongly of armpit. Kyle tried breathing through his mouth, a trick he'd learned from visiting nursing homes in the past. It helped a bit. He turned away from Kalibar, spotting a crowd forming around them…men and women in black or white uniforms stopping to stare. Luckily, the mere presence of the armored guards surrounding Kalibar and Kyle kept the crowd at bay. Kyle stared at the floor, profoundly uneasy with the sudden attention. Then he felt a bolt of panic, and checked his pants zipper discretely. It was in the upright position, much to his relief.

"This is the Tower lobby," Kalibar explained, gesturing at the huge room. Then he nudged Kyle, pointing up at the ceiling. Kyle looked upward; the ceiling was, he found, one giant mirror. People's reflections walked busily to and fro on the ceiling, upside-down, of course. Kyle arched his back, looking straight up, and searched for his own reflection. But he couldn't find it.

"Hey, I don't see us," Kyle observed, turning to Kalibar. "Where are we?" Kalibar smirked.

"We're down here," the old man replied. He pointed upward. "They're up there."

Kyle frowned, looking upward again. Then realization struck; the ceiling wasn't a mirror at all…there were actual *people* standing upside-down on the ceiling! Kyle gasped, pointing upward.

"Are they really…?"

"Yes, they're standing on the ceiling," Kalibar confirmed. "Every floor in the Tower except the top three has a reverse-polarity ceiling. A magical field reverses gravity halfway up, making each floor a ceiling...and each ceiling a floor."

"Whoa," Kyle said, hardly believing his eyes.

"Even the stairways are two-sided," Kalibar continued. "People come from all over the Empire to see the Great Tower at least once in their lifetime."

Kyle stared at the ceiling, marveling at the sight. There were upside-down tables and chairs, and people sitting on upside-down couches. Upside-down candles flickered with upside-down flames. There was even a giant fountain in the center of the ceiling, with water shooting downward, then falling back upward, splashing into an upside-down pool.

"Kalibar!" a voice shouted. Kyle looked down from the ceiling, spotting a short, older man in crisp white robes power-walking toward them. The man's smile was enormous...as was his pot-belly.

"Kalibar, you old bastard!" the man exclaimed, grabbing Kalibar's hand and pumping it vigorously. Kalibar let go of Kyle and gave the man in white a big hug.

"Erasmus!" he replied, finishing the embrace and holding Erasmus at arm's length. He gave Erasmus a big grin. "Where's the rest of your hair? You look terrible!"

"And you smell terrible, you old bag!" Erasmus scoffed, an even bigger grin on his lips. He *was* mostly bald, with white hair at the temples. He had a big white bushy mustache and beard, and the top of his head was almost disturbingly shiny. "Still rotting away in Bellingham?" he asked. When Kalibar nodded, Erasmus rolled his eyes. "Surprised you haven't died of boredom," he muttered. "Heard it was the leading cause of death there." Then he noticed Kyle standing next to Kalibar, and his brow furrowed. "And who is this?"

"This is Kyle," Kalibar introduced, pulling Kyle close to his side again. "He's my great-nephew. Kyle, this is my good friend Erasmus." Erasmus's bushy eyebrows rose, and he considered Kyle with merry blue eyes.

"Good to meet you, Kyle," Erasmus greeted, bending down and extending a hand. Kyle stepped forward and shook it. Erasmus turned to Kalibar with a wry smile. "I see he inherited your stench," he observed, letting go of Kyle's hand. Kyle blushed, squeezing his elbows to his sides to seal his armpits. "Now tell me, what can I do for you, Kalibar? Other than providing a shower, of course."

"I wanted to speak to you about something important," Kalibar replied, his voice turning serious. "Somewhere private," He added. Erasmus's smile vanished, and he nodded quickly.

"Of course," he replied. "We'll go to my office at once." Erasmus gestured for Kalibar to walk with him. Kalibar kept his iron grip on Kyle, and Kyle was forced to come with them. Erasmus paused at this, looking questioningly at Kalibar.

"It's all right," Kalibar stated. "He's part of it." Erasmus's eyebrows rose, but he said nothing, continuing forward instead. The three walked across the lobby toward a long hallway on the other side, the black-armored guards following close behind. Here, as everywhere, there were carvings in the stone walls. Kyle studied them as they passed; these carvings were painted, and so skillfully made that they were nearly photorealistic. On one wall, groups of soldiers in black armor were carved in meticulous detail, facing a brave group of men and women in black and white robes, like the one that Erasmus wore. At the head of the black-armored soldiers, a man in black robes stood, a ball of fire in one hand.

"So how have you been?" Kalibar asked Erasmus as they walked.

"Oh, never better," Erasmus replied jovially. "Damn elections have turned everyone into raving lunatics, as usual. Everyone's drawing lines in the sand, spewing fancy speeches, and declaring all the other candidates to be evil, plotting bastards. Which they are." He grinned impishly. "It's been a hell of a lot of fun!"

"Can't say I miss it," Kalibar admitted. "I take it Orik is still the favorite for Grand Weaver?" Erasmus nodded, his expression souring.

"The vainglorious bastard," he spat. "He's going to win, of course." He gave Kalibar a sidelong glance. "Unless you've come to your senses..." Kalibar gave Erasmus a look.

"No," he replied. "My political days are over." Erasmus gave Kalibar an exasperated look.

"Kalibar the old recluse, pissing his life away in his quaint country manor," he replied. "Limitless potential, and you hole yourself up in Bellingham, of all places!" Kalibar gave a tight smile, but said nothing. They reached the end of the hallway, and stepped onto a large stone platform, walking to the center of it. Then they all stopped...including the guards, who stood around them.

"Orik will be delighted, of course," Erasmus sighed. "You're the only man who could beat him, and he damn well knows it." Again,

Kalibar said nothing. He did shoot a warning glance at Kyle, who had been about to ask if it was the same Orik who'd tried to have Kalibar killed.

"Erasmus is talking about the upcoming elections," Kalibar explained. "The Secula Magna itself is small, but it is the political center of a vast empire. Its government is ruled by the Grand Weaver and Grand Runic, who act like equal kings. Every six years, an election is held to have a new Grand Runic and Weaver."

Erasmus frowned at Kyle. "You mean he doesn't know already? Are you so destitute now that you can't afford to send your own relatives to school?" Kyle felt his cheeks burning, but Kalibar only smiled, patting Kyle on the shoulder.

"Kyle has gaps in his education, but he is quickly filling them," Kalibar replied. "He's an able student."

Without warning, the platform they were standing on started to rise upward. Kyle tensed up, crouching low to the ground...and heard Erasmus chuckle. He stared upward, seeing a vertical shaft extending as far up as he could see. His stomach lurched as the platform accelerated rapidly, shooting upward at gut-wrenching speed. He grit his teeth, watching as the floors whizzed by in front of him. Unlike a real elevator, there was no door to block his view of each floor. He felt a wave of nausea, saliva pooling in his mouth.

Suddenly the platform slowed, making Kyle's stomach lurch again. It came to a quick stop, and Kyle staggered off of it as soon as it did so, reaching the safety of the hallway beyond. He heard more chuckling from behind, and turned around, seeing Erasmus and Kalibar exchanging bemused grins.

"Never been on a riser before, eh?" Erasmus observed, his blue eyes twinkling. Kyle shook his head sheepishly. He didn't know what color red and green made, but he was pretty sure anyone looking at his cheeks would know!

The two older men passed him by, walking down the hallway away from the platform – the riser – and motioning for Kyle to follow. He complied, following the two men – and the black-armored guards – down the long hallway. Like the hallway far below, there were carved murals on the walls. These were different, however. The carvings were of stern-looking older men, painted with muted colors. On the right, the men wore black clothes, on the left, white.

"These are carvings of some of the former Grand Weavers and

Grand Runics," Kalibar explained. The carvings were intricately detailed, so much so that he half-expected them to come to life at any moment. At the end of the mural, the last two carvings stood. On the left was a man who looked an awful lot like Erasmus, but with more hair. On the right...

Kyle slowed his pace, staring at the carving. It was of a handsome older man with short white hair and a trimmed goatee, dressed entirely in black. The man looked terribly familiar.

He stopped in his tracks, a chill running through him.

"Kalibar!" he blurted out.

"A good likeness," Kalibar agreed. "But I think they did a better job on yours," he added, nodding at Erasmus. Erasmus snorted.

"Mine looks like a bloated pig!" he retorted. Kalibar smirked.

"Like I said..."

"Wait," Kyle interrupted. "Why..." He gestured at Kalibar's statue. "What...?"

"Erasmus and I governed the Empire together until about six years ago," Kalibar stated matter-of-factly.

"Governed my ass!" Erasmus interjected. "We ruled the most powerful nation in the world! Modernized the entire military, brought all the neighboring tribes under our rule, and nearly quadrupled our treasury...all in six years!"

"That too," Kalibar conceded.

"We were the most celebrated Grand Runic and Grand Weaver in the history of the new Empire," Erasmus continued heatedly. He gestured at Kalibar. "And *this* clown won't even consider a second term!"

"We've talked about this," Kalibar replied wearily.

"If we ran for office together, no one could possibly beat us," Erasmus insisted, clearly unable to help himself. "We could usher in a second Golden Era for the Empire!"

"Erasmus, please," Kalibar pleaded. Erasmus clenched his fists, biting his tongue. Then he sighed.

"You're a stubborn old bastard," he grumbled.

"That I am," Kalibar agreed. "But I didn't come to talk about the election," he added. "I have something that I think you'll find even more intriguing."

"Doubtful," Erasmus retorted. Then he flashed Kalibar a mischievous grin. "I bet a few glasses of wine would change your mind," he wagered, rubbing his hands together eagerly. "I'll get you smashed and you'll wake up having won the election!"

"Fat chance," Kalibar retorted. "But you're welcome to try." The two men resumed walking down the hallway, and Kyle followed close behind. They passed several doors, stopping at the last door of the hallway, on the right. Kyle noticed that none of the doors had keyholes, or even doorknobs, including this one. Erasmus closed his eyes for a moment, and the door opened suddenly, without being touched.

"Well, go on," Erasmus urged, ushering Kalibar and Kyle into the room. The guards remained standing by either side of Erasmus's door. Kyle followed Kalibar through a short hallway that quickly opened up into a much larger room. It had stone walls and a polished granite floor, much like the lobby had, and majestic paintings hanging on the walls. A huge bookcase – extending all the way up to the ceiling some twelve feet above, and covering the entirety of one wall – stood before them, filled to the brim with books, crystals, small statues, and other odds and ends. And on the lowest shelf, nothing but a long row of bottles. Full suits of armor – including a set of black armor identical to the ones the guards wore – were mounted on another wall. Before the bookcase was a large wooden desk, its surface littered with papers, books, and various objects Kyle couldn't identify. Erasmus cleared these from his desk hurriedly, then pulled two chairs up to the desk, gesturing for Kalibar and Kyle to sit down.

"Ah, just a minute," he stated, turning to face the bookcase. He grabbed a bottle and two glasses from the lowest shelf, uncorking the bottle and pouring red liquid into each glass. That done, he flopped into his own chair opposite them, handing Kalibar one glass while taking the other for himself.

"To surprises," Erasmus proclaimed, raising his glass and tapping it against Kalibar's. "The few that we old men have left," he added, then took a sip of his drink. "Speaking of surprises," Erasmus said with a devilish grin, "...have you found yourself a scandalously young lady to settle down with yet?" Kalibar shook his head.

"I'm too old for that sort of thing," he replied.

"A man is *never* too old for that sort of thing," Erasmus retorted. "Think of it...you're rich and famous, in marvelous physical condition, and you still have your hair, lucky bastard that you are. You could have your pick...start a family, have a few kids…"

"Erasmus…" Kalibar warned, his expression darkening.

"All right, all right," the former Grand Runic replied. "I'm just trying to help." He took another sip of his drink, then leaned back. "So, enough suspense," he declared. "Reveal to me your glorious surprise!"

"We are secure?" Kalibar asked. Erasmus frowned, then nodded.

"Of course," he snorted. "I *am* a Runic, remember? All the usual security measures are in place." He smirked then, his blue eyes twinkling mischievously. "And a few unusual ones as well."

"No doubt," Kalibar murmured. "What we discuss must remain between us. I need your word on this." Erasmus leaned forward in his chair, a frown on his face.

"You have it," he replied. "What the hell is going on, Kalibar?"

Kalibar paused for a long moment, then turned to face Kyle.

"Kyle, please give Erasmus your ring," Kalibar requested. Kyle hesitated, looking down at his left thumb. His ring…his *dad's* ring, was there, the gemstone glittering dully. He pulled it off reluctantly, laying it on top of Erasmus's desk. Erasmus picked it up, staring at it for a long moment. Then his eyes widened.

"Dear god!" he exclaimed, grabbing a magnifying glass off of his desk and using it to get a closer look at the ring. "The runes are so small!" he breathed. He inspected it closely, then looked up at Kalibar. "I don't recognize these runes," he stated, almost accusatorily. "Where the hell did you get this?"

"From him," Kalibar answered, nodding in Kyle's direction. Erasmus's blue eyes shifted to Kyle. Kyle squirmed in his seat, unable to make eye contact with the man.

"*Him?*" Erasmus exclaimed incredulously. Kalibar nodded. Erasmus gave a short, barking laugh. "You're kidding, right?"

"Not at all," Kalibar replied. "And that's not all," he added, turning to look at Kyle. "Kyle, please go over there," he requested, gesturing to the corner at the far end of the office, farthest away from Erasmus's desk. Kyle hesitated, then did as Kalibar had ordered.

"Turn around and face us," Kalibar instructed. Kyle did as he was told, turning about silently.

"What's this all about?" Erasmus asked.

"Why don't you join him?" Kalibar replied, gesturing at Kyle with one hand. Erasmus's bushy eyebrows knit together, and he glanced at Kyle, then back at Kalibar.

"What..."

"Go on," Kalibar urged. Erasmus sighed, finishing his glass and standing up. He walked over to Kyle, stopping a few feet away. Kyle glanced at Kalibar, then at Erasmus, feeling enormously confused. Suddenly Erasmus's eyebrows went up, a huge smile splitting his face.

"Kalibar!" he exclaimed joyously, turning about and facing the man. "You devious old bastard! I can't believe I didn't notice it earlier..." He turned back to Kyle, staring him up and down. Kyle backed up instinctively, but had nowhere to go...he was already cornered.

"My dear, dear boy!" Erasmus exclaimed, grabbing Kyle's shoulders with both hands. "My, my...what a glorious find!" He let go, turning to Kalibar. "How clever of you to hide the boy by keeping him so close to yourself!"

"I want to keep this between you and me for now," Kalibar explained. Erasmus nodded, walking back to his desk and sitting down. He poured himself another glass from the bottle, taking a sip.

"Of course, of course," he assured Kalibar. "Does anyone else know?"

"No," Kalibar replied. He turned to Kyle. "You can sit down now," he added. Kyle complied, walking back to his chair beside Kalibar and sitting down. He glanced at Erasmus, then at Kalibar, feeling utterly lost.

"Kyle, I understand that you must be very confused," Kalibar stated. "I apologize for keeping you in the dark," he continued, "...but I felt that you'd already suffered enough trauma in the last few days, and I didn't want to add to your burden until you had time to...adjust." Erasmus frowned at this.

"You mean he doesn't know?" he blurted out incredulously. "You can't be serious!" Kalibar sighed.

"He doesn't know, but it's time I told him."

"Told me *what?*" Kyle asked. Kalibar chuckled, putting a hand on Kyle's shoulder.

"Erasmus, do you have a Finder Stone here?" he asked.

"You know I do," Erasmus answered. An orange-sized, perfectly clear crystal ball rolled off of one of Erasmus's shelves, then floated through the air until it landed in his left hand. He placed this on his desk in front of Kalibar and Kyle.

"The Finder Stone," Kalibar explained, "changes color based on the intensity of magical power it detects. Small amounts cause it to turn gray. Larger amounts turn it red, then orange, then yellow, then green, then blue, and then violet. Each color change indicates an exponential increase in magical energy." Erasmus nodded, placing his right hand on the sphere. It turned gray, then shifted through the spectrum until it reached a dark green, where it stayed.

"Every year," Kalibar stated, "...the Secula Magna sends emissaries to the cities and towns of the Empire, rounding up children between the ages of eight and sixteen. They line up, and touch the Finder Stone. Those with enough magic to get it to change color are offered free room and board, and free tuition, at the Secula Magna."

"Wait, they're taken away from their parents?" Kyle asked incredulously. Kalibar nodded.

"It's a great honor for their families," he replied. "When their children are done with their training, they will be highly respected, well-compensated members of their communities. Most parents desperately want their children to be chosen...but few children have the ability."

With that, Kalibar placed *his* hand on the Finder Stone. It turned red almost immediately, then rapidly moved through the spectrum, ending at a deep violet. Kalibar winked at Erasmus, a smirk on his face. Erasmus rolled his eyes.

"Show-off," he grumbled.

"Now you try," Kalibar told Kyle. Kyle frowned, then reached forward, placing his hand on the crystal. The surface was surprisingly cool, the countless facets on the gemstone shimmering dully in the sunlight streaming from the large windows above. Slowly, the crystal changed color, turning a dull gray. Kyle gasped.

"I can make magic?" he exclaimed, glancing up at Kalibar. Kalibar smiled, a twinkle in his eyes. Then he gestured back at the Finder Stone. Kyle turned back to look at it...and realized it was slowly shifting from gray to red. The red brightened to orange, then yellow, and slowly turned a light green. Erasmus gave a low whistle.

"Remarkable," he breathed, leaning back in his chair, his right hand smoothing out the curls in his long beard. The Finder Stone remained a light green. "Simply remarkable!"

"What does that mean?" Kyle asked Kalibar, who shook his head slowly, his eyes staring into the depths of the glowing crystal. He ran a hand through his short white hair.

"It means you can make a great deal of magic," he answered.

"Oh," Kyle mumbled. Erasmus snorted.

"Oh?" he replied. "*Oh?*" He jabbed one finger at the Finder Stone. "The most powerful Weaver in the known world touched the same Finder Stone fifty years ago when he was about your age, and do you know what color it turned?" Kyle shook his head.

Kalibar leaned back in his chair, clasping his hands in front of him. He regarded Kyle with a critical eye.

"I made it turn yellow," he replied.

Chapter 7

"Would you kindly tell your protégé to pick his damn jaw off my desk?" Erasmus quipped. Kalibar chuckled, putting a hand on Kyle's shoulder. Kyle realized that his mouth was indeed open, and snapped it shut.

"Wait," he stammered. "You mean...?"

"You make more magic than any boy who's ever been tested," Kalibar confirmed. Kyle's jaw went slack again, and he shut it a second time.

I can make magic?

He glanced at Erasmus, whose blue eyes were twinkling merrily, then back at Kalibar. He could hardly believe what he was hearing.

"Any more surprises?" Erasmus asked. Kalibar shook his head. "Good," Erasmus replied, taking another sip from his glass. "I think I've had all my old heart can take for one day." He peered at Kyle from underneath his bushy eyebrows, then glanced back at Kalibar. "So tell me, who is he, really?"

"Hmm?"

"You're a single child, Kalibar," Erasmus stated impatiently. "If he's your grand-nephew, I'm your sister!" Kalibar gave a rueful grin.

"I couldn't say in front of the guards," he admitted. Then he turned to Kyle. "Why don't you tell him your story," he suggested. Kyle glanced at Erasmus, suddenly none too eager to follow Kalibar's suggestion. Erasmus arched an eyebrow at him.

"Oh ho! You don't trust me, boy?" he exclaimed. But he said it with an impish grin, his blue eyes twinkling merrily. Kyle couldn't help but smile back.

"Sorry," he mumbled. "I'm just nervous."

"You should be!" Erasmus replied. Then reached forward,

patting Kyle on the shoulder. "Your secrets, whatever they may be, are safe with me," he added, his tone suddenly serious. Kyle glanced at Kalibar.

"Go on," Kalibar prompted. Kyle took a deep breath, then repeated the same story he'd told Kalibar, talking about his father giving him the ring, the forest, the rip-vines, the Ulfar, and his near-drowning. He mentioned waking up in Kalibar's mansion, meeting Kalibar and Darius, and their harrowing trip here. When he was done, he leaned back in his chair, feeling spent. Erasmus remained silent throughout, much as Kalibar had when he'd heard the story, stroking his white beard. When Kyle finished, Erasmus smiled.

"Thank you, Kyle," he said. He drummed his fingertips on the top of his desk, then looked up at Kalibar. "What do you make of this?"

"Not much," Kalibar admitted ruefully. "You?"

"Doesn't make any sense to me," Erasmus replied. "But it sure raises a lot of questions." Kalibar nodded.

"Too many," he replied. Erasmus snorted.

"Oh bull," he stated. "You're enjoying every minute of this!" He slapped the surface of his desk with one hand. "An impossibly complex runic ring, a boy with power like nothing we've ever seen...you've been desperate for something like this ever since you retired!"

"True," Kalibar admitted. "As have you." He took a sip of his wine. "I'd like your help," he added.

"Ask and you shall receive," Erasmus replied, spreading his arms out wide.

"I'd like to leave Kyle's ring with you," Kalibar stated. "Maybe you can figure out what it does, and who made it." Erasmus grinned broadly.

"Done!" he exclaimed. Then his grin faded. "And what are you planning on doing?"

"I'm going to take Kyle to Crescent Lake to start his apprenticeship," Kalibar answered. Erasmus's bushy eyebrows rose.

"You're training him personally?" the Runic asked in disbelief. He glanced at Kyle, then back at Kalibar, who nodded.

"That's right," he confirmed. Erasmus leaned back in his chair, running a hand through his long white beard. Then he nodded to himself, patting his impressive belly. "I see," he murmured. Kalibar frowned.

"See what?"

"You're taking this one under your wing," Erasmus observed. "A perfect coincidence, you and him meeting up, eh? You both have something the other needs."

"I don't *need* anything," Kalibar replied rather testily. "I'd have Master Owens teach Kyle, but unfortunately we have to leave Stridon tomorrow.

"Why so soon?" Erasmus asked, clearly disappointed. "I was hoping you'd stay a bit longer."

"I would like to, but I don't think it's safe," Kalibar replied. Erasmus arched one bushy eyebrow.

"Not safe?" he exclaimed incredulously. "You're a damned national treasure! There's no safer place for you."

"I wish that were true," Kalibar muttered darkly. Erasmus's eyes narrowed, and he leaned forward in his chair, pushing his glass of wine off to the side.

"Kalibar, what's going on?"

"I was attacked a few weeks ago," Kalibar admitted, his expression grim. "A group of Weavers came to Bellingham in the middle of the night, killing all of my Battle-Weavers and half of my guards."

Erasmus stared at Kalibar incredulously, his mouth agape. Then he stood up from his seat suddenly.

"They *what?*" he nearly shouted.

"They tried to assassinate me," Kalibar said. Erasmus paused, then slammed his fist onto his desk, making Kyle jump.

"Those bastards!" he swore. He started to pace then. "They dared to attack *you?*"

"It didn't end well for them," Kalibar interjected.

"I don't care!" Erasmus replied. "I'm notifying the elite guards. And Bartholos! He'll ferret out the traitorous weasel that planned this."

"Erasmus..." Kalibar began.

"We'll post a contingent of elite guards with you at all times," Erasmus interrupted, still pacing. "I'll..."

"Erasmus," Kalibar interjected, his voice firm. Erasmus paused, turning to face him. "Sit down."

"But..."

"Please," Kalibar insisted. "...I have more to say." Erasmus nodded, sitting back in his chair reluctantly. Kalibar sighed. "I was attacked a second time three days ago," he continued. "During the carriage ride here. The first attempt on my life was well-coordinated, and the second was even more so."

"What?"

"One of the Weavers that attacked me during the second attack was surprisingly powerful," Kalibar explained. "He disabled all of the runic wards on my carriage in seconds."

"What?" Erasmus repeated. "That's impossible! I made those wards myself! No one could have..."

"I know," Kalibar interjected. "But they did."

"But you still beat him," Erasmus deduced. Kalibar shook his head.

"I don't think so," he replied. "I never saw the Weaver...he disappeared early in the attack, and the other Weavers killed themselves."

"Damn," Erasmus swore.

"All I know is that the Weavers I *did* see were wearing red uniforms," Kalibar stated. Erasmus frowned.

"Did they have black sashes?" the Runic asked. "With green diamonds on the front?" Kalibar nodded.

"You've heard of them?"

"I have," Erasmus confirmed. "There have been reports of small villages east of here being razed by men with similar uniforms...apparently led by a man in black."

"Any idea who they might be?" Kalibar asked. Erasmus shook his head.

"Not really," Erasmus replied. "Few witnesses survived the attacks. The few that did were absolutely terrified of the leader – the man in black. We've sent patrols to the towns, and they've confirmed that the towns have been destroyed...but no official sightings of these red Weavers have been made," the former Grand Runic replied. "In fact, you're probably the first reliable witness to confirm that they actually exist."

"Interesting," Kalibar murmured.

"You've made a lot of enemies in your time," Erasmus stated. "...but I find it hard to believe anyone would be dumb enough to try to kill you."

"One person would," Kalibar countered grimly. "I questioned the Weavers before they killed themselves," he continued. "They confessed that Orik ordered my death."

Erasmus's jaw went slack.

"That bastard!" he exclaimed, clenching his fists. "That two-faced son-of-a-"

Kalibar cleared his throat loudly, glancing at Kyle. Erasmus paused for a moment, then slammed his fists on his desk, nearly tipping over his wine glass.

"Of course he'd attack you, the idiot," he seethed. "When I tell Rivin and Bartholos, they'll string Orik up like the common criminal he is!"

"Don't," Kalibar countered.

"Don't what?"

"You can't tell anyone about this," Kalibar clarified. "Not yet."

"Don't *tell* anybody?" Erasmus retorted. "You're mad! I'm going to shout it from the rooftops! The whole damn Empire thinks Orik's a saint...it's about time they found out who he *really* is."

"Erasmus..." Kalibar cautioned. He stared silently at Erasmus for a long moment, and Erasmus stared back, until finally the former Grand Runic sighed, slumping back into his chair.

"Go ahead," he grumbled.

"We have to think strategically," Kalibar insisted. "I know Orik will. We can't give in to a knee-jerk reaction with him...he's too clever for that." He leaned forward. "Remember what happened the last time we tried to prosecute him?"

"I remember," Erasmus muttered.

"Orik is rich, well-liked, and well-connected," Kalibar continued. "We'll need hard evidence to convict him."

"He has a damn good motive," Erasmus offered. Kalibar shook his head.

"Motive isn't enough," he countered. "All we have is the testimony of a dead man." Erasmus sighed again, rubbing his eyes, then resting his palms on his desk.

"Fine," he muttered. "You're right, if we rush into this, Orik will skewer us...again." He stared at the top of his desk for a long moment, then looked up at Kalibar. "So what do we do now?"

"There are two options," Kalibar answered. "We can either report the assassination attempts to the authorities, or keep them to ourselves. If we report them...without implicating Orik...then there will be an official investigation. Orik – as he has done in the past – will stay above the fray while his underlings plant evidence implicating someone else. Or, Orik will find someone willing to take the fall for him and admit to the crime."

"They'd be executed!" Erasmus retorted. Kalibar shrugged.

"People have done it for Orik before," he replied calmly. "Orik has a strangely fanatical following." Erasmus nodded grudgingly at that.

"He's got a damned cult is what he has," he grumbled.

"So alerting the authorities may not ultimately be useful," Kalibar concluded.

"So what," Erasmus retorted. "We let him get away with murder?"

"I'd prefer *attempted* murder," Kalibar corrected with a smirk. "We have to consider his ultimate motive in trying to kill me."

"That's easy," Erasmus replied. "You're the only one who can win against him in the election, so he's eliminating the competition."

"Right," Kalibar agreed. "But now he needs me dead regardless," he added. "I've already thwarted two assassination attempts...and he'll assume his men have talked."

"Ah."

"Orik has considerable resources," Kalibar continued, tapping his chin with his finger. "And a great many allies here that are depending on his winning the election. Powerful men and women."

"You've got allies of your own," Erasmus protested. "A lot more than he does!"

"Perhaps not," Kalibar countered. "Many of our allies were allies out of self-interest, after all."

"Bull," Erasmus retorted. "You've got a lot of friends in the Council," he added. "Like Jax."

"True," Kalibar conceded. "Maybe I'll set up a meeting with him and let him know what's going on. In the meantime, I need to consider my own safety."

"Ha!" Erasmus snorted. "No one would stand a chance against you and you know it."

"Not in battle," Kalibar agreed. "But there are many ways to kill someone. Even I have to sleep sometime," he noted. "And he could always poison my food, or my drink."

"Cheery thought," Erasmus grumbled, glancing at his wine glass.

"I've thought about this ever since the second attack," Kalibar stated. "I think the best course of action is for me to...disappear for a while."

"What?" Erasmus blurted. "You're going to hide away in some cave while that evil bastard wins the election? Great plan, old boy!"

"I'm going to Crescent Lake," Kalibar corrected. "And I'm going to bring Kyle there to teach him magic."

"Crescent Lake?" Erasmus pressed. "Where the hell is that?"

"Exactly."

"And what if Orik has you followed, and sends more of these red assassins after you?"

"I'll take precautions against being followed, of course," Kalibar replied, "...and I can protect myself quite well."

"That you can," Erasmus admitted grudgingly. Then he chuckled. "Poor bastards wouldn't stand a chance!" Then he frowned, his expression troubled. "But I still don't like the idea of a celebrated Grand Weaver hiding from his political enemy, allowing a murderer to claim the throne!"

"Orik will win," Kalibar replied calmly. "And despite his lack of ethics, we both know he'll make a competent ruler," Kalibar added. "You have to admit he's done a great deal of good for the Empire."

"Yes he has," Erasmus admitted. "But we can't forget that he's in league with these red Weavers who're demolishing towns across the Empire...what about that?"

"They'll be stomped out eventually," Kalibar replied. "I assume the Council is already addressing the issue." Erasmus sighed, rubbing his bald head with one hand.

"This isn't right," he muttered. "I think you should fight back...you'd win, Kalibar. You always were the best."

"I lost to Orik before," Kalibar countered. "And besides, I'm retired now," he added. "It's not my fight anymore."

"Not your fight?" Erasmus snorted. "Not your *fight?* You spent your entire damn life fighting for the Empire! Now you're just going to hide away in the forest like some invalid while your life's work is corrupted by that slimy bastard?"

"The Empire must endure without me," Kalibar stated firmly. "I sacrificed the best years of my life for it. I'd like to enjoy what little time I have left."

"All right, fine," Erasmus grumbled. "So what do we do now?"

"We go to bed," Kalibar answered. "I'll meet you in the Runic Archives tomorrow. I need more of your wards for my carriage." He yawned, stretching his arms out to the sides. "You will of course take Kyle's ring?"

"Hell yes I will," Erasmus replied, picking it up from his desk. Kyle stared at it, feeling suddenly uneasy. His ring was all he had left from Earth…his last link to his father back home. The thought of leaving it with Erasmus made him profoundly uneasy. But it was too late; Erasmus got up from his chair, walking over to a safe on the wall closest to his desk. Without a word, the safe opened itself – more magic? – and Erasmus deposited the ring inside. The safe door closed, again by itself.

"Thank you old friend," Kalibar stated, rising from his chair and walking up to Erasmus. The two men hugged, and then Kalibar turned to Kyle. "Let's go," he prompted. Kyle got up from his chair, then followed Kalibar out of Erasmus's office. The two black-armored guards were still standing on either side of Erasmus's door, and followed close behind Kalibar and Kyle as they made their way back down the hallway toward the magic elevator…the riser. Kalibar remained silent, seemingly lost in thought. It was just as well; Kyle could have hardly concentrated on anything Kalibar might have to say. He was still trying to process what had just happened, after all.

I can make magic!

He followed alongside Kalibar, feeling absolutely giddy with the possibilities. Imagine being able to make fire from thin air…to levitate above the earth! It hardly seemed possible that he could be capable of such things.

He snapped out of his reverie, realizing that they'd reached the riser at the end of the hallway. Kalibar turned to the guards.

"Thank you," he stated. "I'll go alone from here." The guards nodded, and Kalibar and Kyle stepped onto the center of the riser. It rose shortly thereafter, traveling upward a few more stories before coming to an uncomfortably abrupt halt. Kalibar stepped off of the riser, and Kyle followed alongside.

"Where are we going?" Kyle asked.

"To my suite," Kalibar answered. "As a former Grand Weaver, I have a room on the 41st floor of the Tower," he explained. "The current Grand Weaver and Grand Runic have suites on the top floor of the Tower, on the 42nd floor."

"Oh," Kyle replied.

"Have I told you about the Council?" Kalibar asked.

"No."

"The Council is composed of a dozen people," Kalibar

explained. "They are the second-most powerful people in the Empire, below the Grand Weaver and Grand Runic," he added. "They have living quarters on the 40th floor."

"But why is Erasmus's office down below?" Kyle asked. After all, as a former Grand Runic, Erasmus should have a suite on the 41st floor, like Kalibar.

"He has a suite on this floor," Kalibar replied. "But unlike me, he hasn't retired yet. He's the Head Archivist for the Tower's runic artifact collection."

"The what?"

"We've collected thousands of runic artifacts in the last two hundred years," Kalibar explained. "Some of them as old as the Ancients. Erasmus oversees this collection – the Runic Archives."

"Wait," Kyle said, struck by a sudden pang of fear. "What about my ring? He's not going to keep it in the Archives, is he?"

"No," Kalibar replied. "Erasmus is one of the only men I would trust *not* to take the ring for himself."

Kalibar strode down the hallway, and Kyle walked at his side, glancing about. There were painted sculptures of various men on the walls, but also of women as well. All had stern looks on their faces. One of the male statues looked oddly familiar for some reason.

"These statues were recovered from the ruins of the first Tower," Kalibar explained. "We think they're of Ancient Council members," he added. He gestured for Kyle to continue down the hallway, until they reached a large, ornate door on the left wall. The door opened without being touched, just as Erasmus's had earlier. Kalibar walked inside, with Kyle following. They came into a large room – easily thirty feet square, with a ceiling twenty feet high. The room was ornate, almost beyond description. The floors were made of polished granite, and massive windows as tall as the ceiling lined the outer walls. Beyond these, the entire city lay spread out in a magnificent vista far below. Huge bookshelves lined the walls, filled with important-looking tomes. Numerous large white couches had been placed throughout the suite, surrounding glass-topped tables. Kalibar motioned for Kyle to sit on one of these couches, and Kalibar sat on the couch opposite Kyle.

"Well then," Kalibar stated. "You've been given quite a bit to think about." He leaned forward. "Do you have any questions for me?"

Kyle paused, then shook his head. He was sure he had a lot of questions for Kalibar, but he couldn't think of any at the moment.

"All right," Kalibar replied. "I suppose I should tell you more about the Empire...and about the Ancients." He leaned back on the couch, draping one arm over the armrest. "The Ancients were just like us," he explained. "Or rather, we modeled our government after theirs. They had an Empire with a Secula Magna, and a Great Tower like this one," he continued. "Their empire flourished for thousands of years, until the Great War."

He leaned forward, rubbing his eyes wearily.

"The Great War was the most devastating ever recorded. Back then, the Secula Magna was the center of civilization, the ruling body of a vast empire...one even larger than the Empire today. The political structure was the same as it is now, with a Grand Weaver and Grand Runic. However, back then, they ruled for life instead of just six years. The Grand Runic at the time – a man named Nespo – was middle-aged, making it unlikely that any Council member at the time would ever achieve Grand Runic status in their lifetime. An ambitious Council member named Sabin wanted desperately to become Grand Runic, and arranged to have the current Grand Runic assassinated. The plot was discovered, and Sabin was arrested for treason."

Kalibar leaned back in his seat.

"Our understanding of what happened next is somewhat hazy," he admitted ruefully. "Most of the histories have been lost to time, or were destroyed in the war. What we do know is that Sabin was an unusually creative and powerful Runic, and managed to escape from prison before his execution. He fled to a rival country, and convinced their leaders to amass an army against the Empire. He trained their Runics and Weavers for several years. He was also a brilliant inventor, and created massive war machines of enormous power. He marched this army into Stridon, ambushing the city."

Kyle's eyes widened. It was just like his dreams...the Behemoth destroying the city, killing everything in its path. But how could he possibly have dreamt of something that had happened two thousand years ago?

"The Secula Magna was surprised, but it had the finest Runics and Weavers, and thousands of years' worth of powerful runic technology at its disposal. The battle was fierce. Sabin's army demolished the city itself, but once they reached the Secula Magna, they met enormous resistance. Most of the rebel army was defeated by the Secula's superior Weavers, but the giant war machines were unstoppable. The Great Tower fell, and the remaining members of the Secula Magna fled. Those that survived went into hiding, but most were found and murdered. The Ancient Empire fell."

Kalibar let out a sigh.

"When the Ancients died, their knowledge – thousands of years of technological advances – was lost. Only fragments of their works remain. Our most sophisticated runics are nothing compared to what the Ancients created."

"What happened after the Ancients lost?" Kyle asked.

"Sabin overreached," Kalibar answered. "He succeeded in destroying the Empire, but the majority of his forces were destroyed...even his Behemoths, although no one knows how. His forces were unable to defend their newly won territories from the countries bordering the Empire, and they were forced out."

"So the Empire was rebuilt?" Kyle asked. Kalibar shook his head.

"Not right away," he replied. "The Ancient Empire was carved into various countries. These degenerated into numerous tribes, each warring with each other to defend or expand their borders. The new Empire – and the new Secula Magna – weren't formed until about two hundred years ago. They were recreated in an attempt to bring human civilization back to its former glory and sophistication."

"Oh."

"But the Empire wasn't just created to mimic the Ancients' technological advances," Kalibar continued. "The Ancients represented the pinnacle of philosophy and ethics. Their Empire was one where all men were free, where human dignity was respected above all else. This Empire," Kalibar stated, gesturing around him, "...was built on those principles."

"So what happened to the tribes?" Kyle asked.

"Some of them joined the Empire voluntarily," Kalibar answered. "Others rebelled, declaring war. I fought against the last of the tribes during my stint in the military, and Erasmus and I finally defeated them during our tenure as Grand Runic and Grand Weaver."

Kalibar stopped then, and Kyle's stomach growled so loudly that even Kalibar heard it. Kalibar smiled.

"I forgot we haven't eaten since breakfast," he stated. "Let's order dinner." Kalibar leaned over the side of the couch, resting his hand on what looked like a glass orb laying on an end table. The orb glowed faintly when touched, then turned clear again. Moments later, a knock came at the door. Kalibar touched the glass orb again, and the door opened, a man dressed in a blue shirt and black pants stepping through.

"Good to see you again, Jenkins," Kalibar greeted. The man in the blue shirt froze in his tracks, looking startled. He quickly regained his composure, closing the door behind him.

"Your Excellency," he replied, bowing deeply. "Young sir," he added, giving Kyle a shallower bow.

"Jenkins," Kalibar stated, "...my young friend and I would like to order dinner. I'll have the roasted duck with a salad. Kyle here will have the same." Jenkins bowed again, then left as quickly as he'd come. Kyle watched him go, then turned to face Kalibar.

"Why did he look so surprised?" Kyle asked.

"Jenkins?" Kalibar asked. Kyle nodded. "Well, I met Jenkins only once, over a year ago," Kalibar explained. "I made a point to remember his name. Now, I certainly didn't have to...I was a former leader of the Empire, and he was just a servant."

"So why did you?" Kyle pressed.

"Because Jenkins is a person, just like you and me," Kalibar answered. "As the leader of the Empire, my duty was to serve *him*...and everyone else. And I've found that if you treat people as if they're important to you, you will become important to them."

"Oh."

"*That* is how you win loyalty," Kalibar declared. "It can be as simple as caring enough to remember someone's name." He raised an eyebrow then, reaching into his pants pocket. "Or as simple as keeping a promise," he added, pulling out a small, dark brown bottle.

"What's that?" Kyle asked.

"The feathergrass extract I promised you," Kalibar replied with a wink. Kyle's eyes widened, and he broke out into a huge grin.

"All right!"

"I'll let you try it out later," Kalibar promised, placing the bottle back in his pocket. A knock came at the door then, and they both turned to see Jenkins walking back into the suite, his arms overloaded with silver platters. Kalibar got up to help the butler –

despite Jenkins' protests – taking a platter and placing it on the table. Jenkins whisked the covers from the platters, and poured a red liquid into two cups. Kalibar thanked the butler, who bowed and left as efficiently as he'd come.

Kalibar took his cup, and motioned for Kyle to take the other. They clinked glasses in a silent toast, and drank. Kyle almost spewed the red liquid onto the table – it was terribly sour and bitter. Kalibar laughed.

"Sorry," Kyle apologized. He glanced down at his glass with disgust. "What *is* this?"

"It's wine," Kalibar answered. "You've never had wine before?"

Kyle gasped, recoiling in horror. He was drinking *alcohol?* He pushed his glass far away, leaning back in his seat. Kalibar frowned, pushing the glass back toward Kyle.

"Drink it! We're celebrating," the old man insisted.

"I'm not supposed to," Kyle countered. "I don't want to get drunk," he added sagely. Kalibar snorted.

"Ridiculous!" he exclaimed. "It's good wine, and you won't get sick with such a small glass. I insist you drink it, and enjoy the warmth and cheer it brings." But Kyle folded his arms in front of his chest. He'd heard about such tactics in school. He wouldn't give in to peer pressure!

"Oh for pity's sake," Kalibar grumbled. He finished his own glass, then focused on his dinner. Kyle did the same, his stomach growling almost painfully. The aroma of roasted duck was mouth-wateringly good…especially compared to the stale bread and dehydrated meat they'd been eating for the last three days. Kyle dug in, devouring the meal. It tasted every bit as good as it smelled, and it wasn't long before he'd cleaned up every morsel from his plate. When he looked up, he found Kalibar finishing his own meal. The old man leaned back in his chair afterward, dabbing his lips with a napkin. Then he let rip a loud burp, making Kyle laugh.

"Your turn," Kalibar proclaimed.

"Uuuuuuhhrp!" Kyle belched.

"Impressive!" Kalibar exclaimed. "A good, strong belch is considered a compliment for the meal," he explained. He touched the clear orb at his side again, summoning Jenkins. The butler arrived with remarkable alacrity, removing plates and silverware. Then he offered Kalibar more wine, which the former Grand Weaver accepted graciously. When the butler had finally left,

Kalibar turned to Kyle, raising his glass – now filled with wine – in front of him.

"To fond memories already made, and those still to come," he toasted, motioning for Kyle to raise his own glass. Kyle did so, clinking the rim against Kalibar's. Kalibar sipped from his own glass, then set it down. Kyle paused, holding his glass up in the air. Kalibar smiled.

"You know," he stated, "the trick to drinking wine is to have enough to raise your spirit, and not a drop more." He glanced at Kyle's glass, then at Kyle. Kyle hesitated, then shook his head, pushing the glass away.

"I've had enough," he stated. Kalibar nodded.

"I believe we both have," he replied, standing up from his couch and gesturing for Kyle to do the same. "Come, I'll show you to your room, and your bed. Enjoy it…we'll be back on the road soon enough."

Chapter 8

The next morning, Kyle was awakened by the sound of knocking on his door. He yawned, stretching his arms out wide, grimacing as his back twinged. It was much less painful than it'd been a few days ago, but now it was itching…maddeningly so. He resisted the urge to scratch his bandages, rolling carefully out of bed and walking up to the door. It took him a moment to remember where he was: in one of the several guest bedrooms in Kalibar's suite. He reached the door, grabbing for a knob that wasn't there. Then he remembered; most of the doors here were magically opened and closed. There was a blue crystal imbedded into the center of the door, glowing a faint blue to indicate that it was locked. There was no way for him to open it.

"Come in," Kyle called out.

The blue light vanished, and the door swung open, revealing Jenkins. The butler gave Kyle a short bow.

"I trust you slept well, young sir?" he inquired.

"Uh, yeah," Kyle answered. "Yes, thanks."

"His Excellency requests that you join him for an early lunch," Jenkins stated. "If you will get dressed," he added, gesturing to a neat stack of folded clothes on a nearby bureau, "…I will take you to him."

Kyle nodded, and Jenkins shut the door. Kyle took off his pajamas – an amazingly soft set of silver pants and a shirt – and changed into the clothes Jenkins had provided. A simple gray shirt and loose pants, they fit perfectly.

"Okay," Kyle called out. The door opened promptly, and Jenkins gestured for Kyle to follow him into the main room of Kalibar's suite, where he'd eaten with Kalibar the night before. They left the suite, traveling down the hall to the riser at the end. It dropped them rapidly downward, stopping rather abruptly at the 32nd floor. This, Kyle realized as he followed Jenkins down another hallway, was the same floor Erasmus's office had been on. He walked past the carvings of former Grand Runics and Grand Weavers on either wall, striding past Erasmus's door and reaching a large door at the end of the hallway. Jenkins opened this, stepping through, and Kyle followed the butler into the room beyond. Kyle's eyes widened, his breath catching in his throat.

It was, in a word, *huge*.

The room was three stories high, and before him stood a long row of shelves going almost all the way to the top. Each shelf was filled to the brim with books, small trinkets, and gemstones of every color and shape. On either side of the room's entrance were long desks with white-robed men and women standing behind them. Two men in black armor stepped in front of Kyle and Jenkins, barring their way forward.

"His Excellency former Grand Weaver Kalibar requests this boy's presence," Jenkins stated crisply. One of the guards turned about, disappearing behind one of the shelves, while the other remained. Some thirty seconds later, the guard returned, nodding at Kyle.

"I'll take him," the guard stated. Jenkins bowed, then turned and left. Kyle followed the black-armored guard into the huge room, walking between two of the massive bookshelves. Beyond these were more rows of shelves, and beyond those, even more. The guard led Kyle rightward at one of the gaps between rows, and then up a large spiral staircase. They reached the second floor, which was a balcony of sorts. There were bookshelves here too, although much shorter than the ones below, and there were rows of rectangular wooden tables as well. The guard led Kyle past these to a closed door. The guard knocked on the door, and it opened, revealing a small conference room with a table in the center, around which Kalibar, Erasmus, and even Darius were sitting. Darius looked, as usual, dreadfully bored.

"Ah, there you are Kyle," Kalibar greeted as Kyle stopped before them. Kalibar patted the seat of the chair next to him. "Come, sit down with us."

"Morning," Kyle mumbled. He sat down, scratching his head idly. Then he realized that his hair was askew...he'd forgotten to brush it! He patted his hair down, feeling his cheeks turn warm, and withered into his chair.

"Don't worry about your hair," Erasmus said with a mischievous grin, his blue eyes twinkling. "Enjoy it while you can," he added, running a hand over his bald head.

"Here," Kalibar stated, pushing a plate filled with bread and slices of cheese at Kyle. Kyle realized that there were similar plates – all empty – in front of each of the men. Kyle mouthed a silent "thank you," nibbling on some bread.

"We were just talking about you," Erasmus stated jovially, smirking at Kyle's suddenly suspicious expression. "Oh, nothing too terrible," the old Runic added. "We were just brainstorming some theories as to how you might have gotten here."

"That's right," Kalibar agreed. "That's why we met here, at the Archives." Kyle stared at the massive bookshelves beyond the balcony.

"Wait," Kyle said, "...*this* is the Archives?"

"Right you are," Erasmus confirmed. "Finest collection of runic artifacts and books ever assembled!" Then he paused. "Well, except for the Ancients," he admitted. "They had a far better collection."

"I told Erasmus about Urth," Kalibar explained. "I remembered reading a book here about ten years ago," he added. "About teleportation. Erasmus found it for me." Kalibar pointed at a book before him, which was open, a bookmark between its pages.

"Poppycock," Erasmus retorted. "Renval was as mad as his father before him."

"Perhaps," Kalibar replied. "But he was damned brilliant."

"So was his father," Erasmus countered.

Kyle stared at both of them, utterly confused. It must have shown.

"Back in Ancient times," Kalibar began, "...a few years before the Ancient Empire fell, a Runic scholar and inventor called Renval became enormously popular. He is said to have created floating cities in the sky, among other ingenious inventions."

"Renval's father," Erasmus piped in, "...was just as brilliant, but he wasted his life with mad ravings about other planets and teleportation."

"Right," Kalibar agreed. "Publicly, Renval denounced his father's delusions. But after the Empire fell, Renval's journals were discovered in the Citadel on Meros."

"Showing that he was just as mad as his father," Erasmus concluded dismissively.

"Perhaps," Kalibar stated.

"Wait," Kyle interrupted. "What's Meros?"

"An island west of here," Kalibar answered. "The island I talked about earlier, where almost all of the Ancient artifacts in these Archives were discovered. Renval's journals were found in the ruins of an ancient city there."

"Following in his father's footsteps, no doubt," Erasmus muttered. "Wasting his life chasing tall tales."

"Renval was just as interested in teleportation and astronomy as his father," Kalibar continued, ignoring Erasmus. "But unlike his father, Renval's journals claim that he actually succeeded in creating a remarkable invention."

"What invention?" Kyle asked.

"A teleportation device," Kalibar answered. Erasmus rolled his eyes, but Kalibar ignored him. "According to his journals, Renval's device actually worked...and he used it to travel all over the world."

"What a load of crap," Erasmus grumbled.

"Probably," Kalibar agreed. "But he was a formidable inventor, and absolutely brilliant." He sighed. "In any case, Renval's journal ends with his writing about using the teleportation device to travel much, much farther." He turned to Kyle then. "Another planet."

Kyle's eyes widened.

"Wait, what?" he blurted.

"The last entry in Renval's diary," Kalibar stated, flipping a page, "...says this:"

"Unexpected complication re: travel at massive distances. Time contraction/expansion problematic. All test subjects died. Multistep travel may prevent. Will calibrate and test."

"What does that mean?" Kyle asked. Erasmus shrugged.

"Who the hell knows?" he replied. "The device was never found, because it ever existed in the first place. And most of Renval's notes have been lost to time."

"Great," Kyle mumbled.

"The device *may* have existed," Kalibar countered, ignoring Erasmus's sour expression. "Renval mentioned something in his journals...something I didn't read until today."

"And what's that?" Erasmus asked.

"He had an apprentice," Kalibar explained. "A young man who later became – if you believe the histories – the greatest Runic in recorded history."

Erasmus's face brightened, and the portly Runic leaned over the table, his white beard spilling onto the wooden surface.

"Ampir!" he exclaimed. Kalibar nodded.

"Exactly."

"Ampir?" Kyle asked. The name sounded awfully familiar, but for some reason he couldn't quite place it.

"He *was* Renval's apprentice," Erasmus agreed, ignoring Kyle's question. "But only for two years…and Ampir was just a kid at the time," he added. "No offense," he stated, glancing at Kyle.

"Correct," Kalibar stated. "But Renval's journals suggest that Ampir helped him with the teleportation device…and that they worked together long after Ampir's apprenticeship."

"Damn," Erasmus swore. "If Ampir worked with Renval for that long, the bastards might've actually made the thing after all!"

"He was really that good?" Kyle asked.

"Ampir was so good," Erasmus answered, "…that he could win wars just by showing up on the battlefield. Countries would surrender at the mere sight of him."

"Wait," Kyle interjected. "I thought he was a Runic, not a Weaver."

"He *was* a Runic," Erasmus confirmed. "A Battle-Runic, in fact…one of the few that has ever lived." His blue eyes twinkled. "He created his own armor from scratch, making himself the most powerful weapon the Ancients had ever seen. His armor was said to have been so advanced – even for the Ancients – that no one could even understand how it worked, much less defeat it!"

"Indeed," Kalibar agreed. "Legend has it that rival countries placed bounties on Ampir's head. One offered as much as a hundred times Ampir's weight in diamonds to whoever killed him and brought them his armor to study." Erasmus nodded.

"There isn't a single source that questions Ampir's ability," he stated authoritatively. "He was the greatest Runic – perhaps the greatest wielder of magic – the world has ever known!"

"History tends to exaggerate when it comes to heroes and villains," Kalibar countered. "Unless you're forgetting how the 'greatest Runic' abandoned his people, allowing millions to die…and setting humanity back thousands of years." Erasmus sat back in his chair, crossing his arms and glaring at Kalibar.

"There's no proof of that," he retorted. Kalibar raised an eyebrow.

"Do you honestly think the Ancients would have lost to Sabin if Ampir had defended them?"

"Why would he have betrayed them?" Erasmus countered testily. "He spent his entire life defending the Empire!"

"Perhaps Ampir was in league with Sabin all along, and defected to join him in destroying the Empire."

"Oh, don't even mention that hare-brained theory," Erasmus snorted. "Everyone knows Sabin hated Ampir! Ampir had always been the better Runic, and Sabin…"

"How can we know?" Kalibar interrupted. "How can anyone know what really happened two thousand years ago?"

"History tends to exaggerate when it comes to heroes and villains," Erasmus reminded him.

"Granted," Kalibar admitted rather grudgingly.

"But wait," Kyle interjected. Both men turned to him. "So what?"

"Hmm?" Erasmus asked.

"The teleportation device is gone now," Kyle reminded them.

"True," Kalibar agreed. "But such technology might explain how you got here…if you really do come from another world."

"That's a big 'if,'" Erasmus piped in.

"If we entertain the idea," Kalibar stated, "…then perhaps someone managed to recreate Renval's teleportation device, or something like it, to bring you here."

"But why?" Kyle pressed. "Why would anyone bring *me* here?"

"I don't know," Kalibar admitted. "It could have something to do with that ring of yours. You say that there is no magic on your world, which – if it's true – means that your ring must have originally come from *this* world."

"It most certainly did," Erasmus concurred. "It has all of the qualities of the period it was made in, even if it *is* uncommonly advanced. The style of the runes, the metals used, the way the crystals were cut…it dates unerringly back to the Ancient times, right before the Empire was destroyed."

"Wait, what?" Kyle asked.

"Your ring is two thousand years old," Kalibar explained. "And it was made by the Ancients. So if you come from another world, then that means someone must have sent the ring there...and then brought it back here, with you."

"What if the *ring* were the teleportation device?" Erasmus proposed. Kalibar turned to him, arching an eyebrow. "Well, why not?" Erasmus asked.

"It's an idea," Kalibar admitted. He leaned back in his chair, tapping his chin with one finger. "This is all assuming that Kyle was teleported here from another world."

"How else can you explain that device you showed me earlier?" Erasmus asked. Kyle frowned, turning a questioning eye to Kalibar, who reached into his pants pocket.

"He's talking about this," Kalibar said, pulling something out of his pocket and placing it on the table. It was, Kyle realized, his watch...the survival watch he'd gotten for his birthday. He'd completely forgotten about it.

"How did you...?" Kyle stammered.

"I took it from your wrist when you were first brought to my house," Kalibar confessed.

"Remarkable device," Erasmus stated, picking it up and staring at it. "Never seen anything like it. No magic at all...yet it glows when I press this button!" He pressed a button on the side of the watch, and the display began to glow green. Erasmus leaned forward, his blue eyes twinkling at Kyle from below bushy white eyebrows. "Tell us...what does it do?"

"It uh...tells time," Kyle answered. "It's a watch."

"A timepiece?" Erasmus asked. "Is that what these symbols represent? Numbers?" Kyle nodded. Of course Kalibar and Erasmus wouldn't be able to understand Earth numbers or letters...just as he himself hadn't been able to read the signs when they'd ridden through Stridon.

"Fascinating," Erasmus murmured, seemingly in a trance while he stared at the watch. After a long moment, he tore his gaze away from the gadget, handing it over to Kyle.

"No, you can have it," Kyle said. Erasmus paused, glancing at Kalibar, then back at Kyle.

"You're sure?"

"It's the least I can do," Kyle insisted. Erasmus nodded, placing the watch in his pants pocket.

"Thank you Kyle," the former Grand Runic said. He broke out

into a grin, elbowing Kalibar in the side. "Damn if the last few years of our lives aren't going to be the most interesting! Imagine...other worlds, strange technology...teleportation..."

"I knew you wouldn't be able to resist," Kalibar said with a grin of his own. "But first thing's first...we need to figure out what Kyle's ring can do."

"I agree," Erasmus replied. "And I plan on losing a great deal of sleep doing just that," he added zestfully, his blue eyes twinkling. "I tell you, this whole business makes me feel like a young man again!"

"One last adventure," Kalibar murmured. He got a faraway look in his eyes for a moment, and Erasmus cleared his throat.

"Yes, well then," the portly Runic said. "I'd love to stay and chat, but I do have some work to do."

"Of course," Kalibar replied. Erasmus stood up, and Kalibar joined him. The two men hugged, then separated.

"Dinner tonight?" Erasmus asked. Kalibar nodded.

"Of course."

"See you then, old friend," Erasmus said. He nodded at Kyle. "And thanks for the timepiece," he added. Then he turned about, leaving the room. Kalibar sighed, stretching his arms out, then turning to face Kyle.

"Let's go back to my suite," he stated, gesturing for Kyle to stand. Kyle did so, as did Darius. Kalibar grabbed two books from the tabletop, then made his way to the door. Darius followed close behind, and Kyle fell in line behind the bodyguard. They exited the room, making their way down the spiral staircase, then out of the Archives. They strode down the long hallway toward the riser, staying to the right as a line of people passed them on the left, going in the opposite direction. Suddenly Kalibar stopped short, making Kyle nearly bump into Darius from behind.

"What..." Kyle began, but Kalibar held up one hand. Kyle's teeth clicked shut, and he followed Kalibar's gaze, spotting a man approaching them...a tall, well-built man wearing a black cloak. He had short black hair and a thin black mustache, and strode down the hall with an unmistakable air of confidence, his black cloak rippling behind him. Two guards flanked him, their boots clicking sharply on the granite floor. The man spotted Kalibar and slowed, stopping a few feet in front of him.

"Your Excellency," he greeted, giving Kalibar a short bow.

"Councilman," Kalibar replied, giving a curt nod in return.

"I heard of your return," the Councilman stated, glancing at Kyle and Darius, then returning his gaze to Kalibar. "It's been too long since we've had the pleasure of your company."

"Yes, well," Kalibar replied. "...I've found retirement to be preferable to politics."

"Is that so," the Councilman stated. He glanced down at Kyle, then Kalibar. "What brings you to Stridon?"

"Just visiting some old friends," Kalibar answered.

"I see," the Councilman replied. "I can't imagine what it must be like to live in a town like Bellingham after being in Stridon for so long," he added. He gave a tight smile. "I'd be bored to death there."

"I've found the politics here to be far more deadly than boredom," Kalibar countered. The Councilman considered this, then nodded.

"Touché," he conceded. "One has to be careful during election season."

"Very careful," Kalibar agreed. The Councilman paused, then glanced down at Kyle, as if noticing him for the first time.

"And who is this?" he asked. Kyle looked up at Kalibar, who put an arm around Kyle's shoulders.

"One of Master Owen's new students," Kalibar answered. "A distant relative."

"Ah," the Councilman stated, reaching out with one hand. Kyle extended his own; the Councilman shook it, his grip firm but not painfully so. "Always a pleasure to meet an up-and-coming Weaver."

"Thanks," Kyle mumbled, feeling rather awkward. The Councilman let go of Kyle's hand, turning to Darius. "And who is this?" Darius stared back at the man, saying nothing. Seconds passed, the Councilman's smile becoming strained.

"That's Darius, my bodyguard," Kalibar answered. He reached over and patted Darius on one metallic shoulder-plate. "We've been keeping you awfully busy recently, haven't we Darius?"

"Nothing I can't handle," Darius replied, his unnerving blue eyes still locked on the Councilman's. The Councilman lowered his hand, his smile fading. He turned back to face Kalibar.

"Are you staying long?" he inquired.

"Not likely," Kalibar answered. "I've no interest in the circus of the elections."

"A shame," the Councilman replied. "A lot of people would love for you to run for a second term."

"Not everyone," Kalibar countered. The corner of the Councilman's mouth twitched.

"Granted."

"I've no interest in running," Kalibar stated firmly. The Councilman smiled, folding his arms over his chest, his eyes locked on Kalibar's.

"If I were you," he replied coolly, "...I'd strongly consider it."

He nodded at his guards then, then gave Kalibar a curt bow.

"Your Excellency," he murmured. Then he left, striding down the hallway, leaving Kalibar, Darius, and Kyle standing there.

"Who..." Kyle began, but Kalibar strode forward before he could finish, forcing Kyle to sprint to catch up with the old man. Moments later, they stopped in the middle of the riser at the end of the hallway. It shot upward with unnerving speed, zipping past floor after floor of the Great Tower before slowing, then stopping. Kalibar stepped off of the riser, Darius and Kyle following alongside. They walked in silence to one of the doors on the left. It opened by itself, and Kalibar stepped through. They were, Kyle realized, back in Kalibar's suite; Kalibar walked up to one of the couches, sitting down and gesturing for Kyle to take a seat on a couch opposite him. Kyle complied, glancing at Darius, then Kalibar in confusion.

"What's going on?" he asked. "Who was that?" Kalibar leaned forward, his elbows on his knees. His jawline rippled.

"*That*," he replied, "...was Orik."

* * *

Kyle stared at Kalibar in disbelief.

"That was him?" he asked incredulously. Kalibar nodded, rubbing his eyes.

"It was," he replied wearily. "And we're in trouble," he added, leaning back into his couch and staring off into the distance.

"What do you mean?" Kyle asked, feeling a sudden pang of fear. Kalibar focused on Kyle, then sighed.

"Orik practically announced his role in my attempted assassination," he replied. "And I suspect he is going to make the attempt again."

"What?" Kyle blurted out. "Why?"

"That should be obvious."

"But he can't attack you *here*," Kyle protested. Kalibar raised an eyebrow.

"And why not?"

"He'd get caught," Kyle answered. Kalibar considered this for a moment, rubbing his goatee absently.

"He can't know whether I've told anyone else of his involvement," Kalibar reasoned. "He has to assume that I have. He'll know that I've talked to Erasmus, and no one else thus far…which means Erasmus is also in danger."

"You mean…" Kyle began.

"He might try to kill both of us," Kalibar stated grimly. "And you, and Darius, for good measure."

Kyle glanced at Darius, who didn't appear to be paying attention to either of them. Then he turned back to Kalibar, swallowing past a sudden lump in his throat. Kalibar drummed his fingers on the table between them.

"As I said," he muttered, "…we're in trouble."

"Can't we just tell everyone what Orik did?" Kyle pleaded. Kalibar sighed.

"We could," he admitted. "But Orik has already prepared for that possibility."

"What do you mean?"

"Orik is a very dangerous man," Kalibar explained. "He's one of the best political strategists I've ever met. I've got no proof that he was involved in the attacks against me…only my word, and my reputation. And that," he continued, "…was not enough the last time I tried to take him down."

"Wait, what?"

"It's a long story," Kalibar admitted. "But I'll make it short. It was ten years ago or so, while I was still Grand Weaver. At the time, Orik was running for governor of Stridon." He gave a rueful smile. "Even then, he was enormously popular. He'd served as mayor of a nearby city already, with incredible success. You see," Kalibar continued, "…Orik is unbelievably wealthy…one of the wealthiest men in the Empire. He spent massive sums of money donating to charities, building parks, renovating buildings, organizing events…that sort of thing. It made him incredibly popular with the general public."

"Oh."

"He also invested heavily in local businesses, and passed legislation to ease regulations on them, making himself popular with the wealthy," Kalibar continued.

"Doesn't sound like a bad guy to me," Kyle had to admit. Kalibar chuckled.

"He wasn't...until his money wasn't enough to make him win," Kalibar replied. "As I said, after his turn as mayor, Orik ran for governor of Stridon. He would have won easily, but his opponent happened to be a popular and respected career politician...one with powerful friends." Kalibar smiled then. "Including me."

"I see."

"My friend – Orik's opponent – was clearly going to win the election," Kalibar explained. "But then evidence surfaced that implicated him in conducting illegal campaign activities."

"Like what?" Kyle asked.

"Oh, like accepting bribes from various special interests," Kalibar answered. "And men started coming forward, claiming that my friend had...strayed from his marriage."

"Like cheated?" Kyle asked, remembering Ben's father. Kalibar nodded.

"None of it was true," he continued. "The evidence was entirely fabricated. But it was enough to destroy my friend's political career, and Orik won the election handily."

"Oh."

"My friend committed suicide shortly thereafter," Kalibar stated, his tone solemn. "Leaving a wife and three children behind."

Kyle said nothing, unable to meet Kalibar's gaze any longer. He stared at the table between them, not knowing what else to do.

"I suspected Orik immediately, of course," Kalibar said. "My friend's wife made me promise to take Orik down. And as the most powerful man in the Empire at the time, I was one of the few people who could do it."

"What did you do?"

"I launched a private investigation against Orik," Kalibar replied. "I even had my informants investigate his past – his businesses, tax paperwork, business partners, records of his time as governor, even his school records and birth certificate – everything. And everything came back squeaky clean."

"You didn't find *anything*?" Kyle asked.

"Nothing," Kalibar agreed. "His record was impeccable.

Perfect." He shook his head. "But the fact that all of these allegations against my friend came up only after Orik started losing in the election was too obvious to ignore. Orik *had* to be involved...everyone in the Council believed it, and so did Erasmus and I."

"So what happened?"

"I investigated the men who accused my friend of infidelity," Kalibar replied. "And found that they'd been nowhere near my friend during the times they claimed to have...been involved with him."

"So they *were* lying!"

"Right," Kalibar confirmed. "But it was too late...the damage had already been done. Orik himself never endorsed the allegations against my friend. He even went as far as to insist that voters ignore the scandal. After my friend's death, Orik denounced the men who'd wrongly accused my friend, and revealed – from his own investigation, supposedly – that they had indeed been lying all along."

"Oh."

"The thing is," Kalibar continued, "...that the evidence Orik supplied was identical, document for document, word for word, to the evidence my own investigation had revealed."

"So?"

"So Orik was sending me a message," Kalibar explained. "That he'd been aware of my secret investigation the entire time, and that he almost certainly had informants among the men I'd trusted to carry out that investigation."

"What did you do?"

"I accused Orik of stealing classified documents, and implicated him in the smear campaign against my friend," Kalibar answered. "I hoped that with my evidence and my reputation, I could force Orik out of office." Kyle sighed then, shaking his head. "I was wrong."

"What happened?" Kyle asked.

"Orik didn't get involved, as usual," Kalibar answered. "But his supporters accused me of using my office as Grand Weaver to influence elections in favor of my personal friends. No one believed it, at first." Kalibar lowered his gaze. "Then two high-ranking men – men I'd been friends with for decades, men I trusted – came forward to confirm those accusations...and to claim that I'd illegally influenced other elections as well."

"What?" Kyle blurted out. "Why?"

"Good question," Kalibar replied. "The accusations were false, of course. To this day, I can't fathom why those two men did that to me...whether Orik threatened them, or paid them. It doesn't matter now," he added glumly. "The whole thing became such a scandal that I was forced to abandon my investigation of Orik." He shook his head, a rueful smile on his lips. "Orik himself came forward to defend me after I agreed to let the investigation go. He 'found' evidence that my two former friends had lied, and they left Stridon, never to be seen or heard from again. My reputation remained intact, and Orik went on to be a highly successful governor."

"Wow," Kyle breathed.

"Wow is right," Kalibar agreed. "So now you see what kind of man we're up against."

"Isn't there something we can do?" Kyle pressed. Kalibar sighed.

"Orik beat me when I had the full power of a Grand Weaver," he replied. "Now I'm just a citizen of the Empire, and he's even more influential now as a Councilman than he was as governor." He shook his head. "There's no telling what lengths he might go to protect himself," Kalibar added. "Trying to out him might put my friends and family at risk."

"Like Erasmus," Kyle reasoned. Kalibar nodded.

"Like Erasmus."

Kyle stared at the tabletop before him, mulling it over. Then he sighed.

"So we just let him win?" he asked. Kalibar nodded.

"Yes."

"But he's a murderer!" Kyle exclaimed. Kalibar shrugged.

"And he's a skilled public servant who's done a great deal for the Empire," he countered. "You'd be surprised," he added with a smirk, "...but most politicians aren't as concerned about morals and ethics as I am."

"I still don't like it," Kyle grumbled.

"Neither do I," Kalibar agreed. "But I'm going to follow Orik's advice."

"What advice?" Kyle asked.

"He told me to run."

Chapter 9

The Behemoth stands near the ruins of the Great Tower, the city in flames around it. Dozens of airships zoom over the wreckage, laying waste to what remains of Stridon with barrage after barrage of bombs.

My god.

Ampir stares at the devastation, slowing his flight above the Great River. He looks down, seeing Vera turn her head to look at the carnage. She puts a hand to her mouth.

"Oh god," she cries. "Oh god!" Then she turns to Ampir. "Stop them," she orders. "You have to stop them!"

Ampir says nothing, scanning the remains of the city. The heart of the Empire has been crushed. There is no saving Stridon now.

"Stop them!" Vera yells, slamming a fist into his armored chest.

"It's over," Ampir retorts, his voice sharp and cold. Vera stares at him mutely, rage and disbelief in her eyes. He veers to the right, flying over the Great River, following its course now. "There's nothing left to save."

"You don't want to save the Empire," Vera retorts. "You *wanted* this to..."

"Shut up."

Vera stops, her mouth hanging open. Then she shuts it, turning away from him. Refusing to look at him. He feels the distance between them growing, and for a moment he doesn't care. Then he feels his son's arms tighten around him, hears the boy sobbing.

"I'm sorry Vera," Ampir says, more softly now. "I've lost everything. My friends, our home. Dad," he adds. He sees Vera swallow. "I can't lose you."

Vera closes her eyes, taking a deep breath in. Then she turns toward him, putting a hand on his chest and resting the side of her face against him.

"I'm sorry," she says, almost too quietly to hear.

"I love you," he replies, pulling her up and kissing her on the forehead. She hesitates, then lifts her chin, kissing him on the lips.

"I love you too."

Then she grimaces, pulling away. Her face looks pale, fine beads of sweat glistening on her forehead. Ampir feels fear grip him.

"We need to get you to a surgeon," he says, accelerating as he flies low over the river. With the Tower gone, the nearest trauma center is nearly two hours' flight away.

Vera says nothing, gritting her teeth against the pain. She shivers, clutching her arms close to her chest.

Shit.

Ampir glances back at the Behemoth, then turns to gaze down the river. With his vision augmented by his visor, he spots a cliffside far in the distance, a mile or so from the main bridge leading to the city. He feels a sudden burst of inspiration.

Renval!

He aims for the cliffside, flying faster, the wind screaming in his ears. Renval had been his mentor, long ago. They'd invented a device nearly two decades ago, something that could teleport objects vast distances. It had only been a prototype the last time Ampir had seen it, but Renval had spent decades working on it since. He'd sent Ampir letters about his progress a few years ago…that he'd teleported himself hundreds of miles.

"Where are we going?" Vera asks. "Spero?"

"Too far away," Ampir replies. "I'm going to use Renval's device."

"The teleporter?"

"Yep."

"But that's near the evacuation tunnels," Vera protests. "We don't know if the tunnels collapsed when the Tower fell."

Ampir grimaces, realizing that she's right. Renval had built the device in a large underground chamber a quarter-mile from the Tower above.

"Renval warded the chamber," he counters. The room was heavily fortified with magical defenses…and powered by backup magic generators. "We have to try."

"Okay," Vera replies. She gives him a weak smile. "I trust you."

Ampir smiles back. He spots something in his peripheral vision, a ship zooming toward them hundreds of feet above. Dark shapes fly out of the sides of the ship, arcing downward toward them.

What the...

He magnifies the image with a thought, his visor zooming in on the dark shapes. They're men in black uniforms, surrounded by translucent blue shields.

"Shit," Ampir swears.

"What?" Vera asks, alarmed.

"Weavers," he answers. "They've spotted us."

"Well kill them."

Ampir grits his teeth, flying ever-faster over the Great River. The Weavers follow, gaining on them slowly. He knows Vera is right...he *can* kill them, and easily at that. But if these Weavers identify him, the enemy will know where he is...and that he's still alive. Even if he kills the Weavers, more will come. The enemy won't stop until he's dead. And while they almost certainly won't be able to kill him, they *will* be able to slow him down.

He looks down at Vera, at the sweat pouring down her temples. At the rapid pulsing of the vessels in her neck. He feels his own pulse quicken, fear gripping his heart.

Time was of the essence...and hers was running out.

* * *

Kyle cried out, bolting upright in bed. He clutched his blanket to himself, his heart hammering in his chest.

Jesus!

He let go of his blanket, wiping the slick sweat from his forehead with one hand. He closed his eyes, then opened them, staring into the murky darkness of his room. Suddenly his bedroom door burst open, and the room was instantly flooded in bright light. Kyle cried out again, throwing up his hands to shield his eyes.

"Kyle!" he heard a voice shout. "Kyle, are you okay?"

It was Kalibar's voice, Kyle realized. He lowered his hands, squinting against the light. Indeed, it *was* Kalibar standing beside his bed, his eyes wide, a ball of white light floating above the old man's head.

"Are you alright?" Kalibar repeated, his voice tense.

"I'm fine, I'm fine," Kyle answered sheepishly. "I just had a nightmare," he added. Kalibar visibly deflated.

"Hell boy, I thought you were being attacked!" he exclaimed, sitting down on the edge of the bed. He ran a hand through his short white hair. "You scared the daylights out of me," he added.

"Sorry," Kyle mumbled. Kalibar's expression softened.

"Must've been a hell of a nightmare," he mused. He reached over, patting Kyle on the shoulder. "Come, tell me about it, and it will lose its power over you."

Kyle hesitated, staring at Kalibar. He'd never actually told anyone about his dreams...not in any detail. He'd told his mom and dad that he'd been having nightmares, and that was about it. But he remembered how Kalibar had listened – truly listened – to him when he'd recounted his harrowing adventure in the forest with the Ulfar. He remembered how good that had felt.

"Okay," Kyle said at last. And then he told Kalibar everything. Every nightmare, down to the last detail...except for the black-armored man's name. For whatever reason, he couldn't remember it. When he was done, he felt utterly drained...but also, somehow, better. Kalibar sat there for a long moment after Kyle was finished, staring off into space. Then, without warning, he stood, and started pacing back and forth before Kyle's bed.

"When did you start having these dreams?" he asked.

"Um, three weeks ago, maybe four now," Kyle replied.

"Fascinating," Kalibar murmured. He stopped pacing, staring at Kyle for a few uncomfortable moments. Then he sighed. "I want to hear more about your dreams later," he added. "I was hoping for a few more hours' sleep, but seeing as we're both up anyway, we should get going."

"Get going?" Kyle asked. "What do you mean?" Kalibar grimaced, running one hand through his short white hair. He had bags under his eyes from lack of sleep, and his beard was starting to grow in haphazardly.

"We need to leave," he answered. "Wash up and change into these clothes," he ordered, pointing to a neatly folded pile of clothes Jenkins had placed on his end-table. "Meet me in the living room in ten minutes."

With that, Kalibar left the room. Kyle got out of bed, closing his bedroom door and doing as Kalibar had ordered. Then he turned to the bed, thinking to make it, but then decided against it…no doubt Jenkins would see to it. He went to his small bathroom, walking up to the sink. There was a faucet just like on Earth, with knobs for hot and cold water. He splashed water on his face, then wet his hair, finding a comb in a drawer and combing his hair quickly. Then he ran out of the room and into the living room. Kalibar was already there, dressed in his usual black clothes, his goatee neatly trimmed.

"Come on," Kalibar prompted. "Darius is waiting outside of the Tower." He strode toward the front door of the suite, and Kyle followed behind, stepping into the hallway. Two armored guards stood on either side of the door, saluting Kalibar as he passed, then falling into step behind him. Kalibar led Kyle and his guards down the hallway to the riser, which dropped them with unnerving speed to the ground floor. The hallway and lobby beyond were nearly deserted given the early hour. Their footsteps echoed through the huge lobby as they made their way to the front double-doors. The guards opened the doors for Kalibar, and the former Grand Weaver led Kyle outside.

There, parked in front of the double-doors, was Kalibar's carriage. The side doors were already open, and Darius was perched atop the driver's seat. Rain poured from the sky, pattering on the cobblestones at their feet.

"That will be all, thank you," Kalibar told the two guards. They both saluted, then walked back into the Tower, the double-doors closing behind them. Kalibar gestured for Kyle to hop in the carriage, then walked around to the other side, getting in himself. Kyle got in, sitting down on the now-familiar seat cushions. Kalibar slid open the small window between them and Darius.

"Let's go," he ordered.

With a snap of the reins, the carriage jolted forward, turning down the wide road leading away from the Great Tower. The campus and road were lit by tall, elegantly tapered black street lamps with softly glowing white globes on top. The lamps cast the wide expanses of manicured lawns in a pale, ghostly light. They passed the dormitories, making their way after several minutes to the front gate of the Secula Magna. Darius stopped the carriage there, and an armored guard ran out to greet them. This time, however, they merely opened the gate, waving Darius through. The carriage moved forward, leaving the Secula Magna behind.

Kyle yawned, stretching his arms to the sides, then glanced at Kalibar. The former Grand Weaver was staring out of the rear window of the carriage silently. Kyle followed his gaze, seeing nothing but the gate receding into the distance. Lightning flashed in the sky, followed by the low rumble of thunder.

"What's wrong?" he asked.

"I'm checking to see if we're being followed," Kalibar replied. Kyle's eyes widened, and he turned to look out of the rear of the carriage again, peering into the darkness.

"Are we?" he pressed, feeling suddenly uneasy.

"Not that I can tell," Kalibar answered. "But we have to assume we will be."

"What?"

"Orik will want to make sure I'm leaving," Kalibar explained. "And he'll need to know where I'm going if he attempts to have me killed again."

"I don't see anyone following us," Kyle countered. Kalibar shrugged.

"I'm one of the most recognizable people in the Empire," he explained. "And the two guards outside my room, the guards at the gate, and anyone who sees us riding through the city will know that I'm leaving...and the direction we're going."

"Why didn't we just fly out of the Tower then?" Kyle asked. After all, if they'd flown out of one of the windows in Kalibar's suite, no one would have seen them leave.

"The only way out of the Secula Magna is through the front gate," Kalibar explained. "We'd never be able to get past the Gate shield."

"Oh, right."

"Don't worry," Kalibar said, patting Kyle's knee. "Erasmus let me borrow some Ancient wards from the Archives." He smiled reassuringly. "I can defeat anyone Orik sends to hurt us...and our wards will make sure we're safe when we sleep."

"Okay," Kyle mumbled, hardly feeling reassured. Kalibar chuckled.

"I won't let anyone hurt you," he insisted.

"I don't want anyone hurting *you*," Kyle countered. "I don't know what I'd do if something happened to you." The thought of being alone here without the old man to help him was terrifying.

"Oh, you'd still have Darius," Kalibar replied with a wicked grin.

Kyle rolled his eyes.

"Great," he muttered. He glanced through the small sliding window at the bodyguard's golden back, remembering how Darius had acted at the gate to the Secula Magna a few days ago. "Why do you put up with him, anyway?"

"That's a good question," Kalibar admitted. He sighed then. "I suppose it's out of respect for an old friend." He turned away from Kyle, staring out of the side window for a long moment...so long, in fact, that Kyle assumed he'd finished speaking. Then he cleared his throat. "When I was still a young man – not much older than you – I was studying to be a Weaver at the Secula Magna," he stated. "It is customary that a student be matched with a mentor at that age, and I had the great fortune of being matched with a man named Marcus."

The carriage made a rather sharp turn as it wove through the city streets, throwing Kyle against his side door. Kalibar didn't so much as budge.

"Marcus was the finest man I have ever met," Kalibar explained. "He taught me the importance of virtue, of self-reflection." He gave a rueful smile. "I've spent my entire life since trying to emulate him, I suppose."

"What does he have to do with Darius?" Kyle asked.

"Well," Kalibar answered, "...he hired Darius about a decade ago, I think. Darius must have made quite an impression. After the first attempt on my life a few weeks ago, I flew to Marcus's house – he lived a few miles away – to ask for advice."

"What'd he say?"

"He said to hire Darius," Kalibar replied.

"Oh," Kyle mumbled. Then he shook his head. "I don't get it."

"Neither did I," Kalibar admitted. "I *still* don't," he added. "But it hardly mattered...Darius refused to come with me...at least at first. Then, three days later, Darius arrived – unannounced – at my doorstep, as charming and talkative as he is now. When I sent a letter asking Marcus why Darius had changed his mind, he wrote two sentences. One was: 'Infinite patience will bring you infinite rewards.'"

Kalibar became silent then, staring off into the distance.

"What did the other sentence say?" Kyle asked.

"Hmm?" Kalibar replied, turning back to Kyle. "Oh. It said: Until we meet again, Kalibar.'" Kalibar turned to look out his window again. "But Marcus died that day."

"Sorry," Kyle mumbled.

"Oh, it's alright," Kalibar stated. "It wasn't totally unexpected," he added. "The man lived an unusually long life. Darius accompanied me to his funeral. It was…" he began, then swallowed with some difficulty. "It was very hard for me. He'd been more of a father to me than my own father." He shook his head. "I only wish I could have sat with him when he died."

Kalibar fell silent then, and Kyle glanced out of his own window, spotting the familiar stone walls of the huge building Kalibar had pointed out earlier – Stridon Penitentiary. Then he heard Kalibar clear his throat.

"Anyway, Darius has been with me ever since," the old man stated. "He refused to sign a contract, saying his word and mine were enough. And he hasn't said much else since," he added wryly.

"Fintan said Darius asked for a lot of money," Kyle said. "And that he was a coward," he added quietly, glancing at the sliding glass door between them and Darius. It was closed, of course.

"Actually, he asked for a minuscule salary," Kalibar corrected. "And as to the latter, well…it's human nature to magnify the faults of our enemies and the virtues of our friends." He yawned. "In any case, don't put too much trust in the beliefs of others. A belief isn't any truer just because it's felt strongly. In fact, the opposite is more often true."

"So he's not a coward?" Kyle asked.

"I've never seen him put to the test," Kalibar admitted. "But I trust my mentor. I suppose it's out of respect for Marcus that I ignore Darius's mannerisms." He smirked. "Besides, one of the first things I learned when I started ruling the Empire was that it's far better to hire a competent ass than a kind fool."

Kalibar fell silent then, and Kyle turned back to his window, watching the buildings pass by. The streets were still deserted, allowing their carriage to speed through the city unimpeded. Kyle twisted around to look out of the rear window, ignoring the twinge in his back as he did so. Again, there was only an empty street behind them. He turned forward, glancing at Kalibar.

"So we're going to Crescent Lake?" he asked. Kalibar nodded. "Where's that?"

"East of Stridon," Kalibar answered. "About one-and-a-half days from here by carriage. No road goes all the way there, not anymore."

"Why not?"

"It was deserted a long time ago," Kalibar replied. "The roads became overgrown by forest, and no one knows it even exists...not even Orik."

"How do *you* know about it?" Kyle pressed.

"I'm much better-read than Orik," Kalibar answered with a smirk. "The lake can still be found on antique maps, but not on current ones," he continued. "Only Erasmus and I know about it...and maybe a few old cartographers and historians."

"Why are we going there?" Kyle asked. "I thought you said we were going to be followed anyway."

"True," Kalibar replied. "No need to make it *too* easy for them. Besides, it's a beautiful, peaceful place...a perfect place to teach you how to use magic."

He twisted around in his seat then, reaching back into the trunk. After rummaging around for a bit, he retrieved a small book with red and brown binding, then sat back to read it. Kyle realized that the conversation was over...and right when it had started to get interesting.

I'm going to learn magic!

He stared out of the window, barely noticing the buildings passing by. It was the stuff of his wildest daydreams, to have extraordinary powers...to be able to fly, to wield fire with a single thought! He closed his eyes, imaging himself lifting a flowing stream into the air with his mind, just as Kalibar had earlier.

The carriage jolted suddenly, snapping Kyle out of his reverie. He realized that they'd reached the long, wide bridge that spanned the Great River. The carriage angled upward as they made their way across the beginning of its gentle arc, and Kyle glanced out of the rear window, spotting Stridon's skyline in the distance, barely visible in the darkness. But the Great Tower's pyramidal peak glowed brightly against the inky blackness. He had a sudden, powerful sense of déjà-vu. He pushed the feeling aside, turning back to Kalibar.

"Can I start learning magic now?" Kyle asked eagerly. Kalibar glanced up from his book.

"No," he answered. "When you first start learning, you need to have absolutely no distractions. We'll wait until we reach Crescent Lake."

Kyle nodded, doing his best not to look disappointed. He kicked himself for asking the question in the first place; if he seemed too eager to learn, Kalibar might end up not wanting to teach him magic at all. That was how older people were, for some reason Kyle didn't understand. Kalibar twisted around again, grabbed something else from the trunk of the carriage. It was a small white pillow.

"Here, try to get some rest," he urged, handing Kyle the pillow. Kyle placed it behind his head, laying back on it. He sighed, turning to look out of his window again. Huge fields of tall golden grass extended far into the distance, with tall, rocky hills rising upward beyond, blacking out the stars. Kyle yawned, suddenly exhausted. He'd only gotten a few hours of sleep, after all...no wonder that he was so tired. He closed his eyes, snuggling into the soft pillow. And with that, he fell asleep.

* * *

Kyle opened his eyes, squinting against the sunlight. He stretched his arms out wide, then glanced to his left, expecting to see Kalibar sitting there beside him in the carriage. But Kalibar's seat was empty. He frowned, realizing that the carriage had stopped. He sat forward, feeling a twinge in his neck. The pillow Kalibar had given him earlier was nowhere to be seen either. Kyle yawned, looking out of his window, and saw Kalibar and Darius standing outside at the side of the road, munching on some pieces of bread. Kyle opened the carriage door, easing himself to the ground. He walked up to the two men, rubbing his sore neck with one hand. Darius didn't bother to greet Kyle, mutely handing him a piece of bread and a warm cup of soup.

"Thanks," Kyle mumbled, biting into the bread. He immediately regretted it – the bread was as hard as a rock! He rubbed the side of his jaw gingerly, doing his best to ignore Darius's amused smirk, and glanced at Kalibar. The old man was dipping his bread into his soup before eating it. Kyle did the same, waiting a few moments before testing the bread. It was softer this time, although still chewy. He ripped off a piece with his teeth, chewing vigorously. Roast duck it most definitely was not! But he was terribly hungry, and ate the meager meal gratefully.

After he finished, Kyle felt an all-too familiar pressure in his bowels. He groaned, realizing it'd been a while since he'd gone to the bathroom. He cursed himself for not having gone back at the Tower; he'd never had to take a dump outside before, and the prospect was daunting. A few years ago, a kid from school accidently wiped himself with poison ivy during a camping trip; he'd been called "cheeks" ever since.

The pressure in Kyle's bottom grew more insistent, and he excused himself, walking toward the tall grass at the side of the road. He parted the blades with his hands, pushing through, until he was surrounded. Kalibar and Darius must have guessed what he was about to do, because they didn't even ask where he was going. He walked forward some more, then stopped, glancing backward to see if they were watching. They weren't, of course...Kyle couldn't see anything but the tall grass, which meant that they couldn't possibly see him. He yanked his pants down, squatting a foot above the ground. At first, he couldn't go, but after a while things loosened up. Within moments, the dirty deed was done. He ripped a few broad blades of grass off, making a face as he cleaned up...and hoping fervently that there was nothing like poison ivy here.

With that, he pulled his pants up, rejoining the others. Kalibar held out an empty metal pot, and Kyle watched in amazement as the pot filled itself with water, the liquid welling up from the bottom of the pot and filling it rapidly. Kalibar handed the pot over to Kyle, who brought the pot to his lips, drinking greedily. When he was done, Darius and Kalibar were staring at him with odd expressions on their faces. Kyle frowned.

"What?" he asked. Darius glanced down at the pot, then back up at Kyle.

"That's poop bucket," Darius replied, biting into another piece of bread. "I used it this morning," he added. He glanced down at the pot again, a smirk on his face. "A lot."

Kyle glanced down at the pot. Then he gagged, turning away quickly and sprinting back into the tall grass. He barely had time to stop before he puked, hunks of bread gushing out of his mouth and onto the dirt. He vomited again, then again, until there was nothing left in his belly. He stood there, hearing muffled laughter in the background, his cheeks burning furiously. Then he imagined the pot's former contents, and dry heaved, his stomach cramping painfully, tears stinging his eyes.

That son-of-a…!

He stood there, hunched over, waiting for his belly to calm down. Eventually it did, and he turned about, trudging back through the grass until he rejoined Kalibar and Darius by the side of the road. He refused to make eye contact with either one of them, crossing his arms over his chest. Kalibar tried handing the pot to Kyle again, but Kyle refused to take it.

"Darius was just kidding," Kalibar stated, holding back a chuckle with the greatest of effort. "I gave it to you to wash your hands," he explained. Kyle blinked, then looked down at the pot. It filled up with water again, and Kalibar held it out to Kyle. This time, Kyle took it, his cheeks burning, and squatted on the ground, dipping his hands in the pot and scrubbing vigorously. In short order, his hands were clean – or as clean as they could be without soap. He dumped the water on the ground, then brought the pot back to Kalibar, pointedly ignoring Darius.

"Let's go," Kalibar ordered, gathering up the cups into the pot. "We'll be leaving the main road shortly. There's a smaller path that goes about a day's ride to Crescent Forest. After that, we'll have to travel on foot through the forest to get to the lake."

Kyle complied, hopping back into the carriage. Kalibar joined him, and Darius resumed his post at the driver's seat. With a snap of the reigns, they were off. Kalibar immediately got back to reading his book, and Kyle turned to stare out of his window. Fields of tall grass gave way to dense forest beyond, the terrain rising to steep hills miles away. He sighed, his mind wandering. He pictured his dad stepping out of the tall grass, waving to the carriage as it passed by. Imagined the carriage stopping, imagined himself opening the door and running out. His dad hugging him close, telling him that everything was going to be okay.

That he could go home now.

Kyle shook the image away, taking a deep breath in, then letting it out. He felt a horrible sinking feeling, knowing that he would very likely *never* go home. That he would never see his dad or his mom again.

I'm going to be stuck here forever, he realized.

Suddenly the carriage veered to the left, and the carriage began to bounce up and down. Darius had steered them off of the main road and down a narrow dirt path. A thin strip of tall grass grew on either side of the path, with trees beyond. Kyle braced himself at first, then relaxed slowly into his seat cushions, leaning his head back. The jostling was mildly annoying, but tolerable. He stared idly out of the window, watching the scenery go by. His eyelids became heavy, and he closed them, imagining what it would be like to go home. He fell in and out of consciousness, jolted awake from time to time by the carriage hitting a particularly deep pothole. The sun swept slowly across the sky, until dark, gloomy clouds rolled in to hide it from view. A light drizzle fell, quickly intensifying into an all-out downpour. Rain pattered loudly on the carriage roof, a flash of lightning arcing jaggedly through the sky. The deep sound of thunder rattled the carriage, setting Kyle's hair on end. The wind howled around them, sending the rain flying at the carriage almost horizontally. Darius, he noted with guilty satisfaction, was getting utterly soaked.

Another thunderclap rattled the carriage, and this time Kalibar jerked his gaze up from his book, noticing the rain for the first time. He closed his eyes for a moment, and suddenly the patter of rain on the carriage stopped. Kyle glanced out of the window, spotting a shimmering blue half-sphere hovering above the carriage like an ethereal umbrella. It moved with the carriage, rain pouring down its sides.

"How did you do that?" Kyle asked. Kalibar glanced up at him, having already gone back to his book.

"You'll learn soon enough," the old man replied, returning immediately to his book. Kyle turned away, taking the hint...Kalibar didn't want to be disturbed. He tried resting his head against the side window, but the road was far too bumpy. He sighed, resting his head back against the rear cushion, wishing that seatbelts had already been invented here. He imagined himself creating one, then selling it to everyone. There was no one to stop him from doing so, after all...and if he did, he would probably become rich. He could buy a mansion just like Kalibar's, and even have a butler to attend to all his needs, like Jenkins.

More time passed, and the sky continued to darken, until it was so dark that Kalibar had to conjure up a small ball of light that floated above his head just to keep reading. The light cast stark shadows throughout the carriage, bathing the surrounding forest in a pale glow. Kalibar closed his book, the light above his head winking out. He leaned forward, sliding the small front window open.

"Let's make camp," he shouted over the din of the storm. Darius waited a while, then steered the carriage off the path and into a large clearing in the forest, avoiding the occasional tree. The carriage bounced violently as they went off-road, rattling Kyle's bones and vividly reminding him of his injured back. Eventually Darius pulled on the reigns, and the horses came to a halt. Darius immediately dismounted, and Kalibar opened the door on his side, stepping outside. Kyle paused, then did the same, his boots sinking into the muddy ground. He grimaced, taking a step forward, the muck sucking stubbornly at his feet. While Darius tied the horses to a nearby tree, Kalibar used his staff to create a large shimmering hemisphere over the clearing, deflecting the rain. Then he walked – or rather, levitated a few inches above the mud – to the rear of the carriage, opening the trunk. He pulled out a large, pale yellow stick with a few closed buds jutting out of its sides – the same stick he'd used before, on their way to Stridon. Kalibar handed the stick to Darius, who went to the edge of the sphere, and scooped a hole in the mud with his hands. The hole filled up almost instantaneously with water. Darius ignored this, and passed the stick over the hole. The water jumped up to the stick like nails to a magnet, surrounding it. Then Darius jammed the stick into the hole, packing mud onto the base of the stick. Almost immediately, the parts of the stick where the bark had worn off started to glow a soft green color.

"What is that?" Kyle asked.

"A branch from a mummy tree," Kalibar answered. Kyle stared at the branch, watching as the green glow pulsated in the darkness.

"What does it do?"

"It attracts water to itself," Kalibar replied. "It pulls it out of the ground, and even out of the air around it, ensuring a constant supply for itself."

"So why is it called a 'mummy' tree?" Kyle pressed.

"Well, some cultures take their dead and rest them near a tree," Kalibar explained. "The tree extracts all of the water from the bodies."

"Turning them into mummies," Kyle reasoned. "Got it." He eyed the glowing branch warily, taking a few steps back from it. Kalibar chuckled.

"Don't worry," he reassured. "We'll sleep far enough away from it. We'll all be a little thirsty tomorrow though."

"What's it for?" Kyle asked. After all, if they were going to use the levitating sleeping bags again, there was no point in drying out the ground.

"I may be able to levitate back to the carriage tomorrow," Kalibar replied. "But you and Darius can't." He smirked. "I don't need mud in my carriage."

"Oh."

Darius distributed their levitating sleeping bags, and Kyle towed his as close to the edge of the magical shield as he could...and as far away from the mummy tree branch at the opposite end of the dome. There was a definite breeze here, sucking inward toward the shield's translucent blue surface. Kyle stared at it, then reached up with one hand, touching the shield.

"Wait! Don't..." Kalibar cried.

Kyle's fingertips touched the shield's curved surface, and suddenly his hand was yanked forward. The rest of his body followed, sucked into the powerful shield. He flew right through it, hurtling forward through the air. He barely had time to cry out before he slammed belly-first into the mud, the air bursting from his lungs. He pushed himself upward onto his knees, grimacing in disgust. The entire front of his body was covered in mud, cold rain drenching his hair and clothes.

Kalibar took one look at him, and burst out into laughter.

Kyle lowered his gaze, staring helplessly at his soiled clothes, flicking mud off of his hands. His cheeks burned something fierce, which only made Kalibar laugh even more. Even Darius was smirking. Kyle sighed, ignoring the two and slogging back to the edge of the shield, his clothes heavy with muck. He stopped before the shield, then hesitated. He lifted his hand up to it, brushing the surface with his fingers. His hand was thrown backward instantly, spinning him around and tossing him back into the mud.

For the love of...!

Kalibar was laughing so hard he was wheezing now, and broke into a fit of coughing. Kyle staggered to his feet again, cursing under his breath. Kalibar tried desperately to compose himself, staring at Kyle with a grave expression. Then his lips started to quiver, and he burst into laughter again.

"Ha, ha, ha," Kyle grumbled, putting his hands on his hips. Rain coursed down his body, slowly rinsing off the mud on his clothes. Kalibar tried to compose himself again, and succeeded this time.

He lifted his staff from where it was embedded in the ground, and the shield lifted from the ground with it. Kyle ducked underneath it, and Kalibar returned the staff back to where it had been.

"Here," Kalibar offered, gesturing at the mummy tree branch. "Stand near it for a bit so you can dry off. Then Darius can get you a new set of clothes."

Kyle complied, trudging up to the mummy tree branch. To his surprise, the ground around it was completely dry and hardened. He peeled off his boots, his shirt, and his pants, standing there in his underwear feeling ridiculous...and terribly exposed.

"Sorry about that," Kalibar apologized, walking up to Kyle and putting a hand on his bare back. "This shield pulls air outward, pushing the rain away," he explained. "Air comes back in through the few inches between the ground and the shield," he added. "If you touch it, it'll...well, you know."

"Thanks," Kyle muttered, hugging himself. The air was chilly, his skin covered in goosebumps. Kalibar concentrated, and suddenly the air was much warmer.

"Consider this your first lesson in magic," Kalibar stated with a grin, patting Kyle on the back. "Every application has consequences...and sometimes the best way to learn of them is to experience them." The old man turned away from Kyle then, grabbed a folded pile of clothes from Darius and handing them to Kyle. Kyle took them, dressing quickly.

"Let's go to bed," Kalibar stated. He sat down on his levitating sleeping bag, then laid down on it. Darius did the same, and Kyle put on his boots, trudging back to his sleeping bag. He towed it a few feet from the shield's edge, then laid down, snuggling in the warm softness. It wasn't long before the sting of his shame gave way to the comfort of his sleeping bag. Sleep beckoned for him, pulling him downward into its otherworldly embrace. He gave in readily, and within moments fell fast asleep.

Chapter 10

Ampir races above the Great River, the wind screaming in his ears. The black-cloaked Weavers fly after him, closing the distance between them steadily. There is only so fast Ampir can fly with Vera and Junior; alone, the Weavers would never have been able to catch him.

Ampir sees the Weavers in the rear-view section of his visor, in the periphery of his vision. A burst of red light shoots from one of the Weavers toward him. Ampir veers to the left and downward, mere feet from the surface of the river, and the missile soars past him. Ampir spins around in mid-air, facing the fast-approaching Weavers. He *pulls* magic into his mind's eye, seeing threads of power appear at the edges of his vision. He wills the threads into a tight knot, then throws it outward. A ball of blue light shoots outward toward the Weavers, growing rapidly. The Weavers are sucked into the sphere, as is water from the river, forming a ball of water just above the river's surface. Without warning, the water flash-freezes, trapping the Weavers in ice…and instantly killing them.

Ampir spots two more airships converging above him, Weavers leaping out from the sides of the ships and zooming down toward him.

Damn.

He could take them down, but more would come. There was a chance – admittedly small – that the enemy didn't know who they were dealing with. The more attention he drew to himself, the more likely they would find out…and send an army to stop him.

They won't be able to stop me, he knows. *But they can slow me down.*

He turns forward, facing the cliffside in the distance, still miles away. The exit for the evacuation tunnels is there...and will lead him under the Great River, to the center of the city...and Renval's teleporter.

"Ampir," he hears Vera shout, feels her hand on his chest. He glances down at her, then follows her gaze to the center of the city. The Behemoth stands there, its legs hidden in the massive cloud of dust and smoke left by the fallen Tower. As Ampir watches, the Behemoth's head rotates, its diamond-shaped eye turning toward him.

"Well shit," Ampir swears.

The Behemoth faces him, tracking him as he hurtles over the river.

Then its eye flashes.

* * *

Kyle opened his eyes, the pale blue sky greeting him. He rubbed his eyes, which were crusted over and itchy, then yawned and rolled onto his side in his sleeping bag. His mouth was terribly dry; he licked his dry, cracked lips, then looked about, spotting Darius and Kalibar still sleeping in their levitating sleeping bags. It took him a moment to remember where he was...and why he was so thirsty.

The mummy tree, he thought, turning to look at the branch. It was still glowing a faint green, the ground around it...indeed, the ground around the entire camp...completely dry. Kyle slipped his legs out of his sleeping bag, dangling them over the edge.

"Good morning," he heard Kalibar greet. He turned to Kalibar, who was sitting upright in his own sleeping bag. The former Grand Weaver yawned, stretching just like Kyle had moments ago. He glanced up at the sky, then lowered his gaze to Kyle. "You're up early," he observed.

"I had another nightmare," Kyle admitted.

"I see," Kalibar replied. "Tell me about it."

Kyle did so, recounting the dream. Kalibar listened silently but intently, in that comforting way he had, until Kyle was finished. Then he ran a hand through his short white hair, staring off into space for a while.

"What are you thinking?" Kyle asked.

"The woman," Kalibar prompted. "Describe her."

Kyle blushed, remembering the way the woman's thin white

gown had clung to her body. Kalibar arched an eyebrow. "Is something wrong?"

"Uh, no," Kyle mumbled. "She, uh…"

"Yes?"

"She was, um, pretty," he stated, his cheeks turning red-hot. As hot as Desiree had been back home, she couldn't hold a candle to the woman in his dreams.

"I see," he replied. "Well then, describe the man…the woman's husband."

"Well, it's more like it's *me*," Kyle admitted. "Or I mean, I'm him in the dreams." He shook his head. "I did something weird this time," he added. "I mean, *he* did."

"Explain."

"Well, I sort of looked inside my own head," Kyle replied, recalling that strange sensation of manipulating threads of power in his mind's eye. "Then I…I don't know, I pulled this like, thread or something with my mind." He described how he'd twisted it into a tight knot, then thrown it outward. When he'd finished, he realized that Kalibar was staring at him, his mouth agape. "What?" Kyle asked.

"Incredible," Kalibar breathed. "I don't believe it!" Kyle spotted Darius shifting in his sleeping bag, turning about to glare at Kyle and Kalibar with his piercing blue eyes. Then he rolled away from them, pulling the sleeping bag over his head.

"What?" Kyle repeated.

"Well, that sensation – pulling energy into your mind and twisting it – is exactly what Weavers do to use magic," Kalibar explained.

"Oh," Kyle replied. "Really?"

"Really," Kalibar confirmed. He stood up, slipping into his boots. He began to pace then, tapping his chin with one finger as he did so. "I was too distracted back in the Tower," he mumbled.

"What do you mean?" Kyle asked.

"When you first told me about your dreams," Kalibar replied. "I was so distracted by the need to escape that I forgot all about them." He shook his head. "It's clear that they're much more than simple dreams."

"Tell me about it," Kyle grumbled.

"In fact," Kalibar continued, pacing back and forth, "…I don't think they're dreams at all."

"Huh?"

"Hear me out," Kalibar urged, continuing to pace. "Remember the Ancients...how Stridon fell during the Great War?" Kyle nodded. "Well, your dreams...the Tower being attacked by the...what was it?"

"The Behemoth."

"Right," Kalibar said. "The Tower being destroyed...it's all consistent with what we know happened to the Ancients two thousand years ago."

"Wait," Kyle interjected. "You're saying that my dreams really happened?"

"I'm saying they're not dreams at all," Kalibar countered. "They're *memories*."

Kyle just stared at the man blankly.

"It's the only explanation," Kalibar concluded. "You began dreaming of the Ancients and the Great War before you even came here," he added. Then he stopped pacing, turning to Kyle. "When exactly *did* you start having these dreams?"

"A few weeks ago."

"How many weeks exactly?" Kalibar pressed. Kyle frowned, mulling it over. He knew that he'd been having them for at least two or three weeks...

"My birthday," Kyle exclaimed. "Three weeks ago...it was on my birthday!"

"Good," Kalibar replied. "And what happened that day? What did you do?"

"I went to school, and then I came home," he answered. "I had dinner, then cake. Then I opened my presents, and watched a movie, then went to bed." Kyle paused, trying to think if there had been anything else that had happened that day, but couldn't think of anything. "And then I had the nightmare."

"Hmm," Kalibar murmured. "What presents did you get?"

"Some money," Kyle replied. "And..." He glanced down at his left thumb, flexing it. Suddenly it all made sense. "My ring!"

"Pardon me?"

"My *ring*," Kyle repeated. "It was my dad's...he gave it to me for my birthday." Kalibar's eyes widened, and he snapped his fingers.

"Of course!" he exclaimed. "The ring!"

Darius rolled over in his sleeping bag, glaring at the two of them. Kalibar didn't even notice.

"I don't know why I didn't think of it earlier," Kalibar continued excitedly. "Your ring is clearly too advanced to have been made recently…it must have been made by the Ancients." He tapped his chin. "What if whoever made it stored his memories inside of it?"

"You mean the man from my dreams?"

"Exactly," Kalibar replied. He stopped pacing. "What was the man's name again?"

"Um…" Kyle began, frowning. He remembered every detail of his dreams, but for some reason, he couldn't remember the man's name. "I can't remember."

Kalibar's shoulders slumped a bit, but he waved the question away.

"Don't worry about it," the former Grand Weaver stated. "Memories are like women; the harder you try to hold on to them, the farther you push them away. When you ignore them, they come for you with a vengeance."

"Huh?"

"Never mind," Kalibar replied. "You say the man wore a suit of armor?"

"Yeah," Kyle confirmed. He described the armor to Kalibar, with its blue runes and magical visor. Kalibar's eyebrows rose.

"That's Battle-Runic armor," he exclaimed, clearly surprised. Kyle stared at him blankly. "Battle-Runics were Runics who created their own weapons and suits of armor, and fought alongside Weavers in the military during Ancient times," Kalibar explained. "There were only a handful that existed during the Great War, three that we know of." He shook his head. "There haven't been any since…not really."

Kyle heard a *thunk*, and saw Darius lowering himself to the ground from his levitating sleeping bag. The bodyguard had apparently slept in his armor. Darius turned to Kalibar.

"We're burning daylight," he grumbled. "You want to go on foot from here or take the carriage to the end of the path?"

"Hmm?" Kalibar replied, turning to the bodyguard. "Ah yes. We'll go on foot from here. If someone is following our route, they'll expect us to leave the carriage at the end of the path." He walked up to his staff, grabbing it. The magical domed shield around them vanished instantly. "I'll fly the carriage overhead."

Darius nodded brusquely, then collected the sleeping bags and the mummy tree branch, placing these back in the trunk of the carriage. Then he unhitched the horses from the carriage, and loaded each with a few packs from the trunk. He grabbed a pair of reins in each hand, leading them to the edge of the forest. Kalibar walked up to the side of the carriage, his eyebrows furrowing. A translucent blue sphere appeared around the entire carriage, and suddenly it lifted off of the ground, rising into the air. Up it went, ten feet high, then twenty, then thirty, until it was floating well above the treetops. Kalibar turned to Darius and Kyle at the edge of the clearing, striding forward to meet them. The carriage followed Kalibar overhead.

"Let's go," Kalibar stated, passing Darius and Kyle and walking into the forest. Darius fell into stride alongside his boss, while Kyle trailed a few yards behind. The forest was similar to the one Kyle had woken up in only a few days ago, but with Kalibar and Darius there, it seemed far less sinister. He spotted a tree with a few rip-vines hanging off of its branches, but Kalibar steered them around it, clearly aware of the forest's dangers.

They trekked through the forest for what seemed like hours, going up and down gentle hills, dodging the occasional boulder and fallen tree trunk. Kyle's calves and knees started to ache from the hiking, and after a while he found himself desperately hoping for a break. But Kalibar and Darius were clearly in much better shape than he was, and didn't seem to mind their exertions one bit. Kyle found it striking that a man Kalibar's age could be so fit. He'd always thought of older people as being frail.

Eventually Kalibar did stop, retrieving a few cups from the pack on one of the horses and filling it with water conjured from thin air. He handed one of the cups to Kyle, and Kyle drank greedily, the ice-cold water feeling absolutely marvelous. He finished it in one go, and asked for seconds. Kalibar obliged, and Kyle drank until his thirst was quenched. But the break was short-lived, and Kalibar set off again, forcing Kyle to follow from behind. As they walked, the sun rose higher over the treetops in the east, until it hung directly overhead, casting blurred shadows of rustling leaves on the forest floor below. Kyle's stomach began to grumble so loudly that even Kalibar could hear it, and to Kyle's immense relief, Kalibar decided at last to stop for lunch.

Darius tied both horses to a nearby tree, then retrieved a few pieces of dried meat and bread from one of the horse's packs, handing them out. Kalibar filled a few bowls with powdered soup base and conjured water, and had them magically boiling hot within seconds. Kyle took his bowl, dipping the bread and meat into the soup, then chewing vigorously. He walked up to a tree so that he could sit down with his back against it, and noticed a familiar red caterpillar-like bug climbing up its trunk. It was exactly like the one he'd seen on his first night in this strange world…the one that had flashed red, then split in half. He eyed it curiously, then turned to Kalibar.

"Hey Kalibar," he called out. The former Grand Weaver turned to him. "What kind of bug is this?" Kalibar walked up to Kyle, peering at the insect. Then he lurched backward, crying out. The caterpillar immediately burst into flames, falling off of the tree and onto the forest floor. A tiny wisp of smoke rose from its blackened corpse.

"Jesus!" Kyle exclaimed, backing away from the insect. "What happened?"

"That," Kalibar answered, pointing at the smoldering corpse, "…was a killerpillar!"

"A what?"

"A killerpillar," Kalibar repeated. "If it's threatened, it flashes bright red." He shook his head, running a hand through his hair. "And once it does, you're dead."

"No," Kyle countered. "I saw one in the forest before the Ulfar attacked me, and it flashed red, then split in two."

"Are you sure it was the same bug?" Kalibar asked. Kyle nodded.

"It was."

Kalibar stared at the killerpillar's tiny smoking body, then glanced at Kyle. He tapped his chin with one finger.

"Interesting," he murmured. "First the rip-vine died, then the killerpillar. Then the Ulfar, we assume." His eyebrows knitted together. "Something must have been protecting you."

"Like what?"

"Perhaps it was your ring," Kalibar proposed. He went silent then, brooding over the killerpillar. Then he turned away from the tree, taking a bite of his soup-soaked bread. "Finish your food," he ordered. "We need to get going."

Kyle did just that, eating the rest of his meager meal in silence. He finished, handing his bowl back to Darius. The bodyguard untied the horses, then followed Kalibar deeper into the forest,

Kyle trailing behind. They made their way forward, small twigs and dead leaves crunching underfoot in a steady marching rhythm. After what seemed like an hour, Kyle thought he heard the sound of rushing water in the distance. Indeed, the sound grew louder as they progressed, and the air became cooler and a little damp. It felt quite refreshing on his sun-baked skin.

Ahead, the forest ended abruptly, opening up to reveal a lake whose sandy shore lay no more than a hundred feet beyond the tree line. The lake was shaped like a large crescent, the sun shining brilliantly off of its rippling blue water. At the far end of the lake stood a sheer cliff at least fifty feet high, a large waterfall flowing down to the lake below. The waterfall sparkled in the sunlight, its continuous roar drowning out the sound of Kyle's footsteps. He passed the tree line, stepping out into the bright sunlight, then stopped.

"Is this...?" he began. Kalibar turned to him, nodding once.

"It is," he answered. "We've made it...welcome to Crescent Lake!"

* * *

Kyle stretched his legs out before him, sitting on the warm sand of the shore with his bare feet dipping into the warm water at the lake's edge. He glanced back at Kalibar, who had lowered the carriage onto the grass near the lake's shore. The former Grand Weaver was already bringing out the magical wards Erasmus had let him borrow to defend their camp. They looked like short metal stakes, runes inscribed on their shiny surfaces. Darius, on the other hand, had tied the two horses to a tree, and was busy feeding them. Kyle turned back to face the huge waterfall across the lake. He wiggled his toes in the water, feeling quite content. After days of travel, and all the tension and intrigue of the Tower, it was nice to settle down and enjoy the scenery. For Crescent Lake was a small paradise, wild and colorful and free. It was wholly different than the strict order of Kalibar's mansion and the Great Tower. Kyle smiled, gazing up at the tall cliffside before him, listening to the dull roar of the waterfall crashing into the lake below. What a perfect place to learn magic, he though...in a place that had a natural sort of magic of its own.

Magic!

Kyle's heart skipped a beat, and he leapt to his feet, sprinting up to Kalibar, who was still extracting various items from the trunk of the carriage. The old man saw him coming, and straightened up, regarding Kyle quizzically.

"Yes?" he asked.

"Hey," Kyle replied, stopping before him. "I was wondering, you know, now that we're here..." He trailed off, and Kalibar smirked.

"You'd like to start learning magic?" he asked. Kyle nodded. "Soon enough," Kalibar promised. He sat at the edge of the open trunk, gesturing for Kyle to do the same. Kyle sat next to the man, using all of his will to hide his eagerness. "I wanted to talk to you about something first."

"What?"

"We never got a chance to finish talking about your last dream," Kalibar explained. "You said that the man in your dreams wore Battle-Runic armor."

"Right."

"Well, there were only a few Battle-Runics that we know of during Ancient times," Kalibar stated, rubbing his chin. "There was Kovus, who died before the Great War. Then there was Pranon, and of course Ampir." Kyle's eyes widened.

"Ampir!"

"Hmm?" Kalibar asked.

"The man from my dreams," Kyle explained. "It was Ampir!" Kalibar stared at Kyle, his jaw hanging open. He shut it quickly.

"You're sure?" he pressed. Kyle nodded.

Kalibar stared at him for a moment longer, then turned to the waterfall in the distance. He nodded to himself.

"It all makes sense," he said. "Ampir was incredibly skilled...if anyone could have figured out a way to store memories in your ring, it would've been him."

"So you think Ampir made my ring?" Kyle asked. Kalibar nodded again.

"It would explain how you managed to survive the rip-vines and the Ulfar," Kalibar reasoned. "And the killerpillar. As a Battle-Runic, Ampir would've added protective runes to just about anything he made."

"But I don't get it," Kyle protested. "How did I get his ring?"

"I have no idea," Kalibar admitted. "But everything you described in your dreams makes sense now. Ampir was the youngest man to ever be elected to the Council in Ancient times...and according to your dreams, he was in Stridon when the Behemoth struck."

"Oh."

"Ampir allowed millions of innocent people to die, just to save his wife," Kalibar muttered, shaking his head.

"I don't know," Kyle countered. "It happened so fast...by the time Ampir got into his armor, the city was already destroyed. I don't think he could have stopped it."

"Really," Kalibar replied, clearly unconvinced.

Kyle shook his head, amazed by the thought that his dreams had actually *happened*...that Ampir had truly lived once. Kyle had always thought of the past as boring, on account of the tedious and senseless memorization of names and dates that passed for history class at school. His dreams proved that utterly wrong...history was vibrant, alive with real people and real feelings...terror, love, hope, and heart-wrenching loss. How many other stories were lost to history, having never been recorded? Would *his* whole life be forgotten when he died? In a hundred years, would anyone remember that he even existed?

"What happened to him?" Kyle asked. "To Ampir?"

"Nobody knows for sure," Kalibar answered. "In any case, we still don't know how Ampir's ring got to Urth...and how, or why, you got here. And we're not going to figure it out today." He gestured for Kyle to stand up from the back of the carriage. "Take off all of your clothes except your underwear," he ordered.

Kyle froze, unsure of how to react to this rather disturbing request.

"Go on," Kalibar prompted. "Get to it. It's about time I started teaching you some magic!"

* * *

Kyle stood in the shallow end of the lake, just opposite the waterfall, his arms folded modestly across his chest. He'd removed all of his clothes save for his underwear – which on this world were luckily just like shorts – as requested. The water was surprisingly warm, like bath water, and so clear that Kyle could easily see all the way to the bottom, even at the deeper parts of the lake. The bottom was mostly light brown sand and small, rounded pebbles that hurt his feet a little when he'd walked over them.

"Go further in," Kalibar was saying. He was standing at the shoreline, his black boots inches from the water. "Deep enough that you can float on your back." Kyle obeyed, grimacing as a pebble jabbed into the sole of his foot. He paused as the water went up to his mid-thighs, dreading what was to come. He grimaced as his groin dipped into the water, but luckily the lake was warm enough that it wasn't too uncomfortable. He continued onward until he was up to his belly-button in water.

"Stop," Kalibar ordered. "Turn around." Kyle obeyed, facing Kalibar. "Now, I will use this staff…" Kalibar pointed to the tall, metallic staff in his left hand, "…to send a large amount of magic near you."

"Okay," Kyle replied. Then he frowned. "So what do I do?"

"To use magic," Kalibar answered, "you have to first know what magic *feels* like." He gestured at Kyle. "You make a great deal of magic, so you're used to having your mind filled with it. Water wicks magic away from your body, depleting you. It's far easier to feel magic when you're relatively low on it…just like it's easier to hear someone whisper when a room is quiet than when it's loud."

"Ohhh," Kyle replied. "Got it."

"The part of your mind that senses and uses magic is asleep, if you will," Kalibar continued. "Learning to feel the magic inside of you is called your 'Awakening.'" He tapped the butt of his staff on the sandy shore. "Now, you're going to lay on your back and float in the water with your ears submerged." Kyle started to do this, and Kalibar held up his hand. "Not yet," he corrected. "When you're submerged, try to clear your mind of all distractions. Concentrate only on what you are feeling."

"What will it feel like?" Kyle asked.

"You'll know when you feel it," Kalibar answered. He motioned for Kyle to lay back, and Kyle did so, easing into a Dead Man's float. The water tickled his ears as his head dipped into the water, then lapped at his temples. It certainly felt refreshing after his sweaty, sticky trek through the woods. He concentrated on his breathing, holding his breath for a while, then letting it out, and then quickly taking another deep breath in to remain floating. Then he remembered that he was supposed to be concentrating on what he was feeling. He did so, focusing on the warmth of the sun on his face and chest, and the muted sound of the water in his ears. After a minute, his mind started to wander, and he found himself thinking of his dreams. He shook the thoughts from his mind, trying to focus on what he was feeling. But it was no use...his mind kept wandering. He began to wonder if Kalibar was getting annoyed with him. What if he *couldn't* feel magic? What if he failed? Then Kalibar would have brought him here for nothing. Darius would have a field day making fun of him, no doubt.

Kyle sighed, then kicked himself out of the Dead Man's float, standing up.

"Did you feel anything?" Kalibar asked. Kyle shook his head.

"No," he admitted. "I can't stop thinking," he added morosely. "Sorry."

"Don't be sorry," Kalibar replied good-naturedly. "If this were easy, everyone would be doing it. Don't mind me, just relax. Sometimes it takes days – or even weeks – to have your Awakening."

Kyle nodded, feeling relieved. He laid back down in the water, closing his eyes. This time, he tried to relax, as Kalibar had instructed. It wasn't hard to do; the sun felt warm on his skin, a pleasant contrast to the relative coolness of the water. It reminded him of last summer, when he'd gone to the beach with his dad. Of buying ice cream on a cone, then trying – and failing – to eat it before the ice cream melted and dribbled down over his hand. Of running into the ocean next to his dad, both yelling as the ice-cold water lapped at their legs. He smiled, remembering the delicious lobster dinner they'd had afterward. The night in the hotel overlooking the ocean, the stars twinkling in the sky. He imagined that sky, pictured one of the stars exploding into a shower of rainbow-colored candy. One of the candies sprouted legs and galloped away. He threw a lasso out at the candy-beast, but missed it. The thing grew wings and flapped them, flying away. And then...

...and then he felt water rushing into his mouth and down his throat!

Kyle burst up from the water, spewing water out of his mouth. He took a deep gulp of air, then coughed violently, his lungs and throat burning. He heard laughter, and looked up, spotting Kalibar at the shoreline laughing at him. Kyle lowered his gaze, his cheeks flushing. Kalibar's laughter died down...eventually.

"When I told you to relax," the former Grand Weaver called out at last, "I didn't mean fall asleep!" He chuckled, shaking his head. Then he gestured at Kyle. "Lay back again," he ordered.

Kyle obeyed, laying back in the water again. He closed his eyes, spreading his arms out wide, feeling the water resist the movement. He took a deep breath in, feeling himself rising a little in the water as he did so, then let it out a bit, sinking back downward. He fell into a steady rhythm of breathing.

In, two three four...out, two three four...

His mind started to wander, but this time he resisted the urge to fall asleep. Thoughts came to him, but he didn't pay them any mind, and they slipped away quickly. He let them come and go, enjoying the warm sun beating on his exposed skin and the water lapping at his ears. He heard...or rather, *felt*...a slight humming to his right, as if there was a motorboat idling in the water far away. He opened his eyes and turned his head, but only saw the rippling surface of the lake against the bright blue sky. He closed his eyes again, resting his head back into the water.

In, two three four...

He felt the humming vibration again, this time to his left. He paused, then raised his head, turning toward it. But again, there was nothing there.

Weird, he thought.

"Kyle!" he heard Kalibar shout. He frowned, swinging forward out of the Dead Man's float. Kalibar was standing by the shore as before, but this time he was grinning.

"What?" Kyle shouted back.

"You felt it, didn't you?"

"Felt what?" Kyle asked.

"What you were turning your head toward," Kalibar clarified. "*That*, my boy, was magic!"

"It was?" Kyle gasped. He felt his heart leap in his chest, a giddy thrill invigorating him. "*That* was magic?"

"That's right," Kalibar confirmed. "That's how it feels. I sent a stream of magic to your right, and then to your left, and you turned toward it each time."

"Awesome!" Kyle exclaimed. He could hardly believe it...he'd actually felt magic!

"I agree," Kalibar said. He shook his head. "I've never seen a student sensitize to magic so quickly...well done, Kyle."

Kyle felt a flush of pride, and couldn't help but grin. Kalibar smiled back.

"Try it again," Kalibar instructed. "I'll send magic to you, and you do as you did before. Turn your head to wherever you feel it."

Kyle complied, sinking down into the water and kicking his legs up again to float on the surface. He closed his eyes, waiting for the humming sensation to come again. And come it did; within seconds, he sensed it to his left. He turned his head, keeping his eyes closed. The vibration ended as soon as it had begun, then reappeared to his right. He turned his head dutifully, causing the sensation to disappear once more. Then he felt it behind him, and he tilted his head backward.

"Excellent," he heard Kalibar exclaim. Kyle stood up in the water. "You're a natural," Kalibar added. Kyle grinned again, and Kalibar smirked. "Having talent is a lucky way to start," he cautioned, "...but real accomplishment is only achieved through hard work."

"Yes sir," Kyle replied, feeling a bit of the wind come out of his sails.

"You've sensed magic outside of you," Kalibar continued. "The next step is to sense your *own* magic...the magic inside of your brain. This will be much harder to sense than the magic I streamed to you."

"What do I do?" Kyle asked.

"We'll sensitize you to smaller and smaller amounts of magic over time," Kalibar answered. "I'll send a magic stream to you, then send a weaker and weaker stream, until you can't feel it anymore. When that happens, let me know. Eventually, you'll become attuned to even minute amounts of magic – including your own."

"Got it."

"Lay back in the water then," Kalibar ordered. Kyle complied, and waited for Kalibar to start. He felt a vibration directly above him.

"I feel it," he called out.

The sensation began to fade, becoming dimmer and dimmer, until he wasn't sure if he was still feeling it or not.

"I think maybe I lost it," he admitted, swinging forward onto his feet. Kalibar nodded.

"Not bad," he said. "Now I know where your limit is. We'll do it over and over again, and see how you improve."

They did just that, repeating the process again and again. For a while there was no change – he was still losing the sensation at the same amount of magic. But, after the umpteenth time, Kalibar said he noted improvement...a little. Kyle couldn't help but feel frustrated and a little dismayed. Kalibar must have noticed.

"Don't worry," he reassured. "Sensing magic takes time. It's like a muscle," he added. "Even with a great deal of exercise, it takes time to grow."

Kyle nodded, feeling only a little better. He held his arms against his chest, realizing that he was shivering. The water had become a bit chilly; he looked up, spotting the sun hovering just above the horizon. They must have been practicing for hours; indeed, his stomach grumbled at him, complaining bitterly at his neglect.

"I'm starving," he admitted. "Can we take a break?"

"Of course," Kalibar answered, gesturing for Kyle to get out of the water. "It's time for dinner anyway." Kyle stepped out of the water, and they both walked back to the carriage. They both looked around for Darius, but the bodyguard was nowhere to be found. Kalibar cooked up a meal of spinach-like leaves in a hot soup, with small pieces of meat mixed in. Kyle ate his food greedily, slurping every last drop of the soup up, then asking for seconds. By the time the two of them finished their meals, the sun had kissed the horizon, sending brilliant swathes of orange and red across the twilight sky.

"I think we've had enough training for today," Kalibar decided. He yawned, stretching his arms out to the sides. "I'm going to turn in for the night." He walked up to the carriage, pulling two sleeping bags from it and handing one to Kyle. Just then, they heard footsteps approaching in the darkness. It was Darius, back from wherever he'd been all day.

"Welcome back," Kalibar greeted. "Any signs we've been followed?" Darius shook his head.

"Nope."

"Good," Kalibar replied. "We're going to turn in," he continued. He gestured at the metallic, stake-like wards he'd hammered into the ground in a loose circle around the camp. "Once I activate these wards, you'll have to stay inside their circle until I deactivate them." He smirked. "I suggest you...relieve yourselves before then."

Darius declined the advice, but Kyle took it, walking a short distance into the woods to do his duty. Then he returned, curling up inside of his sleeping bag. Kalibar did something with the wards, and suddenly the entire camp was surrounded by a faint blue gravity shield, easily fifty feet in diameter. Kalibar and Darius went into their respective sleeping bags, and with that, the day was done.

Kyle yawned, then closed his eyes, feeling absolutely exhausted. He'd never had trouble sleeping after a day filled with exertions, and he'd rarely exerted himself more strenuously than he had today. Within moments, sleep claimed him.

Chapter 11

Kyle jerked himself awake, opening his eyes. The sun hovered just above the tree line in the distance, its rays peeking between dark, ominous-looking clouds approaching slowly from the east. Kyle squinted against the light, rolling over onto his belly in his sleeping bag. He rubbed his eyes, then crawled slowly out of the bag, his legs and lower back terribly sore and stiff from yesterday's hike. The gravity shield protecting the camp had vanished, the stake-like wards still stuck in the ground in a wide circle around them, their runes glowing a faint blue. Kalibar and Darius were already up; Kalibar was sitting on the edge of his own levitating sleeping bag, an open book floating in the air in front of him. Darius, on the other hand, was sitting cross-legged on the ground, eating some bread and soup.

Kyle yawned, stretching his arms up and out. His stomach growled at him, and he eyed Darius's meal, walking up to the bodyguard.

"Morning," Kyle greeted. Darius didn't respond...he didn't even look up.

Jerk, Kyle thought, doing his best to hide his irritation.

"Can I have some too?" Kyle asked, gesturing at Darius's food. Darius brought his bowl of soup to his lips, slurping loudly.

"Go ahead," he replied tersely.

Kyle paused, waiting for Darius to get up and grab him some, but the bodyguard didn't budge.

"Uh, where is the...stuff?" Kyle asked. Again, Darius didn't reply, biting a hunk out of his piece of bread and chewing it leisurely. Kyle stood there for a moment, staring down at the armored meat-head, and briefly entertained kicking the man's bowl right out of his hands. He resisted the urge, more out of self-preservation than anything else, and stomped off to the carriage in the middle of the camp instead. A few of the packs from the trunk had been set on the ground beside the carriage, and Kyle squatted before these, rummaging through them. Within moments, he found a bowl, a canteen filled with water, a packet of dried soup base, and a loaf of bread wrapped in wax paper. He retrieved these, mixing the soup base with the water inside of his bowl, then soaking the bread in his concoction. Cold and soggy, it was far from appetizing, but it settled his complaining belly.

When he'd finished, he rinsed his bowl with leftover water from the canteen, then put each item back where it belonged. He glanced back at Kalibar – still engrossed in his book – then turned to gaze across Crescent Lake. Sunlight glittered off of its waters like tiny diamonds, fluffy clouds hovering far above overhead, pleasant puffs of white floating in the infinite blue. He spotted a flock of birds flying in a loose ring above, and followed them with his gaze as they crossed the sky, disappearing beyond the cliffs and the waterfall at the far end of the lake. He glanced down at his left thumb, feeling suddenly naked without his father's ring there.

Not just my dad's ring, he reminded himself. It had been Ampir's ring, after all, long ago. A ring filled with the long-dead man's memories, and with the power to send Kyle here, to this world. And maybe – just maybe – to send him back home.

He gazed up at the sky, into that endless expanse of blue.

Where am I?

He sighed, walking across the camp – pointedly ignoring Darius – and stepping beyond the ring of wards. He walked all the way up to the edge of the lake, then sat down on the coarse, damp sand there. He felt a sudden pang of sadness, wondering how long it'd been since he'd been away from home. Seven days? Eight? Either way, his parents had to be fearing the worst now. That wherever he was, he wasn't coming back...ever.

That he was dead.

Kyle took a deep breath in, letting it out slowly. A wave of grief threatened to overtake him, and he clenched his teeth, forcing it down. There was no point in wallowing in his misery, after all...and he sure as hell wasn't about to let Darius see him cry. He grabbed a pebble, standing up and winding his arm back, then whipping the stone over the lake. It skipped off the glittering water, once, twice, and then a third time before sinking below the surface, leaving a string of expanding ripples in its wake.

"Good morning, Kyle," a voice behind him said.

Kyle jumped, whirling around to find Kalibar standing there behind him. Kalibar gave him a rueful smile.

"Didn't mean to startle you," he apologized. "Did you sleep well?"

"Uh, yeah."

"Any dreams?" Kalibar pressed. Kyle shook his head.

"Not that I can remember," he admitted. He was thankful for the reprieve from his usual nightmares, but Kalibar seemed disappointed.

"Ah well," Kalibar said. He scratched the side of his face, where white stubble was already starting to grow. "I had a hard time getting to sleep myself," he confessed. "I couldn't help but think of all the things we could do if we learned to store our memories like Ampir did, in his ring." He shook his head, staring across the water. "Imagine…to be able to hand down your experiences to your children, to let them learn from your mistakes without ever having to make them themselves! That," he added, pausing for a moment. "That would change *everything*."

"Yeah," Kyle mumbled. They both stared at the lake silently for a bit. Then Kalibar stirred.

"We don't know everything about the Ancients," he said, "…but we have a good handle on the extent of their runic technology. Storing one's memories in a ring is far beyond even *their* capabilities, but somehow Ampir managed to do it."

"He was that good?" Kyle asked.

"He was," Kalibar confirmed. "Even his worst critics knew that he was the very best at what he did…that no one before him, or since, even came close." He shook his head again. "I have no doubt that it was Ampir who invented teleportation, and that his mentor Renval was only along for the ride."

Kyle nodded absently, staring down at his left thumb. He heard Kalibar sigh.

"As much as I hate Ampir for what he did, I can't help being fascinated by him," he murmured. ""What I wouldn't give to meet the man," he added wistfully. "Or to have lived in Ancient times."

Kyle heard footsteps behind him, and turned around to see Darius walking across the camp to one of the packs in the trunk of the carriage. The bodyguard retrieved a small, flat stone, then sat down on the ground, pulling out a huge sword from a scabbard at his hip. It looked like a cross between a machete and a standard sword, and had a sharp, wicked-looking edge. Darius began sliding the stone over the edge of the blade, making a metallic ringing sound with each scrape. The sun, now rising above the dark clouds on the horizon, made the man's golden armor shimmer with every movement.

"Well then," Kalibar stated, clearing his throat. "We should continue your training. No point in wasting daylight." Kyle nodded eagerly, feeling positively giddy about the prospect, and started taking off his shirt, but Kalibar stopped him. "We'll get back to the lake in a bit," he stated. "First, I'd like to go over some magic theory."

"Okay…" Kyle replied, pulling his shirt back on. Kalibar led Kyle back to the camp.

"Before we begin, do you have any questions?" Kalibar asked. Kyle frowned, mulling it over.

"Those shields you make with your staff," Kyle answered. "How do they work?"

"Good question," Kalibar replied. "Magic can do many things, but they all come down to manipulating substances and forces. Gravity is a type of force, and magic can create it, strengthen it, or weaken it." He smiled. "It can even *reverse* it."

"Like make things fall up?" Kyle asked. Kalibar nodded.

"Sort of," he agreed. "Gravity shields are reverse-polarity gravitational fields…meaning they shove things away instead of attracting them. They're usually less than an inch thick, and shaped into a sphere…but they're not blue, they're clear," he corrected. "In any case, using them can get tricky if you don't know what you're doing."

"What do you mean?"

"Well, can you imagine what might happen if you surround yourself with a force that pushes everything outward?"

"Um…you'd get pushed out too?"

"Well possibly," Kalibar replied. "But more importantly, the *air* around you would get sucked out, leaving you in a relative vacuum…and you would suffocate."

"Oh."

"That's why most gravity shields have two layers," Kalibar

explained. "An outer layer that pushes outward, and an inner layer that pushes inward. If they're the same strength – exactly the same strength – air won't get pulled out."

"Makes sense," Kyle conceded.

"And you'd still die," Kalibar continued.

"Huh?"

"You'd be breathing the same air over and over again, until you suffocated," Kalibar explained. "And no one would be able to hear you, since sound wouldn't be able to escape the inner gravity field. Can you think of a way to solve that problem?"

Kyle thought it over for a bit, then shrugged helplessly.

"I dunno," he admitted, feeling a familiar sense of despair come over him. He'd figured that magic would just...well, *work*. It was sounding more and more like science.

"You'll figure it out," Kalibar replied, patting Kyle on the shoulder. "Did you have any other questions?"

"No," Kyle mumbled. He heard a dull *thunk*, and turned to see Darius standing at the edge of the camp, unlatching his golden armor piece by piece, until it lay in a heap at his feet. Underneath his armor, he wore a simple black shirt and a pair of shorts. He removed his shirt, revealing a heavily muscled torso and chest. The sun shone on his well-tanned skin as he strode leisurely toward the lake, wading, then diving into the water. Within a remarkably short period of time, the bodyguard had swum half the length of the lake, his head barely visible in the mist formed by the waterfall.

"I think that's the first time I've seen him enjoying himself," Kalibar observed, watching as Darius swam right up to the waterfall, getting immediately shoved beneath the surface of the lake by the force of the falling water. The bodyguard emerged a few dozen feet away after a long moment, then swam up to the waterfall and did it again. Kalibar turned to Kyle. "Except of course when he's needling you," the old man added with a wink.

"Great," Kyle muttered.

Kalibar watched the bodyguard for a moment longer, then turned to Kyle.

"In any case, let's start your first lesson in magic theory," Kalibar said. He strode up to his still-levitating sleeping bag, retrieving his staff from the ground beneath it. He handed it to Kyle, who grasped the cool metal with both hands. The staff was surprisingly light, with countless small symbols carved into the surface. The runes were all glowing a faint blue, and when Kyle looked up close, he could swear he saw something shimmering in each symbol's tiny furrows.

"Now," Kalibar stated, "...what is a Weaver?"

"Uh..." Kyle began, then hesitated. "Someone who uses magic?"

"They do," Kalibar agreed, "...but so do Runics."

"Someone who uses magic to do things like make gravity shields?"

"True," Kalibar said. "And many other things. Weavers use magic to make what we call 'patterns' in their minds. It's a little like weaving a thread of yarn into a pattern to make fabric, which is why we call it *weaving* magic."

"And that's why you're called a Weaver?"

"Exactly," Kalibar replied. "Different patterns do different things. One might create a gravity shield, while another creates fire."

"Okay," Kyle said. He looked down at Kalibar's staff. "So what exactly do Runics do?"

"Runics create objects – called 'runics' or 'runic devices' – to do the weaving for them," Kalibar answered. "Now remember, you have to weave magic into particular patterns in order for it to do anything. The pattern determines the nature of the magic – how it will alter matter and energy. While a Weaver weaves magic patterns in his mind, a Runic weaves magic using runes," he continued, gesturing at the runes carved into his staff.

"I don't get it," Kyle admitted. "How do runes weave magic?"

"Runes are essentially threads of minerals," Kalibar explained. "When magic flows through these threads, it's the same as weaving magic in the mind. So the same pattern that makes fire when woven in the mind..."

"Makes fire when it flows through the rune," Kyle finished. Kalibar nodded. "But wait," Kyle protested. "Why make uh, runic devices if you can just weave in your mind?"

"Well, weaving takes time and effort," Kalibar answered. "Remember the gravity shield I made with my staff, the one that protected us from the rain a couple days ago?"

"Yeah."

"Well, my staff has magic stored within it," Kalibar said. "And this was automatically sent to the runes that created the gravity shield. If it hadn't been for the staff, I would have had to stay awake all night to keep that shield up."

"Oh, gotcha," Kyle replied. It made perfect sense, now that he thought about it. "So Runics are just like Weavers, but they just let runes do the weaving for them?"

"It's a bit more complicated than that," Kalibar admitted. "Runes can do more than just weave magic." He frowned, tapping his chin. "For example, if I were to weave the pattern that makes fire in my mind, and I were anywhere near a type of rune with the same pattern, that rune would generate a small magical current."

"What do you mean?" Kyle asked.

"Well, runes can 'sense' when patterns identical to them are being woven. No one is quite sure how or why, but nonetheless it is so...and it is extraordinarily useful." He reached into his breast pocket then, retrieving a pair of sunglasses. They were, Kyle realized, the same glasses Kalibar had worn earlier, the night when their carriage had been attacked. He'd wondered why the man had worn his sunglasses at night.

"Put them on," Kalibar urged. Kyle did so. They were too big for him, and he strongly suspected that they looked ridiculous on him. "Now, I'm going to weave the pattern that makes fire," Kalibar explained. Almost immediately, a small flame danced in the air between them. Kyle saw a small red symbol start glowing at the left upper edge of the sunglasses on the left lens.

"Whoa," he breathed.

"Did you see the red symbol?" Kalibar asked. Kyle nodded. "The glasses have a fire rune that senses anyone weaving the fire pattern nearby," Kalibar explained. "This is connected – by a metallic thread – to a rune that weaves a pattern to make red light. We call the sensing rune a *sensory* rune...and stimulating it makes it send magic to the rune that creates the light...the *effector* rune."

"Oh, I get it," Kyle exclaimed.

"Good," Kalibar replied, clearly pleased. "These glasses have sensing runes," Kalibar explained, "...for almost every known magical pattern. They are connected to effector runes that make light of varying colors and positions. By knowing the particular location and color of a pattern when it appears on my glasses, I can tell what pattern an enemy is weaving. The outer surface of the lenses have a reflective coating," Kalibar added, "...so that only the wearer can see the glowing runes."

"Cool," Kyle breathed. The flame between them vanished, and so did the red symbol on the inner surface of the glasses. Kalibar gestured for Kyle to take them off, and he did so, handing them back to the man.

"Now, you can connect any sensory rune to any effector rune." He gestured at his staff. "This staff has hundreds of sensory and effector runes in it. The staff automatically senses potential magical attacks, and counters with the appropriate effector runes to generate a defense...or a counterattack." He smiled. "Not only that, but you can even link one sensory rune to many effector runes," he added. "I could make a runic device that linked dozens of effector runes together. With a single thought, the entire chain of runes could be activated. If the runes happened to create bolts of lightning, dozens of bolts would be generated within seconds. Or I could use a variety of runes, disabling my opponent's shields, then coordinating dozens of unique attacks, one after the other."

"Wait, doesn't that mean a Runic is more powerful than a Weaver?"

"Not at all," Kalibar replied. "A runic device can only do the same thing over and over...a Weaver can be unpredictable, using magic much more flexibly and creatively from moment to moment. In a battle, a good Weaver will almost always triumph over a Runic."

"Oh, good," Kyle said, feeling relieved. After all, he *was* training to become a Weaver.

"Now, there are only so many known patterns," Kalibar continued. "And no one really knows why these patterns do what they do, although many people – myself included – have tried to figure it out." He sighed. "The Ancients probably understood how magical patterns did what they did. That's likely how they came up with new patterns. But that knowledge died with them; now, we only know the patterns that managed to survive in writing, or in their runic devices. Nowadays, nobody knows how to make new patterns."

"Why not just experiment?" Kyle asked. "Just make random patterns and see what happens?" Kalibar smirked.

"Oh, that's been tried," Kalibar replied. "But random patterns have unpredictable effects...and plenty of scholars have died attempting such things."

"Ah," Kyle murmured. Then he frowned. "Wait, if there are

only so many patterns, couldn't someone just make a staff that countered every possible attack?" he asked. "They'd be invincible!"

"Not really," Kalibar countered. "As a Weaver, I test my enemy's runic devices, and figure out their counterattacks early, so I know how to beat them. In practice, Weavers fighting each other have to guess their enemy's next few moves, and act accordingly. We always try to be a few steps ahead of our opponents."

"That sounds hard," Kyle replied, suddenly feeling a bit depressed. It sounded a great deal like chess, and he'd never been good at that.

"It is," Kalibar replied with a chuckle. "But don't worry," he added, patting Kyle on the shoulder. "With practice, everything hard becomes easier."

Kyle heard footsteps coming up from behind them, and turned about, seeing Darius walking back to the camp. The bodyguard was dripping wet from his swim, but he didn't bother to grab a towel from one of the packs to dry off. Instead, he reached for his various pieces of armor, putting them back on. Within a few minutes, the bodyguard was a gilded warrior once again, his armor shining almost painfully bright in the sunlight. Even after days of travel through muck and grime, Darius's armor was spotless. The oaf must have spent as much time polishing his armor as he did sharpening his weapons, Kyle mused. It was a shame he hadn't spent more time working on his personality.

"I think we've had enough theory for today," Kalibar declared. He took his staff from Kyle, and gestured for Kyle to follow him out of the camp and to the water's edge. "Take off your clothes and go into the water again," he instructed. Kyle complied, stripping off his shirt and pants, and wading into the water. It was considerably cooler than it had been yesterday afternoon. He winced as his delicate areas dipped into the water, then took a deep breath in, steeling himself before dropping himself neck-deep into the lake.

"We'll continue where we left off yesterday," Kalibar stated, standing at the shoreline, staff in hand. "We need to continue sensitizing you to magic, until you are able to sense the magic within your own mind."

Kyle nodded, forcing himself to kick his legs up into the Dead Man's float. He lay there suspended in the water, immediately feeling the vibration of magic a few feet to his left. He waited for that vibration to wane, trying not to sigh. If today was anything like yesterday's sessions, it was going to be a long, long morning.

* * *

The sun shone down on the camp from directly overhead by the time Kalibar let Kyle step out of the water and onto the sandy shore, shivering despite the warmth of the sun's rays. Kalibar grabbed a towel from one of the packs by the carriage, handing it to Kyle. Kyle dried himself off, grateful to be out of the water...and to finally have a break from his training.

"Not bad, Kyle," Kalibar declared, patting him on the shoulder. "You're improving."

"I guess," Kyle replied, skeptical of just how much he'd accomplished. Despite hours of practice, it felt like he'd gotten nowhere.

"Are you hungry?" Kalibar asked. Kyle nodded, his stomach grumbling in agreement. Kalibar retrieved some dried meat and soup mix from the packs, magically filling two bowls with hot water and handing one to Kyle. Kyle accepted his gratefully, warming his cold hands on it. They ate in silence, and Kalibar returned the bowls to their pack. The former Grand Weaver paused over the pack, then reached in and grabbed something...a dark brown glass bottle. A loop of twine was tied to a ring attached to the neck of the bottle, and Kalibar handed this to Kyle.

"Wrap this around your arm," Kalibar stated. Kyle complied, and then Kalibar handed Kyle the bottle. Kyle took it, then gasped as the bottle rose upward, pulling out of his grasp and floating upward into the air. The twine around Kyle's arm went taught, stopping the bottle from rising any further.

"What the...!" Kyle exclaimed, hastily grabbing for the bottle, holding it in both hands. The slick, cool glass continued to pull upward. Kalibar grinned.

"That's the feathergrass extract I showed you earlier, remember?" he explained, gesturing at the bottle. "It floats – and so does anything it's kept in," he added. "I thought you'd want to try it out." Kyle's eyes widened, and he couldn't help but feel a burst of glee.

"Can I try it now?"

"I don't see why not," Kalibar replied with a wink. "Here, hand it back," he instructed. "I'll show you how to drink it...it takes a bit of practice." Kyle handed the bottle back – carefully – and Kalibar held the bottle upside-down, twisting off the cap. Nothing poured out of the neck of the bottle, of course. Kalibar tipped his head back, then brought the upside-down bottle to his lips. With his mouth sealed around the opening, Kalibar brought his head down, and the bottle right-side-up, taking a gulp of the extract. Then he tipped his head back up, holding the bottle upside-down before twisting the cap back on.

"That's how you do it," Kalibar explained. Then he handed the bottle over to Kyle, wrapping the rope around Kyle's wrist. "You try," he prompted. "First, tip the bottle upside-down, so the liquid doesn't float up and out." Kyle did so. "Now, untwist the cap."

Kyle untwisted the cap, tipping his head back, then bringing the neck of the bottom to his lips, just as Kalibar had done. Then he slowly brought his head back down and forward. As the bottle went right-side up, thick liquid floated up and out, filling his mouth. Kyle nearly spit the fluid out – it was a bit bitter – but managed to stop himself from doing so. He swallowed, then tipped his head back, re-capping the bottle. He handed it back to Kalibar.

"This is the hard part," Kalibar cautioned, putting the bottle back into the pack. "The extract is going to float up from your stomach and into your mouth if you're not careful." Kalibar was right; Kyle felt the fluid filling up in the back of his throat, the bitter taste making him want to gag. He swallowed it back down with some difficulty, but it came right back up. He swallowed it again, feeling queasy.

"Here, lay on your right side," Kalibar explained, pulling Kyle down onto the ground. Kyle complied, lying on his right side on the sparse grass of the camp. He immediately felt better; the feathergrass extract was still making his stomach feel weird, but it was no longer refluxing into his mouth.

"How long do I have to do this?" Kyle asked, feeling a little awkward. Kalibar chuckled.

"Only a few minutes," he reassured. "The extract is quickly absorbed through the stomach. Once it gets into your blood, your stomach will calm down."

Kyle waited. His belly gurgled, and then he felt something *shift*. The upper right part of his belly felt as if it were pulling upward, then he felt his chest do the same. From there, the sensation spread to his head, then his arms, and finally, his legs. He felt as if at any moment, he might float away, falling forever upward into the infinite blue sky. He panicked, rolling onto his stomach and grabbing on to tufts of grass with both hands. He heard Kalibar chuckle.

"Don't worry," Kalibar reassured. "Everyone does that the first time. You can let go…I promise you won't fly away."

Kyle hesitated, then slowly let go of the grass with one hand. To his relief, he didn't float upward. He paused, then tried pushing himself up onto his hands and knees. The motion catapulted him a few feet above the ground, and he flailed his arms wildly, crying out. To his relief, he fell slowly back to the ground, landing gently onto his belly in the tough grass.

"Try using small, slow, gentle movements," Kalibar suggested. "The slower you move, the less likely you are to lose control." Kyle complied, getting into a push-up position, then carefully pushing himself off of the ground. With his feet as the pivot point, he swung upward until he was standing straight up, his feet firmly planted on the ground. He stood there for a moment, then glanced at Kalibar, who was watching Kyle with a grin.

"What now?" Kyle asked.

"Now," Kalibar replied, "…we have some fun!"

With that, Kalibar bent his knees, then leaped upward. High into the air he went, until he was soaring above even the treetops around them. He sailed over Kyle's head, then fell slowly downward, landing some fifty feet away, near the lake shore. Then he turned around, gesturing for Kyle to follow suit.

"Come on!" he yelled. Kyle took a deep breath, then bent his knees all the way down, like Kalibar had done. But then he hesitated.

"Go on," Kalibar urged.

Kyle took another deep breath in, and then jumped!

Or rather, he chickened out at the last minute, hopping a few feet into the air, then landing on his hands and knees on the ground. He heard Darius chuckle from a few feet away, and felt his face flush.

"Oh come on," Kalibar called out with a grin on his face. "Don't be afraid…just let yourself go!"

Kyle heard footsteps approaching, and turned just in time to see Darius lean over and grab him under the armpits. Before Kyle could react, the bodyguard heaved him up into the air!

"Ahhhh!" Kyle screamed, hurtling upward. He flailed his arms and legs madly, the world dropping out from under him at a terrifying speed. Still upward he went, until the camp was easily forty feet below. His ascent slowed, and then stopped.

Then he fell.

"Craaaaap!" Kyle yelled, his stomach doing cartwheels in his belly. Downward he went, slowly at first, then more quickly. He closed his eyes as the shore rose up to meet him, throwing his arms in front of his face. His feet struck the ground, and threw his arms in front of him, his palms hitting the moist sand. He tensed up, fully expecting to feel a burst of horrible pain...but he only heard laughter.

"See?" Kalibar exclaimed between guffaws. "You can't get hurt!" The older man walked up to Kyle, offering him a hand, and Kyle took it, allowing Kalibar to pull him to his feet. "Now," Kalibar stated, "...ready to try without Darius throwing you?"

"Yeah," Kyle grumbled, wiping the sand off of his hands. Kalibar grinned, crouching down low, then leaping back toward the camp. He traveled in a slow arc, landing a few feet beside Darius. Kyle hesitated, staring at the two men, then grit his teeth, bending down low. He crouched down as Kalibar had, taking a few short breaths in and out.

Here goes...

He paused for a moment longer, then jumped!

"Whoaaa!" he cried as he shot upward into the air, higher even than Darius had thrown him. His stomach lurched again as he reached the top of his leap, then fell downward toward the camp. He overshot Darius and Kalibar by a few dozen feet, landing just beyond the perimeter of wards opposite the lake.

"Well done," Kalibar exclaimed, walking up to Kyle. "Try again...follow me," he added, leaping upward again, gliding through the air in a gentle arc and landing a few feet from the shore. This time Kyle barely hesitated, crouching low and leaping into the air toward Kalibar. He felt giddy as he flew through the air, the wind whipping through his hair as he went.

I'm flying!

Forward and upward he went, sailing over the camp. He laughed as he passed over Darius, imagining himself pooping on the bodyguard's head like a bird. Then he began to fall toward

Kalibar...or rather *beyond* him. He'd overshot again...and this time, he was headed right for the water! He cried out, crashing into the water, feeling cool wetness envelop him. He bounced upward clear out of the water, flying through the air like a skipping stone, landing again, then flying upward, until he settled on top of the water at last. He rolled over from his back onto his stomach, floating effortlessly on the surface. He paddled toward Kalibar, making his way awkwardly to the shore.

"You did that on purpose," Kyle accused as he stepped out of the water, crossing his arms in front of his chest. Kalibar gave him an innocent look.

"Me?" he replied in mock astonishment, holding back a smirk with little success.

"Yes you," Kyle retorted, unable to hold back a smile of his own. Kalibar chuckled.

"Now you can imagine," he said, putting an arm around Kyle's shoulders, "...that feathergrass is especially helpful for people who can't swim. Sailors use it so that if they fall overboard when performing risky tasks, they'll float on the surface instead of drowning."

"Huh," Kyle replied. Then he frowned. "Wait, how long does this stuff last?"

"It's most powerful for the first half-hour or so," Kalibar answered. "The effects fade afterward, and are gone by an hour or two." He paused, then smirked.

"What?"

"I thought about not warning you, but that would be too cruel," Kalibar admitted.

"Warn me about what?"

"Well, most of the extract is...released in the urine and stool," Kalibar explained. "I recommend being very careful when you...remove the extract from your body."

"What do you mean?"

"Everything floats," Kalibar replied rather cryptically. "It takes a bit of practice to deal with properly. I'll tell you more when the time comes."

Kyle frowned, trying to imagine just how he'd deal with floating...stuff.

"Come on," Kalibar said. "We've still got time before the extract starts to weaken!" With that, the former Grand Weaver jumped high into the air, landing further along the shore. The two spent the better part of the next hour leaping to and fro. It wasn't long before Kyle's aim improved, and soon he was following behind Kalibar as the older man leapt from the ground to a large tree branch, then to another, and another. They jumped up to the top of the cliff where the waterfall began, then sailed over the edge. Kalibar had enough forward momentum to land on the shore over fifty feet below, while Kyle landed somewhere in the middle of the lake. They both whooped and laughed as they played, leaping about their slice of paradise with abandon. It was, without a single doubt, the most exhilarating time of Kyle's life.

But as all things good and bad come eventually to an end, the effects of the extract waned, and Kyle soon found that he had some rather urgent matters to attend to. He quickly sought Kalibar's advice about matters eliminatory, and thankfully, the old man was rapid and very clear with his instructions. After expelling the extract from his system, Kyle realized that Kalibar had been right. Without his expert consultation, Kyle would have had quite a mess on his hands...and everywhere else, for that matter. Luckily, everything fell into its proper place at the end.

Afterward, they ate, then spent the rest of the afternoon and evening with Kyle back in the lake, practicing sensing magic. By the time the sun had set, and the brightest of the stars had become visible in the night sky, Kyle was all too eager to be done with his practice, and left the now-cool water to join Kalibar in the camp. The former Grand Weaver set their sleeping bags in a ring around a small campfire, and Kalibar set it alight with his magic. Darius, Kyle, and Kalibar sat down on their respective bags, their legs dangling over the edge, their faces lit from below by the orange-red flames. The heat of the fire was heavenly after hours in the cool lake, and Kyle soaked up the warmth with a contentment he hadn't felt in a long, long while.

"I can't remember the last time I sat by a campfire," Kalibar stated, clearly enjoying it as much as Kyle. The former Grand Weaver smiled, looking more at ease than Kyle had ever seen him. Darius, however, his armor glittering in the light of the flickering flames, was no better than his usual self.

"Today was awesome," Kyle said, swinging his legs back and forth over the edge of his sleeping bag. Kalibar chuckled.

"Indeed it was," he agreed. "I haven't played like that since I was a boy," he added. He shook his head then, staring into the fire. "My father always said that having children reminded him of what true joy was."

Kyle nodded absently, then stared across the fire at Kalibar.

"Do you have any children?" he asked.

Kalibar paused for a long moment, then shook his head.

"No."

"Oh," Kyle replied. Kalibar stared into the fire for a bit, then cleared his throat.

"I had a son," Kalibar confessed. "But that was a long time ago."

"What happened?" Kyle pressed. Kalibar sighed, picking up a small stick and throwing it into the fire. The flames engulfed it, the bark slowly blackening in the intense heat.

"He died," Kalibar answered at last. He paused, then threw another stick in, watching it burn alongside the first. Kyle swallowed, turning away from Kalibar and staring into the fire.

"Sorry," he mumbled.

"So am I," Kalibar murmured. He stood up from his sleeping bag then, throwing one last stick into the campfire. "We'd better get to sleep," he added. The wards around the camp activated, a huge domed gravity shield appearing around them. He walked up to Kyle, putting a hand on Kyle's shoulder. "You did well today."

"Thanks," Kyle mumbled. Kalibar turned to walk back to his sleeping bag, and Kyle followed him with his gaze. "Kalibar?" he asked. Kalibar paused, turning to look over his shoulder.

"Yes?"

"Thanks," Kyle stated. "For everything."

Kalibar smiled, turning about and ruffling Kyle's hair with one hand.

"The pleasure," he replied, "...is mine."

With that, Kalibar went back to his sleeping bag, as did Darius, and the two men turned in to sleep. Kyle went to his own sleeping bag, snuggling inside its warm confines. Utterly exhausted, he closed his eyes, and was lulled to sleep by the gentle crackling of the dying fire.

Chapter 12

Ampir bursts upward and to the left just as the Behemoth's eye flashes far in the distance. A beam of unholy green light burns across the night sky, missing Ampir by less than a yard. The wide beam strikes the Weavers behind him, annihilating their gravity shields. Their bodies explode, hunks of burning flesh falling to the Great River below.

The beam fades, its purple afterimage seared into Ampir's vision. The Behemoth's head turns slowly, still tracking him as he accelerates over the River. For the first time in over a decade, he feels vulnerable despite wearing his armor. He designed it to withstand any assault...but after seeing what the Behemoth's beam did to those Weavers, eating through their gravity shields as if they didn't exist...

Focus.

He pushes forward, keeping an eye on the Behemoth, even as the gargantuan weapon tracks him. That lone, green eye shines brightly against the black metal of its domed head. The image evokes a long-forgotten memory...a memory that makes Ampir's breath catch in his throat.

I know who made you, he realizes, staring at the Behemoth. *I know who's behind this.*

A chill runs through him.

Then the Behemoth's eye flashes.

* * *

The morning sky was a dull gray when Kyle awoke, dark clouds rolling in from the east high above the camp. The air was cool and thick with moisture, leaving the ground slightly damp. The campfire had long since burned itself out, blackened logs and sticks all that remained of last night's merry blaze.

Kyle yawned, swinging his legs over the side of his sleeping bag. He stretched his arms out to his sides, feeling even more stiff and sore today than he had yesterday. He glanced about the camp, spotting Kalibar – already awake, as usual – sitting cross-legged on the ground, hunched over a glittering brown crystal as big as Kyle's fist.

"Morning," Kyle mumbled, rubbing the crust from his eyes. Kalibar looked up from the crystal, smiling when he saw Kyle.

"Good morning Kyle," he greeted.

"What are you doing?" Kyle asked, gesturing at the brown crystal.

"Making runic wards," Kalibar replied, hunching back down over the crystal. As Kyle watched, a tiny dot of blue light appeared on the surface of the gem. The dot moved slowly across its surface, leaving a thin orange line behind it, tracing a complicated pattern. When Kalibar was done, he offered the gem to Kyle, who walked up next to Kalibar and sat down beside him, taking it. He stared at the orange pattern.

"Is this a rune?" he asked. Kalibar nodded.

"Erasmus taught me how to make simple runes a few years ago, after I retired," Kalibar explained. "I may never become an expert at it, but I enjoy the challenge." He stretched his neck from side to side, then smiled. "I highly recommend doing things you're bad at from time to time…it keeps you humble…and keeps your mind sharp."

Kyle heard footsteps approaching, and turned to see Darius walking toward them. The bodyguard held a large pack in his arms, which he prompted dropped onto the ground in front of Kalibar. Then he squatted before it, unzipping the pack to reveal a large collection of thick white roots, like pale carrots but three times as long.

"What's that?" Kyle asked.

"Those are sweetroots," Kalibar replied, setting his brown crystal aside and standing up to look down at Darius's bounty. "They're highly nutritious," Kalibar added. He grabbed a root, snapping off a small piece and handing it to Kyle. "Here, try it."

Kyle complied, biting a tiny piece off and chewing it. It was a bit tough, and surprisingly bland. Kyle frowned.

"It's not sweet at all," he complained. Kalibar chuckled, throwing the remainder of the root back in the pack.

"It's called sweetroot because of its magic, not its taste," he replied. "The root has a rather pleasant calming effect on anyone who eats it…making them sweet, in a manner of speaking. A few species of insects pollinate the sweetroot flowers, deliberating planting the small seeds in their territories. Then they dig underground to chew the roots, taking small pieces and bringing them to the surface. They place these pieces in a perimeter around their territories; any predator that tries to enter the insects' territories will be enticed by the sweetroot, eating it…and will become completely disinterested in fighting. It's an elegant relationship, really."

"Wait, what's it going to do to me?" Kyle asked, suddenly regretting having swallowed the stuff.

"That depends," Kalibar replied. "The effect is powerful on insects, but in humans, it takes quite a bit of sweetroot to have an effect." He paused for a moment, then continued. "Sweetroot has something of a checkered past," he admitted. "By grinding down a large amount of it, and concentrating the extract, alchemists can make a powerful potion indeed. One sip can completely nullify a man's desire for violence. Sweetroot potions are used in maximum security prisons to make dangerous prisoners – some of them Weavers – docile."

"That doesn't sound like a bad idea at all," Kyle opined.

"Yes, well that's what we thought during the first few years of the second Empire," Kalibar agreed. "The Secula Magna heavily subsidized sweetroot farming, and used the massive crop yields to make unheard-of quantities of extract. They thought that, by spraying the extract in a fine mist above enemy towns and armies, they could easily subdue, then dispatch them. They were right; it worked extraordinarily well…that is, until the enemy used the same tactic back on them. It became a critical strategy to find and eliminate enemy stores of the extract, and burn their fields of sweetroot."

"Wow," Kyle exclaimed, staring warily at the pack full of roots. "Are we really going to eat that?" he asked. Kalibar smiled.

"Of course," he replied. "At most, you'll feel a pleasant peaceful feeling – if you eat a half-dozen of them." He grabbed a root from the pack, biting off a good-sized piece and chewing it. "Nowadays, sweetroot cultivation is heavily regulated by the government. Mass-farming is illegal, and heavy personal use is frowned upon – except in certain circumstances."

"What do you mean?" Kyle asked.

"Well, doctors use the concentrated extract as medicine for people with violent tempers," Kalibar replied. "Particularly in domestic abuse situations. The root has saved many marriages," he added. "And it's used on maximum-security prisoners. But the use of sweetroot for crowd control is forbidden." Kalibar took another bite of sweetroot, and chewed on it thoughtfully. "About fifty years ago, the Empire experimented on using sweetroot extract on their own citizens...secretly, through the drinking water. It was for a supposedly noble purpose – to see if it would improve civility among the people, decreasing the murder rate and criminal activity. But when the population at large found out about it...well, it was far from a 'sweet' response."

"The Empire experimented on its own people?" Kyle exclaimed in disbelief.

"Often with good intentions," Kalibar answered. "In this case it was a noble cause. But without the consent of the people, good intentions often yield unfortunate results. Very few leaders truly appreciate that."

Kalibar walked back to his crystal then, sitting down before it once again.

"I'd like to keep working on this, if you don't mind," he said. "We'll start your training in an hour or so." He glanced up at the sky. "Those storm clouds are closing in fast," he observed.

"I'll get more firewood," Darius offered. Kalibar nodded.

"A fire like last night would be nice," the Weaver agreed.

"Let's go," Darius said, turning to Kyle. Kyle stiffened.

"What?"

"Yes, why don't you go with Darius for a while," Kalibar agreed. "Try to be back in an hour or so."

Darius nodded, picking up an empty pack from the back of the carriage, then shoving it into Kyle's arms.

"Come on princess," the bodyguard growled, turning away from Kalibar and walking out of the camp toward the woods. Kyle grit his teeth.

"Princess?" he shot back. Darius didn't reply, continuing to stride toward the forest.

"Jerk," Kyle muttered under his breath.

Kyle gripped the empty pack tightly, stomping out of the camp behind the armored oaf. Darius was already past the tree-line now, and Kyle had to sprint to catch up with him.

"Have fun," Kalibar called out after them.

Yeah right, Kyle muttered to himself. He doubted that Darius even knew what fun was, much less how to have it.

He reached the tree-line quickly, catching up to Darius and falling into step behind the bodyguard. Despite Darius's armor – which had to weigh a ton – the man maneuvered through the rough terrain easily and quickly, forcing Kyle to struggle just to keep pace. A thick fog hung above the trees over their heads, blocking their view of the overcast sky. As the terrain led them up a slight incline, they rose to meet the fog. It made the forest seem dull and gray, and anything more than thirty feet away was swallowed whole by it. The air was chilly, but the coolness was a welcome reprieve from the heat of his exertions.

They strode silently, Kyle trailing a few feet behind, weaving through the trees. Fallen leaves and small branches littering the forest floor crunched underfoot in a cadence that became almost hypnotic. The forest took on an otherworldly appearance, disappearing on all sides into the oblivion of the gray mist surrounding them. Darius kept silent as he walked, not slowing his pace one bit. It wasn't long before Kyle was huffing and puffing, sweat pouring down his flanks. His legs began to burn, the already sore muscles complaining bitterly. He found himself falling behind, the distance between him and Darius growing with every step. Before long, he could barely see the man's outline in the fog ahead.

"Wait up!" Kyle gasped, breaking into a run. But if Darius heard him, he didn't acknowledge it. Kyle grit his teeth and pushed forward, ignoring the pain in his legs.

"Slow...down!" Kyle gasped as he fell into step a few feet behind the man. Darius didn't so much as turn his head.

"Speed up," he countered.

"I can't!" Kyle protested. Darius raised an eyebrow, glancing back to where Kyle had been a moment before, then turning back to Kyle. Kyle felt a flash of anger.

"Would it kill you to be nice for once?" he blurted out. He didn't care what the bodyguard did to him...enough was enough.

"That's not my job."

"Then what is?" Kyle shot back. As if it had to be in the man's job description to be nice! Darius didn't respond; instead, he quickened his pace slightly. Kyle groaned, pushing himself to the limit just to keep up.

The earth dipped downward, gently angling toward a narrow path flanked by steep, nearly vertical cliffs on either side. Darius led them down the path, the cliffs looming nearly twenty feet tall. Kyle glared at the golden metal plates of the bodyguard's armored back.

Not his job!

Suddenly Darius jerked to the left, nearly stumbling into the side of the cliff wall. He grunted, catching himself. There was something sticking out of the back of his right shoulder.

An arrow.

"Get down!" Darius shouted, running up to Kyle and shoving him to the ground. Something whizzed by Kyle's head, and he heard a *thunk* as another arrow embedded itself into the cliff wall to his left.

"Darius!" he cried.

The bodyguard grabbed Kyle's arm, pulling him back the way they'd come. Darius broke out into an all-out sprint, pulling Kyle along with him. They ran down the narrow path between the cliffs, their footsteps echoing off of the stony walls.

"Come on!" Darius yelled, letting go of Kyle's hand and sprinting even faster. Kyle ran as fast as he could, his heart pounding in his chest. Another arrow whizzed through the air behind them.

Oh crap oh crap oh...

His right foot landed on a small stone, and his ankle rolled out from under him. He careened toward the ground, landing on his outstretched hands. He scrambled to his feet, hearing a dull *thunk* to his right.

An arrow was embedded into the ground, inches from where his head had been.

Kyle limped forward, each step sending a stabbing pain through his ankle. His ankle gave out again, and he stumbled into the cliff wall to his right, bracing himself against it.

"Help!" he cried at Darius's retreating back. Darius spun around, spotting Kyle. The bodyguard cursed, sprinting back to him and grabbing him by the arm. He turned around, then froze.

Dark shapes moved within the fog some twenty feet from where they stood.

"Back!" Darius shouted, whirling Kyle around and wrapping an arm around his waist. They ran in the other direction, Kyle hopping on his good ankle. Then Darius skid to a halt.

More shadows in the fog ahead…moving right toward them.

Kyle glanced behind him, and saw the dark shapes closing in, hazy figures in the fog.

They were surrounded!

Kyle clutched at Darius's arm, watching as the shadowy outlines on either side of them grew sharper, more distinct. They were men, Kyle realized…nearly a dozen of them. Out of the mist they came, big, burly men wearing armor made of thick leather over chain mail, most carrying a sword and shield, one holding a crossbow. They surrounded Kyle and Darius, still huddled against the cliff wall. Darius stepped in front of Kyle, shielding him. One of the armored men – bald, with a scar over his left eye – strode forward, pointing the tip of his sword at Darius.

"Hand over the boy," he ordered.

Darius said nothing, not budging from where he stood. The man with the crossbow raised it, aiming it at Darius. The bald man sighed.

"Come now, give us the boy," he stated. "We had an agreement."

Kyle's blood went cold.

"What?" he blurted out.

"Ignore him," Darius stated, still staring at the bald-headed man, who smirked.

"Looks like our *friend,*" he said, "…is having second thoughts about our agreement." His smirk faded. "The terms have changed. You give us the boy," he ordered, "…or you die."

Still Darius stood there, saying nothing. Kyle slipped to the side away from the bodyguard, his back pressed against the cliff. He stared at Darius, hardly believing what he was hearing. The bald man sighed again.

"I don't have time for this," he muttered, turning to the man with the crossbow. "Kill him already."

The crossbow *clicked.*

Darius jerked to the left, his hand going to his thigh. He swung his arm forward just as a crossbow bolt slammed into the cliff wall inches from his head, something flying out of his hand. The man with the crossbow jerked backward, the hilt of a dagger jutting out of the center of his forehead.

He collapsed to the ground with a *thump*.

"Go!" the bald man shouted.

Two of the armored men stepped forward, shields raised, swords in hand. They inched forward toward Darius, spreading apart to flank him on either side. Kyle hesitated, staring at the men, then at Darius.

Give us the boy...we had an agreement.

The men continued inching forward, their eyes on the bodyguard. Despite every fiber of his being telling him not to, he ducked behind Darius, his heart hammering in his chest. Darius took a step forward, shielding Kyle, his fists clenched at his sides...and his sword still in its scabbard on his back.

One of the men lunged forward, raising his sword, then swinging it down at Darius's head.

"Darius!" Kyle cried out.

Darius raised one armored forearm, and the sword slammed into it, sparks flying from the impact. The cruel blade slid down Darius's arm, and Darius reached out with his other hand, grabbing the man's shoulder and yanking on it. The man stumbled forward, and Darius brought his knee up into the man's chest with a horrible crunching sound.

The man fell to the ground like a rag dog, bloody pink froth bubbling from his lips.

The other swordsman hesitated, glancing down at his fallen comrade. Darius reached for the hilt of his sword, slowly unsheathing the massive blade from its scabbard. The swordsman roared, swinging his sword at Darius. Darius stepped aside, the blade narrowly missing him, and swung his own sword, chopping at the man's neck. The man's head separated from his shoulders in a spray of red, falling to the ground. His headless corpse struck the ground next to it, limbs twitching once, then again. Darius stood over the body, staring coolly at the nine remaining men.

"What are you waiting for?" the bald man growled. "Get him!"

The men charged.

"Run!" Darius yelled, grabbing Kyle's arm and yanking him to the right. The bodyguard bolted, sprinting toward one of the swordsman rushing him. Darius swung his sword just as the other man did, his massive machete-like blade sending the man's sword flying from his hands. Darius shoved the man out of the way, sprinting past him, pulling Kyle along with. Kyle stumbled after the bodyguard, hearing shouting behind them. Pain shot through his ankle with every other step, and he cried out, his leg buckling underneath him.

"Darius!"

Darius cursed, stopping to pull Kyle up onto his feet.

"On my back, *now!*" he barked.

Kyle scrambled onto Darius's back, and the bodyguard sprinted forward again, running down the narrow corridor between the cliffs. Kyle glanced over his shoulder, seeing the swordsmen rushing toward them, only a few feet behind.

"Go, go!" Kyle yelled.

Darius picked up speed, bursting out of the corridor and into the open woods, dodging trees as he made a mad dash into the misty forest. Voices shouted behind them, men spilling out of the valley after them.

Kyle clung onto Darius's back, watching as they slowly pulled away from the men running after them, gaining distance with every step. He felt a surge of hope…they were going to make it!

Then he felt something *slam* into him, saw the world spinning madly around him. His shoulder smashed into the ground, air exploding from his lungs. He saw Darius land a few feet away, his temple bouncing off of the hard dirt.

The bodyguard lay there on the ground, lifeless.

Kyle gasped for air, loose dirt filling his nose and mouth. He coughed, his nose and throat burning, tears welling up in his eyes. He rolled onto his back, falling into a fit of coughing again. He blinked away his tears, seeing a shadowy figure descending through the mist from high above.

Black boots, then a hint of red fabric. A blood-red cloak, its thick fabric billowing in the breeze. Pulled tight at the waist by a thick black sash, a green diamond-shaped symbol sewn into it.

It was a man, Kyle realized. A man in a red cloak, his features hidden behind a deep cowl. The cloaked figure continued to descend, landing a few feet away from where Kyle and Darius lay. Kyle heard the clamoring of footsteps behind him, arched his neck to see the swordsmen forming a ring around them.

The man in the red cloak stared down at Kyle and Darius. The bald swordsman walked up to Darius, kicking him onto his back with a shove of his boot.

"Nice try," he muttered. He glanced up at the cloaked man. "Bastard managed to kill Ricart and Goff." He stepped on the bodyguard's right forearm, reaching down and taking Darius's sword from him. Or at least he tried to; he struggled to lift the massive sword, barely able to do so, even with two hands.

"He'll be dealt with," the cloaked man replied.

"I'll deal with him right now," the bald man promised, dropping Darius's sword and grabbing the hilt of his own with both hands. He raised the sword above his head, then swung it down in a vicious arc at Darius's exposed neck.

"No!" Kyle screamed, turning away at the last minute and squeezing his eyes shut. He heard a loud *clang*, and then a shrill scream.

"Enough!" the cloaked man shouted. Kyle opened his eyes, staring up at the man. "Move again," he growled, "...and these men will spend the rest of the day scraping you off of these trees."

Kyle turned his head, seeing Darius kneeling on one knee, his sword in his right hand. The bald man stood a few feet behind, clutching at his right wrist. Blood spurted from the stump where his hand used to be, the ends of his forearm bones jutting from his flesh, gleaming impossibly white.

Kyle gagged, bitter fluid filling his mouth.

"I told you," the cloaked man said, turning his shadowy gaze to the bald man, "...that he would be dealt with." He gestured at the severed hand lying on the ground beside Darius. "Did you learn your lesson?"

The bald man grimaced as another man pressed a wadded-up cloth against his stump, then nodded once, his eyes on the ground.

"Yes sir," he muttered between clenched teeth.

The red-cloaked man turned to face Darius again, his face still half-hidden in the shadows thrown by his cowl. Kyle noticed a faint, familiar blue light surrounding the man. His eyes widened.

"Darius, he's a Weaver!" he warned.

"No shit," Darius grumbled, rising slowly to his feet. Men surrounded him immediately, their swords bared.

"Rest assured," the Weaver stated, "...that you will pay for those you've killed." His jaw rippled. "With a greater cost than your own worthless life." He turned to Kyle. "Grab him."

Kyle saw two leather-clad arms reach down for him, felt hands grabbing him under the armpits and hauling him to his feet. A man grabbed his chin, forcing it upward and exposing his neck. Kyle felt cold, sharp metal press against his throat.

The Weaver stepped up to Kyle, pausing before him. The almost imperceptible gravity shield surrounding the man pressed up against Kyle's chest, forcing him to take quick, gasping breaths.

"Remarkable," the Weaver breathed.

The pressure on Kyle's chest vanished.

The Weaver hurled backward through the air, slamming into a tree twenty feet away. The knife at Kyle's neck yanked away, flying straight toward the Weaver, burying itself hilt-deep in the man's chest.

"What the...!" the man holding Kyle yelled. His grip on Kyle's neck loosened, and Kyle ducked down and forward, breaking away. He made a mad dash toward Darius, hearing men shouting behind him.

"Darius!" he cried, nearly colliding with the bodyguard. Darius shoved Kyle behind him.

"Down!" Darius barked. Kyle ducked, turning around to see a swordsman rushing at them, sword bared. He felt the wind of the bodyguard's blade as it passed mere inches above his head, saw the dull flash of the metal as it cut in an arc toward the swordsman's neck. The swordsman's head toppled backward, a gaping red gash in his throat. Then he burst into flames, hurtling backward through the air like a rag doll.

Darius looked at the burning body rolling to a stop on the forest floor, then stared at his own sword in bewilderment.

"Darius!" Kyle cried, spotting two more swordsmen rushing them. Darius raised his sword, but before the men could reach him, they too burst into flames, then flew upward high into the air, well above the treetops. Their burning bodies fell to the ground with a dull *thud*, their flesh spitting and crackling as the fire consumed them.

The six remaining swordsmen stared at their fallen comrades, their eyes wide. Then they turned and ran.

A shadow descended through the mist ahead of the fleeing men, bursting through the thick veil of white. It was a man dressed all in black, with short hair white as snow, a long metallic staff in his right hand.

"Kalibar!" Kyle cried, his heart bursting with elation.

Kalibar landed on the forest floor, cutting the swordsmen off. They skid to a halt in front of Kalibar, their weapons bared. The former Grand Weaver stared at the half-dozen men, his eyes as hard as steel.

"Good morning, gentlemen," he called out. His gaze swept over them. "Do you know who I am?"

One of the men glanced at the others, then turned to Kalibar, nodding. Kalibar's lips curled into a smile, but his eyes remained hard.

"Good," he replied. "Then you understand how very dead you are."

Kyle felt a slight vibration in his skull, saw a faint blue gravity field appear around himself and Darius.

The air before the six men *exploded*.

Kyle flinched backward, colliding with Darius. He squeezed his eyes shut against the sudden flash of light, hearing what sounded like dozens of hailstones striking the ground and trees all around them.

Then there was silence.

Kyle opened his eyes, spotting Kalibar still standing there, fifty feet away or so. The swordsmen, however, were gone.

"Kalibar!" Kyle cried again, rushing forward as the gravity shield around him vanished. He ran up to the former Grand Weaver, slamming into him and giving him a big bear hug. Kalibar hugged him back, not even budging with the impact. After a moment, Kyle pulled away, grinning up at the man.

"Are you two all right?" Kalibar asked. Kyle nodded.

"We're okay," he answered. He turned around, seeing Darius walking toward them. A chill ran down his spine as he remembered what the bald-headed man had said.

We had an agreement.

"What happened?" Kalibar asked.

"A dozen men surrounded us," Darius answered, stopping before Kalibar. "I killed a few, then ran for camp. The Weaver stopped us." He glanced at the dead Weaver in his blood-red robes, still pinned against the tree trunk by the dagger in his chest. Kalibar followed his gaze, his jawline rippling.

"They're wearing the same uniforms as the men who attacked our carriage," Kalibar observed. "We *were* followed." He turned back to Kyle and Darius, shaking his head. "I can't believe I let you two leave the camp," he muttered. "You almost died...and for what? Firewood?"

Darius said nothing, and Kyle lowered his gaze. Kalibar hadn't been the one to suggest that they go into the woods, after all...that had been Darius.

Give us the boy.

"I apologize," Kalibar said, turning to Kyle. "I allowed myself to grow complacent, and it nearly cost you your life. I will not make the same mistake again."

"It's okay," Kyle said, not looking up. "You saved us."

"Barely," Kalibar retorted. "It was pure luck that I managed to hear your screams and get here in time." He sighed, then turned around, gesturing for them to follow him. "Let's get back to camp."

Kyle walked beside Kalibar staying close to the man. Darius walked ahead of them, his golden armor gleaming dully with each step. The bodyguard passed the red-cloaked Weaver's corpse, kicking it as he passed. It fell from the tree, landing face-first in the dirt with a *thump*.

They walked through the dense fog back toward the camp, Kyle's eyes on Darius the entire way. He *had* to tell Kalibar about what had really happened...about Darius. Not now, of course...not with the bodyguard present. But the minute Kyle and Kalibar were alone, Kyle would tell the former Grand Weaver the truth.

* * *

The camp was just as they'd left it, with the bag of sweetroot still laying on the ground next to the burnt-out campfire. Darius walked into the ring of wards, Kalibar and Kyle following close behind. Kyle glanced up at Kalibar; the older man was lost in thought, his eyes downcast. He hadn't said much of anything since the attack. Kyle was about to ask what he was thinking when Kalibar cleared his throat.

"I'm activating the wards," he warned. The wards flashed a faint blue, and the half-dome of the camp's gravity shield appeared all around them. Kyle sat down on his still-floating sleeping bag, feeling a little lightheaded. He looked down at his hands, realizing they were shaking a bit.

"Are you all right?" Kalibar asked. Kyle nodded.

"I'll be okay."

Kalibar sat down next to Kyle, putting an arm around his shoulders.

"You haven't seen much death in your life, have you," Kalibar stated. Kyle nodded again. He'd seen the bodies littering the ground after the attack on Kalibar's carriage days ago, but it'd been dark...he hadn't really seen much. But today...

"Combat is nasty business," Kalibar admitted. "But the deepest wounds are often to the mind." He sighed. "If you don't tend to them, they can leave scars far more damaging than any to the body."

Kyle said nothing, remembering the swordsman that Darius had decapitated, how the man had gone from alive to dead in a fraction of a second. He touched his throat, remembering the knife that had been pressed there. To think that *he* could have died that easily...that if Kalibar had been a few seconds later, he'd almost certainly be dead.

"We soldiers don't win wars," Kalibar said, interrupting Kyle's thoughts. "Politicians do. Soldiers *survive* wars. Wounds to the flesh heal with time, and wounds to the mind heal with words." He patted Kyle on the shoulder, smiling at him. "If you ever want to talk, I'm here."

"Thanks," Kyle mumbled. He shot a glance at Darius. The bodyguard was staring off into the forest, his massive sword back in its sheath on his back. Blood stained his golden armor.

"*Can* I talk to you?" Kyle asked Kalibar, turning to the old man. Kalibar smiled.

"Of course."

"I mean, alone," Kyle added in a near whisper, glancing at Darius again. Kalibar nodded.

"Yes, we..." he began.

"Guys," Darius interrupted, his voice terse. Kalibar frowned, turning to face the forest. Then he stood abruptly. Kyle followed Darius and Kalibar's gaze.

There, at the edge of the forest, white fog was flowing toward them. It wrapped around the tree trunks, spilling onto the ground beyond the forest, forming misty fingers that hovered low to the ground. Onward it came, until it struck the edge of the camp's wards, wrapping around the protective dome. Within moments it had completely encircled them, a sea of fog no more than a foot tall, but so dense that nothing could be seen beneath it.

And there, at the edge of the tree line, a man in a black cloak stood.

Kyle felt a chill run through him.

The man stared at them, his black cloak rippling in the breeze. Mist surrounded his black boots, licking at the edges of his cloak. The hood of his cloak was pulled forward, hiding his face in shadow.

And then he began to move toward them.

"Kalibar…" Kyle warned, taking a step backward. Kalibar said nothing, watching as the cloaked man approached. He didn't walk through the fog toward them, he *floated* over it, as if he were standing on an invisible conveyor belt. The fog swirled behind him, stirred up by his passage.

He reached the edge of the wards, and stopped.

"Identify yourself," Kalibar commanded, his tone icy. "Or die."

The cloaked man paused, then reached up with both hands, grasping the front edges of his hood. His fingers were long and thin, and terribly pale. He drew the hood back.

Kyle gasped.

The man's face was as pale as his hands, his skin appearing as if it had been pulled tight against his bones. His cheeks were hollowed, his lips thin. His hair was short and black, and impeccably groomed. And in the center of his forehead was a large, diamond-shaped green crystal, its innumerable facets shimmering dully.

He stared at them silently, his black eyes moving from one person to the next, until they rested on Kalibar.

"You can call me," he stated, his voice surprisingly deep, "…the Dead Man."

"We will," Darius growled.

The Dead Man ignored Darius's remark, his eyes still on Kalibar. Kyle swallowed in a dry throat, unable to help himself from staring at the man. He carried himself with an eerie sort of calm, and would have been considered handsome if he hadn't resembled a freshly exhumed corpse. The Dead Man's eyes flicked over to Kyle, and Kyle drew back involuntarily, the hair on the nape of his neck standing on end.

"Do you know who I am?" Kalibar asked, holding his staff before him. The Dead Man's lips twisted into something that resembled a smile.

"How could I not?"

"Then you know what I'm capable of," Kalibar warned. The Dead Man said nothing for a moment, his eyes dropping to regard Kyle. Kyle found himself unable to hold the man's gaze, and dropped his to the ground.

"You are capable," the Dead Man replied, his eyes turning back to Kalibar, "...of greatness." He smiled again. "And unlike most men, you have achieved it."

Kalibar frowned.

"Why are you here?" he asked.

"I admire you, Kalibar," the Dead Man stated. "You must understand that I hold you in the highest respect."

"I asked you a question," Kalibar retorted. The Dead Man paused, then nodded.

"Of course," he apologized.

"Then *answer* it," Kalibar growled.

"I am here," the Dead Man replied, "...because of Orik."

Kalibar took a step forward, his eyes locked on the Dead Man's, the gravity shield of the camp's wards shimmering between them.

"So you work for Orik," he deduced, drawing himself up to his full height. The Dead Man smirked.

"Quite the reverse," he replied. "Orik was my student," he added. "...and like any good teacher, I want for him to succeed."

"So *you* ordered my assassination?" Kalibar pressed. The Dead Man shook his head.

"Not at all," he countered. "Orik disobeyed a direct order when he moved against you. He was not to disturb you, or interfere if you sought re-election. But he is unwise, and has exercised his free will. What is done is done." He sighed. "Now I have to clean up the mess he made."

"And who do *you* work for?" Kalibar inquired.

"That," the Dead Man answered, "...is...complicated."

The fog around the camp grew heavier, now rising several feet above the ground. It spilled over the lake behind them, obscuring the water. Kyle stared at the Dead Man, realizing that the fog was pouring out from all around the man...that it was coming from *him*.

"I've got time," Kalibar retorted. The Dead Man shook his head.

"Oh no," he countered. "I'm afraid your time has run out."

Rays of blue light shot outward from the green crystal on the

Dead Man's forehead.

"Kalibar!" Kyle warned, ducking low.

The rays extended to each of the wards around the camp, to the crystal atop Kalibar's staff...and even to Kalibar himself. Kyle took a step back, then looked down, seeing rays of the blue light shining on *him*.

"Kalibar..." Kyle repeated, looking up at the former Grand Weaver. Kalibar was staring at him, clearly confused.

"The..." Kyle began...and then the gravity shield around them winked out.

"Get back!" Kalibar cried. Fog spilled into the camp from all sides, rushing toward them. Gravity shields appeared around Kyle and Darius. Kalibar put his mirrored sunglasses on with one hand, then raised his staff toward the Dead Man. Then he frowned, staring at his staff in disbelief. The staff's runes were no longer glowing.

The Dead Man smirked.

Kalibar threw his staff to the ground, a ball of fire appearing in front of him. It shot out at the Dead Man with incredible speed.

Layer after layer of gravity shields sprung up around the Dead Man, the fireball deflecting to one side of them. The fireball traveled around the man in a tight arc, hurtling right back toward Kalibar.

"Watch out!" Kyle cried.

Layered gravity shields appeared instantaneously around the former Grand Weaver, and the fireball splashed against them, disintegrating on impact.

"Go on," the Dead Man offered.

Suddenly four massive boulders shot up from the fog around the Dead Man, sending sprays of dirt and mist high into the air. The boulders hovered there for a split second, then crushed inward, slamming into the Dead Man's layered shields.

The Dead Man didn't so much as blink.

More dirt and rocks shot up from the fog all around the Dead Man, coalescing onto his shields. Within seconds, the man was completely covered in a thick sphere of earth and stone.

Kalibar's eyes narrowed.

One of the boulders in the earthen sphere began to glow a faint red. The redness spread across the sphere until the entire thing was glowing. The air around it rippled with the immense heat, and even with the gravity shield surrounding him, Kyle could feel the intense warmth on his exposed flesh.

The sphere *exploded*.

Kyle jerked backward, flinging his arms in front of his face. Red-hot debris flew outward in all directions, ricocheting off of his gravity shield. The fog blew backward from the explosion, exposing the ground below. Lumps of glowing stone scattered onto the ground, setting fire to the grass.

And almost instantly thereafter, the fog slithered inward, suffocating the flames. Kyle watched as it filled the gaping hole left by the blast. Watched as it gathered around the still-rippling cloak of the Dead Man.

Who still hadn't moved.

"Elegant," he congratulated, nodding slightly at Kalibar. "Crush, suffocate, immolate." He smiled. "So refreshing to meet an intelligent Weaver."

"I'm just getting started," Kalibar shot back. The Dead Man gestured at Kalibar with one hand.

"By all means."

Kyle felt something *shift*, felt the hairs on his arms rise up.

A jagged bolt of lightning shot down from the sky, slamming into the Dead Man's shields with an ear-splitting *boom*. The fog burst back from the impact, its surface rippling violently. Thunder echoed off of the cliffs in the distance, the trees at the edge of the forest blowing backward, leaves tearing free from their branches. The ground around the Dead Man glowed bright white for a split second, then faded, leaving a black, charred scar in the earth.

The fog rolled inward, slowly filling the void.

"Impressive," the Dead Man murmured, a smile on his thin, pale lips. "Attempting to bypass my shields with an electrical gradient." Kalibar nodded back.

"Equally impressive that you survived."

Kalibar's eyes narrowed, and suddenly the outermost layer of the Dead Man's gravity shields winked out...and promptly reappeared.

The Dead Man smirked.

Kalibar grimaced, and the outer gravity shield winked out again...and then the next layer vanished. The third layer disappeared, but within a fraction of a second, all three reappeared again. Kalibar took a step back, and frowned, staring at the crystal in the center of the Dead Man's forehead.

"Interesting," he murmured.

"My turn," the Dead Man declared. Before he'd even finished speaking, a column of white-hot light shot outward from him at Kalibar, instantly dissolving the fog in its path. The impossible brightness seared Kyle's eyes, forcing him to squeeze them shut, the afterimage burned across his vision. The light vanished as quickly as it had come, and Kyle opened his eyes, blinking rapidly. He stared at the spot where Kalibar had been a second ago, fear gripping him.

He was gone.

"You'll have to do better than that," a voice called out from above. Kyle saw the Dead Man look up, the green gem on his forehead glittering as he tilted his head back. Kyle followed his gaze, spotting Kalibar floating some thirty feet above the lake.

"Very well," the Dead Man replied.

Boulders shot upward through the fog, sending misty contrails into the air, raining dust on the ground below. The boulders shot toward Kalibar, homing in on him. At the same time, huge spheres of water burst through the fog over the lake, crystallizing into pure ice as they flew up toward the former Grand Weaver. A half-dozen trees at the edge of the forest – nearly a hundred feet away – ripped up out of the ground, bursting into flames as they careened after Kalibar.

Kalibar dodged to the side as the volley shot toward him, but the missiles followed him, flying at him with formidable speed. He spun around in mid-air, facing the barrage. One of the boulders struck his shields, bouncing off. Another exploded into pieces before him, a sphere of ice shattering behind it. The burning trees split before him like water at the prow of a boat, sending burning chunks raining down into the fog-covered lake.

Kalibar stared down at the Dead Man, smiling grimly at his opponent.

"You've got power," he observed, "…but no strategy."

Then all of his shields vanished.

The Dead Man smiled.

A fist-sized stone hovering in the air behind Kalibar – a remnant of one of the shattered boulders – flew toward him, striking him in the back of the head. His head jerked forward, his body going limp.

And then he fell.

"Kalibar!" Kyle screamed.

The former Grand Weaver plummeted toward the thick fog below, slamming into it. A plume of mist shot up from the impact, followed by a spray of water. Kyle's heart leapt into his throat.

No!

Kyle broke out into a run, aiming for the plume of fog where Kalibar had landed. But a hand grabbed him from behind, hauling him backward. He twisted around, finding Darius standing behind him. The bodyguard held Kyle by the upper arms, his grip like iron.

"Darius!" he cried. "What are you doing?"

Darius remained silent.

Kyle struggled against the bodyguard, trying to free himself, but it was pointless. He gave up, watching as the fog swirled where Kalibar had fallen, feeling utterly hopeless. Darius pulled him backward, and Kyle felt a burst of anger.

"You traitor!" he spat, clenching his fists. "You're just going to let him die?"

Suddenly Kalibar burst upward through the fog, gravity shields glowing a faint blue in layers around him. He flew through the air in a tight arc, landing a dozen feet in front of the Dead Man. Kyle felt his heart soar.

"Kalibar!" he cried, straining against Darius's grasp.

Kalibar stared down the Dead Man, his brown eyes cold.

"You want to see power?" he asked, his voice icy calm. His lips curled into a tight smile. "I'll show you power."

A large blue sphere surrounded the Dead Man, far brighter than the man's layered shields. A powerful wind slammed into Kyle, nearly ripping him from Darius's grasp. Air shrieked past Kyle, the sound growing louder and louder, sucking the fog toward the Dead Man. Darius's grip on Kyle tightened, the bodyguard planting his feet on the ground. Small stones rolled across the exposed ground, shooting into the large blue sphere. They slammed into the Dead Man's shields, some of them penetrating the outermost layers.

The blue sphere grew brighter, the howling wind almost deafening now.

More stones flew at the Dead Man, penetrating further into his shields. Blacked logs flew up from the campfire, shattering as they struck the shields. Kalibar's carriage began to slide across the ground toward the glowing blue sphere, its wheels digging deep furrows in the earth.

The Dead Man's jawline rippled.

The sphere around him faltered, going suddenly dimmer. The wind began to die down, the stones around the Dead Man's shields falling to the ground. Kalibar smirked.

The sphere flashed bright blue.

Wind ripped into Kyle, knocking him off of his feet and pulling him toward the sphere. Kyle cried out, Darius's hands gripping his upper arms the only thing preventing him from flying away. The stones around the Dead Man flew inward, popping through layer after layer of his shields. His black cloak sucked flat against his gaunt frame, a few stones making it past his innermost shield and slamming into his body.

Yes, Kyle thought. *Yes!*

Then Kalibar's shields vanished, and his staff flew up from the ground, whipping through the air and slamming into the side of his head. The sphere around the Dead Man vanished instantly, and Kalibar slumped to the ground.

The Dead Man stared down at Kalibar, his black cloak falling loosely against his frame, the edges still rippling sinuously. Fog spilled outward from around his feet, obscuring the ground and swirling around Kalibar's motionless body.

Kalibar's arm twitched, and he groaned. He slid his hands and knees underneath him, and pushed himself up off of the ground. Blood oozed from his left temple, trickling down the side of his neck.

"Kalibar!" Kyle shouted. Kalibar's head turned, and he stared at Kyle for a moment, looking dazed. Then his eyes focused, and he looked up at Darius.

"Darius," he yelled back, waving with one arm. "Run!"

Darius didn't budge.

"Darius!" Kalibar repeated.

The Dead Man moved forward, his boots levitating above the ground, until he was standing over Kalibar.

"I was hoping for a challenge," he lamented. He shook his head. "How you managed to kill one of the Chosen is beyond me." He sighed, gripping the sides of his cowl with both hands and pulling it over his head, obscuring his face.

"Take them," he murmured.

Shadows burst through the fog at the tree line, flying through the air toward the camp. A dozen men in blood-red cloaks, hoods pulled forward over their faces, flanking two levitating black rectangular objects, each as large as Kalibar's carriage. The Weavers landed in a loose circle around Kalibar, Kyle, and Darius, gravity shields appearing around them. Kalibar took a step backward, facing one of the Weavers.

That Weaver's shields vanished, and then he exploded.

Another Weaver walked up to Kyle, grabbing him by the throat. Kyle tried to raise his hands to pull the Weaver off of him, but Darius's grip on his arms was unbreakable.

"Stop," the Weaver shouted. "…or we kill the boy!"

Kalibar spun around, his eyes meeting Kyle's, and froze. He stared at Kyle for a long moment, then drew himself to his full height, dropping his hands to his sides. Two Weavers strode up to Kalibar, grabbing his arms and pulling them behind his back.

The Weaver let go of Kyle's throat.

"Release him," the man ordered Darius, grabbing Kyle's arm. Darius complied immediately, and the Weaver pulled Kyle away, toward one of the black rectangular objects levitating a few inches above the fog-covered ground. Another Weaver grabbed Darius, pulling him in the same direction. The Dead Man raised one hand, and the Weaver holding Darius stopped.

The Dead Man floated up to Darius, his face hidden in the shadows of his hood.

"A wise man fights for the winning team," he stated, putting a hand on Darius's armored shoulder. "You are clearly a wise man."

"You're a traitor!" Kyle yelled, resisting the Weaver pulling at his arm. Darius ignored the comment, his eyes on the Dead Man. The Dead Man removed his hand from the bodyguard's shoulder.

"Unfortunately the boy is correct," he agreed. "You have no loyalty. I can only trust you as much as your former friends do." He nodded at the Weaver holding Darius. "Bind him and take him."

Darius stood still as the Weaver tied his wrists behind his back, his eyes still on the Dead Man. Kyle, Kalibar, and Darius were herded toward the two rectangular objects. Each had a pair of double-doors at the back, and they swung open without warning, revealing a plain gray interior, much like the inside of a moving van. Kyle and Kalibar were led into one of them, and Darius into the other.

The double-doors closed behind Kyle and Kalibar, leaving them alone inside.

Kyle stared at the double-doors, then turned Kalibar. The old man was turning in a slow circle, taking stock of his surroundings. There were no seats to sit on, and the ceiling was barely high enough for them to stand without their heads hitting it. Horizontal slits were built into each side wall at Kyle's eye-level, letting in a sliver of light.

"Are you okay?" Kyle asked, glancing at the still-oozing wound on Kalibar's left temple. Kalibar nodded.

"I'll be fine," he replied, putting a hand to his head and leaning back against one of the side-walls. He slid down onto his butt. "I've got one hell of a headache," he admitted. He sighed, looking up at Kyle wearily. "And you?"

"I'm okay," Kyle answered. He sat down beside Kalibar, and seconds later felt a sudden lurch, as if he were in a rising elevator.

"We're moving," Kalibar observed. His eyes narrowed. "These are flying carriages."

"Where are they taking us?" Kyle asked. Kalibar shrugged.

"I don't know," he admitted. "Frankly, I'm surprised we're still alive." He sighed, then put a hand on Kyle's knee. "I'm sorry, Kyle."

"For what?"

"I failed you," he answered bitterly. He shook his head again. "I thought I was the best Battle-Weaver in the world," he added. "Until today."

Kyle said nothing at first, feeling the carriage start to accelerate forward. He shivered in the relative coolness of the carriage, crossing his arms over his chest.

"You didn't fail me," Kyle countered. "Darius did." He turned to Kalibar. "I should have told you," he muttered.

"Told me what?"

"Back when me and Darius were attacked," Kyle explained, "...one of the bad guys said that Darius had been in league with them all along. That they'd had an agreement."

Kalibar stared at Kyle, saying nothing.

"He was in on it all along," Kyle continued. "I wanted to tell you...I was going to do it when we were alone."

"It's okay," Kalibar replied. "It wouldn't have mattered."

"What?"

"The Dead Man would have captured us anyway," Kalibar reasoned. "He's unlike any Weaver I've ever fought against." He lowered his head into his hands, rubbing his forehead. "That gem in his forehead...it must be a runic device."

"How can you tell?"

"It countered all of my attacks almost instantaneously," Kalibar answered. "I've never seen a runic device react like that...not even an Ancient device."

"Who do you think he is?" Kyle asked. Kalibar shrugged.

"I have no idea," he admitted. "All we know is that he's in league with Orik." He tapped his chin with one finger. "He said Orik was his student...but that Orik defied his orders when he attacked me." He frowned. "So Orik is – or was – controlled by the Dead Man."

"Wait," Kyle interjected. "So if Orik wins the election..."

"Then he might be just a puppet," Kalibar deduced. "The Dead Man – or someone above him – will be in control of the Empire." He shook his head. "And no one will be the wiser."

"We can't let that happen!"

"I agree," Kalibar said. "We have to find a way to notify the Empire of what's happening."

"But how?" Kyle asked. Kalibar sighed.

"I don't know," he admitted. "But I do know one thing...we're not going to win through brute force. I'm better than the Dead Man at making magic...much better. But that crystal on his forehead..." He shook his head. "I need to be smarter than that damn gemstone."

Kalibar fell silent, and Kyle stared at the sunlight shining through the horizontal slit in the opposite wall of the carriage. He felt the carriage accelerate forward gently. It moved without a sound, without even the howling of wind. The utter silence was unnerving.

"Where are they taking us?" he asked, knowing full well that Kalibar didn't know.

"I don't know," Kalibar replied. "Crescent Lake lies near the foot of a small chain of mountains," he added. "There used to be a few towns nearby, but they were abandoned over a century ago."

"Why?"

"Well, they were mining towns," Kalibar answered. "There were large kimberlite pipes underground..."

"Wait, what?"

"Kimberlite pipes," Kalibar repeated. "Columns of rock containing diamonds. The townsfolk mined them. Diamonds make excellent magic storage devices," he explained.

"Oh."

"The mines were very profitable," Kalibar continued. "That is, until strange things began to happen. Some miners went missing…at first just a few, but then more and more. A few men were found wandering the mines in a daze, covered in orange dust and screaming utter nonsense. When they recovered, these men claimed to have seen terrible things in the mines…huge monstrosities that attacked the miners, spitting acid and killing off many of the men."

"Wow."

"The Empire sent Weavers into the mines, but none returned," Kalibar stated. "Eventually, everyone became so terrified of the mines that people left to find other work. The nearby towns were abandoned."

"And now no one even knows that Crescent Lake exists," Kyle said. "Does anyone know about these mines?" If not, no one from Stridon would even think to look there…unless Erasmus eventually told them where they'd gone. It was a perfect place for the Dead Man to hide.

"Erasmus knows," Kalibar countered. Then he sighed. "But he thinks we'll be at Crescent Lake at least until after the election."

And that meant, Kyle knew, that they were on their own.

They fell into silence then, and Kyle stared idly at the slit-like window opposite him. He felt a sudden dip, his stomach lurching. He caught a glimpse of green through the window, and realized they were descending through the forest. The light shining into the carriage became dimmer…and then it winked out.

The carriage was thrown into utter darkness.

Kyle slid closer to Kalibar, felt the old man's arm slip around his shoulders. Faint orange light shone through the slits on either side, then went dark. Moments later, the orange light reappeared…then vanished again.

"Where are we?" Kyle whispered. Kalibar stood up, looking out of one of the slits.

"We're underground," he answered. Kyle stood as well, looking out of the slit. He saw a flash of orange – a glowing lantern – in the distance, set against an irregular stone wall. "The mines," Kalibar murmured. "We must be in one of the abandoned mines."

It made perfect sense, Kyle realized. No one would think to look for them in a mine that had been abandoned for a century…a mine that wasn't even on the map anymore. Even if someone *did* find them…if the Secula Magna sent Weavers to come and rescue them…they had no hope of ever succeeding. Not against the Dead Man.

Fear gripped him, and he stepped back from the slit, his heart pounding in his chest.

We're trapped, he realized. *We're never getting out of here.*

Suddenly the carriage jerked to a halt, throwing Kyle forward into Kalibar. Kalibar kept his balance, gently pushing Kyle back. He turned to Kyle, bending down and putting his hands on Kyle's temples, staring at him intently.

"We're prisoners now," he stated. "They're probably going to separate us."

"What?"

"You must survive," Kalibar continued. "You *must* survive. Do as they say, follow their rules…no matter what." He leaned in closer. "But no matter what they make you do, don't forget who you really are."

Kyle nodded, a lump rising in his throat.

"Survive," Kalibar repeated, staring at Kyle with unnerving intensity. "One day at a time."

There was a *click*, and then the back doors of the carriage swung open. Kalibar stepped in front of Kyle, and Kyle peered past the man's shoulder. Beyond the open double-doors was a long underground tunnel. It was as wide as a three-lane highway, the ceiling over two stories high. The floor, walls, and ceiling were made of jet-black rock intermingled with small white crystals that looked like quartz. Lanterns had been bolted to the walls in regular intervals, bathing the large tunnel in an orange glow.

Two red-cloaked Weavers stepped into view on either side of the carriage, followed by the Dead Man. He pulled his cowl back, revealing his pale face. The green crystal in the center of his forehead shimmered in the lantern-light as he turned to stare at Kalibar and Kyle.

"Exit the carriage," he commanded, his deep voice echoing through the tunnel. Kalibar stared back at the Dead Man, staying right where he was.

"The boy stays with me," he stated.

"I'm afraid not," the Dead Man retorted. He gestured for Kalibar to come forward, but Kalibar didn't budge.

The Dead Man smirked.

Suddenly Kalibar lurched to the side, slamming into the opposite wall of the carriage. A shield appeared around him just in time, and he ricocheted off harmlessly. Kyle heard a loud *crunch*, and looked up, spotting a few large black stones and hunks of quartz falling from the ceiling...right toward the Dead Man.

Who didn't even flinch.

The rocks bounced harmlessly off of his shields, and suddenly Kalibar's shields vanished, and he was flung sidelong into the carriage wall again. This time, his shoulder struck with a loud *thump*, and he cried out with the impact, grabbing his shoulder and falling to his knees.

"Kalibar!" Kyle cried. He ran up to the former Grand Weaver, putting a hand on his good shoulder. The Dead Man's eyes turned to Kyle.

"Come," he commanded.

Kyle froze, his hand still on Kalibar's shoulder. He stared back at the Dead Man, his heart thumping in his chest. Then he began to slide forward, pulled by an invisible force. He tried to plant his feet on the floor, but it was no use; he slid right out of the carriage, levitating a few inches above the ground in front of the Dead Man. The force holding him vanished abruptly, and he fell to the ground, stumbling a bit before catching himself.

"What is your name?" the Dead Man inquired, his black eyes glittering in the lamp-light. Kyle swallowed in a dry throat, staring up at the gaunt Weaver.

"Kyle," he mumbled.

"Well Kyle," the Dead Man replied. "I am taking you in to my family. I have high expectations of all of my children," he added. He lifted one pale hand, touching the side of Kyle's neck. Kyle flinched despite himself; the man's flesh was ice cold. "One of those expectations," he continued, "...is obedience."

He dropped his hand from Kyle's neck, making a slight gesture. The two red-cloaked Weavers stepped into the carriage, grabbing Kalibar by the arms and lifting him to his feet. They pulled him out of the carriage, stopping before the Dead Man. The Dead Man regarded Kalibar with his cold, black eyes.

"If you try to escape, the boy will suffer unimaginable torture," he murmured. "And you will die," he added with a finality that left no doubt in Kyle's mind that he would do exactly what he promised.

"I'm a dead man anyway," Kalibar countered, staring back at the Dead Man defiantly. "We both know that."

The Dead Man smiled.

"I think you'll find us more...creative than that," he murmured. He made another gesture, and one of the red-cloaked Weavers withdrew something small and white from his cloak, pressing it onto the nape of Kalibar's neck. Kalibar flinched, pulling his arm free of the other Weaver and reaching around to touch the back of his neck. But before he could even reach it, his eyelids fluttered, then closed, and he went utterly limp. The Weavers caught him before he fell, holding him upright.

"Take him," the Dead Man ordered.

A faint blue sphere appeared around Kalibar, and the former Grand Weaver rose upward, levitating a few feet above the ground. The Weavers flanked him, walking past the Dead Man and down the long tunnel.

"Kalibar!" Kyle cried. He tried to run after them, but the Dead Man stopped him with one chilly hand on his shoulder. The man's touch made Kyle freeze in place, a chill running through him.

"I regret that we had to meet like this," the Dead Man lamented. His voice – deep, yet gentle – was in stark contrast to his ghastly appearance. "You must understand how it pains me to treat a great man like Kalibar so callously." He sighed. "He has accomplished so much for our Empire."

"Just let him go," Kyle urged. "He doesn't want to be Grand Weaver!"

"True," the Dead Man agreed. "If only Orik could have believed that." He sighed again, then gestured down the long hallway. "Come," he added. "Walk with me."

"Where did you take them?" Kyle demanded, staying right where he was.

"Kalibar and the traitor are being held in separate rooms," he replied. "They will be treated with the dignity they deserve. If they behave, no harm will come of them." He leaned in then, his smile fading. "If *you* misbehave," he added coldly, "...they will suffer greatly for it."

Kyle felt the blood drain from his cheeks, and he swallowed in a suddenly dry throat. The Dead Man turned, moving forward down the long tunnel, his black boots levitating a few inches above the ground. His black cloak rippled sinuously behind him, despite the still air. Kyle followed alongside the man, his footsteps echoing off of the walls.

"You are one of us now," the Dead Man declared. He turned to regard Kyle, his eyes unblinking. "In time, you will understand how great an honor this is."

Kyle said nothing, lowering his gaze.

"You have enormous potential, Kyle," the Dead Man continued. He put a cold hand on Kyle's shoulder, and it took everything Kyle had not to pull away from the man's touch. "You will do great things for our cause."

"What cause?" Kyle asked.

"To guide the Empire," the Dead Man answered. "To nurture its people." He smiled, patting Kyle's shoulder. "One day, the Empire will far surpass the one that came before…the people you call the Ancients. Xanos wills it."

"Xanos?" Kyle pressed. The Dead Man nodded.

"The one true God," he clarified, his tone reverent. "We are his people. He has chosen us to do His work."

"To guide the Empire," Kyle mumbled.

"To save humanity from itself," the Dead Man corrected.

"Right," Kyle muttered under his breath. It all sounded like a crazy, twisted cult to him. But he held his tongue. They continued down the long, dark tunnel silently, following it for what seemed like an eternity. The floor angled downward slightly, and Kyle couldn't help but feel like he was walking into the very bowels of the earth…into Hell itself.

"You doubt the existence of our God," the Dead Man observed, breaking the silence at last. Kyle said nothing, his eyes downcast. "Understandable," the Dead Man conceded. "It is difficult to believe in something you have never seen."

"Have *you* seen him?" Kyle countered. The Dead Man smiled.

"Xanos is a divided God," he explained. "We Chosen carry a piece of Him within us. We cannot see Him, but we feel His presence."

"Chosen?"

"Those who are like me," the Dead Man clarified. "Those who bear a shard of Xanos," he added, tapping the crystal on his forehead.

"Wait, there are more people like…you?" Kyle pressed. The Dead Man smiled, but said nothing. They walked in awkward silence for a few more minutes, until the tunnel abruptly ended. There were two narrow paths leading left and right, and the Dead Man turned down the right one, continuing along it. Kyle followed, trailing behind the ghoulish Weaver. The path winded up a slight incline for a bit, leading to an even narrower tunnel carved into the dark stone. The long line of lanterns ended here, the tunnel beyond utterly black. Kyle hesitated, resting his palms on the rough, cool rock walls on either side of him.

"Ah, forgive me," the Dead Man said.

There was a flash of light, and Kyle squinted, spotting a small sphere of pure white light floating in the air a foot above the Dead Man's head. The light cast long, inky-black shadows up and down the length of the tunnel. The Dead man continued forward, forcing Kyle to follow close behind.

"Where are we going?" Kyle asked, peering over the Dead Man's shoulder. Even with the magical light, he couldn't see to the end of the tunnel.

"To the Arena," the Dead Man replied.

"The what?"

"The place where you will live from now on," the Dead Man clarified. "I train all of my Death Weavers there."

"Death Weavers?" Kyle asked. "Like the men in red?" The Dead Man nodded.

"They are my children, as you have become my child," he explained. "I will teach you as I have taught them, and as I taught their parents, and their grandparents, and their great-grandparents."

Kyle stopped in his tracks, staring at the Dead Man's back. The Dead Man paused, turning to face him.

"What?" Kyle asked. "You trained their *great-grandparents?*"

"And their great-great-grandparents," the Dead Man confirmed.

"But..." Kyle began, then stopped. He stared at the Dead Man, feeling his skin crawl.

"I am young, for a Chosen," the Dead Man explained. "This body will be one hundred and eighty-two in two weeks."

"That's impossible," Kyle protested. "No one can live that long!" The Dead Man smirked.

"I never said I *lived* that long," he countered.

"What?"

"I *am* the Dead Man," the Dead Man deadpanned.

With that, he turned back down the tunnel, continuing forward, his black cloak rippling slowly behind him. Kyle followed from behind, hardly believing what he'd just heard.

One hundred and eighty-two!

The Dead Man led them down the narrow, winding tunnel. After another minute, it took a sudden, sharp right turn, and opened up abruptly...into a massive underground cavern.

Kyle froze in his tracks, his eyes widening.

The cavern before him was truly enormous...beyond anything he had ever seen. It was larger than a football stadium, and similarly structured. It was as if he were standing at the very top row of a stadium, with row after row of seats descending down to a central, circular field made of packed dirt far below. Each row of seating was carved from the same black stone as the rest of the cavern, with cushions bolted to the rock for each seat.

Kyle looked upward.

The ceiling rose easily a hundred feet above the field below, short, thick black stalactites hanging down from it. In the center of the Arena, floating midway between the ceiling and the field below, a huge glowing sphere levitated. It was so bright that it lit the entire chamber, making it as bright as day. It pulsated ever so slightly, like a beating heart.

Beyond the circular field, opposite from where he stood, the ring of stadium seating was cleaved in two by a path that led from the field below to four large buildings carved into the rock walls of the cavern beyond. Each building was seven stories tall; a large pond divided the two pairs of buildings, its dark waters utterly still. A narrow bridge arched over the pond, connecting two streets that lay before the buildings.

And while the stadium was empty, the streets around the buildings far below were bustling with people...*hundreds* of them.

The Dead Man put a hand on Kyle's shoulder, gesturing at the massive cavern before them.

"Welcome to the Arena," he exclaimed, his deep voice echoing off of the stone walls. He smiled down at Kyle. "And welcome to your new home," he added. "Your past is behind you...and your future is here, with your new family."

Chapter 13

The Dead Man led Kyle down a narrow set of stone steps cutting through the stadium seats on either side, toward the empty field of the Arena below. Kyle followed behind the black-cloaked Weaver, the cool, damp air of the cavern giving him goosebumps. The voices of the crowds of people milling about beyond the Arena echoed throughout the huge chamber, getting louder as they descended. They reached the bottom of the stairs, and the Dead Man led Kyle to the center of the field. He stopped then, turning to stare down at Kyle with his glittering black eyes.

"How far along are you in your studies, Kyle?" he asked.

"Uh…" Kyle replied, "…you mean with magic?"

"Yes."

"I was learning how to sense magic," Kyle answered. The Dead Man frowned.

"You haven't learned how to weave yet?" he pressed, his tone incredulous. Kyle shook his head. The Dead Man's frown deepened. "I see," he murmured. "You've wasted a great deal of time."

Kyle dropped his gaze to his feet, feeling ashamed despite himself. It wasn't *his* fault he'd been born on Earth, after all. But he could never tell the Dead Man that.

"Close your eyes," the Dead Man commanded. Kyle glanced up at the Dead Man, then complied. "Tell me when you feel a vibration in your mind."

Kyle nodded, trying to clear his mind like he had before, when he'd been in the lake training with Kalibar. He felt a faint cool breeze on his skin, smelled the strong odor of dust in the air. He could hear the voices of the crowd beyond the field, and found himself trying to figure out what individual people were saying. Then he felt a familiar vibration in his skull, at his right temple.

"I feel it," he stated, opening his eyes and pointing to his right temple. "Here."

"Good," the Dead Man replied. "Now, keep your eyes open and do it again."

Kyle complied, and it wasn't long before he felt a vibration at his left temple. He pointed to it.

"Good," the Dead Man repeated. "Can you sense your own magic?"

"Not yet," Kyle admitted.

The Dead Man reached into the recesses of his black cloak, retrieving a clear gemstone roughly the size of an egg. Its facets sparkled brilliantly in the light from the levitating orb far above, and a pale blue glow emanated from within. The Dead Man handed it to Kyle, who held it in one hand, regarding it curiously.

"What is this?" Kyle asked.

"A diamond," the Dead Man answered. Kyle stared at the crystal, his eyes widening. A *diamond*! It was bigger than any diamond he'd ever seen…and he'd seen the Hope diamond at the Smithsonian the year before. He held it gingerly, afraid he might accidentally drop it.

"Close your eyes again," the Dead Man ordered. Kyle obeyed, holding the diamond out in front of him. "Bring the diamond to your forehead." Kyle did so, pressing the crystal against his skin. He sensed a slight vibration there.

"It's vibrating," he observed.

"No," the Dead Man countered. "You're merely sensing the magic radiating from the diamond."

"Oh," Kyle replied sheepishly. The man was right…the sensation was identical to when he'd felt magic earlier.

"Keep the diamond at your forehead," the Dead Man continued. "Sense the magic *within* it. Pull that magic into your mind."

"But how?" Kyle asked, opening his eyes.

"I didn't tell you to open your eyes," the Dead Man chided. Kyle felt a twinge of fear, and snapped his eyes shut. He stood there in front of the Dead Man, the diamond still pressed to his forehead.

"Will the magic into your mind," the Dead Man ordered. Kyle nodded, concentrating on the vibrations at his forehead. He tried pulling at it with his will, imagining the magic coming into the center of his brain.

Nothing happened.

Kyle grimaced, resisting the urge to give up and open his eyes. He tried again, but again, nothing happened.

Sense the magic within *the diamond.*

He concentrated on the vibration at his forehead, then followed it into the center of the diamond, and to his surprise, he felt a more powerful vibration there. He frowned, then pulled the diamond away from his forehead, and sensed the vibration move away at the same time. It was strange...he could *feel* the magic in the diamond, sense its exact position in space, even with his eyes closed.

Weird.

He tried *tugging* at the magic there, imagined his mind reaching out to grab it and pull it into his brain. He felt the vibration within the diamond shift, felt it move through the air toward the center of his forehead. He felt it *inside* of him then, humming in his mind's eye, and could almost *see* it there, pulsing like a tiny blue light in his brain.

"Open your eyes," the Dead Man commanded.

Kyle did so, feeling the magic dissipate. He found himself smiling. The Dead man smiled back.

"Well done," he murmured. "Now you know what magic feels when your mind has summoned it. Later, you will learn to summon magic from yourself, as you did with the diamond."

"From myself?" Kyle asked. The Dead Man nodded.

"Yes," he confirmed. "This diamond can store magic, like other gemstones. You can pull the magic from the diamond to store it within yourself, or even to weave it. But ultimately you must learn to use the magic your own mind generates."

"Okay."

"But first," the Dead Man stated, "...close your eyes again."

Kyle did so, the diamond still clutched in his right hand. His palm was sweaty despite the coolness of the Arena.

"Pull magic from the diamond again," the Dead Man ordered. "And hold it within your mind's eye."

Kyle complied, bringing the diamond back up to his forehead. He *felt* the magic within it, and brought it into himself again. This time it was far easier than the first, and within moments he could feel the power in his mind's eye...could *see* it pulsating there.

"Pull the magic to the back of your mind, then return it to the front," the Dead Man ordered.

Kyle nodded, concentrating on the tiny light in his mind's eye. He tried pulling it backward, and to his surprise it came easily, creating a thin, glowing thread in his mind's eye going front to back. He pushed it forward then, seeing another blue thread run parallel to the first.

"Got it," Kyle stated.

"Now pull it backward again," the Dead Man instructed, "…then left, then right, then forward."

Kyle obeyed, seeing more blue lines appear in his mind's eye…threads of magic vibrating slightly there, like strummed guitar strings. As he watched, the threads snapped inward, forming a pulsating knot of light in the center of his mind's eye.

"Whoa," Kyle breathed.

"You feel the knot?" the Dead Man asked.

"I do."

"Throw the knot outward in front of you," the Dead Man commanded.

Kyle complied, *pushing* the knot forward, and it shot outward immediately. There was a sudden flash of white light, so bright that he could see it behind his closed eyelids. He flinched, opening his eyes, but the light was already gone. He looked up, seeing the Dead Man staring down at him, a smile on his lips.

"What was that?" Kyle asked. The Dead Man put a cold hand on Kyle's shoulder.

"That," he answered, "…was weaving."

"Wait," Kyle replied. "…you mean I…?"

"Yes," the Dead Man interjected. "You weaved your first pattern…the light pattern."

"Cool!" Kyle exclaimed, feeling downright giddy. He'd woven magic!

"Well done, Kyle," the Dead Man murmured.

"That was pretty easy," Kyle stated. The Dead Man smirked.

"Yes it is," he agreed. "In fact, any eight-year-old here can do it." Kyle's smile faded, his pride wilting.

"You have a lot of catching up to do," the Dead Man stated, his hand remaining on Kyle's shoulder. "We expect a great deal from you," he added. Kyle lowered his gaze, unable to match the Dead Man's unblinking stare.

"Yes sir," he mumbled.

The Dead Man gestured down the path to the four buildings beyond, the street crowded with people.

"Come," he stated. "Walk with me."

Kyle complied, falling into step beside the Dead Man as the ghoulish Weaver levitated forward. They made their way out of the stadium-like Arena, taking the wide path toward the bustling street beyond. Men and women walked up and down the street; some were dressed in the blood-red cloaks of the Weavers Kyle had seen earlier, while others wore armor like the soldiers that had attacked him and Darius. Still others wore plain white uniforms. Kyle even spotted a few children in simple gray uniforms running about. Everyone turned to regard Kyle and the Dead Man curiously, and everyone gave the two a wide berth.

"This is our campus," the Dead Man explained, gesturing at the four buildings. "One thousand one-hundred and five people live here. Many of them are students, like yourself."

"A *thousand?*" Kyle asked incredulously. The Dead Man nodded.

"Only a fraction of them can use magic, of course," he stated. "There are two hundred and fourteen Death Weavers here...the rest are children or those who can't use magic." He gestured at one of the children, a girl in a gray uniform. "That is one of your peers, a student Weaver."

The Dead Man led Kyle across the campus, toward the leftmost building. People parted before them, bowing at the Dead Man as he passed.

"You will join your peers in their studies tomorrow," the Dead Man declared. "You will learn magic with them, eat with them, and live with them. They will become your brothers and sisters, as I have become your father."

Kyle said nothing, staring at his own feet as they walked, glancing at his left thumb.

You're not my father, he thought.

They reached the leftmost building, and the Dead Man walked Kyle up to the front doorway. There was no door, which Kyle supposed made sense...there was no rain here, after all. The Dead man stopped before a boy wearing a gray uniform.

"Jayce," he stated, gesturing at the boy, "...will show you to your room. You will obey him," he added. He turned to Jayce. "This is Kyle. Take him to his room and drill the light pattern." He turned back to Kyle. "Use the diamond today. Tomorrow I will teach you to use your own magic."

With that, the Dead Man turned and left.

Kyle turned to face Jayce, clutching the Dead Man's diamond in his right hand. Jayce was maybe a year or two older than him, and a few inches taller. Kyle gave him a weak smile.

"Hey," he greeted. Jayce stared back at him coldly.

"Follow," he ordered, turning around and walking through the doorway into the building. Kyle hesitated, then sprinted after the boy, falling into step behind him. They weaved through long, stone-walled corridors, passing other students as they went. The other students stared at Kyle as he passed them...and all of them looked as happy to see him as Jayce was.

Great, Kyle muttered to himself.

They turned down another corridor, this one leading to a wide staircase going up. Jayce led Kyle up the stairs, turning down yet another long corridor at the top. Eventually they came to a dead-end hallway with doors lining the walls on either side. Jayce stopped at one of the doors, pushing it open.

"Get in," he ordered, gesturing inside.

Kyle complied, stepping into the room beyond. It was tiny, barely big enough to fit the small cot within. The only other piece of furniture in the room was a small dresser. A single lantern bolted to the wall illuminated the small room. There were no windows, the walls made of the same black stone as the rest of the cavern.

Jayce sat down on the far end of the bed, glaring at Kyle.

"Weave the light pattern," he commanded.

* * *

Kyle slumped onto his narrow cot, staring at the door Jayce had just left through. He laid down gingerly, the wound on his back aching slightly as it pressed against the stiff mattress. He sighed, staring up at the black stone ceiling.

Thank god that's over, he thought.

Jayce had done exactly as the Dead Man had ordered, making Kyle weave the light pattern over and over again. And again...and *again*. He must have woven that damn pattern a hundred times. At *least* a hundred times. He'd gotten it wrong the second time...and Jayce had lunged forward, slapping him across the face...hard. He'd never been hit like that before. It'd made him see stars.

He hadn't screwed up after that…not once.

Jerk, Kyle muttered to himself.

He rolled onto his side, trying to find a comfortable position on the narrow cot. His stomach growled, but he didn't feel like eating. He closed his eyes, visions of bright threads of power weaving themselves in his mind's eye. Weaving the light pattern had become rote…mundane, even. The joy he'd felt in using magic had faded completely.

How terrible that Jayce could have taken something as awesome as using magic, and make it tedious and boring. Like school on Earth, but with beatings.

He wondered where Kalibar was…how the old man was doing.

He felt his stomach growl, and sighed, rubbing his eyes. He hadn't had anything to eat since he'd been captured, and when he'd asked Jayce, the older boy had ignored him. It had to be at least midnight, if not later, but he was so hungry that he doubted he'd be able to fall asleep. He laid there on his side, staring at the wall.

I'm never getting out of here, he realized.

He glanced at his left hand, flexing his thumb. It felt naked without his ring there. Without his *father's* ring there.

A lump rose in his throat, moisture blurring his vision.

I'm never going home.

He closed his eyes, rolling onto his belly. Silently, his face buried in his pillow, he wept.

Chapter 14

The Behemoth's eye flashes.

Ampir veers downward, flying straight at the black waters of the river. He slams through the surface and deep into the water, the river parting around his gravity shield. Darkness envelops him, and then a brilliant flash of green pierces the water behind him, creating a mass of bubbles and foam.

Vera and Junior scream, and Ampir feels Junior's arms tighten around his neck in a death grip.

Ampir flies upward, bursting from the surface of the water. Behind him, a wide swathe of the Great River is boiling, steam rising from its surface. The Behemoth's eye remains fixed on that boiling surface, no longer following him.

It thinks it got me, he realizes, feeling a surge of hope. He turns forward, seeing the cliffside less than a mile away now. The entrance to the evacuation tunnels is hidden along the cliffside, invisible to the uninitiated. But Ampir knows where it is.

"Ampir," Vera yells, pointing upward.

He looks up, spotting another airship flying a few hundred feet above them. More Weavers spill out of the ship. They follow him, but keep their distance...no doubt afraid of the Behemoth's deadly beam. As if sensing his thoughts, the Behemoth's eye turns toward him, tracking him once again.

Damn it!

Ampir looks to the rapidly approaching cliffside. Neither the ships nor the Behemoth will be able to follow him through the narrow evacuation tunnels once he gets there. Only the Weavers will be able to follow...and they won't stand a chance.

He hears Vera moan, and glances down at her. Her eyes are squeezed shut, grimacing against a wave of pain.

"Almost there baby," he says, flying low over the river. "It's almost over."

* * *

Kyle woke up to find Jayce staring at him from the doorway. He bolted upright, pulling his blanket to his chest. Jayce walked into the room without saying a word, and threw a stack of neatly folded clothes on the dresser opposite Kyle's bed.

"Put these on," he ordered. "Meet me outside." He turned, striding out of the room and closing the door behind him. Kyle watched him go, then turned to the dresser, seeing the clothes sitting there next to the Dead Man's diamond. The reality of his situation came flooding back to him – the attack, the abduction – and his heart sank.

He sat there for a long moment, staring at the clothes. He felt utterly exhausted...he couldn't have gotten more than a few hours of sleep.

"Hurry up!" he heard Jayce shout from behind the door.

Kyle sighed, dragging himself out of bed. He stood over the stack of clothes, then grabbed a shirt from the top. It was dark gray, and made of a thick, rough fabric. He took off his own shirt, putting the gray one on. Then he grabbed a pair of matching gray pants, unfolding them. He removed his own pants, slipping the new ones on. Then he stared down at the dresser, at the last remaining item. A black sash, with a green diamond woven into the fabric. He reached to pick it up, then stopped, his hand hovering over it.

"Come on!" he heard Jayce yell.

Kyle grabbed the sash, wrapping it around his waist, then tying it tight. He hurried to the door, opening it. Jayce glared at him from the doorway, then grabbed his sash, undoing the knot roughly.

"That's not how you tie it, moron," he admonished, re-tying the sash so that the knot was at Kyle's left hip. This made it so that the green diamond faced forward. "Grab the diamond," he ordered, gesturing at the dresser. Kyle turned around, spotting the diamond the Dead Man had given him yesterday. He grabbed it, then faced Jayce again. Without another word, Jayce turned around and walked down the hallway, gesturing for Kyle to follow.

Kyle trudged along, following the boy through the maze-like hallways of the dormitory. They weaved this way and that, going down one staircase, then another, until they emerged at the entrance to the building. Kyle shuffled through the doorway, staring at the Colosseum-like Arena in the distance. The huge stone sphere floating above the field glowed brightly, like a full moon in the center of the cavern.

"This way," Jayce ordered, turning left and walking down the street. Kyle followed along, being sure to stay close behind. The street was relatively empty compared to last night, with only a few dozen people milling about. Jayce led Kyle to the stone bridge arching over the large pond dividing the campus. In the middle of the bridge, at the top of its arch, stood a familiar figure.

The Dead Man.

Kyle felt a chill run through him, and hugged his arms to himself, letting Jayce lead him up the bridge toward the pale, gaunt Weaver. The Dead Man's black boots hovered inches above the stone bridge, his inky cloak rippling endlessly in the still air. The man's dark eyes followed Kyle as he followed behind Jayce, until the two were standing before the dark Weaver.

"Good morning Kyle," the Dead Man greeted, his deep voice giving Kyle goosebumps.

"Morning," Kyle mumbled. The Dead Man turned to Jayce, putting a pale, slender hand on the boy's shoulder.

"Thank you Jayce," he stated. "Wait for Kyle back at the entrance to Vortair."

Jayce bowed, then turned back the way he came. Kyle stared at the older boy's back, then turned – reluctantly – to face the Dead Man. The Dead Man looked Kyle up and down, a smile curling his pale, thin lips.

"Your uniform suits you," he opined. He reached out with one hand, smoothing out a wrinkle in Kyle's shirt. "Did you sleep?"

"A little."

"It will get easier," the Dead Man reassured. He glanced down at the diamond in Kyle's right hand. "Show me the light pattern."

Kyle paused, then closed his eyes, bringing the diamond up to his forehead. He *pulled* magic from it, weaving the thread of power in his mind's eye. After doing it so many times, the pattern came easily, almost automatically. He finished the pattern, throwing it outward. There was a flash of pure white light, fading in a fraction of a second. He opened his eyes, looking up at the Dead Man.

"Good," the ghoulish Weaver murmured. Then he held out his hand, palm up. "Give me the diamond." Kyle did so, handing it over. The Dead Man placed the diamond into the recesses of his cloak. "You've learned to weave with the diamond's magic," he continued. "But as a Death Weaver, you'll need to learn to use your *own* magic."

Kyle nodded, wiping his hands on his pants. Despite the cool air of the cavern, he was sweating.

"Magic," the Dead Man stated, "...is created in the brain. But it doesn't stay there unless you force it to," he added. "It is pulled into the bones of your skull." He gestured at Kyle. "Close your eyes."

Kyle did so.

"Focus your mind's eye," the Dead Man commanded. "Then concentrate on the very edges of that vision."

Kyle frowned, focusing inward. He pictured the same mental space he'd woven the diamond's magic in earlier. He followed the Dead Man's instructions, concentrating on the outer edges of that mental space. After a long moment, he opened his eyes.

"I don't see anything," he confessed.

"Don't look," the Dead Man replied. "*Feel.*"

Kyle sighed, closing his eyes again. He turned inward, focusing his mind's eye again. Seconds passed, then nearly a minute. Still, he felt nothing. He paused, then opened his eyes again.

"I don't feel anything," he muttered. "Sorry."

"Try again," the Dead Man pressed. "Be patient."

Kyle complied, closing his eyes yet again. He focused on the center of his mind's eye, seeing nothing but darkness. He waited, feeling his heart beating in his chest, his breath coming in and out of his lungs.

Still nothing.

He kept his eyes closed, keeping his focus on the blank space of his mind's eye. He thought he sensed a vague, almost imperceptible sensation just out of reach, a vibration in his skull. It was as if he were humming, but without the sound.

"I think I feel it," Kyle stated, keeping his eyes closed.

"Pull it inward," the Dead Man commanded. "...like you did with the diamond."

Kyle complied, reaching out with his will and *pulling* the vibration into the center of his mind's eye. He saw streaks of light converge inward from all directions, forming a small, pulsing pinpoint in the blackness. He held it there with his mind, feeling it struggling to escape his grasp.

"Got it," Kyle said.

"Weave the light pattern."

Kyle did so, pulling the light backward, then forward, seeing the pinpoint stretch into a thin thread. He pulled it back again, then left, then right, then forward. Within moments, the tangled thread snapped inward, forming a throbbing knot in the center of his mind's eye. He threw it outward, seeing the familiar burst of light through his closed eyelids.

He opened his eyes, and despite himself, he grinned.

"Well done, Kyle," the Dead Man congratulated. "You learn quickly."

"Thanks," Kyle mumbled, feeling his cheeks flush.

I did it, he realized. *I had my Awakening!*

He lowered his gaze, unable to keep the smile from his lips. He thought of Kalibar, and suddenly wished that the man was here. He would have been so proud. He pictured Kalibar standing there at the edge of Crescent Lake, and his giddiness seeped away.

"Is something wrong?" the Dead Man inquired. Kyle hesitated.

"Just wondering about Kalibar," he admitted.

"Kalibar is fine," the Dead Man reassured. He put a cold hand on Kyle's shoulder, and Kyle resisted the urge to pull away. "I have no desire to harm him," the Dead Man added.

Kyle glanced up at his captor, seeing those sunken, glittering eyes staring down at him.

"I admire Kalibar," the Dead Man continued. "He is a good man...one of the best I've ever met. We share the same goals," he added. "We both want what is best for the Empire."

Kyle dropped his gaze, saying nothing.

"It was never our intention to kill Kalibar," the Dead Man stated. "Or any of you...other than the traitor."

Right, Kyle thought.

"Kalibar and the traitor murdered a dozen of my children," the Dead Man murmured. He gestured at Kyle. "Yet I've let them live, given them a home. And now I've given Kalibar a new purpose, one that any man would enjoy." He smiled. "And you...I've treated you as one of my own."

Kyle swallowed, keeping his eyes on his feet. He couldn't argue with what the Dead Man was saying, but he knew the truth. This wasn't a home...it was a prison.

"The men that Kalibar and the traitor killed had wives and children who loved them. Friends who cared for them. They must be honored, and remembered. There will be a funeral for them tomorrow evening. I expect you to attend."

Kyle nodded.

"All actions have consequences," the Dead Man counseled. "If we don't witness the consequences of our actions, then we will never learn from them." He paused for a moment. "Is that clear?"

"Yes sir."

"Good," the Dead Man replied. "Weave the light pattern again," he ordered, "…using your own magic."

Kyle hesitated, then closed his eyes, focusing on his mind's eye. He waited, trying to feel the vibrations at the edges of his consciousness. He felt them much more quickly than before, and reached out to them, pulling them inward towards the center. They coalesced into a tiny sphere, which he wove into the light pattern. He threw the pattern outward, and was rewarded by a brief flash of light.

"Well done," the Dead Man congratulated. "The next step is to learn how to create light for a longer period of time." The Dead Man gestured, and a globe of white light appeared above his outstretched palm. "To understand how to do this, you have to understand more about how magic works."

The globe of light vanished suddenly, and the Dead Man lowered his hand.

"Magic is energy," the ghoulish instructor explained. "Like light, or heat, or magnetism. But magic is unique in that it can control all other forms of energy. When you throw out the light pattern, you are using magic to force the particles of air to release light."

Makes sense, Kyle thought. He'd learned a little about light in school, about how it was made of photons emitted from excited electrons.

"The light pattern requires magic to power it," the Dead Man continued. "The magic you weave to create the light pattern is only sufficient enough to power it for a split–second. You must continue to supply magic to the pattern if you want the light to last longer."

"How?"

"You have to send a 'stream' of magic to the pattern after you throw it out," the Dead Man explained. "Weave the light pattern, but hold it in your mind instead of throwing it out."

Kyle did so, closing his eyes and pulling magic into his mind's eye. He wove the pattern, then held it there.

"Got it," Kyle said.

"Now pull another strand of magic into your mind's eye," the Dead Man instructed "…and push it to the pattern."

Kyle front, knitting his eyebrows together. He concentrated, trying to hold the light pattern in place as he drew more magic from the edges of his consciousness. He pulled the magic inward, but the light pattern unraveled, sucking back beyond the edges of his mind's eye. Kyle grimaced, opening his eyes.

"I lost it," Kyle apologized.

"Try again."

Kyle did so, closing his eyes and weaving the light pattern once again. He held it there carefully, pulling more magic into his mind's eye. This time, he managed to hold the light pattern in place; it was a bit like trying to rub your belly and tap your head at the same time. He pushed this second dot of light towards the pulsating light pattern, and the dot stretched into a thin thread which fused with the pattern.

"Got it," Kyle said.

"You should sense a thread connecting to your pattern," the Dead Man stated. Kyle nodded. "This thread will connect your mind to the pattern after you throw the pattern out," the Dead Man continued. "Then you will be able to stream magic to the pattern through this thread."

"Okay."

"Throw out the pattern now."

Kyle did as he was instructed, *pushing* the pattern outward. He saw the remaining thread of magic in his mind's eye, watched it thin out like a stretched rubber band. There was a flash of light, but this time it did not fade away.

"Pull more magic from your mind, and send it through the magic stream towards the pattern," the Dead Man commanded. Kyle did so, and the light grew painfully bright. He turned his head away, losing control of the stream. The light winked out immediately.

"Well done Kyle," The Dead Man murmured. Kyle opened his eyes, looking up at the Dead Man, and saw a smile on the man's lips. "You have a gift for weaving."

Kyle smiled back; despite everything, he felt rather proud of himself.

"Again," The Dead Man ordered.

Kyle nodded, closing his eyes and weaving the pattern again. He grabbed another strand of magic – it was a bit easier this time – and pushed it to the pattern. Then he threw the pattern outward, and pushed magic to it through the stream. This time, he managed to keep the light going for a few seconds before he lost control of it.

"Again," the Dead Man ordered. "Longer this time."

"It's hard to do two things at once," Kyle protested. He thought he was doing pretty good, after all; Kalibar would have been amazed with his progress.

The Dead Man said nothing, staring down at Kyle for a long moment. Suddenly a globe of light appeared above the Dead Man's head. Then a second, and a third. More and more lights appeared, until there were a few dozen globes shining above him, illuminating the bridge.

Then they all vanished.

"*Again*," the Dead Man commanded.

* * *

Kyle stretched his arms up over his head, twisting his aching back left, then right. He glanced up at the Dead Man, waiting for more instructions. The ghoulish Weaver had made Kyle practice streaming magic to the light pattern dozens of times, until he had proven that he could hold the magic stream for as long as he wanted. His stomach grumbled loudly; he was practically starving. The Dead Man put a chilly hand on Kyle's shoulder, patting it gently.

"That's enough practice for this morning," he declared. "You still have a great deal to learn, but you're ready to join your peers in class today." He raised his hand from Kyle's shoulder, snapping his fingers loudly. Within moments, Kyle saw Jayce sprinting towards them. The older boy reached them at the center of the bridge, bowing to the Dead Man. The Dead Man nodded at Jayce. "Take Kyle to Mr. Maywind's class," he ordered.

"Yes sir."

Jayce turned around immediately, walking back toward the leftmost building. Kyle followed after the older boy, sprinting down the arched surface of the bridge to the street below. They made their way to the entrance to the building, walking inside. Jayce led Kyle through a maze of hallways, then up a flight of stairs, eventually stopping at an open door. Kyle peeked beyond the doorway; the room beyond appeared to be a classroom, with desks organized in rows facing a chalkboard. Every one of the desks was already taken by someone – girls and boys that looked to be about

Kyle's age – except for one at the front of the class.

"Sit," Jayce ordered, shoving Kyle through the doorway toward the empty desk. Kyle obeyed, walking up to the desk and sitting down. Two dozen eyeballs followed him as he sat. Kyle glanced to his right, seeing a short, black-haired boy to his right. The boy glared at him, then turned away.

Okay, Kyle thought.

Kyle turned to his left, spotting a girl sitting next to him. She was a little taller than him, and slender, with dark brown hair in a long ponytail. She had big, almond-shaped brown eyes…and it wasn't until she glanced over at him that he realized he was staring. He turned away quickly, his eyes on his desk.

Idiot, he muttered to himself.

A man strode through the doorway into the room, walking up to a long wooden desk at the front of the classroom. He sat down, staring at the students in front of him. He was a Death Weaver, dressed in the familiar blood-red uniform. He had long black hair and beard, with a pale white scar running down his left cheek.

"Good morning Mr. Maywind," the class greeted in unison.

"Good morning, class," Mr. Maywind replied. He leaned forward, propping his elbows on his desk, and turned to Kyle, gesturing with one hand. "We have a new student today," he announced. "Stand and introduce yourself."

Kyle hesitated, then stood, twisting around to face the class. The whole class stared back at him, each student looking as excited to see him as the boy to his right had been.

"I'm Kyle," he mumbled.

"Louder," Mr. Maywind ordered.

"I'm Kyle," he stated.

"Sit," Mr. Maywind commanded. Kyle did so, slouching in his seat. He could *feel* the other students' eyes on him.

"This," Mr. Maywind stated, standing up from his chair and pacing in front of the class, "…is Introductory Magic Theory." He stopped in front of Kyle's desk, looking down at him. "In this class, you will learn what magic is, how it works, and what you can do with it."

"Yes sir," Kyle mumbled.

Mr. Maywind turned away from him, pacing once again.

"Today we will continue talking about magic production," he lectured. "Yesterday we learned that magic is generated in the brain, and that some Weavers can naturally make more magic than others. Some make a large amount," he stated, glancing at Kyle as he strode by, "...while others make hardly any at all." He paused for a moment, a smirk curling his lips. "And these people become magic teachers."

Kyle heard nervous laughter from the back of the room.

"Luckily," Mr. Maywind continued, "...many of us who have little talent for producing magic can train ourselves, over time, to produce more. Now, how do we make our muscles grow?"

The dark-haired boy to Kyle's right raised his hand, and Mr. Maywind nodded at him.

"You lift weights," the boy answered. Mr. Maywind nodded again.

"Correct, Pipkin," he replied. He turned to Kyle. "And how do you produce more magic?" he pressed. Kyle stared back at the man, his mind going blank. Suddenly he didn't even remember the question. He heard more snickering coming from the back of the room...and from Pipkin, who smirked at him.

"By using magic," a feminine voice called out. Kyle turned to his left, seeing the pretty brunette sitting there. She glanced at him, smiling faintly. Unlike Pipkin's smirk, her smile seemed genuine...apologetic, even. He found himself smiling back, and blushed, turning away.

"Partially correct, Ariana," Mr. Maywind replied. "Using magic already stored in one's body does little to improve production," he added. "And using magic stored in a crystal does nothing to improve it. But if you use up enough of the magic stored in your body, you'll force your mind to produce more to replace it." He clasped his hands behind his back. "Only by taxing one's ability to *generate* magic can one improve that ability. Understood?"

"Yes, Mr. Maywind," the class stated in unison.

"Good," Mr. Maywind replied. "Now, unlike muscle, with magic there is no known upper limit as to how much a Weaver can make." He turned to another student in the front row. "Where is magic stored?"

The student stared at Mr. Maywind blankly.

"Perhaps our slower students would benefit from a hint," Mr. Maywind stated. "Magic is stored in the largest repository of crystals in your body. Which is?"

"Our bones," the girl to Kyle's left – Ariana – answered. Mr.

Maywind nodded, clearly pleased.

"Correct," he replied. "Magic is generated in the mind, and if not used, it flows through the skeleton." He pressed the fingers of both hands to his temples. "It flows to the closest bones to the brain first, the bones of the skull. When those bones are filled, magic flows from them to the bones of the spine, and then the rest of the skeleton. Understood?"

"Yes Mr. Maywind," the class replied. Kyle found himself answering along with the rest of the students.

"Now, the larger the bone, the more magic it can hold," Mr. Maywind continued. He gestured at a girl sitting a few seats to Kyle's right. "If I were to break your arm, what would happen?"

The girl said nothing, but turned very pale, no doubt worried that her teacher would resort to a demonstration.

"An *intelligent* student," Mr. Maywind stated, "...would deduce that breaking a bone would prevent a Weaver from accessing the magic stored in the bone past the break. In battle, you can use this to your advantage. Removing or breaking limbs will weaken your opponent significantly."

Kyle found himself glancing furtively to his left, at Ariana. She was writing something down on a small notepad, a few strands of hair falling in front of her face. She brushed them away, tucking them behind her ears, which were a little small. She looked to be as old as Desiree back home, but without the curves he'd found so utterly fascinating. She was almost the opposite of his blue-eyed, blonde-haired crush on Earth. Still, he found himself having a hard time looking away.

"Now," Mr. Maywind said, forcing Kyle out of his reverie. "We've all learned the simplest pattern of all – how to make light. But how does one make the light larger or smaller?"

The sound of shuffling feet echoed through the small classroom. No one answered.

"To make the light bigger, put more magic into the light pattern itself," he said. "The less magic you use while weaving, the smaller it will become. Understood?"

"Yes Mr. Maywind."

"And how do you make the light brighter?" he asked. There was silence, and then Ariana raised her hand again. "Ariana?"

"Put more magic into the magic stream," she answered. Mr. Maywind nodded.

"Precisely," he agreed. "I'm glad at least *one* of my students possesses the ability to think." Kyle found himself staring at Ariana again, and turned to look down at his desk. He thought about Ariana's answer; it made sense, in a way. It was like a flashlight...the bigger the light bulb, the bigger the light. The more electricity going to the light bulb, the brighter it would become.

"Now, don't try it here," Mr. Maywind said as lights popped up all around the room. The lights winked out almost immediately. "This is a class about magic theory, not application." He smirked then. "Mr. Tenson will be more than happy to have you practice during his class."

There were a few groans around the room.

"We've run out of time," Mr. Maywind declared, walking back to his desk and sitting down. "Never forget that Xanos is with all of you, watching you through His Chosen. Make Him proud."

"Yes Mr. Maywind," the class droned.

"Class dismissed," Mr. Maywind stated, waving them away.

The students rose up out of their seats around Kyle, bowing at Mr. Maywind, then filing toward the exit. Kyle stood, bowing awkwardly at his teacher, then following the line out of the classroom. He stepped out into the hallway, which was packed with students in gray uniforms. They were all walking down the hallway in the same direction, and Kyle followed the crowd, having no idea where he was going...or what was to come next.

Suddenly he felt someone elbow him in the ribs, and he doubled over, his breath catching in his throat. He turned, spotting a taller boy glaring at him. He stared back, rubbing his side. The boy disappeared into the crowd.

What was that *for?*

Someone smacked him in the back of the head...*hard.*

Kyle spun around, looking behind him. He saw a sea of faces staring beyond him, none of them paying him any mind.

The hell?

Kyle turned forward...and felt someone shove him to the side. He lost his balance, slamming his right shoulder into the wall. Two boys grabbed his arms, pinning them to the wall. A third boy stepped out of the crowd, cocking his fist back, and punched Kyle square in the belly.

Kyle doubled over, the breath exploding from his lungs. Bitter fluid rushed up into his mouth, and he nearly vomited. The hands holding his arms let go, and he sank to the floor, clutching his aching belly.

The boy who'd punched him leaned down, his lips at Kyle's ear.

"*That's* for my father," he growled.

The boy straightened up, then gestured for the other two to follow him. They rejoined the crowd, leaving Kyle sitting on the floor, his head between his knees.

Kyle grimaced, feeling moisture welling up in his eyes. He wiped it away with his sleeves, pushing himself up to his feet. He braced himself against the wall, holding his belly with one hand. The crowd moved past him, nobody so much as looking at him.

Great, he thought. *Just great.*

He sighed, then rejoined the crowd, shuffling down the hallway. He'd gone a few dozen feet when he felt someone grab his right hand. Kyle jerked it away, hugging his arms to his belly defensively. Then he realized who was grabbing him. It was the pretty girl from class...Ariana.

"Come with me," she said, holding out her hand.

Kyle hesitated, then took her hand. She pulled him to her side, walking down the hallway with him.

"Where are we going?" he asked.

"Cafeteria," she answered. "It's lunch time."

The hallway ended in a wide staircase, and Ariana led him down it to the first floor of the building. They turned left, then right, walking down another long hallway toward a pair of open double-doors. This doorway led to a huge room filled with rows of long tables. The room was easily four times as big as the cafeteria in Kyle's school back on Earth. Ariana guided Kyle to the left, joining one of several lines of students. At the front of the line, a few older men and women stood behind a line of tables brimming with food, doling out portions to each student at the front of the line. Although the line that Kyle was in was long, it moved surprisingly quickly, and it wasn't long before he and Ariana were at the front of it. Ariana took two plates, handing one to Kyle. She spooned various bits of food onto her plate, and then his, filling both. She then led him to one of the few remaining empty lunch tables in one corner of the cafeteria. She sat down opposite him, gesturing for him to sit as well.

"Better eat quick," she counseled. "We only get twenty minutes."

"Thanks," Kyle mumbled.

"I'm Ariana," she greeted, holding out a hand. Kyle shook it. "I'm Kyle."

"I know," she stated. She let go of his hand, staring at him for a long moment. Kyle held her gaze for a few seconds, then felt his cheeks burning, and lowered his gaze to his food. He didn't recognize anything on the plate, although it smelled appetizing enough. He picked up a glob of orange slop with his spoon, and nibbled at it. It tasted like mashed potatoes. His stomach growled at him, and he slurped down another spoonful.

"You're the boy they caught outside," Ariana stated. "Your friends killed a Death Weaver."

Kyle nodded, remembering the boy who'd punched him.

"How did he die?" Ariana pressed, leaning forward eagerly. Kyle hesitated, staring at her guardedly. "Tell me everything," she pleaded.

Kyle paused, then told her how Kalibar had arrived to save him and Darius in the forest, killing the soldiers and the Death Weaver. Ariana listened intently, leaning back in her chair when he'd finished.

"Good," she declared.

"What?"

"Good," she repeated, leaning forward again. A few strands of hair fell down fetchingly in front of her face.

"But..."

"I'm a prisoner here too," she interrupted, her tone hushed. "They kidnapped me like they did to you and your friends." She paused, then leaned forward a bit more, her big eyes staring into his. "Everyone here hates you."

"Wait, what?"

"The other students," Ariana answered. "They hate you." She gave a conspiratorial smile. "They hate me too. We're outsiders...the only ones who weren't born here." She gestured for Kyle to eat some more of his food, and Kyle obeyed, spooning up a piece of something that looked like chicken. He sniffed it, then took a bite. It tasted like chicken, too.

"They hate you more," Ariana continued. "Your friends killed a dozen soldiers and a Death Weaver," she added. "The boy that hit you, his dad was the Death Weaver."

"Ah," Kyle muttered. "Great." He paused, taking another bite of meat. "So...how long have you been here?"

"A year," Ariana answered. "I used to live in Mortown. They took me away and brought me to this...*place.*"

"Who took you?"

"The Dead Man," Ariana replied, spooning a gob of food into her mouth. She had rather full lips, which Kyle imagined would be enormously pleasant to kiss. He blinked, looking down at his plate, feeling his cheeks turn red-hot. He cleared his throat, trying desperately to think of something to say.

"He kidnapped you?" he asked rather lamely.

"And you," Ariana replied matter-of-factly.

"I'm sorry," Kyle mumbled, glancing up at her. She leaned back in her chair, crossing her arms over her chest.

"I'm angry," she retorted. "Sorry didn't get me anywhere." She leaned forward. "They feed off of sorry here."

"Huh?"

"They keep you afraid," she explained. "That's how they get you." Then she leaned back, regarding Kyle with a critical eye. "They already have you."

"No they don't," he retorted.

"Uh huh," Ariana replied. "You're even scared of the food." Kyle glanced down at his plate, realizing she had a point. "Finish up," she advised. "Lunch is almost over...and unless you do well in Mr. Tenson's class, that's all you'll get today."

Kyle did as he was instructed, polishing off as much of his lunch as he could. Then Ariana stood up, taking Kyle's plate and stacking it on top of hers.

"Come on," she urged.

Kyle stood as well, and followed Ariana to a table where students were putting their dirty dishes. She dropped their plates off, then joined the line of students heading for the exit. They went back upstairs, returning to the hallway where Mr. Maywind's class had been. But instead of going into that classroom, Ariana led Kyle two doors down.

"In here," she said, pulling him in. The classroom beyond was much larger than Mr. Maywind's, and there were no desks, no chairs...no furniture of any kind. At the front of the room stood a short man in a Death Weaver uniform. He looked older than Mr. Maywind, with short, salt-and-pepper hair. His face was lined with fine wrinkles, which deepened as he scowled at the students entering the class. The students lined up against the wall opposite the Death Weaver, and Ariana led Kyle to stand next to her in line. She leaned over, her lips near Kyle's ear.

"That's Mr. Tenson," she whispered. "He hits. Do exactly what he says. Don't talk back."

A few more students filed in, until they were all lined up against the wall facing Mr. Tenson. The Death Weaver glared at the last student who'd entered the room. It was Pipkin, the black-haired boy from Mr. Maywind's class. Pipkin stared back at Mr. Tenson, the color draining from his face.

"What are we forgetting?" Mr. Tenson growled, striding up to stand in front of the boy. Before Pipkin could answer, Mr. Tenson swung his hand, slapping him across the face. The loud *smack* echoed off of the stone walls, and Pipkin spun to the floor, landing on his hands and knees. Mr. Tenson turned away from the boy, turning to face the rest of the class. Pipkin rose shakily to his feet, then walked to the front door, closing it. He resumed his place in line, staring at his own feet.

"Who are you?" Mr. Tenson growled, pointing right at Kyle. Kyle's heart jumped up to his throat.

"Kyle, sir," he replied, his voice cracking. He blushed, half-expecting Mr. Tenson to walk up to him and hit him like he'd hit Pipkin, but the man just lowered his hand.

"I am Mr. Tenson," Mr. Tenson said. "You will obey me or you will end up like him," he added, gesturing at Pipkin, who was still rubbing the side of his face. "This is Introductory Weaving. I am your instructor. Show me the light pattern."

Kyle's mind blanked, terror seizing his gut. He saw Mr. Tenson's right hand go up.

Show me the light pattern.

Kyle closed his eyes, *yanking* magic into his mind's eye, then weaving it rapidly. He threw it outward, and saw a light flash briefly from beyond his closed eyelids, winking out almost as soon as it had appeared. He paused, then opened his eyes, seeing Mr. Tenson scowling down at him.

"Attach a magic stream next time," Mr. Tenson ordered. He walked down the line of students, stopping at Pipkin. "Boy," he spat, glaring down at Pipkin, "...show me the light pattern."

Pipkin closed his eyes, and a few moments later, a small, weak ball of light appeared in front of him. Mr. Tenson sneered, gesturing at the rest of the class.

"Your *colleague*," he growled, "…is demonstrating a weakly woven pattern with a pathetic magic stream." He gestured at Kyle. "Notice how impotent his light is compared to our newest student's."

Kyle swallowed in a dry throat, glancing at Pipkin, who was staring at the floor. A large, angry-looking welt was rising on his cheek.

"Mr. Maywind," Mr. Tenson declared, "…taught you how to change the size and intensity of your light." He strode past Kyle, stopping in front of Ariana. Kyle immediately tensed up. "Make a large, weak light," Tenson ordered.

Within less than a second, a pale light, easily twice the diameter of Pipkin's, appeared in front of Ariana.

Mr. Tenson nodded sharply. Kyle relaxed, realizing he'd been holding his breath. He threw a smile at Ariana, but she didn't react.

"Boy," Tenson growled, turning back to Kyle. Kyle stiffened, his smile vanishing instantly. "Make a small, bright light."

Kyle stared at Tenson, then closed his eyes, trying to remember what Mr. Maywind had said. A small light meant weaving the pattern with a small amount of magic. He wove the light pattern as instructed, using as little magic as he could. Then he attached a magic stream, throwing the pattern outward and *pushing* as much magic as he could through it. He'd never used so much magic before; it was light trying to lift a heavy weight, but with his mind.

A burst of impossibly bright light seared his eyes, even through his closed eyelids.

"Stop!" he heard Mr. Tenson shout.

Kyle dropped the magic stream, and the light winked out immediately. He opened his eyes, seeing large dark spots in the center of his vision. He glanced to his right, seeing Ariana – and many of the other students – blinking rapidly and rubbing their eyes.

Then he felt the right side of his face explode in pain, felt himself falling to the floor. He landed on his left shoulder, his left temple smacking against the stone floor. He didn't even have time to cry out. He grunted, looking up to see Mr. Tenson looming over him.

"Never," he growled, "…show off in my classroom again."

Kyle nodded, rising shakily to his feet.

"Yes sir."

"Boy," he said, pointing to a small, blonde-haired boy, "make a big, bright light." The boy closed his eyes, and quickly produced a softball-sized light that was as bright as a light bulb. Mr. Tenson shot a glare at Kyle, then continued down the line.

Kyle's face throbbed, and he resisted the urge to reach up and touch it. He glanced at Ariana, who stared back at him wordlessly.

Mr. Tenson commanded each student in the class to perform a variation of the light pattern, until each had performed nearly a dozen times. At the end of the class, he reiterated what Mr. Maywind had said – that the more magic put into the pattern, the greater the area of affect, while the more put into the stream, the greater the intensity.

It was a lesson that Kyle doubted he would ever forget.

When the class ended, Mr. Tenson excused his students. Everyone bowed, then formed an orderly line at the door, walking out into the hallway. Once safely out of the classroom, Kyle leaned against the wall, taking a deep, shaky breath in, then letting it out slowly.

Ariana leaned in, her lips brushing up against his ear. Her touch sent a shiver down his spine.

"Don't try so hard," she whispered. "You don't want to stand out here."

Chapter 15

The next morning, Kyle woke to the sound of Jayce knocking at his door.

"Coming," he yelled, sliding out of bed groggily. He'd been kept up late again last night being instructed by Jayce, and had hardly gotten any sleep...again. He yawned, hastily changing into his uniform. He tied his sash around his waist, making sure that the green diamond was properly centered. He'd just finished changing when Jayce opened the door.

"Took you long enough," the boy muttered, eyeing Kyle's uniform critically. Then he turned around, walking down the hallway. Kyle followed close behind, and after a short while found himself standing before the door to Mr. Maywind's class. He frowned, having expected a morning lesson with the Dead Man.

"Go, idiot!" Jayce prompted, shoving Kyle through the doorway. Kyle stumbled into the classroom, then caught himself, glancing at row after row of desks. His fellow students stared back at him.

He lowered himself into his seat, blushing furiously.

"Hey," he heard a voice whisper. He turned to his left, seeing Ariana smiling at him.

"Hey," he whispered back.

Mr. Maywind strode through the doorway, closing the door behind him and walking to his desk, sitting down before it.

"Good morning, class," he greeted.

"Good morning, Mr. Maywind," the class – including Kyle – replied.

"Today we learn a new pattern," Mr. Maywind declared. "The water pattern, to be precise." He walked up to the blackboard at the front of the room, grabbing a piece of white chalk. He scribbled a strange symbol on the board, and turned back to look at the class. Two dozen blank stares looked back at him.

"I'll draw it again," Mr. Maywind stated, moving to the right of his previous drawing and placing a dot there. "Remember that *this* is the center of your mind," he added. Then he drew a line downward. "...and this is you pulling magic backward." Then he drew an "S," bringing the chalk upward. "Then you move it right, then left, then right, all the while bringing it forward," he continued. Then he drew a line straight down. "Then you pull it back. *That* is the water pattern. Understood?"

"Yes Mr. Maywind," a few voices replied in unison. The rest of the class looked like Kyle felt...lost.

Mr. Maywind reached into his desk, bringing out something that looked very much like a real human skull. He placed it on his desk with a *thunk*.

"Let me demonstrate again," he stated, "...for the *slower* students in the class." A tiny bright ball of light appeared an inch above the skull, in the middle. "*This* is the path the magic should take," he explained. The light slowly moved to the back of the skull, then traced a slow "S" forward, ending at the front right, just above the right eye socket. Then the light moved slowly backward across the middle of the skull.

Ohhh, Kyle thought. Suddenly the symbol on the blackboard made sense. He glanced at Ariana, who was busy coping the symbol into her notebook. Mr. Maywind demonstrated the technique a few more times, until everyone in the class seemed to get it.

"Now you know *how* to weave the water pattern," he stated. "But without knowing how it works, you'll never be able to use it to its full potential. Understood?"

"Yes, Mr. Maywind."

"No you don't," he retorted. "But you will. The water pattern forces a substance within air – it only works with air – to come together to make water. This requires a great deal of heat. Anything nearby will be substantially cooled as a result."

Kyle stared at the symbol on the blackboard, then closed his eyes for a moment, weaving the pattern in his mind. But instead of sending it outward, he let the magic dissipate.

Got it.

"The more magic you put into the pattern," Mr. Maywind continued, "...the broader the stream of water you'll create. The more magic you put into the stream, the faster you'll make water. Any questions?"

Ariana raised her hand, and Mr. Maywind nodded at her.

"How much air does the pattern use?" she asked.

"An intelligent student asks intelligent questions," Mr. Maywind replied, nodding approvingly. "It takes an enormous amount of air to make even a small amount of water." Ariana raised her hand again.

"But couldn't you suffocate if you make too much water?"

"In theory," Mr. Maywind agreed. "But only if you were in a sealed room." He paused, then turned to face the rest of the class. "I suggest you commit this pattern to memory," he warned. "Mr. Tenson will have high expectations of you."

The class groaned, and Mr. Maywind smirked.

"Good luck," he stated. "Never forget that Xanos is with all of you, watching you through His Chosen. Make Him proud."

"Yes Mr. Maywind," the class droned.

"Class dismissed."

* * *

Kyle sat down opposite Ariana at the lunch table, setting his plate on the table-top. He dug into his meal eagerly, having eaten nothing since waking that morning. It seemed like no one ate breakfast here...only lunch, and dinner if they did well in class. Any disobedience, or a failure to perform to their teachers' expectations, would mean no dinner. With portions strictly doled out by the cafeteria workers, it was no surprise that not a single student here was overweight.

"You're not scared of the food anymore," Ariana observed, digging in to her own meal. Kyle smiled.

"Guess not," he agreed.

"You should practice the water pattern," she advised. "Before Mr. Tenson's class. But be careful."

"What do you mean?"

"If you weave it wrong," Ariana answered, "...you could get hurt."

Kyle nodded, taking another bite of his food. He'd already practiced the pattern – in his mind's eye – a few dozen times, while they'd been walking toward the cafeteria. No one had come to beat Kyle up this time, to his relief. He suspected that Ariana's presence had something to do with that. She was clearly the best student in her class...and everyone knew it.

"Hey," Kyle said, swallowing another mouthful of food.

"Yes?"

"So what's the point of all of...this?" he asked, gesturing around the cafeteria. Ariana raised an eyebrow.

"The cafeteria?"

"No, this whole place," he clarified. Ariana shrugged.

"I don't know," she admitted. "They don't really tell us students much," she added. "I do know that once we become Death Weavers, we'll get to go back out to the surface."

"How long does that take?"

"We graduate when we're eighteen," Ariana answered. Kyle blanched.

"*Eighteen?*" he blurted out. Ariana nodded. Kyle stared at her incredulously, then lowered his gaze to his half-empty plate. Suddenly he wasn't hungry.

"The funeral is today after class," Ariana said, thankfully changing the subject.

"Are you going?" Kyle asked, his tone hopeful. It would be far less intimidating with her there. Ariana hesitated, then nodded.

"*Everyone* is going," she answered.

"Everyone?"

"Yeah," she confirmed. "They take death very seriously here."

"Oh."

Kyle took another bite of food, relieved that he wouldn't be one of the few people there. If he was just another member of the audience, it wouldn't be so awkward.

"Are your parents still alive?" Ariana asked, staring at him. Kyle nodded.

"Yeah."

"That's good," she replied. She pushed her plate away then. There was still some food left on it. "Almost finished?"

"Uh, yeah," Kyle mumbled. He ate faster, wolfing down the rest of his food. When he was done, Ariana stood up, grabbing their plates and bringing them to the table where the rest of the dirty dishes were. She dropped them off, and they walked out of the cafeteria, back to Mr. Tenson's classroom. When they got there, however, they found the door locked, the other students standing around it.

"What's going on?" Kyle asked Ariana.

"I don't know," she admitted. She turned to an older-looking boy. "What's going on?"

"We're waiting for Mr. Tenson," the boy answered. "He's going to take us to the Arena."

"Wait, what?" Kyle asked.

"For the funeral," Ariana explained. The older boy gave Kyle a dirty look, then turned away. Kyle swallowed, glancing at Ariana, who seemed lost in thought. Moments later, Mr. Tenson arrived.

"Follow me," he ordered, turning about and striding down the hallway. The class followed behind, and Mr. Tenson led them down the hallway, then downstairs, until they'd left the building. The Arena stood before them, the huge stone sphere glowing some fifty feet above the field below.

"What *is* that?" Kyle asked, pointing at the sphere.

"The Timestone," Ariana answered. "It's like the sun. It gets brighter during the day, then dark at night."

"Oh."

Mr. Tenson led them toward the Arena, whose seats were already starting to fill. Groups of other students, led by their Death Weaver teachers, made their way toward the underground stadium. It wasn't long before Kyle was walking across the field, toward one of the stairways leading upward.

Without warning, Mr. Tenson stopped. He turned around, pointing right at Kyle.

"You," he barked. "Stay there. The rest of you, come with me."

Kyle froze in place, staring at Mr. Tenson. He felt a warm hand on his arm, and turned to see Ariana there.

"I'll see you," she promised.

"See you," he mumbled. Then he watched as she joined the rest of the class, climbing up the stairs, then sitting down in one of the seats some thirty feet up.

Kyle stood there near the center of the Arena, sensing hundreds of eyes staring down at him. He lowered his gaze to his feet, sweat dripping down his flanks.

More students walked across the field, ascending the stairs to find their seats. Then came the Death Weavers, hundreds of them, filling the front rows of the Arena.

And still, Kyle stood there, alone.

After a few minutes, the last of the Death Weavers took their seats. The stadium was full now, all eyes on the field below. On Kyle. He heard hushed voices from the stands, saw a few people pointing at Kyle. Or rather, *behind* him.

Kyle turned around, spotting a dark figure moving across the field toward him. It was the Dead Man; he floated slowly toward Kyle, his cloak rippling sinuously behind him. The Dead Man stopped a few feet in front of Kyle, staring down at him with those black, sunken eyes. Then he turned, gazing across the field.

There, levitating a full foot above the ground, a line of brown coffins moved forward into the Arena, each flanked by a Death Weaver. They stopped a few feet from the Dead Man, forming two rows of six coffins each, with a dozen feet between rows. Another coffin entered the field, this one red, and much more ornate, flanked by two Death Weavers. It moved between the two rows of coffins, stopping right in front of the Dead Man.

The Death Weavers bowed before the Dead Man.

A man entered the Arena, flanked by two armed guards. A man dressed in shabby, dirt-smudged clothes, his short brown hair in disarray. His wrists were bound behind him, wrapped around a tall, heavy post on his back. His bare feet slipped in the dirt as the soldiers dragged him forward between the coffins. They stopped before the Dead Man, pulling the man upright until the bottom of the post lined up with a small hole in the floor of the Arena, sinking into it. Kyle stared at the man, his breath catching in his throat.

It was Darius.

The bodyguard stared back at Kyle, tethered to the upright post, his blue eyes unblinking. Kyle looked away, unable to face that gaze.
Traitor.

Kyle saw movement in the periphery of his vision, and looked up, gazing down the length of the Arena. He saw a dozen Death Weavers walk into the stadium in a loose circle, surrounding a single man. Even from across the Arena, Kyle recognized the man's black shirt and pants, his short white hair. His equally white goatee, scruffy from days of unfettered growth.
Kalibar!

Kyle stared at the former Grand Weaver, his heart soaring. Kalibar stood tall from within the ring of Death Weavers, his hands at his sides, unbound. He spotted Kyle, his stony expression softening. He smiled faintly, nodding once. Kyle smiled back, resisting the urge to run to the man. He felt relief course through him, relief that Kalibar was okay. That he was alive and unharmed...just as the Dead Man had promised.

Kalibar stopped before the Dead Man, the Death Weavers surrounding him dropping back to form a line behind him. Darius stood a dozen feet to Kalibar's right, his eyes locked on the Dead Man, who regarded the two men silently, then turned to face the crowd above.

"We are here today," he bellowed, his deep voice echoing throughout the massive cavern, "...to celebrate the lives of these heroes." He gestured at the coffins lined up behind him. "We are here to thank them for their sacrifice, as they gave up their lives in service to you, to the Empire, and to their God."

The crowd was utterly silent.

"You are also here," the Dead Man continued, "...to mourn the loss of your brothers." He paused, his expression darkening. "And I am here to mourn the loss of my children."

The Dead Man turned to face the caskets behind him, his gaze sweeping over them.

"My children were murdered," he stated, turning back to the crowd. "Taken from me by the treachery of one man and the ignorance of another."

He lowered his gaze to the field, and as if on cue, the Death Weavers flanking the brown caskets began to move back out of the Arena, the caskets levitating at their sides. Only the red casket remained. The Dead Man turned to Darius, gesturing at him with one hand.

"This man murdered three of your brothers," he declared.

"Four," Darius corrected.

The Dead Man stared at Darius for a moment, his black eyes unblinking. Kyle saw his jawline ripple.

"...and he betrayed the very people he promised to protect," the Dead Man continued. "A murderer and a traitor, yet we feed him, clothe him, and house him." He gazed at the crowd. "Is this just?"

The crowd booed, countless voices echoing off of the massive stone walls of the cavern.

The Dead Man turned to Kyle, gesturing for him to come forward. Kyle obeyed, stopping a few feet in front of his teacher. He wiped his sweaty hands on his pants, staring into the Dead Man's eyes.

"Gather magic in your mind," the Dead Man ordered. Kyle did as he was told, closing his eyes and *pulling* magic into his mind's eye. "Make a full circle clockwise, front to back."

Kyle did so, holding the pattern in his mind. It contracted, forming a pulsing knot there.

"Pull the magic backward, then forward," the Dead Man ordered. "Then attach a magic stream and throw the pattern outward."

Kyle obeyed, then opened his eyes, seeing a small flame – about the size of a candle's – dancing in the air between them. His eyes widened.

"Do it again."

Kyle did so, creating another flame. The Dead Man nodded in approval, then turned back to the crowd.

"Fire," he shouted, his voice carrying over the crowd, "…is our symbol for justice. Man's discovery of fire elevated him above the beasts, just as justice gave rise to civilization." He gestured toward Kyle's flame. "Fire can give us warmth, and life. Or it can kill," he added. Then he turned back to Kyle, putting a cold hand on Kyle's shoulder.

"Kyle, make the fire pattern," he ordered. "Larger this time."

Kyle closed his eyes, weaving the fire pattern with more magic this time. He attached a magic stream, throwing the pattern outward, and opened his eyes to see a ball of flame the size of a soccer ball roar to life a foot in front of him, tongues of flame licking the air hungrily. He stepped back, the heat of the fire almost unbearable on his exposed skin.

The Dead Man smiled, nodding at Kyle in approval. Then he gestured at the guards flanking Darius. The guards grabbed pails next to them, lifting them up and emptying them on Darius. Dark liquid spilled over the bodyguard, soaking his hair and clothes. The stench of oil assaulted Kyle's nostrils.

"Now," the Dead Man stated. "Send the flame to the traitor."

Kyle froze, staring at the Dead Man. His concentration broke, the flame between them going out. The Dead Man's eyes bored into Kyle, his pale lips drawn in a frown.

"Weave the fire pattern," he commanded.

Kyle obeyed, weaving the pattern again. A large ball of flame appeared before him, as before.

"Send it to the traitor," the Dead Man repeated.

Kyle hesitated, turning to Darius. The bodyguard stood there, staring back at Kyle silently. Kyle swallowed in a dry throat, his eyes drawn to the flame between them.

He stood there, doing nothing.

"Do it," the Dead Man pressed.

Kyle shook his head silently, staring at Darius. He cut the magic stream to the fire, and it vanished abruptly.

"No," he replied.

The Dead Man shook his head.

"I'm disappointed in you," he stated. He took a step forward, looming over Kyle, his black eyes locked on Kyle's. Kyle turned to face him, staring right into his eyes.

"I won't do it," he stated. "And you can't make me."

"Defiance," the Dead Man murmured, raising an eyebrow. "I see. Very well then. I told you what would happen if you defied me."

Kyle felt the hairs on the back of his neck stand on end. The Dead Man turned to the crowd once again.

"Mercy," he declared, his voice booming through the cavern, "…for the traitor." The crowd booed again, and the Dead Man paused, letting the voices fade away before continuing. "This," he stated, gesturing at Kalibar, "…is the man who murdered so many of your brothers, and the children of another of Xanos's Chosen," He turned to Kalibar, regarding the former Grand Weaver with a pitying gaze. "His is a crime of ignorance, mistaking us – and them – for enemies of the Empire."

Kalibar regarded the Dead Man silently, his expression flat.

"His eyes deceive him," the Dead Man continued. He raised one hand in the air, closing it into a fist. The line of Death Weavers standing behind Kalibar closed in on him. Two of the Weavers grabbed his arms, and the Dead Man stepped forward until his lips were only a few inches from Kalibar's ear. His lips moved, but Kyle couldn't hear what he was saying.

Kalibar grimaced, his eyes locked on the Dead Man, who drew back, staring back at the former Grand Weaver.

Kalibar nodded once.

The Dead Man gestured at the Death Weavers around Kalibar, and two more of them strode up to their prisoner, reaching down to grab his legs. They lifted him up off of the ground, carrying him until he was suspended over the levitating red casket in the center of the Arena. They laid Kalibar atop the casket, pulling his arms and legs until he was lying spread-eagled upon its surface.

Kyle's heart hammered in his chest, a chill running through him. He stared at Kalibar mutely, his mouth going dry. Kalibar laid on top of the casket without a struggle, his expression eerily calm. Kyle glanced at Darius, seeing the bodyguard's eyes locked on Kalibar. The traitor's expression was as flat as ever, but Kyle saw the muscles of his jaw ripple, his fists clenched tight at his sides.

The Dead Man walked up to the front of the casket, where Kalibar's head lay. He leaned over the old man's face, staring down into Kalibar's eyes.

"You will never forget my face," he murmured. Then he straightened his back, gazing up at the crowd.

"Xanos required a test," he shouted, pointing at Kyle. "A test that our newest student has failed. Xanos demands that I extract payment for this failure."

The Dead Man turned to Kyle.

"I am a man of my word," he stated, his voice filled with disappointment. "I would not have allowed the traitor to be harmed had you followed my instructions. If you had obeyed me, none of this would have happened. Remember that."

The Dead Man turned back to Kalibar, staring down at the former Grand Weaver. He raised his right hand into the air, the sleeve of his black cloak slithering down his pale arm. Then he rolled the sleeve with his left hand, exposing his right arm up to the elbow.

"Let this man," the Dead Man shouted, pointing down at Kalibar, "...be deceived no more!"

The crowd rose to its feet, cheering wildly. The Dead Man brought his left hand down on top of Kalibar's head, pinning it to the closed lid of the casket. Kalibar grimaced, squirming for a moment, then becoming still. The Dead Man placed his right hand over Kalibar's face, holding it a few inches away, his fingers spread out wide.

The crowd hushed, the Arena utterly silent.

The Dead Man plunged his hand downward, shoving his fingers into Kalibar's right eye socket.

Kalibar screamed, writhing on the casket, jerking his head away. The Dead Man's fingers slipped to one side, and he tightened his grip on Kalibar's head with his left hand, jerking Kalibar's head so that it faced upward again. Tears poured out of Kalibar's right eye, and he squeezed it shut, gritting his teeth in pain. The Dead Man stared down at Kalibar's one open eye, shaking his head in warning.

The ghoulish Weaver brought his right hand forward, hovering an inch above Kalibar's face. Kalibar's chest rose and fell rapidly, the muscles in his neck going taught. But he didn't move, didn't try to resist.

The Dead Man paused, his fingers hovering over Kalibar's right eye.

"No!" Kyle yelled, bolting toward Kalibar. "Stop it!" he cried. Someone grabbed his shirt from behind, yanking him backward. One Death Weaver locked Kyle's arms behind his back, while another grabbed his head, forcing it to face Kalibar. He struggled against their iron grips, a sob bursting from his lips.

No no no!

The Dead Man looked up from Kalibar, staring directly at Kyle. Then he plunged his fingers into Kalibar's right eye socket.

Kalibar shrieked in agony, his arms flailing wildly. The Death Weavers holding his limbs struggled, leaning backward to pull his arms and legs taut. Kalibar sucked in a deep, shuddering breath, then screamed again as the Dead Man's fingers sunk deeper into his orbit, sliding downward past the first knuckle. Blood welled up between the Dead Man's fingers, dripping down the side of Kalibar's face and pooling on the casket below.

The Dead Man paused, gazing up at the crowd. Then he twisted his right wrist slowly. A muffled popping sound echoed throughout the Arena. Kalibar screamed again, his back arching off of the casket.

The Dead Man jerked his hand upward.

Kalibar roared, flailing on the casket, struggling violently against the Death Weavers holding him captive. He jerked free, rolling off of the casket and landing on the ground below with a dull *thud*. He curled into the fetal position, clutching his face with his hands, blood seeping between his fingers and spilling onto the dirt.

The Dead Man lifted his right hand into the air, facing the

crowd triumphantly. A white orb glistened in his outstretched hand.

The crowd roared.

Kyle's legs gave out from under him, and he fell to the dirt floor, his entire body feeling numb. The arms behind him pulled him upward roughly, forcing him to his feet.

The Dead Man lowered his hand, tossing Kalibar's eye onto the dirt floor of the Arena. He nodded at the four Death Weavers, who stepped away from the table. Four new Death Weavers replaced them, surrounding Kalibar. The former Grand Weaver waved them away, rolling onto his belly, then pushing himself up onto his hands and knees. He rose to his feet, swaying slightly, and faced the Dead Man with his remaining eye. He lifted his gaze to the crowd, facing them defiantly.

Then, without a word, he turned to the red casket, hoisting himself upon it. He laid on his back, calmly offering his arms and legs to the Death Weavers surrounding him.

They paused, staring at the Dead Man, who nodded. Then they each grabbed a limb, pulling backward until Kalibar was stretched taught. The Dead Man, still standing at the head of the casket, lifted his right arm into the air.

The crowd went silent.

The Dead Man grabbed Kalibar's forehead with his left hand, then brought his right hand down, fingers hovering over Kalibar's left eye.

He plunged his fingers into Kalibar's left eye socket.

Kalibar screamed, the awful sound echoing throughout the Arena. The Dead Man's fingers sunk downward, and Kalibar cried out again, his back arching in agony. The Dead Man twisted his wrist. Even from where he stood, Kyle could hear the muted *pop* as the muscles anchoring Kalibar's eyeball tore free.

The Dead Man jerked his left hand upward, displaying the white, glistening orb to the crowd. The crowd roared again, cheering wildly.

The men holding Kalibar let go of his limbs, and the former Grand Weaver turned over onto his side, clawing blindly at the edge of the casket. He rolled over the edge, falling hard onto the Arena floor. Kyle heard Kalibar moaning, saw his trembling hands covering his empty sockets.

The Dead Man tossed Kalibar's left eye onto the ground.

Kyle felt bile welling up in his throat, and swallowed it down, turning away from the sight. The Dead Man faced Kyle then, walking up to him and staring down at him with those black, sunken eyes. He reached out, grabbing Kyle's chin with one pale, frigid, blood-smeared hand.

"He suffered for you," the Dead Man murmured. He let go of Kyle's chin, and turned away.

The arms holding Kyle let go suddenly, and Kyle dropped onto his knees. He lowered himself to the ground, weeping into the cold dirt floor of the Arena.

Chapter 16

Kyle woke up, blinking the sleep out of his eyes. His tiny, cramped room was dark, the lantern bolted to the wall glowing ever-so-softly. He laid there on his bed, stifling a yawn.

Someone knocked on his door – hard.

"I said get up!" he heard a voice yell from the hallway. Kyle groaned, rolling out of bed and walking to his dresser. He grabbed his uniform from atop it, pulling his clothes on, still half-asleep. The door burst open, and Kyle started, seeing Jayce standing in the hallway glaring at him. Kyle finished pulling on his shirt, reaching up to rub his eyes.

His *eyes*.

He froze, an image of the Dead Man coming unbidden to his mind, a glistening white globe in the dark Weaver's hand. Kalibar screaming in agony...

"Put on your belt," Jayce snapped, jolting Kyle from his thoughts. He stared at Jayce blankly. "Put it *on*," Jayce repeated, grabbing Kyle's belt and throwing it at him. Kyle obeyed, tying his sash around his waist. When he was finished, he glanced up at Jayce; the older boy was glaring at him.

"What?" Kyle asked.

"You don't deserve to wear that," Jayce spat. Then he turned away, exiting the room. Kyle stared at his back, then lowered his gaze.

Everyone knows, Kyle realized.

He followed Jayce mutely, letting himself be led down the now-familiar maze of hallways. He kept his eyes on the floor, trying to ignore the students they passed as they made their way to class. He could feel their eyes on him, staring at him as he walked by.

Suddenly, Jayce stopped.

Kyle looked up, realizing they were at the open doorway to Mr. Maywind's class. He hesitated, but Jayce shoved him through.

Two dozen students stared at him from their desks.

Kyle dropped his gaze, walking to his desk. He sat down quietly, closing his eyes. An image of the Dead Man's face appeared in his mind's eye, black eyes staring down at him.

He suffered for you.

Kyle opened his eyes, wiping them with the back of his sleeve.

"Kyle," he heard a voice whisper. He turned, spotting Ariana looking at him, her eyes filled with concern. She reached out to touch his shoulder, but he pulled away. He didn't want to be touched. Didn't *deserve* to be touched.

Mr. Maywind walked into the classroom.

"Good morning, class," he greeted.

"Good morning, Mr. Maywind," the class droned. Kyle remained silent, staring at his desk.

"Today," Mr. Maywind stated, "…we will learn the finer points of using the water pattern." He walked up to the chalkboard, and Kyle heard the rhythmic sound of chalk scraping against it. He glanced up at the board, seeing a few symbols there he didn't recognize. He lowered his gaze again. Even the thought of paying attention was exhausting.

Mr. Maywind continued the lecture, droning on about the water pattern. He called on several students to answer questions, but luckily Kyle wasn't one of them. After what seemed like an eternity, the lecture was over.

"Never forget that Xanos is with all of you," Mr. Maywind intoned. "…watching you through His Chosen. Make Him proud."

"Yes Mr. Maywind," the class replied.

Kyle stood up with the other students, bowing mechanically to his teacher. He shuffled listlessly out of the classroom, following the other students down the hallway. He couldn't help but notice his peers stepping away from him, giving him wide berth. He felt their eyes on him, heard them whispering to each other.

Then someone grabbed his hand.

He flinched, pulling his hand away, half-expecting a group of boys to corner him again. But when he looked up, he saw Ariana looking back at him.

"Kyle…" she said, giving him a weak smile. She reached out to grab his hand again, but he pulled away. She moved with him, reaching out a third time. This time she was too fast, grabbing his hand before he could react. She gripped his hand tightly, pulling him to her side. She led him down the hallway into the cafeteria, guiding him to their usual table.

"Sit with me," she urged, letting go of his hand.

He hesitated, then sat down. Ariana walked back to the line of students getting their meals. Moments later, she returned with two plates filled with food. This time she sat down next to him instead of across from him. She pushed one plate of food in front of him, keeping the other for herself. Kyle glanced down at his food; the smell of it made him nauseous.

"I'm not hungry," he muttered, pushing the plate away.

"Kyle," Ariana murmured, putting a hand on his shoulder. "I'm sorry about your friend."

Kyle said nothing, swallowing back a lump in his throat. He took a deep breath, blinking away the sudden moisture in his eyes.

"Kyle…"

Kyle wiped his eyes with the back of his sleeve, unable to look Ariana in the eye. He felt her hand touch his, and he pulled his hand away. There was a long silence, and Kyle found himself glancing up at her. She was staring at him, her expression unreadable.

"Why are you shutting me out?" she asked.

Kyle looked down at his plate, then shook his head.

"It's my fault."

"What is?"

"What happened to Kalibar," Kyle replied.

"No it isn't," Ariana retorted. "You didn't hurt your friend…the Dead Man did."

"No," Kyle stated, shaking his head again. "He told me that he wouldn't hurt them if I obeyed him. But I didn't listen."

"Kyle, that's crap," Ariana said, reaching out for his hand again. This time she gripped it firmly, so that Kyle couldn't pull away. Her skin was warm and soft.

"No it isn't," Kyle countered miserably. Ariana stared at him for a long moment, then let go of his hand. She grabbed her fork, stirring her food around her plate for a while. They sat in silence for a few long, awkward minutes. Then Ariana raised her big brown eyes to look at Kyle again. This time, they were moist.

"You were right," she said at last. "They didn't have you, not before." She gave a bitter smile. "But they do now."

* * *

The walk back to Mr. Tenson's classroom was long and silent. Kyle kept his eyes down the whole way, feeling the eyes of the other students following him as he walked. Ariana strode beside him, but said nothing, seemingly lost in her own thoughts. By the time they reached the door to Mr. Tenson's class, the rest of the students had already arrived. Ariana stopped before the door, gesturing for Kyle to go in first. Then she followed, closing the door behind her. Mr. Tenson's sharp gaze locked on Kyle, following him as he made his way to the back of the classroom to line up with the rest of the students.

"You," Mr. Tenson ordered, pointing at Kyle. Kyle looked up at the man, his stomach twisting into a knot. "Come here," his teacher ordered. Kyle obeyed, almost sprinting up to the man. Tenson stared down at him, his expression cold. "You are no longer in this class," he stated dismissively, pointing at the door. "Leave."

Kyle hesitated for a split second, and saw Mr. Tenson's right hand start to rise. He bowed quickly, then turned and nearly ran to the door, opening it and escaping into the hallway. He closed the door behind him, then leaned back against it, his heart hammering in his chest.

What was that *all about?*

"Hello, Kyle."

Kyle jumped, turning to see the Dead Man standing only a few feet away in the otherwise deserted hallway. The hairs on the nape of his neck rose up, fear gripping him. He stood there, frozen in place, staring at the Dead Man mutely.

"You barely ate," the Dead Man murmured, a concerned look on his face. Kyle shrugged, but said nothing. An image of the Dead Man's pale fingers sinking into Kalibar's eye sockets came to him, and he blinked, forcing the vision from his mind's eye.

"I want you to know that I honored your wishes," his ghoulish master stated, "...and spared the traitor's life." He levitated forward, his boots inches from the floor, and stared down at Kyle with his black, unblinking eyes. "My children demanded Kalibar's death," he added solemnly, "...for the murder of their brothers."

He smiled, putting an icy hand on Kyle's shoulder. "I spared his life as well, for you."

Kyle mouthed a silent "thank you," lowering his gaze to his feet. "Walk with me."

The Dead Man turned about, levitating down the hallway, his black cloak ever-rippling behind him. Kyle paused, then strode after the man. He followed his master through the hallways and down a flight of stairs, until they passed through the front doorway of the building. Kyle stepped out into the open cavern, seeing the Arena in the distance.

He turned away from it quickly, fixating on the bridge over the pond.

The Dead Man turned left, moving toward the pond, and Kyle walked after him. But instead of going onto the bridge, the Dead man veered to the side, stopping a few inches from the rocky shore of the pond. Kyle walked up to his side, staring down into the dark, still waters. There were dozens of glowing forms floating near the surface, flitting about to and fro. They were fish, Kyle realized.

The Dead Man turned to Kyle.

"Come closer," he ordered. Kyle obeyed, standing right beside him. The Dead Man levitated forward, his boots hovering above the pond. The water beneath his feet sank inward, forming a large dome below them. Grabbing Kyle's arm, the Dead Man continued forward, pulling Kyle into the pond. Kyle tensed up, expecting the water to rush inward around his feet and ankles, but instead he found himself levitating above the sunken dome in the pond.

Slowly, they descended.

The water parted around them as they sank, forming a sphere of air around them. Within seconds, they were completely underwater, the dim light from the Timestone above barely illuminating them. Fluorescent fish darted to and fro around them, none daring to penetrate the globe of air surrounding them. As they sank, the light became even dimmer, throwing them into near-complete darkness.

"Weave the light pattern," the Dead Man commanded.

Kyle closed his eyes, weaving the pattern and throwing it out, attaching a small magic stream. A white globe of light appeared before them, banishing the darkness. The Dead Man nodded approvingly.

Downward and forward they sank, until the surface of the pond was no longer visible from above.

"Where are we going?" Kyle asked nervously. He felt suddenly claustrophobic, as if the sphere of air around them would collapse at any moment, drowning them in water.

"You'll see."

They continued downward and forward, until the pond bottom was visible only a few feet below. Kyle saw a rock wall ahead, some twenty feet away, into which a smooth, arched doorway had been carved. Kyle's light revealed a rippling, fluid surface at the doorway, with nothing visible beyond.

Still they moved forward, until they were inches from the doorway.

The Dead Man continued forward, the sphere of air following him. He passed through the doorway, vanishing beyond, his passing sending ripples across the watery surface. Kyle felt himself moving forward, and moments later he too was passing through the rippling barrier. As his head passed through, the rippling darkness gave way to a sudden intense brightness. He squinted, losing control of his magic stream to the light pattern. He passed all the way through, feeling a sudden cool breeze on his skin as the Dead Man's protective sphere vanished. Slowly, his eyes adjusted to the bright light.

Kyle stared, his jaw dropping.

He was standing on a narrow, grated metal platform that extended from the arched doorway into a long tunnel beyond. The walls, floor, and ceiling were made entirely of huge, translucent white crystals, their multifaceted surfaces glowing slightly. Each crystal had a broad base some three feet in diameter, and tapered into a sharp point that aimed toward the center of the tunnel. The crystals were at least seven feet long, their stark whiteness contrasting with the black metal platform upon which Kyle stood. The platform hovered a foot or so above the sharp tips of the crystals below.

The Dead Man turned to Kyle, a smile curling his lips.

"Welcome," he stated, his deep voice echoing throughout the tunnel, "...to the Void."

Kyle stared at the tunnel mutely. Then he looked back, seeing the rippling of the water at the doorway behind him. It must have been held back by a force field of some kind.

"Come," the Dead Man ordered, levitating forward over the

metal platform. Kyle paused, then followed, staring at the sharps tips of the crystals above him. Faint rays of blue light shone downward from each tip, aiming unerringly at Kyle…and following him as he walked. He heard a *thunk*, and lowered his gaze, seeing the Dead Man standing on the platform a few feet ahead, his boots no longer levitating above the ground. The dark Weaver's black cloak lay still for the first time.

Kyle stared, realizing he'd stopped walking.

"Follow me," the Dead Man ordered.

They continued forward, their footsteps echoing down the tunnel, until the tunnel opened up into a modest-sized domed chamber. The platform broadened to cover the floor of the circular chamber. There was a large circular hole in the center of the platform, through which a cluster of broad, green crystals jutted out at a forty-five-degree angle. The Dead Man strode up to the green crystal, gesturing for Kyle to follow.

"This is the Void," the Dead Man explained, gesturing at the chamber. "This is where I was reborn into a Chosen of Xanos."

Kyle glanced around the chamber, shivering a bit in the cool air.

"What's with all the crystals?" Kyle asked. He peered at one of the crystals forming the wall to his left, spotting something dark in its base.

"Those are Void crystals," the Dead Man answered. "They were created by Xanos himself, each representing a vanquished enemy of the one God. They hold the secret to His power."

"What do you mean?" Kyle pressed.

"That is for a later time," the Dead Man replied. He stepped to the outer edge of the platform, reaching out and touching the tip of one of the white crystals. "Void crystals," he murmured, "…are Xanos's creations, the conduit through which I receive His gift."

Kyle frowned at the Dead Man, having no idea what he was talking about.

"I no longer generate magic," the Dead Man continued. "It is a…consequence of my rebirth. Xanos provides me with the magic I require, and the means to acquire it for myself." He gestured at his black cloak. "And the means to keep it. Without magic…" he pointed to the green crystal on his forehead with one finger. "…I would cease to exist."

"You mean you would die?" Kyle asked. The Dead Man stepped away from the edge of the platform, walking up to Kyle and staring down at him unblinkingly.

"Xanos provides," he replied. "He is the giver and taker of life. I am loyal to Him, and so He will not forsake me." Then the Dead Man knelt down before Kyle, his black eyes glittering in the soft light the countless white crystals lining the chamber gave off. "Loyalty," he added, placing a pale, cold hand on Kyle's shoulder, "...is what Xanos – and I – value most." He stood up then. "Onas niria rebra," he murmured.

"What?" Kyle asked.

"Teliv trasyc hels," the Dead Man stated. Kyle stared at him blankly, and the Dead Man frowned, his eyes flicking to Kyle's right ear. Kyle brought a hand up to his ear, feeling the earring Kalibar had placed there. He'd forgotten all about it.

The Dead Man walked up to the cluster of green crystals, touching one of them. The white crystals lining the chamber shifted color suddenly, turning light blue, and Kyle felt a powerful vibration in his skull.

"Loyalty," the Dead Man stated, "...is the greatest form of wealth. There is no greater loyalty than that between a father and his children." He sighed then, staring off into space. "Orik violated my trust," he murmured. "The greatest test of a man is to give him unlimited power and wealth."

The Dead Man paused for a moment, staring down at the green crystals. Kyle stared up at the man, saying nothing. At length, the Dead Man stirred, turning to face Kyle.

"Orik failed this test," he stated grimly. "He gave up the possibility of becoming one of the Chosen...and for what?" He shook his head. "Petty revenge."

"Wait," Kyle said. "Orik was going to become...?"

"A Chosen," the Dead Man interjected. "Like me."

A chill ran down Kyle's spine.

"Come," the Dead Man ordered, turning about and walking out of the domed chamber, back down the narrow platform toward the arched doorway. Kyle obeyed, following behind the man. "Your progress is unprecedented," the Dead Man continued. "Attending classes with the other children will only slow you down. You will receive personalized training from myself and our finest Death Weavers from today onward."

They stopped at the arched doorway, and the Dead Man turned to face Kyle, putting an ice-cold hand on his shoulder. His sunken eyes peered into Kyle's, his gaunt features softening for a moment.

"You are destined for greatness, Kyle," he said, raising his hand off of Kyle's shoulder to pat him on the cheek. "We have something very special in mind for you."

* * *

Kyle slumped onto his narrow, stiff mattress, laying on his belly, his head buried in his pillow. He moaned, rolling over onto his side and rubbing his eyes. His head throbbed, undoubtedly from the countless hours of training the Dead Man had put him through.

If I have to weave one more pattern, he thought darkly.

After their trip to the Void, his pale master had grilled him on the light, water, and fire patterns, forcing him to weave each of them over and over again. With eyes closed, then open. Then faster. Then two lights at once, followed by three. Then weaving the light and fire patterns side-by-side, and so on.

And every time, Kyle had been terrified that he'd screw up...and that the Dead Man would do something horrible to punish him.

Kyle rolled onto his back, staring up at the ceiling. There was no doubt in his mind that this was going to be his life from now on. Grueling training all day, every day. The Dead Man had made that painfully clear.

You'll never see Ariana again.

It was true; not only was Kyle going to train with the Death Weavers and the Dead Man, he was to dine with them as well. He would never get a chance to see her, not really...the one person who cared about him in this awful place.

Now he was truly alone.

Tears blurred Kyle's vision, and he wiped his eyes on his blanket, gritting his teeth against the grief that threatened to rise up out of him. More tears came, followed by a muffled sob, and he curled up on his side, burying his face in his pillow. He took a deep, shuddering breath in, clenching his jaw tight.

You have to stay strong, he told himself. *You have to survive.*

Then he pictured Ariana's face, her sweet smile, the warmth of her hand clutching his.

And then the dam broke.

He cried into his pillow, sobs forcing their way out of him, one after the other. He wept until his belly ached, until his nose had stuffed up completely, mucous dripping down his face and onto his sheets. He cried until there were no more tears, not caring if anyone heard him. It didn't matter anymore.

Nothing mattered anymore.

At long last, curled into a ball, his pillow soaked with tears, and his blankets curled tightly about him, he fell asleep.

Chapter 17

The black-cloaked Weavers follow behind Ampir as he races over the Great River, Vera curled up in his arms. He sees the cliffside to his right, beyond a small forest, and turns toward it, leaving the river behind. The Weavers follow him...as does the Behemoth's diamond-shaped eye. Though Ampir is miles away, the monstrosity is somehow able to track him. He can't risk a direct hit from the thing, not with Junior on his back.

Almost there...

Ampir aims for the forest, going in low, weaving between the densely-packed trees. The Weavers behind him fly above the treetops, gaining on him quickly...but he pays them no mind. It's the Behemoth he's worried about.

He sees the thing's eye flash in the distance.

Ampir slows rapidly, diving down to within a foot of the ground, behind a small hill. A wide beam of deadly green light shoots over him, striking some trees a few yards in front of him, igniting them instantly. The trees explode, sending debris flying.

The beam fades.

Ampir bursts forward, flying a few feet from the ground, zig-zagging through the trees. He sees the cliffside, only a hundred feet away now. The entrance to the secret underground tunnels is there, hidden by an illusion of a sheer rock wall. Only the members of the Council – and the Grand Runic and Grand Weaver – know where it is. Luckily, Ampir is still a member of the Council.

He reaches the cliff wall, slowing, then landing on the grass before it. He scans the near-vertical surface, spotting a faint blue light coming from the rock a few dozen feet to the left.

There!

He hears something behind him, turns to see a half-dozen black-cloaked Weavers landing on the forest floor. They face Ampir, their faces hidden by the hoods they wear. One of the Weavers steps forward, but another holds out a hand, stopping the first in his tracks.

"Hold," the second Weaver commands. The voice is deep, obviously male. The Weaver steps forward himself, reaching up with both hands and pulling his hood back.

Ampir freezes, and he feels Vera tense in his arms.

The man reveals a bald head, with skin as black as night. Multicolored tattoos crawl up the sides of his neck, and thin, raised scars run up his temples like the bones of a bat's wing. The man's eyes are black, and hard. He stares at Ampir for a long moment.

Then he smiles.

"Ampir," he greets, giving a curt nod.

"Torum," Ampir replies coolly, his back to the cliffside.

"Forgive us," Torum apologizes. "We did not know it was you."

"Now you do," Ampir counters.

Torum says nothing, glancing at Junior, then at Vera. At her bloodstained nightgown. Then he meets Ampir's gaze.

"The tribes had nothing to do with this," he states, gesturing at Vera.

"That so," Ampir replies, his tone ice-cold.

"The Empire is our enemy," Torum insists. "Not you."

Ampir stares back at Torum, his eyes hidden behind his visor.

"The Empire is dead," he replies. "Are you?"

Torum says nothing for a long moment. Then he pulls his black hood forward over his head, making a sharp gesture to the men around him. He gives a curt nod, then turns his back to Ampir, walking away from the cliffside. Torum flies upward, clearing the treetops in seconds, and the others follow suit.

"Who was that?" Vera asks.

"An old friend," Ampir answers, turning back toward the cliff wall. "From the war."

"A *friend?*" Vera exclaims incredulously.

Ampir ignores the comment, continuing forward until he senses the entrance to the tunnels. A section of the cliff-wall, looking for all the world like real stone…yet the faint blue glow around it betrays the illusion.

He steps through.

* * *

"Wake up!"

Kyle groaned, turning over onto his back, the healing wound on his spine aching slightly. He felt someone grab his shoulder and shake it, and he groaned again, blinking against the murky darkness. The hand shaking him shook harder. He felt a surge of anger, and suppressed it, rubbing his eyes groggily.

Damn Jayce, he grumbled to himself.

"Wake *up*," the voice hissed. Kyle sat up, swinging his legs over the side of the bed. He stood, walking up to the dresser to grab his uniform. Then he remembered that he was still wearing it. He felt dazed, as if he'd slept even less than usual, and his forehead ached.

"I'm up, I'm up," Kyle grumbled, slipping his shoes on. He yawned then, and turned to face Jayce.

Except it wasn't Jayce at all.

The person in front of him was dressed in a red cloak, the hood pulled over his head, his face hidden in shadow. He was far too tall to be the boy who'd woken Kyle up every morning since he'd gotten here. Kyle stiffened, backing up. His legs struck the bed behind him, and he lost his balance, falling onto his butt on the bed.

The figure standing before him reached up with both hands, drawing the hood back over his head. No, not hands...gauntlets. *Golden* gauntlets. Kyle's eyes widened, his breath catching in his throat.

"*Darius!*" Kyle exclaimed.

"Yes, it's me, shut up." Darius whispered back. Kyle nodded mutely, staring at the bodyguard, not knowing how to feel. Despite the terrible things Darius had done, a part of him was relieved to see the man.

"What are you doing here?" he whispered, scooting backward in his bed until his back hit the stone wall behind him. Darius said nothing at first, staring off into space for a moment, as if he was listening for something. Then his eyes refocused on Kyle.

"I'm getting you out of here," Darius replied. "Come on," he added, reaching toward Kyle with one hand. Kyle stayed where he was, shaking his head.

"You betrayed us," he hissed back, glaring at the man.

"Bullshit."

"No," Kyle shot back. "I don't trust you!"

"You trust them?" Darius retorted, pointing at the closed door. Kyle said nothing. *Couldn't* say anything. The man had a point, after all. But he still didn't move.

"Let's go," Darius pressed, his hand still outstretched. "We have to get Kalibar."

Kyle's eyes widened, and he hesitated, staring at Darius's outstretched hand. Even if Darius was lying...even if he *was* a traitor...he was still as much of a prisoner here as Kyle and Kalibar were. He had every reason to want to escape.

Kyle reached forward, grabbing Darius's hand.

Darius pulled Kyle off of the bed, then turned to the door, cracking it open a bit. He peered through, then opened the door all the way, motioning for Kyle to follow him. They snuck out of the room and into the hallway.

It was deserted.

Darius turned to Kyle, putting a finger to his lips. Then he made his way slowly down the hallway, letting go of Kyle's hand. Kyle followed right behind the bodyguard, doing his best to tread lightly. Darius led him down the hallway, then turned at a fork to go down another, making no sound as he went. Eventually they reached a stairwell going downward. Darius started down the stairs, but Kyle hesitated.

"Wait," he whispered.

Darius turned to glare at Kyle.

"*What?*" he mouthed.

"We have to save Ariana," Kyle whispered back.

"Who?"

"Ariana, my...friend," Kyle replied. Darius shook his head.

"Too risky," he argued. "We grab Kalibar and go." He turned back to the stairwell, walking further down. Kyle stood where he was, crossing his arms in front of his chest. Darius stopped, turning back to Kyle and shooting him a murderous glare.

"Then I'm not coming," Kyle stated resolutely. Ariana wanted to leave this hellhole just as much as Kyle did. He wouldn't be able to live with himself if he left her here to rot here while he fled to freedom. And he knew that if their situation were reversed, Ariana would come for him.

"Fine," Darius spat. "What does she look like?"

"Long brown hair, brown eyes, very...um, pretty," Kyle said, blushing at the last part. Darius rolled his eyes.

"Great," he grumbled. "I'll go get your girlfriend. You stay here."

"She's *not* my girlfriend," Kyle whispered back. Darius turned his back to Kyle, walking away quickly. "Wait!" Kyle hissed. Darius turned around, looking supremely annoyed. "You don't know where her room is." In fact, Kyle didn't know either. How were they going to find her now? But Darius only smirked.

"Yours wasn't the first room I checked," he replied dryly. "Stay here," he added. Then he continued down the stairs, disappearing from sight. Kyle crouched behind one of stone columns beside the stairwell, glancing furtively behind him. If he got caught, it was all over...and the Dead Man would almost certainly punish Darius and Kalibar for trying to escape.

He might kill Kalibar, Kyle realized, fear gripping him.

In fact, if they caught Ariana coming with them, they might do something horrible to her, too. Kyle immediately regretted asking Darius to get her. As much as he wanted to save her, he couldn't bear the thought of being responsible for what they might do to her.

Kyle waited there in the hallway, his heart pounding in his chest. Despite the cool air, sweat dripped down his flanks. Minutes passed, and he began to wonder if Darius would ever come back.

Maybe he got caught, Kyle thought, glancing behind him. He considered walking back to his room; if they *had* found Darius, then pretending to sleep in his own bed would remove any suspicion that Kyle had been involved...and Kalibar would be spared.

He heard faint footsteps approaching from below the stairwell, and froze, his heart leaping into his throat. A dark figure appeared at the foot of the stairs.

"It's me," Darius hissed, just as Kyle was about to turn and run. Kyle felt a wave of relief, and realized that the bodyguard was carrying something in his right arm. Not something...*someone.*

"Ariana!" Kyle exclaimed, his eyes widening.

Darius glared at Kyle, putting a finger to his lips as he went up the stairs. His hand was firmly planted over Ariana's mouth, his other arm wrapped tightly around her torso. She struggled against his grip, her big brown eyes filled with terror. Then she spotted

Kyle, and her eyes widened.

"Ariana!" Kyle whispered. "It's okay, it's me, Kyle."

Ariana nodded once, immediately stopping her struggling. "This is Darius," Kyle added. "We're getting out of here. Do you want to come with us?" Another nod. Darius set Ariana down at the top of the stairs, her hand still covering her mouth. He leaned in, his lips inches from her ear.

"Make a noise without my permission," he whispered, "…and you'll never make a noise again."

Ariana nodded a third time.

Darius let go of Ariana's mouth, and she bolted up to Kyle, throwing her arms around him. Kyle returned her embrace, his heart soaring.

"Let's go lovebirds," Darius grumbled, walking back down the stairwell. Ariana let go of Kyle, flashing him a brilliant smile before turning and following Darius. They moved down the stairs, into the hallway below.

It too was vacant.

Darius gestured for them to continue, leading them through the maze of hallways until they emerged at the exit to the building, the massive cavern of the Arena opening up before them. Kyle glanced up at the Timestone, seeing that it was barely glowing. It couldn't be much past midnight. Darius must have woken him up a mere hour or two after he'd gone to sleep.

Darius led them toward the Arena, then through it, the packed dirt floor muting their footsteps. They reached the stairs leading up the stadium seating, making it to the top…and to the small tunnel Kyle and the Dead Man had traveled through a few days ago. Without the Dead Man's light, the tunnel was pitch black. Kyle quickly conjured up a small light to lead the way. Darius turned to Kyle, stopping him for a moment.

"Close one eye, both of you," he whispered. "Keep it closed." Kyle complied, more than a little confused. He wasn't about to question Darius about it, however. The three moved quickly through the tunnel, emerging at the end of the huge tunnel their carriage had stopped in when they'd first come here. On Darius's insistence, Kyle extinguished his magical light. Having been accustomed to the bright light earlier, Kyle could barely see out of his one eye. Then Darius turned around, motioning for Kyle to open his other eye. Kyle did so, and was surprised to find that he could see well in the darkness with it.

Kyle nodded at Darius, feeling a grudging respect for him. No matter how he felt about the man, Kyle had to admit that Darius was damn good at what he did.

Like betraying you and Kalibar, he thought darkly.

Darius peered up the huge tunnel, then gestured for Kyle and Ariana to follow him in a straight line perpendicular to it, toward another small tunnel. They did so, entering the tunnel and weaving through it. The tunnel forked once, then again, and Darius went left both times without hesitation. The tunnel eventually opened up into a large room with a desk in the center, and small prison cells with barred doors lining the walls all the way around. A man in a Death Weaver uniform lay slumped over the desk in a pool of dark red blood. The crimson liquid was still dripping from the edges of the desk to the floor. Kyle turned away from the gruesome sight, feeling woozy.

"Come on," Darius prompted, leading the way to the desk in the center of the room. Kyle noticed that one of the cells across the room already had an open door.

That must have been Darius's, he realized. But how had the bodyguard managed to escape?

Darius walked up to the corpse on the desk, searching through the dead man's pockets. He retrieved a small blue gem, then walked to one of the cells in the back of the room, disengaging the bar locking the door and bringing the blue gem up to it. The door swung inward silently. Kyle saw a small room carved into the stone beyond, with a single four-post bed, chains tied around the posts. On the bed was an old man with a scraggly white beard dressed in fine, if dusty, black clothes. Kyle's heart skipped a beat.

Kalibar!

Darius put a finger to his lips, as if anticipating Kyle's excitement. Kyle nodded, stifling the urge to call out to Kalibar. Darius walked up to the former Grand Weaver, nudging him with one hand. Kalibar stirred a bit, but did not wake up. Darius nudged him again, and Kalibar groaned.

"Kalibar," Darius whispered into the old man's ear. Kalibar turned his head toward the sound, his eyelids sunken into his empty sockets.

"Darius? Is that you?" he whispered. His voice was hoarse, and he broke into a spasm of coughing, his face turning red. After a few moments, he got himself under control.

"Yes, it's me," the bodyguard replied. "I'm gonna get you out of here."

"Did the Secula Magna come to rescue us?" Kalibar asked. Darius put a hand around Kalibar's waist, lifting him up into a seated position on his narrow bed.

"No," he replied. "It's just me and Kyle." Then he glanced at Ariana, who hadn't made a sound since she'd been freed. "And Kyle's girlfriend," he grumbled. Ariana blushed fiercely, and Kyle felt like dying inside.

"Kyle's here?" Kalibar exclaimed, a smile lighting up his features. "Where are you, Kyle?"

"I'm here, sir," Kyle whispered, unable to look at Kalibar's ruined face. Kalibar reached out with one hand, finding Kyle's shoulder, then sliding his fingers across Kyle's cheek.

"It *is* you," he exclaimed, breaking into a smile. He let go of Kyle then, his smile fading. "What do you mean, 'Kyle's girlfriend?'"

"She's a friend," Kyle corrected, blushing furiously. "A student."

"We can't trust her," Kalibar warned. "She may give us away."

"No!" Kyle exclaimed. Darius shot him a warning look, and he lowered his voice. "They kidnapped her, just like us."

"Kyle…" Kalibar began.

"She comes with us," Darius interjected. Kalibar's eyebrows furrowed.

"One traitor vouching for another," he mused. "How comforting."

"Then stay here," Darius retorted. Kalibar put up one hand.

"No need to be hasty," he countered. "I'll go. But why help us now?"

"It's my job."

"Is it now," Kalibar muttered. He broke out into a fit of coughing then, taking a few moments to recover. "Kyle told me about…"

"Don't believe everything you hear," Darius interrupted. He grabbed Kalibar, wrapping one of the older man's arms around his shoulders, and pulled him toward the open cell door.

"What's the plan?" Kalibar asked.

"Follow me," Darius answered.

They made their way past the dead guard laying on the desk, with Darius leading the way. Kyle stole a glance at Kalibar's empty eye sockets, then looked away. An immediate, overwhelming guilt came over him, and he stopped walking, slumping against the wall of the tunnel. Darius stopped, glancing back at Kyle, then disengaged from Kalibar, propping the former Grand Weaver up against the wall. He reached down to the end of his red cloak, and used a small knife to cut a strip from it. He wrapped this around Kalibar's eye sockets, tying it in the back...then walked up to Kyle.

"Hey," Darius said, grabbing Kyle by the shoulder roughly. The bodyguard stared at Kyle for a long moment, pinning him there with his blue eyes. "It's not your fault, kid."

Kyle tried unsuccessfully to break free from Darius's grasp, moisture welling up in his eyes. He turned away from the bodyguard, wiping his face with his sleeve.

"What's wrong?" Kalibar asked. Kyle shook his head silently. Kalibar frowned, reaching blindly outward, until his hand touched Kyle's shoulder. He knelt down before Kyle, gently squeezing Kyle's shoulder. He pointing to his eye sockets, covered as they were underneath his makeshift bandana.

"Darius is right, Kyle," the old man stated firmly. "*This,*" he said, tapping his temple with one hand, "...is not your fault."

Kyle shook his head emphatically.

"It *is* my fault," he retorted bitterly. "The Dead Man..."

"The Dead Man was manipulating you," Kalibar interrupted. He put a hand under Kyle's chin, lifting it slightly. "It was his plan all along to take my eyes," he added. "...for the same reason I was going to blind the Weavers that attacked my carriage; I was too dangerous otherwise." Kalibar sighed. "In one act, he neutralized me, gave his people the revenge they craved, and ensured your obedience through guilt and fear."

"Really?" Kyle asked, daring to hope. He felt a small hand on his other shoulder, and turned around. Ariana stared at him silently, then glanced at Darius, who nodded. She turned back to Kyle.

"I told you they feed on sorry here," she whispered.

Kyle wiped the moisture from his eyes, then smiled weakly, facing Kalibar.

"Thank you," he whispered. Kalibar smiled.

"You're welcome."

"We need to get going," Darius interjected, placing one gauntleted hand on Kalibar's shoulder. Kalibar turned toward the bodyguard.

"The plan," he stated. "What is it?"

"There's a natural series of caves that will take us to the surface," Darius answered. "These tunnels should connect to the caves." Kalibar frowned.

"How do you know this?" he asked.

"My guards liked to talk," Darius replied. He gestured for everyone to follow him, leading Kalibar by one arm down the narrow tunnel. At first Kalibar walked slowly, feeling his way tentatively with every step. After a few minutes, however, he seemed to gain confidence, taking longer strides.

The bodyguard took them a different route down the tunnels then they had come. These had fewer lanterns on their walls, but Kyle supposed that was a good thing; the more well-lit tunnels probably saw more traffic...and that was exactly what they were trying to avoid. Kyle heard a muted clattering coming from behind them, and glanced back as they walked.

"Did you hear..." he began. Darius shot him a glare, putting a finger to his lips. Kyle's mouth snapped shut, and he followed the bodyguard silently, glancing back every once and a while. Then he heard a low, rumbling sound echo through the dark tunnel. It sounded for all the world like thunder.

It can't be thunder, he thought. *We're underground.*

Another low boom rolled through the tunnel.

"They're sounding an alarm," Darius warned. "We need to get moving. *Now.*"

Darius turned forward, moving faster now, Kalibar clinging to his shoulder. Kyle and Ariana followed, straining to keep up with the warrior's quick pace. Another low boom sounded, and Darius went even faster, wrapping a metallic arm around Kalibar's waist, guiding the old man. The lanterns on the walls became fewer and fewer, until there were none at all; the tunnel was pitch black now, making it impossible to proceed safely. Kyle heard Darius whisper something, and a small glowing sphere appeared, hovering above Kalibar's head and bathing the tunnel in the dimmest of lights. The light cast long shadows across the walls of the tunnel, which shifted unnervingly as they continued onward. The tunnel walls soon became rougher, no longer made of smooth, polished stone. Rocky outcrops jutted from the walls and the floor, and Kyle nearly tripped over one in the darkness.

Boom.

Kyle glanced back the way they'd come, seeing shifting shadows extending into the blackness beyond like long, slender fingers stretching into the void. He continued forward, following close behind Ariana.

Suddenly the rough tunnel opened up into a full-blown cavern, with mighty stalactites hanging from the ceiling. The relatively even floor of the tunnel gave way to an irregular cave floor, making it particularly difficult for Kalibar to avoid tripping. Darius was forced to lift the former Grand Weaver up, carrying him on his back. Luckily, Kalibar's weight didn't seem to slow the gilded warrior one bit.

Boom.

Darius broke out into a run, sprinting over the uneven terrain with surprising ease. Ariana grabbed Kyle's hand, her eyes wide with fear. They followed Darius's lead, running hand-in-hand as quickly as they could, following the glowing sphere above Kalibar and Darius's head.

Suddenly Kyle's feet slipped out from under him, and he fell backward, landing butt-first on the hard rock below. A sharp pain shot up his back, and he cried out involuntarily. Darius stopped abruptly, spinning around and bringing a finger to his lips. He glared at Kyle for a moment, gesturing for Kyle to get up. Ariana helped pull Kyle to his feet, and he continued beside her, feeling a slick, slimy substance on his right palm, the same stuff coating the ground he'd slipped on. He wiped his hand on his chest, then continued forward, following Darius through the ever-widening cavern. The bodyguard led them in a zig-zagging course, dodging stalagmites and potholes. Some of the stalagmites were covered by a thin, slimy substance similar to the fluid he'd slipped on earlier. There were erosions wherever the slime lay, and some of these erosions were covered by a moss-like substance that glowed a soft, pale white. Kyle peered at a patch of the moss as he passed by; hundreds of tiny translucent finger-like projections poked up out of the rock.

Boom.

Darius increased the pace again, Kalibar bouncing up and down on his back. Most of the stalagmites they passed were covered with the glowing moss now...as were the walls and the floor. Dense clusters of mushrooms began cropping up all over the cave, growing amidst the patches of moss. Some of the mushrooms were huge, nearly as tall as Kyle, with wide orange caps.

Without warning, a shrill scream came from far in the distance ahead, reverberating off of the rocky walls. Darius stopped abruptly, staring off into the distance. Kyle and Ariana skid to a halt, nearly running into the bodyguard. They all stared...and listened. Kyle glanced at Darius, then at Ariana, his heart pounding in his chest. He rubbed his right hand on his pants...his palm was itching a little.

"What was that?" Kyle asked. Darius glanced at Kyle, then did a double take, staring at Kyle's right hand. "What?" Kyle asked, looking down. His hand was bright red, and a little swollen. Flakes of skin were peeling off of his palm, as if he'd had a bad sunburn. The itching he'd been feeling was quickly turning into a painful burning sensation.

"Oh!" Kyle yelled out, rubbing his hand on his pants. Then he started to feel itching on his chest. Looking down, he saw that his shirt had a big hole in it. "Oh!" he cried out again, frantically pulling his shirt off. He threw it away, scratching his chest. More skin peeled as he scratched, and his chest started to burn too.

"The slime," Darius said, grabbing Kyle's wrist, preventing him from scratching his chest any more. Little spots of blood oozed from his chest where his fingernails had scraped.

"Ow, ow!" Kyle cried. His skin was on fire!

"Make some water, rinse it off!" Ariana urged.

Kyle did so, quickly weaving the water pattern, and soon he had a continuous stream of cold water pouring in front of him. He rinsed his hands, then his chest; wind sucked inward from the water pattern whipped around Kyle, making him shiver. He cut the magic stream to the water pattern, staring down at his chest and hand. The itching and burning, thankfully, had stopped. But now he was shirtless and freezing, little trails of blood dripping down his chest. Ariana, who'd expertly dodged the skin-melting slime earlier, offered Kyle her sweatshirt. Luckily she'd worn layers, and had an undershirt for herself.

Another thunderous boom echoed through the cavern, followed by voices in the distance.

Kyle glanced back, seeing a faint light behind them. His heart leaped in his chest, terror seizing him. Darius swore, breaking into a sprint, carrying Kalibar with him. Ariana snatched Kyle's hand and bolted after Darius, pulling Kyle with her. Kyle pumped his legs as fast as he could, leaping over small boulders and dodging stalagmites as he went. Then his foot slipped on a slick patch on the floor again, and he lurched to the side, his hand slipping out of Ariana's. He slammed his shoulder into a stalagmite, stumbling, then falling headlong onto the ground. His head struck the unforgiving rock, pain exploding across his forehead. He tried desperately to scramble to his feet, but his limbs felt suddenly like jelly, refusing to hold his weight. He fell to his hands and knees, his head swimming sickeningly. He heard someone yelling, and then strong hands grabbed his back. He felt himself being pulled upward, his palms lifting off the ground.

A shrill, ear-piercing scream echoed through the cavern from ahead, followed by the low, thunderous boom from behind.

Darius yanked Kyle forward. Muffled voices called out from behind, much closer now. The light behind them grew brighter, long shadows dancing along the walls.

The four ran down the cavern, soon finding themselves sprinting through a veritable forest of mushrooms. The mushrooms grew taller and wider the farther they traveled, until mushroom caps towered over them on either side, a narrow rocky path barely five feet wide the only way through. The cave floor was almost completely covered in the glowing white moss. An orange, pungent mist hung in the air, making it harder and harder to see the path ahead.

The shrill scream came again, this time painfully loud, forcing everyone but Darius to cover their ears. It died away as it had before, but as it did, the sound of footsteps became audible from behind.

Darius dropped Kalibar from his back suddenly, spinning around and unsheathing his machete-sword from its scabbard.

"Get behind me!" the bodyguard commanded. Kyle huddled behind Darius, with Ariana crouching at his side. The gilded warrior peered into the dimly glowing cavern beyond, orange mist swirling in front of him. There was a shout, and then Kyle spotted them...a half-dozen men in red uniforms rushing forward. His breath caught in his throat.

Death Weavers!

A half-dozen men in red uniforms stopped before them, their faces hidden in the shadows of their cowls. Kyle scrambled backward, his eyes widening in terror. Darius, however, stood his ground, his sword shimmering in the light of the glowing moss.

One of the Death Weavers took a few steps forward, stopping not five feet from where Darius stood. The Death Weaver paused, then pulled his cowl back from his head, revealing short salt-and-pepper hair.

It was Mr. Tenson!

Mr. Tenson glanced at Kyle, who hid behind Darius, unable to meet those cruel eyes. Tenson pointed one hand at Darius's armored chest.

"Surrender or die."

Darius regarded Mr. Tenson with his equally cold blue eyes. "Make me."

An ear-splitting scream burst through the cave, bringing almost everyone – Death Weavers and otherwise – to their knees. Only Darius remained standing. Kyle covered his ears with his hands, and Ariana did the same, her face twisted in agony. The scream ended as quickly as it had come, echoing through the cave in the distance. Kyle's ears rang loudly, even after he uncovered them. Kyle turned to Ariana, who was still on her knees. Her mouth was moving, but he couldn't make out the words. Kyle shook his head.

"I can't hear you!" he shouted. He helped her up from the cave floor, and they both ran to help Kalibar get up from the ground. The old man, unable to see or hear, stood helpless between the two. Kyle glanced at Darius; the burly bodyguard was standing with his machete in hand, facing *away* from the recovering Death Weavers, his head tilted upward.

"What are you *doing*?" Kyle cried.

Darius didn't respond, his eyes locked on something above. Kyle followed the bodyguard's gaze; at first, all he saw were the undersides of massive orange mushroom caps twenty feet up. Then he made out a strange shape through the orange haze...a long beam as thick as a telephone pole, but bent at slight angles at a series of joints. One end was resting on a mushroom top; the other was connected to something very large farther above.

"What's that?" he asked Darius, who continued to ignore him. The beam moved suddenly, lifting off of the mushroom top and descending toward them. It was then that he realized what he was looking at.

It was a leg. Like an ant's leg, but *huge*.

Kyle scrambled backward, pulling Ariana with him. Ariana

followed Kyle's gaze – and screamed.

The leg smashed down between Darius and Mr. Tenson, followed by a massive pale *thing* that descended through the orange mist above. It looked for all the world like a massive maggot, but with six long legs perched on top of the mushroom caps far above. The thing was as big as a bus, its body covered in pale, translucent white skin. It had no eyes, but its mouth was huge, and filled with countless rows of dagger-like teeth.

As Kyle watched, the creature's giant tapered posterior curled up over its back, clear fluid pulsing out of the end, splashing over the creature's pale back and dripping all over the mossy floor. The creature shook like a wet dog, sending drops of the liquid flying. A single drop landed on the tip of Kyle's shoe; ribbons of smoke began to rise from the thick leather.

"Oh!" Kyle exclaimed, scraping his shoe on a rock.

Mr. Tenson stared at the beast, then turned to his fellow Death Weavers.

"What are you waiting for?" he snapped. "Kill the damn thing!"

A gravity shield appeared around him, and the other Death Weavers activated their shields, facing the huge creature. A brilliant flash of light shot out from Mr. Tenson, slamming into the creature's massive head. It jerked backward, emitting another ear-shattering scream. This time, surrounded by his shields, Mr. Tenson and the Death Weavers were unfazed, not even bothering to cover their ears. Kyle, however, dropped to the ground, covering his ears with his hands and gritting his teeth against the pain.

The creature swung one huge leg, slamming it into the stalk of one of the gigantic mushrooms. The stalk snapped, the mushroom-top falling toward Mr. Tenson's head. Mr. Tenson just stood there, the huge mushroom top slamming into his magical shields. It exploded, a dense cloud of orange spores shooting outward in all directions, surrounding Mr. Tenson and the Death Weavers. Darius backpedaled quickly, pulling Kyle, Kalibar, and Ariana to their feet, guiding them well clear of the spores.

Mr. Tenson ignored the orange cloud surrounding him, protected by his gravity shield. A ball of fire appeared in front of the Weaver, growing until it was almost as large as Mr. Tenson himself. The fireball shot forward, slamming into the massive creature's head. The beast lurched backward with an ear-piercing shriek, vanishing into the shadows above the mushroom-tops.

Then, mercifully, there was silence.

Mr. Tenson lowered his gaze to Darius, raising one hand and pointing his finger at Darius's chest. A ball of fire roared to life just beyond the Weaver's shield, growing rapidly. Even from where Kyle stood, far behind Darius, the heat was almost unbearable. Kyle squinted against the searing flames, terror gripping him. He knew that Mr. Tenson would kill Darius; there would be no mercy for the bodyguard this time.

"Stop!" Kyle pleaded.

The fireball grew ever larger, and Mr. Tenson's lips curled into a smirk.

"I said stop!" Kyle repeated.

Mr. Tenson ignored him.

Kyle closed his eyes, tearing a thick cord of magic from his skull into his mind's eye. He tied the vibrating thread of energy into a tight knot, then thrust it outward, right at Mr. Tenson.

The cave exploded in brilliant white light, so eye-searingly bright that it instantly blinded Kyle, even through his closed eyelids. He heard Mr. Tenson cry out, then felt cold, metallic fingers wrap around his right arm, pulling him backward. He opened his eyes, seeing a huge dark spot in the center of his vision. He barely made out Darius's large frame beside him, the bodyguard's hand on his arm. He turned forward, spotting Mr. Tenson dropping to the ground, his shield gone. The Weaver coughed violently, puffs of orange spores coming from his mouth. He recovered quickly, rising up into the air, his shield reappearing around him. He scowled, raising his hand up at Darius.

Then he blinked, his shield vanishing. He paused, then stared down at his hands. His eyes grew wide with terror.

Then he screamed.

Mr. Tenson lurched backward, losing his balance and falling onto his butt on the hard stone below. One of the other Death Weavers rushed to help him, and Mr. Tenson turned on the man, his eyes wild.

The Death Weaver's shield vanished, and he burst into flames.

The other Death Weavers converged around the burning man, a stream of water appeared out of thin air to douse the flames. Mr. Tenson roared at them, a shockwave exploding outward from around him, knocking the other Death Weavers backward and dissolving their shields. They toppled to the ground, the orange spore-cloud swirling all around them.

Darius pulled Kyle backward, motioning for Ariana to grab Kalibar and do the same. Kyle tore his gaze from Mr. Tenson, looking back at the other Death Weavers. Without their shields, the men were exposed to the spores around them, and soon they too were coughing puffs of orange.

Then all hell broke loose.

One of the Weavers stretched out his hand, a geyser of flame shooting right at Mr. Tenson. Mr. Tenson leapt *into* the flames, his clothes igniting instantly. He screamed in agony as the fire ate at his flesh, falling to his knees on the rocky ground. Another Death Weaver shouted something incomprehensible, stumbling away from the others, then tripping over a rocky outcropping, falling flat on his face. He writhed on the ground, flailing his arms and legs wildly.

A shrill scream pierced the air from above.

The massive maggot-creature burst downward through the cloud of spores, its slender legs perched on the mushroom tops above. It swung its long, tapered backside below its body, curling it forward until the orifice at the end was aiming right at the maddened Death Weavers. Its tail pulsed, a jet of clear liquid shooting outward in a wide spray, showering the group of men. Smoke immediately began billowing upward from their red uniforms. Their skin bubbled up, then blackened, the slime eating rapidly through their flesh.

The Death Weavers' screams echoed through the cavern.

Kyle sprinted down the tunnel away from the Death Weavers, following Darius. After a few agonizing moments, the horrible screaming died away, leaving the cavern in silence.

Kyle looked back over his shoulder.

All that remained of Mr. Tenson and the Death Weavers were smoking, blackened husks strewn across the glowing white moss. The monster that had massacred them was nowhere to be seen. Kyle's stomach churned, and he turned away from the horrid sight.

Then, without warning, the huge maggot-creature descended in front of them, cutting them off!

Ariana screamed, skidding to a stop and pulling Kalibar back from the terrible beast. Kyle nearly fell trying to stop, and Darius grabbed him, pulling him backward.

The monster opened its mouth, emitting an ear-splitting shriek.

Kyle cried out, covering his ears with his hands and following

Darius down the corridor toward the fallen Death Weavers. He glanced over his shoulder, seeing the maggot-creature lift its body up above the mushroom-tops, vanishing into the darkness beyond.

Oh god oh god oh...

He felt something crunch under his foot, and looked down, realizing he'd stepped right onto one of the Death Weavers' blackened corpses. He felt a wave of revulsion, but ignored it, sprinting as fast as he could. After a few harrowing minutes, Darius slowed down, then came to a stop. He turned around, peering down the cave behind them. Kyle stopped beside him, bending over and putting his hands on his knees. Sweat poured from him, his heart threatening to hammer through his chest.

"What *was*," Kyle gasped, "...that thing?"

"What's going on?" Kalibar asked. "Darius, describe everything to me."

Darius complied, describing the giant creature, and what it had done to the Death Weavers.

"Sounds like a Dire Lurker," Kalibar replied. "Damn!"

"What?" Kyle asked.

"It's blocking our escape," Kalibar explained. "And it's only a matter of time before they send more Death Weavers...or worse."

Kyle went cold, knowing all too well what that meant.

"Wait," Ariana said, staring down the long, mushroom-lined tunnel. "The orange mist...it made them crazy, right?"

"Yeah," Kyle agreed. "Why?"

"Well..." Ariana began, then gestured around them. Kyle blinked, realizing that the air around them had a slight orange tint to it. His breath caught in his throat; they were surrounded by the stuff! It was far less concentrated than it had been for Mr. Tenson, but still...

A shrill scream came from directly above, sharp pain lancing through his left ear. Kyle clutched his ears, falling onto his elbows and knees on the hard ground, tears streaming down his face. The scream stopped abruptly; Kyle felt hands grabbing him, and turned to see Ariana behind him, her eyes cast upward, wide with terror.

The Dire Lurker burst through the orange mist above them, deadly slime dripping down from its pale body. Its rear swooped down through the mist, curling forward until the hole at the very end was pointing right at them. Clear fluid dripped from the orifice.

"Kalibar," Darius shouted, turning the former Grand Weaver

around to face the horrid creature. "Make a shield in front of you *now!*"

The creature's tail spasmed, a jet of deadly fluid spraying out at them. Kyle screamed, throwing his hands in front of him and squeezing his eyes shut. He waited for the inevitable pain, the agony of feeling his flesh melt from his bones.

But nothing happened.

Kyle opened his eyes, lowering his hands.

There, not two feet from where Kalibar stood, was a translucent blue gravity shield forming a wide arc in front of them, like an umbrella tipped on its side. The Dire Lurker's deadly slime had collided with the shield, bouncing off harmlessly...and leaving everyone perfectly dry.

"Hold that shield!" Darius barked into Kalibar's ear. The Dire Lurker shifted its weight, lifting one massive leg off of a mushroom stalk and swinging it right at Kalibar!

"Kalibar!" Kyle cried.

But it was too late. The creature's leg struck Kalibar's shield, its foot piercing right through. It headed straight for Kalibar, who of course had no idea what was happening.

No!

The foot slowed, then stopped – mere inches from Kalibar's face.

The shield flung the Dire Lurker's leg backward, sending it crashing into a giant mushroom stalk. The stalk shattered, the mushroom cap it supported falling to the ground and exploding into a cloud of orange spores twenty feet from where Kyle stood.

The Dire Lurker lurched to the side, catching itself with its other five legs. Quickly righting itself, it faced them once again, aiming its acid-spewing orifice at Kalibar. A great jet of fluid shot forth, once again hitting the shield, and splattering away ineffectively. Kalibar stood tall against the fierce beast, his jaw set firm. Even in his dusty clothes, with a red band around his eyes and a scruffy beard, the former Grand Weaver looked the part.

The Dire Lurker lowered its orifice then, aiming its deadly secretions onto the ground in front of Kalibar. Pools of the stuff welled up on the mossy ground, rising up to meet Kalibar's shield. The acid sprayed backward where it met the shield, but the rest flowed around the barrier, pooling in the small depression Kalibar was standing in front of. As the shield only covered their front, soon the acid was pouring in from the sides…right toward them.

Darius grabbed Kyle and Ariana, shoving them up the slight slope behind them. The liquid flowed into the depression in front of them, forming a veritable pond on the cavern floor. Darius and Kalibar were left standing on a narrow island of rock, surrounded on all sides by the Dire Lurker's slowly rising pool of acid.

"Kalibar!" Darius yelled, tapping the former Grand Weaver on the shoulder. Kalibar shook his head, clearly unable to hear what Darius was saying; he must have been deafened by the creature's ear-gouging shrieks. Darius stepped back, pulling out two small daggers from his red cloak, clutching one in each hand. He backed up to the far end of the narrow island, crouching low to the ground. "What are you…" Kyle began.

Darius lunged forward, sprinting across the narrow island, right at Kalibar. He leaped into the air, sailing over Kalibar's head…and right into Kalibar's shield. The shield flung him upward and forward, launching him over twenty feet in the air, even higher than the tallest mushroom cap. Kyle turned away, knowing full well the bodyguard would never survive a fall from that height.

He heard a loud *thump*, followed by an agonizing scream.

Kyle heard a gasp, then felt a hand on his shoulder.

"Kyle, look!" he heard Ariana cry.

He did so, his guts twisting into a knot as he peered through the thick orange cloud beyond Kalibar's shield. He scanned the cavern floor for a hint of golden armor, expecting to see Darius's corpse strewn across the rock. But the bodyguard was nowhere to be seen.

Then he heard a shriek from above, and followed the sound upward, seeing the Dire Lurker. It was thrashing its massive head from side-to-side, deadly acid flinging from its pale skin. Something was hanging from the beast's underbelly, barely visible through the mist of orange spores. No, not some*thing*…some*one*.

"Darius!" Kyle cried, his heart near to bursting with elation.

The bodyguard's legs were wrapped around the Lurker's underside, each dagger buried hilt-deep into the beast's pale flesh. Pulling one dagger free, Darius inched up the Lurker's belly, jamming the blade into the side of its throat. The creature screamed, its maw gaping wide. It thrashed again, but Darius hung on, using his daggers to climb up to right below the Lurker's gaping maw. Kyle watched in horror as streams of clear liquid dripped from its mouth, covering Darius's left shoulder in a shiny layer of acid goo. Darius's red cloak blackened, smoke rising from a rapidly expanding hole in the fabric. Darius ignored the deadly stuff, sheathing his left dagger and reaching up with his left hand into the monster's mouth, grabbing onto a tooth. He hauled himself upward, jamming his remaining dagger into the creature's lower lip.

The Dire Lurker shrieked, forcing Kyle to cover his ears again. He watched as Darius hung from the creature's mouth for dear life, even as its massive head swung side-to-side. Despite his gauntlets being coated in slippery goo, Darius somehow maintained his grip, swinging a leg up and over into the gaping mouth.

Then the massive beast raised its head high into the air, slamming its jaws shut!

Darius jerked back, rolling out of the creature's mouth. The Lurker's razor-sharp teeth slammed together, and the bodyguard let go of just in time, free-falling toward the cavern floor far below.

Kyle heard Ariana scream, felt his heart leap into his throat.

Darius twisted in mid-air, unsheathing his left dagger and slamming it into the creature's underbelly, cutting a huge gash in the white, translucent skin. His descent slowed, then stopped, leaving him hanging from the Lurker's underside. The Lurker shrieked, thick yellow fluid gushing from the wound and splashing into the pool of acid before Kalibar. The bodyguard swung his legs upward, wrapping them around the creature's underside, then used his daggers to climb his way up to its mouth again. He sheathed one dagger, grabbing a tooth with his freed hand, then vaulted his legs up into the monster's massive maw. There he crouched, just beyond the rows of sharp teeth. He brought his right arm up to the sword in his scabbard...

...and then the giant mouth snapped shut.

Kyle and Ariana stood there, staring in disbelief as the creature's mouth closed on Darius. A loud, sickening *crunch* echoed off the cave walls.

"Darius!" Kyle screamed. "*No!*"

The Dire Lurker's eyeless head jerked in Kyle's direction, its pale body glistening in the pale glow of the moss-lined cavern.

Kyle's legs wobbled, then gave out. He fell onto his butt on the hard rock below, his eyes glued to the Lurker's horrid mouth. The creature's head shifted, facing Kalibar.

"Kalibar!" Ariana cried, stepping forward, to the edge of the pool of acid.

The creature dropped a leg from its mushroom-top, swinging it at Kalibar. Its huge foot slammed into Kalibar's shield, clipping the former Grand Weaver on the shoulder before being flung backward. Kalibar cried out, spinning around and falling backward onto the narrow island of rock. His temple struck the ground with a terrible *crack*.

"Kalibar!" Kyle shouted.

Kalibar lay motionless on the rock, blood pooling around his head. His shield – the only thing protecting them from the Dire Lurker's deadly acid – vanished.

Ariana backpedaled, stopping twenty feet from the edge of the pool. Then she burst forward.

"Ariana!" Kyle cried. "What are you –"

She sprinted right to the edge of the pool, and jumped, sailing through the air over the lethal liquid…and barely cleared it, landing on the narrow island beyond. She skid to a stop before Kalibar, crouching down and rolling the man onto his back.

"Kalibar!" she yelled, shaking his shoulders. But he just laid there, utterly limp, blood oozing from his temple. She leaned in close, her lips next to his ear. "Kalibar!"

Kyle saw movement from above, and looked upward, spotting the Dire Lurker. The beast's rear swung downward, arcing below its wounded belly, that deadly orifice pointing right at Ariana and Kalibar.

"Ariana, watch out!" Kyle warned.

Ariana turned her head just as the Lurker's rear pulsed, shooting acid at her. The flesh-eating goo struck Ariana and Kalibar, knocking Ariana backward. Smoke began to rise from the front of her uniform.

No!

He weaved magic in his mind's eye, and suddenly a cold gust of wind whipped around Kyle, shoving him from behind. He braced himself, a veritable waterfall appearing out of thin air above Ariana and Kalibar, drenching them both.

The Lurker's acid spray stopped, fluid dripping from its orifice.

Ariana rose to her feet, water coursing down her head and body. Kyle maintained his magic stream to the waterfall for a moment longer, then stopped it. She stood there, shivering violently, her uniform riddled with tiny holes…but her flesh was intact. She nodded at Kyle.

A shrill scream echoed through the cavern, and Kyle flinched, crouching low and bringing his hands to his ears. He glanced up, seeing the Dire Lurker above them still. Its horrible mouth opened, then shut, its jaws quivering. Then its whole body went rigid. Kyle backpedaled slowly, his eyes locked on the monstrous beast.

What the...

Then the Lurker's legs buckled, its spiky feet slipping off of the mushroom caps. Its huge body fell through the air, landing in the pool below. Acid sprayed outward from the incredible impact, showering Ariana and Kalibar. Kyle felt a few drops pelt his shirt, and seconds later smelled smoke. He wove the water pattern frantically, sending it up above his head. Ice-cold water gushed onto him, soaking through his clothes and chilling him to the bone. He gasped, his throat locking up, his whole body going rigid. He turned to Ariana and Kalibar, weaving a second water pattern above them, attaching a magic stream while maintaining his stream to the waterfall above himself. It took everything he had to maintain his concentration, streaming magic to more than one pattern at a time. But he managed to do just that, another waterfall appearing above Ariana and Kalibar, drenching them instantly. He held the streams for a while, until all of the acid had been washed away. Then he dropped them both.

"Kyle," Ariana yelled, pointed at the Lurker. "Look!"

The Dire Lurker lay utterly still in the pool of its own acid, its mouth partly open, thick yellow fluid seeping between its teeth. A muffled crunching sound came somewhere inside the beast, then another. A strange pulsing mass rose from the top of the creature's head, tenting upward to form a sharp peak. Then the Lurker's pale skin ruptured, pus-like yellow fluid streaming down its head. A long, razor-thin spike thrust upward out of the wound. The spike twisted ninety degrees, and it was then that Kyle realized it wasn't a spike at all. It was a long blade.

A *sword*.

As Kyle watched, the blade sawed up and down, slicing down the creature's skull. Then a slick, golden-armored arm shot out of the wound.

"Darius?" Kyle cried, unable to believe his eyes. "Darius!"

Another arm shot out of the creature's head, and then a brown-haired head appeared. It *was* Darius! The warrior pulled himself up out of the creature's skull, then jumped down from the thing, landing feet-first into the wide pool of acid below.

"Darius!" Kyle cried in horror.

The gilded warrior waded slowly toward Ariana and Kalibar, the deadly acid lapping at his upper thighs, the golden metal hissing and bubbling. His red cloak blackened where it touched the pool, dissolving before Kyle's eyes. Darius reached the small island of rock, stepping up onto it and looking down at Ariana and Kalibar. Ariana stared wide-eyed at the man, her jaw slack. Darius sheathed his sword.

"Anyone want to help me here?" the bodyguard asked, gesturing at the acid still eating away at his armor.

Ariana snapped out of her trance, and within moments a stream of water appeared above the bodyguard, splashing over his armored body, flowing down his legs and back into the acid pool behind him. The grim warrior didn't even flinch as the ice-cold water coursed over him, rinsing the deadly acid from his now-pitted armor. After a full minute, Darius raised one hand, and the stream stopped. He dropped to one knee at Kalibar's side, shaking the unconscious man's shoulder.

Kalibar groaned, putting a hand up to his bleeding temple.

"Kalibar," Darius prompted.

"Who is it?" Kalibar asked. "Who said that?"

"Darius," the warrior answered.

"What happened?" Kalibar pressed, pushing himself off of the ground and sitting up. He began to gag, and Darius quickly lowered the former Grand Weaver to the ground again.

"The Lurker is dead," Darius replied.

"Who said that?" Kalibar asked, his eyebrows knitting together. Darius sighed, standing up and facing Kyle and Ariana.

"Wait here," he ordered. Then he lifted Kalibar off of the ground, slinging the older man over his shoulder. He turned about, wading right back into the acid pool, going around the massive corpse of the Lurker and continuing forward until he disappeared in the orange spore-mist that still hung in the air beyond.

"What is he, crazy?" Ariana asked, staring at the spot where Darius had vanished. Kyle said nothing, but he had to agree. If Darius breathed in enough of that orange dust, he *would* go crazy.

After a minute, Darius reappeared – without Kalibar – wading out of the fog and back up to Kyle and Ariana. He stepped up onto the rock, the armor on his feet and legs hissing loudly. Darius cleared his throat, glancing down at his own feet.

Kyle took the hint, weaving the water pattern to create a stream of magic level with Darius's waist. Darius stepped into it, rinsing his legs thoroughly. When the stream stopped, Darius reached out to Ariana, motioning for her to crawl up onto his back. She hesitated, glancing nervously at Kyle, then obeyed, climbing onto the bodyguard's back. Darius stepped down into the pond once again, wading forward until he disappeared beyond the orange mist.

Kyle stood there, now alone, facing the motionless body of the Lurker. It lay in the pool of acid it had created, yellow fluid dripping slowly down the side of its skull. He peered into the mist, trying to find Darius's dark form in the distance, feeling more and more uneasy as the seconds passed.

What if he doesn't come back, Kyle thought. *What if he leaves you here, all alone?*

The thought made his guts squirm.

A dark shape appeared in the mist, wading through the deep pool of acid, coming toward him. Kyle breathed a sigh of relief, watching as the warrior made his way to the shore, climbing up onto the rocky ledge and turning around to present his back to Kyle. Kyle doused Darius again with the water pattern, then hopped onto his back, wrapping his arms around the warrior's neck, being careful not to strangle the man. Darius walked into the pond a final time, wading slowly to the right of the creature's massive corpse. Kyle looked down, realizing that Darius was up to his thighs in acid. Kyle gripped Darius tightly; if he slipped now, he was as good as dead. The only thing preventing Darius from being horribly burned was his heavy golden armor, and even that was slowly dissolving in the deadly fluid. Darius ignored the danger, making his way toward the dense orange mist.

"Hold your breath," Darius ordered. Kyle complied, taking a deep breath in and holding it. They waded through the orange mist, emerging at length into the open air on the other end. Kyle let his breath out, taking a few deep, gulping breaths of the fresh air. It wasn't long before Kyle saw two figures on a rocky shore in the distance. As they got closer, he saw that it was Ariana and Kalibar, safely on the other side of the acid pond. Ariana was standing over Kalibar, who was sitting on the shore, his head in his hands.

Darius waded to the rocky shore, stepping up onto it and dropping Kyle next to Ariana. A stream of water appeared before

Darius – created by Ariana, of course – and the warrior rinsed himself off a final time. Kyle found himself staring at the man; Darius's red cloak, once at ankle-length, ended at hip-level now. The rest had completely dissolved, the edges blackened. Much of the warrior's armor was dull and deeply pitted, corroded by the Lurker's deadly juices.

"He's starting to remember," Ariana said, gesturing at Kalibar, who raised his head.

"Ariana said that you defeated the Dire Lurker, Darius," Kalibar said. "Is that true?"

"Yep," Darius answered.

"Impressive," Kalibar murmured. He rose to his feet then, aided by Ariana. "We should get going; the Death Weavers will send more men after us before long."

"Let's go," Darius stated.

"Are you going to be okay?" Ariana asked, staring at Darius. The man said nothing, offering his shoulder for Kalibar to hold on to. Then he strode forward, leading the way forward through the tunnel. Kyle and Ariana followed side-by-side, their footsteps muted by the glowing moss underfoot. More mushrooms stood throughout the cavern, forcing them to weave around the tall, thick white stalks. Mushroom caps of different colors, some as low as Kyle's hip, and others twenty feet up, topped each stalk. The taller mushrooms grew nearer to the cave walls on either side, while the shorter ones sat nearer to the middle. Kyle stepped around one at belly-height, glancing down at the mushroom cap. It was bright red, with white stripes at the edges...he'd seen several just like it earlier. But something was different about this one; the cap looked swollen somehow, as if it were about to...

The cap *exploded*, sending a cloud of thick orange spores up into the air...and right into Kyle's face.

Kyle jerked away from the mushroom, slamming into Ariana. They both fell to the ground, a huge orange plume expanding all around them. Kyle landed on his back, knocking the air out of his lungs.

He rose to his hands and knees, gasping for air.

Ariana scrambled to her feet beside him, orange dust swirling all around them. She offered her hand, and Kyle grabbed it, rising to his feet. He felt a tickle in the back of his throat, and coughed, a thick cloud of orange shooting out of his mouth.

He stared at it, his blood going cold.

"Kyle?" Ariana said, staring at him. Then *she* coughed, a puff of orange escaping her lips. She stared at this, then at Kyle, her face going pale. Her pupils were *huge*.

"Hold your breath!" Kyle ordered, following his own advice. He brought the front of his shirt over his mouth and nose, squinting in the cloud of orange. Then he grabbed Ariana's hand, pulling her forward. He felt her pull back, resisting him, and turned to find her staring at him, her eyes filled with terror.

She screamed, then tore her hand free, shoving him backward. Kyle stumbled, falling onto his buttocks on the rock floor. He scrambled to his feet, then froze.

Something was wrong.

He closed his eyes, and immediately felt the floor dropping out from beneath him, as if he were falling *upward*. Opening his eyes, he saw his feet standing on the ground, as they should be. He hesitated, then closed his eyes again. Once again, he felt as if the floor were dropping out underneath him. But he still felt his feet on the ground; it was as if the ground were falling and his legs were growing *longer* at the same time. As soon as he opened his eyes, the sensation stopped.

Weird.

He looked forward, spotting Darius's armored back in the distance ahead. He stared at the warrior's golden armor, at the way the metal caught the light of the glowing moss. Darius seemed to freeze in place, as if suspended in time, every detail of the shimmering armor magnified and amazingly sharp. He devoured every detail, even the distorted reflections of the cavern. He'd never seen anything so incredible in his entire life.

He felt a hand on the back of his shoulder, and turned around to see Ariana staring at him. Her lips were slightly open, her big brown eyes staring right into his. He stared back, realizing that her eyes were *growing*, so large that he was afraid he was going to fall into them. He took a step back.

The world *shifted*.

Kyle stumbled to the side, feeling the ground tilt to the left. He caught himself on the wall of the tunnel, righting himself quickly. Taking a step toward Ariana, he felt the ground tilt in the opposite direction, throwing him into a thick cluster of mushroom stalks.

What the...

He staggered away from the stalks, stumbling toward Ariana. The tunnel tilted *backward* then, and he cried out, closing his eyes. He fell back, two streams of brilliant rainbow-colors shimmering in wondrous arcs before him. Time slowed, then stopped.

He fell through infinite space.

Kyle felt his back striking the ground, felt pain there, but it was as if it were happening to someone else. He opened his eyes, and saw two huge blue eyes peering down at him.

"Darius!" Kyle exclaimed.

And it *was* Darius. The man's mouth was moving, but the words were gibberish. He stared at Darius's mouth, watching as it started to grow. It was a perilously deep cavern now, lined by teeth ten feet high. Kyle felt as if he were being pulled upward toward that huge orifice, and cried out.

Hands shook him.

Kyle scrambled backward on the cavern floor, feeling it tilt crazily to the left. He rolled onto his belly, pushing himself up onto his hands and knees, a sudden wave of nausea coming over him. He resisted the urge to puke, gritting his teeth. He could feel the back of his throat with remarkable clarity, all the way down to his stomach. Warm, bitter fluid gushed upward, filling the back of his throat.

Don't puke don't puke...

He vomited, a wave of orange-brown fluid spewed from his mouth in slow motion, flying toward the ground in a graceful arc. He watched in fascination as tiny droplets separated themselves from the main vomit-stream, spinning majestically in space for minutes until they splashed onto the ground. Then he vomited again, but this time the liquid poured from his mouth rapidly, splattering onto the glowing moss underneath him. He vomited until he had nothing left in his belly, and then he retched some more. The world tilted crazily around him.

Then, mercifully, everything went black.

* * *

Kyle's head *hurt*.

He groaned, opening his eyes, and saw Darius kneeling down before him. The bodyguard stood up.

"Welcome back," he grumbled.

Kyle blinked, realizing that he was lying on his back on the cavern floor. He sat up, glancing down at his hands. Glowing moss coated the palms of his hands, the light slowly fading as he watched.

What the heck happened?

Darius stepped away, reaching down and lifting Ariana up from the ground. She was clutching her head in both hands; she looked absolutely miserable.

"What happened?" Kyle asked. He felt the ground tilt ever-so-slightly underneath him, and tensed up. But the sensation vanished as quickly as it had come.

"You passed out," the bodyguard answered. Kyle resisted the urge to roll his eyes.

"I mean *before* that," he clarified.

"Let's go," Darius said, walking forward, Kalibar leaning on his shoulder. Kyle sighed, rising to his feet. He glanced at Ariana, who fell into step beside him. She was a little unsteady on her feet, and bumped into him as they walked.

"You okay?" Kyle asked. She nodded, rubbing her temples gingerly.

"That was really weird," she stated.

"You felt it too?" Kyle pressed. Ariana nodded, but said nothing more. Kyle couldn't blame her. As novel as the experience had been, he would never *ever* want to go through that again. It was no wonder that the Death Weavers had gone insane after the Lurker had exposed them to the mushroom spores. It was pure luck that Kalibar hadn't inhaled the stuff. If he had, they'd all be very dead by now.

They walked in silence, the tunnel ramping slightly upward now. The glowing moss became sparser, making the cave appear darker as they went. At Darius's request, Kyle made another magical light above their heads to guide the way. The underground fungal forest eventually thinned, the mushrooms becoming smaller and smaller until there was only bare rock left. The glowing white moss vanished as well. They marched slowly along the uneven ground, dodging stalagmites carefully. No one spoke.

The silent hike gave Kyle's mind plenty of time to wander, and he found himself contemplating the strange mushroom forest they'd left behind. The Dire Lurker's acid had dissolved the stone floor, and the moss – which seemed immune to the stuff – had grown there. And then there were the mushrooms. Were they the creature's food supply? Maybe the mushrooms needed the glow-moss to grow…and the moss needed the Lurker. With the Lurker gone, would the mushroom forest die off? It made Kyle a little sad to think so. An entire ecosystem might have been destroyed by their actions.

His morbid thoughts were interrupted by a sudden, sharp pain in his right heel. He yelped, stopping abruptly and lifting his foot to inspect his heel. The sole of his shoe had a large hole in it. It must have been eaten away by the acid he'd stepped in earlier. His exposed heel was red and flaking, and stung terribly. He rinsed his foot off with a stream of conjured water, then continued onward. With each step, his heel struck the hard, cold rocky floor, throbbing fiercely.

He limped along, following Darius through the winding tunnel. The ground angled upward sharply at times, making the going particularly difficult. Kyle's legs burned with each step; still, he limped along, trying to keep up with Darius and Kalibar. Ariana was limping too, her undershirt riddled with holes from the acid that had splashed on it. She shivered in the cool breeze, hugging herself closely. Kyle offered his shirt to her, but she refused.

Darius set a tireless pace, leading the group onward and upward. The stalactites and stalagmites become sparser, until there were none at all. The pain in Kyle's right foot intensified with every step, until it became nigh unbearable. He stopped, feeling Ariana bump into him from behind.

"I need a break," he called out, shifted his weight to his good foot. Darius didn't even turn around, continuing his brutal pace.

"You stop, you die."

Kyle stared at the bodyguard, images of the Dead Man flashing in his mind's eye.

He'll come for us, he realized.

Kyle continued forward, limping badly. Ariana squeezed in beside him, wrapping an arm around his lower back. He gave her a weak smile, and they leaned on each other, walking behind Kalibar and the dour bodyguard. Kalibar, who hadn't said much of anything the entire trip, seemed to be concentrating entirely on putting one foot in front of the other. The former Grand Weaver's boots were in terrible shape, eaten away by the Lurker's acid, and he too was limping. Kyle felt suddenly ashamed; Kalibar, having been imprisoned, mutilated, and having suffered greatly at the whim of the Lurker, hadn't uttered a single complaint. Kyle grit his teeth, resolving to be more like the former Grand Weaver. If Kalibar could make it, so could he.

Step by step, pain after pain, he made his way forward. The air, having been dank and musty since leaving the Arena, started to smell fresher. A cool breeze wafted through the cave, giving poor Ariana a chill. The cave became progressively brighter, until Kyle was able to stop his magic stream to the light pattern.

Then, at long last, an impossibly bright light shone in the distance. Kyle squinted at it, his eyes smarting. Slowly his vision acclimated, and he saw a hint of blue and green beyond. He quickened his pace, ignoring the pain in his foot.

Is that...?

He caught up to Darius and Kalibar, squeezing past them as the tunnel broadened, pulling Ariana with him. The light at the end of the tunnel grew larger and larger, until at long last he reached the mouth of the cave. Warm, sweet air greeted him, the sky opening up before him in a magnificent blue vista. Soft, fragrant grass tickled his feet, so green that it seemed unreal. The sun's rays felt wondrously warm on his skin, and Kyle lifted his face to the sky, laughing joyously. He let go of Ariana's hand, lowering himself onto his belly on the grass, embracing the warm earth. Tears of joy streamed down his cheeks.

We did it, he realized, his spirit soaring. *We made it!*

Despite losing all hope, in the face of impossible odds, they had escaped!

Chapter 18

The warm sun shone on Kyle's back as he lay on his belly on the grass just outside the mouth of the cave he'd just escaped, and he basked in its healing rays, closing his eyes and resting his temple on the ground.

"Are we outside?" he heard Kalibar ask. Kyle opened his eyes, rising to his feet and turning to face the Weaver. Kalibar was still holding onto Darius's shoulder.

"We are," Ariana answered, as if she couldn't believe it. She turned in a slow circle, taking it all in. Kyle grinned at her.

"We're free!" he exclaimed.

Ariana nodded, but didn't smile back. She turned to face the mouth of the cave, staring at it for what seemed like an eternity.

"Ariana?" Kyle asked, stepping toward her. She turned to face him, then froze, her eyes going wide. She backpedaled, then tripped and fell backward onto her butt on the grass.

"Going somewhere?" said a voice behind Kyle.

Kyle froze, the hairs on the nape of his neck standing on end. He turned around – slowly – his eyes dropping to the ground before him. He spotted two black boots hovering above the grass, surrounded by a black cloak with ornate gray symbols woven into its thick fabric. His eyes drew upward of their own accord, until he found himself staring into dark eyes sunk into a pale, drawn face...and that green, diamond-shaped crystal, sparkling brilliantly in the sunlight.

"No," Kyle whimpered, feeling his legs wobble underneath him. He fell onto his rear, landing hard, pain shooting up his back. He stared at that horrible face, and scrambled backward in the grass, terror gripping him.

The Dead Man stared down at Kyle, his expression unreadable.

"I'm disappointed in you, Kyle," he murmured, levitating forward toward Kyle, his dark cloak rippling behind him. "I thought we had an understanding."

"Darius, what's going on?" Kalibar demanded. Darius pushed Kalibar away from his shoulder, grabbing his sword and pulling it from its scabbard.

"The Dead Man," the bodyguard growled. The Dead Man turned to face Darius.

"I underestimated you," he stated, his deep voice sending chills down Kyle's spine. "I won't make that mistake again."

"Doubt that," Darius shot back, stepping in front of Kalibar. The Dead Man smirked.

"Wait!" Kalibar exclaimed, stepping from behind Darius and facing the general direction of the Dead Man. "You have me," he stated, stretching his arms out before him. "Take me, take what you want from me. But please, let the others go."

"You are correct," the Dead Man stated, facing Kalibar. "We do have you...and you will continue to contribute to our future." His smirk faded. "And in time, so will Kyle...and Ariana," he added, gesturing at the two.

"Please," Kalibar pleaded, stepping toward the Dead Man. He reached out blindly, grabbing the Dead Man's arms by the sleeves and falling to his knees before the dark Weaver. "They're innocent children!"

"They are *my* children," the Dead Man retorted, pulling his arms away. He grabbed the front of Kalibar's shirt, pulling the former Grand Weaver to his feet with one hand. "Don't grovel," he reprimanded. "It doesn't suit you."

Kalibar's stood there before the Dead Man, his jawline rippling. He squared his shoulders, then faced forward...as if he were staring right into the Dead Man's eyes.

"Your name suits you," the former Grand Weaver stated, his voice icy calm. "Time to earn it."

White-hot light burst forward from Kalibar, shooting right at the Dead Man. Layer upon layer of gravity shields appeared around the dark Weaver instantaneously, the white light slamming into them, then wrapping around them in a mad orbit. Then the light shot outward from the Dead Man's side, slicing through a copse of trees in the distance. The trees split in two, the ends bursting into flames and falling to the forest floor.

The Dead Man shook his head, having not even flinched.

"Not today," he shot back.

"Oh, I'm just getting started," Kalibar growled.

Suddenly a half-dozen layers of gravity shields appeared around the former Grand Weaver. The earth rose up around the Dead Man, huge fingers of stone reaching up and closing on his legs. The Dead Man's shields stopped them.

Then the shields vanished.

The earthen fingers clutching the Dead Man's legs pinched inward, crushing the dark Weaver's legs. The bones at his mid-calves snapped, then crunched as they were ground into bits. The Dead Man howled, his dark eyes wide with agony. Layers of shields appeared around him, then just as quickly winked out.

Kalibar smirked.

A huge explosion burst from between Kalibar and the Dead Man, ripping the Dead Man from his rocky prison and hurtling him backward through the air like a rag doll. His body tumbled madly across the ground, slamming into a large tree trunk a dozen yards away with a sickening *crack*. Pieces of the Dead Man's limbs flew apart from his body, scattering across the ground. What remained of his body fell lifelessly to the ground, unmoving in the short, green grass. Flames licked at the edges of his black cloak.

Kalibar stood tall before his fallen enemy, his acid-worn black clothes rippling in the wind. He pulled his hand out of his pocket, holding a small hunk of quartz. It was covered in tiny runes, barely visible to the naked eye.

"Amateur."

Kyle stared at the limp body in the distance, then at the fingers of stone a few feet in front of Kyle. The Dead Man's severed legs were still clutched between them, bones jutting out of each bloodless stump. Then he stared at Kalibar, his mouth agape.

"Kalibar!" he shouted, scrambling to his feet. He ran up to the man, nearly knocking the former Grand Weaver off of his feet. "You did it!"

"I did?" Kalibar asked.

"You did!" Kyle exclaimed. He let go of Kalibar, shaking his head in amazement. "How did you do that?"

"With this," Kalibar answered, holding out one hand and showing the quartz crystal. "Prison gave me time to work on my

Runic skills...and build a device to neutralize his shields."

"Impressive," a deep voice called out from behind.

Kyle whirled around, seeing a dark figure coming toward them. Where its legs should have been, only ragged pieces of pale flesh remained at the thighs, hanging down to levitate a few inches from the grass. Its left arm was missing entirely below the elbow, as was much of the flesh on the left side of its chest. White ribs glinted in the sunlight beneath charred black flesh. And its face...

Kyle took a step back.

Its face was blackened on the left, deep gashes carved into its temple, exposing the bleached skull that lay below. Two black eyes stared at Kalibar from their sunken sockets, a green crystal shimmering in the sunlight from its pale forehead.

"My turn," the Dead Man declared, his pale lips twisting into a grim smile. The green crystal on his forehead flared to life suddenly, glowing bright green even in the full sunlight, casting its verdant rays across the Dead Man's gaunt features. His arms spasmed once, his eyes going wide.

"Kyle, get back!" Kalibar commanded. Kyle backpedaled, seeing gravity shields appear around the former Grand Weaver. The Dead Man stared blankly off into space for a moment. Then his eyes focused on Kalibar.

Every one of Kalibar's shields vanished.

"So this," the Dead Man's voice boomed, so deep and powerful that Kyle felt it in his bones, "...is the man who would murder My Chosen."

Kalibar took a step back, a shield appearing around him...and almost instantly vanishing. The Dead Man levitated forward, grabbing Kalibar by the neck with one hand. He lifted Kalibar off the ground, and Kalibar grabbed the Dead Man's hand with his own, struggling against that powerful grip. Another shield appeared around Kalibar, then vanished. A dozen bright lights shot outward from Kalibar at the Dead Man, but fizzled out before ever reaching his shields.

The Dead Man stared at Kalibar impassively.

"You're weak," he observed. "And slow." He let go of Kalibar's neck, dropping the former Grand Weaver. Kalibar landed hard, falling onto his back on the ground. He clutched at his neck, gasping for air.

"Kalibar!" Kyle cried, rushing to Kalibar's side.

"You're not the one who killed My Chosen," the Dead Man stated in that strange voice, staring down at Kalibar. Kyle felt Kalibar grip his shoulder, heard the man croak something.

"What?" Kyle asked.

"Run," Kalibar gasped, squeezing Kyle's shoulder hard. Kyle hesitated, glancing up at the Dead Man, then back at Kalibar.

"But..."

"*Run!*"

Kyle felt arms reach around him from behind, turned to see Ariana there. She pulled him from Kalibar and grabbed his hand, bolting past the Dead Man toward the dense forest beyond. Kyle pumped his legs as fast as he could, and Ariana matched him stride for stride. He heard a blood-curdling scream from behind, and turned his head to look back.

"Don't look!" Ariana shouted. "Go!"

Kyle obeyed, keeping his eyes forward. The forest was only a few hundred yards ahead. He pushed himself harder, his legs starting to burn. Tears streamed down his face, blurring his vision.

Kalibar!

Still he ran, his breath coming in gasps now, his lungs on fire.

Then he felt a force pull at him, lifting him upward. His feet left the ground, dangling in midair...and then he flew backward, the ground whizzing by underneath him at dizzying speed. Upward and backward he went, careening helplessly through the air.

Kyle screamed.

He felt himself drop through the air suddenly, and he landed on his back...*hard*. He gasped for air, stars exploding before his eyes. He rolled onto his side, seeing Kalibar lying beside him, blood dripping from the man's right ear. He heard a *thump*, and turned to see Ariana lying on the ground a few feet away.

The Dead Man's mutilated body levitated over them, the gem on the dark Weaver's pale forehead shining like a miniature green sun.

"I must say I'm impressed, Kalibar," that impossibly deep voice boomed. "It takes a lot to impress Me."

Kalibar's mouth opened soundlessly, then closed. He clutched at his right ear, his hand trembling. The Dead Man turned his black eyes on Kyle, his pale lips twisted into a frown.

"You," he stated, pointing one skeletal finger at Kyle, "...have been disloyal to your master." He lowered his hand. "And to Me."

His eyes flicked to the side; Kyle followed his gaze, and saw Ariana lying there in the dirt, her eyes wide with terror. "Now you will see what disloyalty earns you."

"No!" Kyle screamed, scrambling backward. An invisible force slammed into his chest, pinning him to the ground. "No!"

Ariana's feet burst into flames.

"*No!*"

Ariana screamed, kicking her legs wildly, her eyes wide with terror. She tried to lift herself off of the ground, but to no avail. She lay there on her back, her legs flailing, her eyes wide with terror.

"Stop it!" Kyle screamed. "Stop!"

The flames devoured Ariana's boots, crawling up her ankles. They licked at her pants, smoke billowing upward from them. She shrieked in agony, beating at the ground with her hands. Upward the fire went, eating at her shins, then her knees. It engulfed her thighs, growing taller and hotter as it went.

"*Ariana!*"

The heat was so tremendous now that Kyle could feel it scalding his own skin, even from a few feet away. Suddenly the force pinning him to the ground vanished. He rolled onto his hands and knees, sprinting to Ariana's head and kneeling down. The heat stung his eyes, scalding his exposed skin.

"Ariana!" he cried. He ignored the heat, closing his eyes and yanking magic into his mind's eye, weaving it into the water pattern. He thrust it out above Ariana's legs, and opened his eyes.

A waterfall appeared over the burning girl, landing directly on her legs. The fire engulfing her hissed and sputtered angrily, a cloud of white steam rising from her burning limbs.

Then the waterfall vanished.

The fire roared to life again, crawling up Ariana's thighs, all the way up to her hips. Still it rose, engulfing her lower belly. Ariana howled, thrashing wildly on the grass.

Kyle closed his eyes again, weaving frantically. Ariana's hand slammed into his arm, her fingernails raking down it. His concentration faltered, and he opened his eyes, seeing the flames crawling up Ariana's shirt. Tears streamed down his cheeks, evaporating almost instantly in the tremendous heat. He looked up at the Dead Man, grabbing Ariana's hand in his own and gripping it tightly.

"Stop it!" he pleaded. "*Please!*"

The Dead Man stared down at him impassively, the glowing crystal on his forehead casting horrible shadows across his face. Time seemed to slow to a crawl, every second feeling like an eternity.

A shadow rose behind the Dead Man.

Kyle stared over the Dead Man's shoulder, spotting a corner of red cloth billowing majestically in the wind. The cloth was riddled with holes, rays of sunlight piercing through each one as it flew ever upward above the Dead Man. A long, silver blade rose to the right of the red cloak, shimmering like a diamond in the sun.

A shockwave rippled through the air, slamming into Kyle's brain. He fell onto his butt, his hand slipping from Ariana's. The Dead Man's shields vanished.

The blade arced through the air, striking the Dead Man's pale neck. Kyle watched as the pale flesh rippled with the blow, caving inward. Then the blade continued leftward, biting into the flesh. It sliced deep into the Dead Man's neck, severing the muscles, then passing clean through his windpipe. It continued leftward, cutting through to the other side, and exiting in a spray of black fluid.

The Dead Man levitated there for a moment, his eyes wide, his mouth open. Then his head slipped sideways off of his neck, falling to the ground. It struck with a dull thud, rolling in a half-circle until it lay still.

The Dead Man's eyes, wide open with shock, stared lifelessly upward at the sky. The crystal on his forehead flickered, its light fading.

Kyle watched as the Dead Man's headless body fell forward, landing with a dull *thump* on the ground. His black cloak, once ceaselessly rippling, lay still at last.

There, behind the body of the Dead Man, a tall, muscular man in golden armor stood. His eyes, as blue as the sky above, stared down coldly at the corpse lying on the ground before him.

Chapter 19

"Darius!" Kyle cried, scrambling to his feet. His legs wobbled, then gave out, sending him back onto his butt in the grass.

Darius stood tall before them, staring downward at the headless corpse at his feet, his machete-sword dripping with thick black liquid. He grabbed his tattered red cloak, ripping it from his back and tossing it on the ground beside the Dead Man's corpse.

Kyle stared at the gilded warrior, his mouth agape, hardly believing his eyes. Darius ignored him, striding up to Kalibar and kneeling before the former Grand Weaver, who was still lying in the fetal position on the grass, his head in his hands. Darius put one gauntleted hand on Kalibar's temple, frowning slightly. Then he grabbed the older man's arms, lifting him to his feet. Kalibar leaned heavily on Darius's shoulder, raising his head slightly and groaning. His hand went to his temple.

"What happened?" he asked.

"Darius killed the Dead Man!" Kyle exclaimed. Kalibar frowned, lowering his hand.

"He *what?*"

"He killed him," Kyle repeated.

"He did?" Kalibar pressed. "Are you sure?"

Darius said nothing, but moved away from Kalibar, reaching down to grab the Dead Man's head by his black hair. He lifted the decapitated head from the ground, black liquid still oozing from the severed stump of his neck, and handed it to Kalibar.

"What…" Kalibar began. He slid his fingers over the Dead Man's face, stopping at the green crystal embedded in the pale forehead.

"You really did it," Kalibar breathed. The head rolled out of his hands, falling back onto the ground. "You really killed him!" This time it was Kalibar's legs that wobbled, and Darius grabbed him under the armpits, lowering him to the ground, where he sat in stunned silence.

Kyle felt a small, warm hand grab his, squeezing tightly. He turned to see Ariana staring back at him, her face pale, her lower lip trembling.

"Guys!" Kyle yelled, his heart leaping into his throat. Darius turned to Ariana, walking up to her side, leaving Kalibar sitting in stunned silence in the grass. The bodyguard knelt down over her, his blue eyes scanning her body. Her shoes and pants were charred beyond recognition, as was the bottom half of her shirt. She was shivering violently despite the warm air, mute tears streaming down her cheeks. Kyle squeezed her hand, staring at her charred limbs.

Oh god, he thought. *Oh god no…*

Darius stared at Ariana's legs, then rested a gauntleted hand on her knee. She whimpered, clutching Kyle's hand so hard that her knuckles turned white. Darius ignored her, brushing at her scorched pants with one hand. The material disintegrated under his touch, flaking away in brittle black pieces. He removed these until he reached the blackened skin below. Ariana refused to look down, staring into Kyle's eyes instead. Her lower lip trembled, and she whimpered again, wincing as Darius continued.

"Darius, stop," Kyle pleaded.

The bodyguard ignored him, wiping away thick dust until a patch of pale, bone-white flesh appeared. He kept going, moving up until most of her leg had been exposed. Kyle stared at that wide expanse of exposed flesh, hardly believing his eyes.

There, underneath her clothes, her pale skin shone in the sun, completely intact!

"What?" Kyle breathed. Ariana clutched his hand even tighter, cutting off the circulation to his fingers. "No, look!" he urged. Ariana hesitated, then looked down at her leg. Her eyebrows drew together in confusion.

"You're okay!" Kyle cried. And it was true; sure, there were a few blisters here and there, and the skin was awful red in some places, but for the most part, her leg was intact! "How…?"

Ariana gasped, covering her mouth with one hand. She let go of Kyle's hand, propping herself up a bit, and watched as Darius brushed off her other leg. It too was – impossibly, inexplicably –

intact. Ariana began to cry again, but this time they were tears of joy.

Kyle *whooped*, grabbing Ariana and hugging her tightly. She wrapped her arm around him, burying her head into his shoulder, tears wetting his shirt. Then he pulled back, realizing he'd been brazen enough to hug her without asking first. But Ariana didn't seem to mind at all; she was smiling radiantly at him, the tears on her cheeks glittering like jewels in the light of the sun.

"Don't move," Darius told Ariana gruffly, walking up to the headless body of the Dead Man.

"Why not?" she asked. Darius gave her a look, removing the tattered black cloak from the Dead Man's body.

"You want your boyfriend to see you naked?"

Ariana blinked, then stared down at herself. Her condition was scandalous, a thick layer of soot the only thing standing between her and obscenity. She blushed fiercely, curling into a ball. Kyle looked away chivalrously, and Kalibar turned away as well, for what it was worth. Darius walked over to the Dead Man, lifting the tattered black cloak from his corpse, then laying it over Ariana. Despite its condition, the cloak was intact enough to cover the parts that needed covering.

Ariana rose to her bare feet carefully, wrapping the cloak around her waist. Soot poured down around her feet, a cloud of dust rising all around her. She sneezed, backing out of the growing cloud, then shook herself from head to toe, dislodging the remaining soot and debris.

"Is your, um…" Kyle began, then stopped, his cheeks burning. "Um, are you okay…everywhere?" he asked. Darius smirked, and Ariana blushed.

"I'm okay," she answered. Kalibar frowned.

"What happened to her?" he asked. Of course he wouldn't know, being blind. Kyle explained what had happened, and Kalibar shook his head.

"None of this makes sense," he muttered.

Darius walked back up to the Dead Man's head and picking it up. The bodyguard grabbed the green crystal on the corpse's forehead, pulling at it. Kyle looked on in disgust as the crystal pulled out slowly from the Dead Man's skull. Inch after inch of shimmering green was revealed, until finally it was completely freed, leaving a deep hole in the center of the Dead Man's forehead. The crystal was in actuality a spike nearly five inches long. Kyle swallowed, fighting down a sudden wave of nausea. The thing had been buried deep within the ghoulish man's brain.

Darius tossed the Dead Man's head onto the ground, inspecting the crystal for a long moment, turning it over in the sun. Kyle glanced at the decapitated head staring sightlessly upward from where it lay on the ground. He still couldn't believe that Darius had somehow managed to kill the Dead Man.

"Hey Darius?" Kyle asked. Darius glanced up at Kyle. "Um, so, I was just wondering…" Kyle began.

"The suspense is killing me," Darius grumbled.

"Uh, how did you kill the Dead Man?"

"I cut off his head," Darius replied evenly. Kyle rolled his eyes.

"I mean, *how* did you cut off his head?" Before Darius could respond with another glib remark, he added "…I mean, your sword should have bounced off his shields."

"I removed his shields first," Darius answered. He placed the long green crystal into the recess of his armor, then retrieved something small and shiny. He tossed it at Kyle, who caught it. It was a blue crystal set in a silver metal setting, with a delicate chain on one end.

"What's this?" Kyle asked.

"An amulet a Runic made for me," Darius replied. "Gets rid of those pesky shields."

Kyle frowned, looking at the crystal a little more closely. He concentrated, trying to *feel* the magic within the crystal. A slight vibration came from the gem, but nothing more.

"There's barely any magic in this," Kyle pointed out.

"The Dead Man had a lot of shields," Darius shot back.

"Can I see it?" Kalibar asked, holding out a hand. With crusted blood at his temples, and drying blood trailing from his ear, Kyle was amazed the man was so lucid. He'd been splattered with acid, had struck his head on a rock, and been viciously attacked by the Dead Man for good measure. It had been a very bad day for the former Grand Weaver.

"Here," Kyle replied, handing Darius's amulet to Kalibar. Kalibar held it up to her forehead, his eyebrows furrowing in concentration. "I still don't understand how that thing worked on the Dead Man," Kyle admitted.

"Well," Kalibar replied, "…I suspect the gemstone in his

forehead was a runic device itself…like that piece of quartz I used to fight him."

"Oh, right."

"I spent days inscribing the runes in that crystal," Kalibar continued. "I designed it using what I learned the first time I fought him…and by observing his gemstone every time he visited me in my cell."

"Wait, he visited you?"

"Oh yes," Kalibar replied with a grimace. "As did…others." He sighed, handing the amulet back to Kyle, who gave it to Darius. "I only had a few days to work on my crystal. All I had to do was unlock it with my magic, and it did the rest, weaving a few dozen patterns in a matter of seconds." He gave a rueful smile. "I'm a poor substitute for a Runic, however. Whoever made that amulet was a very skilled Runic. It's quite an elegant piece."

Kyle offered the amulet back to Darius, who took it, then shook his head.

"You take it," he stated. "Might come in handy some day." The bodyguard put the amulet's chain around Kyle's neck, tucking the amulet under Kyle's shirt.

"Wait," Kyle interjected, turning back to Kalibar. "How can a Weaver ever beat a Runic then?" After all, if a runic device could weave dozens of patterns in a matter of seconds, what hope would a Weaver have?

"The amulet only worked for a moment," Kalibar answered. "If Darius hadn't struck when he had, the Dead Man would have adapted to the situation, and won anyway…like he did with the runic I made." He rubbed his temples, grimacing slightly. "Anyway, we should get going."

"Agreed," Darius said. He turned away from the mouth of the cave, walking up to Kalibar, who leaned on his shoulder. The bodyguard turned back to Kyle and Ariana, who stared back at him silently. "The Dead Weavers are going to come looking for their master," Darius explained.

"Um…they're called 'Death' Weavers," Kyle corrected. Darius walked by the Dead Man's head, kicking it as he passed by. It rolled a few yards, into some brush.

"For now," he replied.

* * *

The forest quickly engulfed them as they made their way from the mouth of the cave, the sun shining through the rustling leaves in a hundred shimmering rays that danced over the forest floor. The sunlight sparkled merrily off of the surprisingly large waves rippling across the surface of a large lake on their right, just beyond the tree line. Like Crescent Lake, its waters were crystal clear; but it was much deeper, making it impossible to see the lake bottom. Kyle felt a chill run through him as he stared at its depths. He'd always been afraid of very deep water, unable to help himself from imagining what terrible things might lurk below, hidden from sight.

Kyle turned away from the lake, focusing on the path ahead. Darius and Kalibar led the way, occasionally talking amongst themselves, though about what, Kyle couldn't make out. He and Ariana followed a few feet behind. Ariana was still dropping bits of dust between her feet as she walked, even after she'd spent a few minutes away from the group to remove her half-burned shirt. She'd had to run to catch up with the group, as Darius hadn't been considerate enough to stop for her. Kyle couldn't really blame him. After all, if the Death Weavers caught up with them...

"I still can't believe you're okay," Kyle remarked when she caught up with the group. He'd lagged behind a ways so that Ariana wouldn't get lost, keeping an eye on Kalibar and Darius as they'd moved on ahead. He remembered feeling the enormous heat of the flames as they'd engulfed her. Her legs should have been charred beyond hope.

"Me neither," Ariana replied. "I thought I was going to die." Then she shuddered, casting her gaze downward. "I *wanted* to die...at the end, I mean." Kyle nodded in mute understanding. Better to have a quick death than to be slowly burned alive.

"It doesn't make sense," he muttered, absently kicking a small pebble that happened to be in his way. "The fire almost burned *me*, and I was a few feet away. Why weren't you burned?" Ariana shrugged.

"Maybe the Dead Man didn't really want to kill me," she replied. "Maybe he was just punishing me."

"Punishing you?" Kyle asked. Ariana nodded.

"He knows how much I hate fire."

"Oh," Kyle said, not understanding at all. Ariana hardly noticed; she became very quiet, staring down at the ground in front of her as she walked. Kyle realized she was looking at the soot still falling from her clothes. He stared at the dribbles of blackened powder silently, not at all convinced that the Dead Man had been trying to spare her.

"I wish I'd been the one to kill him," Ariana muttered bitterly.

They walked in silence then, following Darius deeper into the forest. The bodyguard kept a quick, steady pace, forcing the others to keep up. It was a not-so-subtle reminder of the danger behind them, the Death Weavers that would almost certainly come looking for their fallen master...and for vengeance. The thought of the Death Weavers made Kyle walk faster, falling into step only a few feet behind Darius. The forest floor began to angle downward, slightly at first, then rather steeply. Kyle nearly slipped more than once, but with Ariana's help, he managed the treacherous terrain without falling. After what seemed like an hour – the front of his thighs burning from walking downhill for so long – the terrain leveled out.

Onward they went, no one saying anything, the only sound the rhythmic crunching of their footsteps on the fallen leaves and twigs littering the forest floor. The sun gradually swung past high noon overhead, throwing steadily longer shadows as it continued westward across the sky. Despite burning legs and lungs, Kyle kept going, having long ago fallen into a trance. He heard the gurgling sound of a stream nearby, and after a time it came into view. Perhaps ten feet wide, and quite shallow, it flanked them on the right. Kyle wondered if it came from the lake he'd seen earlier, near the mouth of the cave.

Suddenly Darius slowed, then stopped. Kyle nearly walked right into the bodyguard's back, snapping out of his reverie and looking around. The forest a few dozen feet ahead came to an abrupt end, leading to a rocky ledge, with only blue sky visible beyond. Darius continued forward, walking out of the forest onto the ledge, and after a moment, Kyle followed. The sound of rushing water grew louder as he neared the forest's edge.

"Where are we?" Kyle asked the bodyguard, not for the first time wondering if the man knew where he was going. Or *how* he would know where he was going. But Darius merely walked to the very edge of the rocky ledge, stopping there and gazing down, Kalibar at his side. Kyle sighed, following Darius up to the ledge, then looking down.

He gasped.

There, in a sheer drop nearly fifty feet below, was a large, crescent-shaped lake. It was bordered by a sandy shore, with the treetops of a dense forest beyond. And there, to Kyle's right, not thirty feet away, the stream they'd been following flowed off of the rocky ledge, forming a large, glittering waterfall to the lake below.

"Kalibar!" Kyle shouted, his heart nearly leaping out of his chest. He laughed out loud, staring at the shore far below, spotting the top of a small carriage there. "Kalibar, we did it!"

"Did what?" Kalibar asked.

"We made it to Crescent Lake!"

* * *

The trip down from the cliff to Crescent Lake was relatively short, Darius leading them leftward down a steep slope to the shore below. Kyle already knew the way, having walked up the path to get to the top of the waterfall with Kalibar during their time experimenting with the feathergrass extract. Once on shore, they made their way quickly to the carriage. It was, to Kyle's surprise, completely intact, including the wards surrounding it. The horses, however, were nowhere to be seen.

"I'm afraid I might not be as useful protecting you from the Death Weavers," Kalibar stated, standing at Darius's side by the carriage. He was clearly frustrated by that fact. "We're going to need a few items from the trunk if we're to stand a chance against them."

"Which bag?" Darius asked.

"The one with the suit of armor on top," Kalibar answered. Darius walked up to the back of the carriage, lifting the door to the trunk. He searched through a few packs, then picked one up, setting it on the ground beside the carriage. Then he took Kalibar's arm, guiding him to the pack. Kalibar knelt down, reaching inside and rummaging around for a moment. "This is the pack," he confirmed. Lifting something silver and shiny from the pack, he handed it to Darius. It was a metallic breastplate. A pale blue crystal was set in the center of it.

"What's that?" Kyle asked.

"The Cuirass Gravita," Kalibar answered. "Armor worn by Ancient infantry. It detects an incoming attack, and generates a burst of gravitational force to repel the attack. The greater the force of the attack, the greater the repelling force. Put it on," Kalibar instructed. Darius handed it to Kyle. It was shockingly light, almost weightless. He lifted the breastplate up, dropping it over his head onto his shoulders. It covered his chest and back more than adequately, having clearly been designed for someone larger.

"Why is it so light?" Kyle asked.

"Ancient magic," Kalibar answered. "It continuously senses gravity and velocity, adjusting to nullify the inertia of the suit. Darius, if you could demonstrate?" Kalibar asked. Darius picked up a small stone from the ground, and tossed it right at Kyle. The stone smacked into his chest with a dull ringing sound. Kalibar smiled.

"Now send a stream of magic to the crystal on your chest piece," he commanded. Kyle did so, and immediately felt a humming sensation all around him. Darius picked up another stone, and threw it at Kyle. This time, the stone never struck him, coming to a stop a fraction of an inch in front of him, then flying away at incredible speed.

"Cool," Kyle murmured. He felt the Cuirass Gravita cinch inward, and realized that it was shrinking to fit his body. Ancient magic, no doubt. He watched as Kalibar rummaged through the pack again, pulling out a sword. It had a straight silver blade about two feet long, with a dull edge on both sides. The handle was black with silver symbols carved into it.

"This is the Spatha Luna," Kalibar said. "The sword of the moon. Its blade is dull, but when activated, its edges light up with the power of lightning, effortlessly cutting into almost any substance." He handed the sword to Kyle hilt first. Kyle took it gingerly, afraid that he might cut himself. Thankfully, Kalibar gave Kyle a sheath for the blade, which could be tied onto his back.

"How do you activate these?" Kyle asked.

"Just push magic into the main crystal on each item," Kalibar replied. "You don't need to weave a pattern. After the first activation, the armor recognizes that the magic comes from you, so only you can activate it while you're wearing it."

"Wait, why didn't we use these earlier?" Kyle pressed.

"You need to send a continuous stream of magic to keep them activated," Kalibar replied. "...and you weren't able to do that yet."

"Oh," Kyle mumbled. "Right."

Kalibar brought out a few more items, this time for Ariana. One was a magical dagger, the other a black suit. Ariana accepted both eagerly...particularly the suit. Having worn nothing below the waist but the tattered black cloak, she was undoubtedly ready for real clothes. She walked off into the forest to change, appearing a few minutes later. While the suit looked a bit too big for her at first, it soon shrank to fit her body, making her look remarkably fetching. Kyle found himself staring, and looked away, blushing furiously.

"Your dagger is similar to the Spatha Luna," Kalibar explained to Ariana. "And your armor generates a form-fitting shield that repels attacks...although not as effectively as Kyle's. It will also allow you to vanish at will – just activate the diamond on your chest piece." Ariana nodded, closing her eyes for a moment. Then she vanished into thin air. A few moments later, Kyle felt a tap on his right shoulder. He spun around, and found Ariana standing behind him, a mischievous smile on her face. He smiled back, suddenly wishing that *his* suit could make him disappear. Useful magic indeed!

"Keep in mind that your dagger will be visible unless it is kept in your suit's sheath," Kalibar warned Ariana.

"Are there any more invisibility suits?" Kyle asked. "If we're all invisible, the Death Weavers will never be able to find us."

"Unfortunately no," Kalibar replied ruefully. "This is one of the few left in existence...and no one knows how it works. If we could reverse-engineer that suit, our military would be unstoppable."

"Oh," Kyle muttered. He glanced at Ariana's suit, suddenly wishing *he'd* been given it. Kalibar continued rummaging through the pack, pulling out another breastplate identical to Kyle's, and put it on himself. Then he pulled out a pair of black boots, putting them on.

"What are those?" Kyle asked.

"An extra pair of gravity boots," Kalibar answered. "Not that I'll make much use of them, being blind," he added ruefully. "We could make it to Stridon in a few hours if I had my sight. I don't have a pair of gravity boots for you, unfortunately," he continued. "But there should be regular boots for you and Ariana in another pack."

Before Kyle could begin to search, Darius was handing Kyle the pair of boots. Kyle took off his acid-worn footwear, slipping the boots on. They fit perfectly.

Kalibar rummaged through the pack again, pulling out a long, curved sword. "This," he explained, "is for you, Darius." He held out the sword in front of him, clearly uncertain as to where exactly his bodyguard was.

"No thanks," Darius replied. Kalibar frowned, but didn't push the matter.

"Your Ancient runics are extraordinarily rare – and hopefully more powerful than anything the Death Weavers will have ever seen," Kalibar explained. "If they catch up to us, these will help even the odds." He summoned Darius to his side then, placing a hand on his gilded armor. "We should go," he stated. "...and quickly."

Darius picked up the pack – which was by no means empty – and placed it back into the trunk of the carriage. He rummaged through the other packs again, and took one, lifting it from the trunk and slinging it over his broad shoulder. Kalibar gestured for everyone to move away from the carriage, and then stood motionlessly for a moment. Kyle felt a subtle vibration in his head; Kalibar must have activated wards to protect the carriage. With the Dead Man gone, it was unlikely that anyone would be able to break past them.

"Ah," Kalibar stated suddenly. "My staff...I almost forgot. Darius, can you find it?" Darius searched the camp, finding Kalibar's staff lying on the ground a ways away. He handed it to Kalibar, who accepted it gratefully. They left the camp then, striding across the sandy shore to the forest beyond. They were soon surrounded by trees, the air much cooler in the shade of the leaves overhead. Darius led them over the uneven terrain, marching at his typical quick pace. Kyle and Ariana walked side-by-side as usual; Kyle found himself stealing glances at her more than once. With her tight black suit contrasting with her pale skin, she looked quite fetching. Luckily Ariana didn't seem to notice his furtive glances, seeming to be lost in thought once again. He wondered what she was thinking.

After a long, silent hike, the sun began to set, sending a splash of pink and purple across the sky. The forest became darker, the leaves on the trees starting to glow faintly. Kyle and Ariana marched together in the growing darkness, dodging trees and avoiding rocks and roots that threatened to trip them.

"We should make camp soon," Kalibar suggested, stifling a yawn. "And I need to eat after using all of that magic."

"I'll find a spot," Darius replied. They walked for a few more minutes, and then Darius stopped. "There," he said, pointing forward, and slightly to the left. Kyle peered off into the darkness, but couldn't see anything. Darius moved forward, motioning for Kyle and Ariana to follow. Soon Kyle saw what Darius had been talking about: a clearing in the forest, covered with sparse tufts of tough, short grass. Darius led Kalibar to the middle of the clearing.

"Let's eat," Kalibar said.

Darius dropped the pack he'd been carrying onto the ground, and reached inside to pull out a few loaves of bread and some powdered soup mix. Kyle's stomach growled, and he realized that he hadn't eaten anything all day. With Darius's help, Kalibar filled some cups with hot water, and soon all four of them were sitting on the ground, dipping their bread into hot soup and eating it zestfully. When they could eat no more, the cups were put away, and Darius put Kyle and Ariana to work gathering branches for a fire. When they'd accumulated a fair amount in the center of the clearing, Darius turned to Kalibar.

"Can you make a shield twenty feet in diameter?" Darius asked.

"Is everyone here?" Kalibar asked tentatively. Kyle and Ariana huddled up close to the old man. Kyle had no desire to be flung into the dirt by Kalibar's shield again.

"They are now," Darius answered. The old man paused for a moment, and Kyle sensed a familiar vibration in the air. A shimmering half-globe appeared around the group, some twenty feet in diameter. A few tree branches that were unlucky enough to penetrate the shield snapped off violently, flying far into the forest beyond.

That done, everyone sat down before the fire, and Kyle had the honor of lighting it. He wove the fire pattern without even having to think about it, sending the flame into the branches. Within moments, the campfire was blazing, nurturing them with its warmth. Ariana stayed farther back from it than everyone else.

"I still can't believe we escaped," Kyle mused, staring into the dancing flames. "I thought we were going to be trapped there forever."

"I know," Ariana agreed.

"What *was* that place, anyway?" Kyle asked. "I mean, what were they doing there? And why did they want us?"

"From what I gather," Kalibar replied, "...it was a cult."

"Yeah," Ariana piped in. "They all worshiped some god named Xanos."

"Yes," Kalibar agreed. "The Dead Man called himself a 'Chosen' of Xanos." He frowned. "From what I gather, the Dead Man isn't the only one of these Chosen."

"He told me Orik was supposed to become one," Kyle offered, remembering his conversation with the Dead Man in the Void. "But he screwed up by attacking you."

"Interesting," Kalibar murmured. Then he shook his head. "If there are more Weavers like the Dead Man, we're in serious trouble." He ran a hand through his short white hair. "After I attacked him with my runic stone, he seemed...different. He started weaving so fast that I couldn't follow him. I've never seen anything like it."

"That gem on his forehead lit up," Kyle said. "And his voice changed too."

"I've seen him do it before," Ariana piped in. Everyone turned to her. "They said when his gemstone glows that Xanos is taking over his body."

Kalibar frowned at this, rubbing his chin thoughtfully.

"I for one don't believe in gods," he confessed. "But *someone* is creating these Chosen. And whoever it is, their magic is beyond anything the Empire has ever seen."

Silence fell over the camp for a while, everyone staring into the campfire. At length, Kyle stirred.

"I still don't understand why they kidnapped us," he muttered. "Shouldn't they have just killed us?"

"No, not necessarily," Kalibar answered.

"What do you mean?"

"Their purpose was to build an army," Kalibar explained. "They wanted their Death Weavers to be stronger than the Empire's...which they weren't, by the way. If it hadn't been for the Dead Man, I might've been able to destroy his army single-handedly."

"So they wanted us in their army?" Kyle pressed.

"I don't think so," Kalibar replied, scratching his beard. He hesitated for a moment. "In order to get the strongest Weavers, they needed to...breed them."

Kyle stared at Kalibar blankly.

"That place was a breeding program," Kalibar continued,

grimacing with distaste. "They were kidnapping people who made the most magic, so that they could breed the strongest ones with each other."

"Oh," Kyle mumbled. He glanced at Ariana, who was staring back at him silently. He turned away immediately, blushing.

"We have to get back to the Empire as quickly as possible," Kalibar stated. "The Grand Weaver and Runic need to know about this cult...and about Orik."

"What about the Death Weavers?" Kyle asked uneasily. "What if they come after us?"

"The Dead Man was their absolute leader," Kalibar answered. "They didn't have much of a hierarchy for leadership below him. I suspect they'll be disorganized for some time."

"But what if they *do* come after us?" Ariana pressed. Kalibar gave a grim smile.

"I may be blind," the former Grand Weaver replied, "...but I'm far from helpless." He stood then, brushing the dirt off the back of his pants. "In any case, I've had enough for one day. Goodnight everyone."

"Goodnight," Kyle and Ariana replied.

"And Darius?" Kalibar added, turning in the bodyguard's general direction.

"Yeah?"

"Thank you," Kalibar said. "For everything."

With that, Kalibar asked Darius for his sleeping bag, and nestled into it, falling quickly asleep. Darius grabbed two more sleeping bags.

"Hey Darius," Kyle said, eyeing the bodyguard.

"Yeah?"

"How did you escape your cell?"

"By using my greatest weapon," Darius answered.

"What's that?" Kyle pressed. Darius smirked, chucking a sleeping bag at Kyle. Kyle flinched, but caught it.

"Surprise."

Kyle frowned, staring at Darius, who pointedly ignored him, handing the other sleeping bag to Ariana.

"I'll stand watch," he said.

Kyle and Ariana set their sleeping bags by Kalibar – Ariana bringing hers as far from the fire as she could. Kyle got into his bag, yawning as soon as he did so. Kalibar was right...it *had* been a long day. He hadn't had a good night's sleep in days, not since he'd been taken by the Dead Man. He was about to close his eyes when he saw Ariana step up to him. She leaned over, giving him a quick peck on the cheek.

"Goodnight," she whispered, standing up and walking back toward her sleeping bag. She got in, then closed her eyes. Kyle touched his cheek with his hand, hardly believing what had just happened. He'd never been kissed before...not by a girl. He smiled, snuggling into his sleeping bag, staring at Ariana as she fell asleep.

"Goodnight," he whispered back.

Chapter 20

Kyle opened his eyes, squinting against the harsh sun streaming through the tree branches above. He groaned, his whole body aching as he sat up. He spotted Ariana sitting at the edge of her sleeping bag. Darius was standing at the edge of the camp's gravity shield, facing away from them, while Kalibar was still fast asleep.

It took Kyle a moment to remember why he wasn't laying on his narrow, uncomfortable cot underground, near the Arena.

We really did it, he thought, feeling a surge of joy.

"Good morning," Ariana greeted. Kyle turned, realizing she was talking to him. A few strands of her long dark hair fell in front of her big brown eyes, contrasting with her pale skin. The full day in the sun yesterday had given her the barest hint of color.

"Morning," Kyle replied, smiling at her. Ariana smiled back, but weakly. "You okay?" he asked.

"I don't know," Ariana admitted, gazing at the forest beyond the shield. "I still can't believe I'm here," she added. "It doesn't feel real."

"Yeah."

"I'd forgotten how beautiful the surface is," Ariana murmured, staring up at the sky. She took a deep breath in through her nose, closing her eyes and letting the breath out.

Kyle heard coughing, and turned to see Kalibar stirring in his sleeping bag. The older man rolled onto his side, then fell still again.

"Everything is so colorful," Ariana said.

Kalibar coughed again, and this time he sat up in his sleeping bag, swaying a little. He grabbed the edge of the bag, swinging his legs carefully over the edge. Then he frowned, extending one hand. His staff – lying on the ground by his sleeping bag – flew up into his hand. He tapped the ground below him with the butt of the staff, then stood up.

"Good morning Kalibar," Kyle greeted.

"Good morning sir," Ariana piped in.

"Morning," Kalibar replied. "Shall we eat breakfast?"

With that, Darius helped Kalibar prepare the same meal they'd eaten the night before. Nobody complained, their stomachs eager for sustenance after their harrowing journey yesterday. After they'd finished their meals, Darius made Kyle and Ariana put everything away.

"Ready to go?" Darius asked Kalibar. The old man nodded, and the shimmering shield surrounding the camp promptly vanished. Darius grabbed the lone pack laying on the ground, and he and Kalibar took their usual positions in front, while Kyle and Ariana trailed a few feet behind. Kyle caught Ariana staring at him, and he frowned.

"What?"

"Your hair," she answered. He felt his hair, realizing that it was sticking up on end on one side. He suspected that he looked fairly ridiculous.

"Let me fix that," Ariana said, creating a small water stream and dipping her hands into the cool fluid. Then she ran her fingers through his hair, smoothing it backward. Then, satisfied with her work, she grabbed his hand, squeezing it gently, and walked with him. It felt marvelous, her hand in his, and he found himself grinning stupidly at her. Luckily, she didn't seem to notice, her eyes on the forest ahead.

Onward they went, trekking through the forest. With the sun peeking just above the horizon behind them, it had to be early morning. Kyle found that he was getting better at judging times without a watch or a phone. Still, it felt a bit strange – and a bit freeing – to not know exactly what time it was. He soon fell into the familiar trance of hiking, idly counting steps to a hundred, then starting over again. It wasn't long before the forest ended, revealing a field of tall, golden-hued grass. It was the same type of grass he'd seen after he'd escaped the Ulfar, before he'd passed on the road so many days ago. In fact, he remembered seeing the grass at the edges of every road he'd been on in this world. He said as much to Kalibar.

"This grass," Kalibar explained, running a few strands through his fingers as he walked, "is called bordergrass. It magically repels trees, preventing trees from blocking their sunlight. Road-builders planted these fields so that trees wouldn't rip through the roads. Most cities are surrounded by similar plants."

"Wait," Kyle replied. "What do you mean, 'rip through the roads?'"

"Without the bordergrass, the trees would slowly migrate through the roads, and into the cities," Kalibar explained.

"Wait, what?" Kyle exclaimed. "Trees can't move!"

"They most certainly can," Kalibar retorted.

"Not where I come from."

"That may be true," Kalibar conceded, "...but here they are in constant motion. Far too slow for the eye to see, but trust me...their roots dig through the soil, pulling them along at a glacial pace. Without bordergrass, roads would be overrun in a matter of months."

"Huh," Kyle muttered. Then he felt a surge of hope. "Wait, does that mean we're close to the road?"

"Very likely."

Darius stopped suddenly, holding up one hand. Kyle and Ariana stopped behind the bodyguard, watching as Darius cocked his head to the side, as if listening for something.

"What?" Kyle asked.

Darius shoved Kalibar backward.

"Get *down!*" the bodyguard yelled...and then a huge black shape slammed into him, knocking him to the side.

He vanished into the tall grass.

Kyle heard a snarling sound to his right, and turned, seeing nothing but a wall of tall grass surrounding him. He crouched low to the ground, his heart pounding in his chest. Ariana did the same, her eyes wide with fear.

He heard rustling to his right, heard Ariana cry out.

Something *slammed* into Kyle's right shoulder, spinning him around and throwing him bodily to the left. He fell to the ground, the air blasting from his lungs. Scrambling to his feet, he turned in a slow circle, seeing nothing but tall grass. Whatever had knocked him over was nowhere to be seen.

"Kyle?" he heard Ariana shout.

"Ariana!" Kyle shouted back. He turned toward the sound of her voice, parting the walls of grass with his hands. Within moments, he found Kalibar. The former Grand Weaver was standing quite still, a gravity shield surrounding him.

"Kalibar!" Kyle exclaimed. "Where's Ariana?"

"I wouldn't know," Kalibar answered. Kyle glanced at Kalibar's blindfolded face, and nearly slapped himself on the forehead. Ask a stupid question...

"I'm right here," a voice called out from behind him.

Kyle whirled around, seeing nothing but tall grass. Then the air in front of him rippled, a slender figure appearing there.

"Ariana!" he exclaimed. "How...?"

"My suit, remember?" Ariana replied, gesturing at her black suit. Kyle paused, then nodded. He'd forgotten all about it...and his own suit, in fact. He streamed magic to the gem on his breastplate, feeling the armor *hum* with power.

"What's going on?" Kyle asked.

"I don't know," she replied. "Have you seen Darius?" Kyle shook his head. "I'll go look for him," she stated. A second later, she'd vanished again.

Kyle turned in a slow circle, peering through the endless waves of rippling grass all around him.

What the heck is going on?

He heard panting from behind, and spun around just in time to see a huge black creature leap through the grass right at him, huge, sharp teeth bared in a terrifying snarl!

Kyle screamed, the stream to his armor vanishing.

The beast slammed into Kyle's chest, knocking him onto his back on the ground. Kyle threw his arms in front of his face just as the beast lunged toward his head, and felt teeth clamp on the armor protecting his right shoulder. He cried out, kicking at the beast's underbelly, and felt it release him from its jaws, backing up. He stared up at the creature, his blood going cold.

A huge, wolf-like creature with iridescent eyes stood over him, thick strands of drool hanging from its massive jaws.

An Ulfar!

Kyle froze, staring at the ungodly creature, his breath catching in his throat. He tried to get up, tried to run away, but his limbs refused to obey him. He could only watch as the huge beast hunched down, low to the ground, gathering its hind legs under it.

Then it pounced.

Kyle squeezed his eyes shut, turning away and throwing his arms in front of him as the beast hurtled toward him. He pulled magic into his mind's eye, and *pushed* it toward the crystal on his armor.

He heard a *yelp.*

Kyle opened his eyes, seeing a large shape hurtling through the air over twenty feet above the ground. It peaked, then fell, striking the ground with a sickening *crunch* somewhere in the grass ahead of Kyle. There was a loud, sharp squealing sound, followed by silence.

Kyle hesitated, then rose to his feet, peering into the grass ahead.

"Took you long enough," he heard a voice say from behind. Kyle whirled about, crouching low…and then relaxed. There, his left arm covered in streaks of blood, with more dripping from his bared sword, stood Darius.

"Thank god," Kyle exclaimed, feeling immensely relieved.

Darius sheathed his sword, walking past Kyle and into the grass toward the fallen Ulfar. Kyle followed close behind, staring at the crimson fluid dripping down Darius's arm.

"You okay?" Kyle asked.

"Better than him," he answered, gesturing toward the Ulfar that had attacked Kyle. It was lying in a bed of flattened grass a dozen feet away, whimpering pathetically. "You going to finish that?"

"Huh?"

"Turn off your armor," Darius ordered. Kyle did so, ending the stream of magic he'd been sending the breastplate's crystal. "Come on," the bodyguard urged, pulling Kyle toward the fallen beast. It was lying on its side, two of its legs obviously broken. Kyle saw a piece of jagged white sticking out of one leg, and realized it was a bone. He tried to step backward, but Darius stuck one brawny arm out to stop him.

"You gonna let him suffer?" the bodyguard asked. The fallen Ulfar lifted its big head up off of the ground, staring at them for a moment, its eyes wide. It growled, then flopped back onto the ground, its chest rising and falling rapidly as it panted. A pool of blood expanded slowly around its shattered body. Kyle turned away from the horrible sight, but Darius grabbed his arm.

"Kill it or torture it," the bodyguard growled, grabbing Kyle's hand and placing it on the Spatha Luna, the sword at Kyle's hip. "Your choice."

Then Darius walked away, disappearing into the grass beyond.

He heard a high-pitched squeal, and turned to face the Ulfar. It stared back at him silently, laying with the side of its head on the ground. The single eye Kyle could see was wide, the pupil enormous.

Kyle tried to swallow in a suddenly dry throat, and found that he couldn't. He stared silently at the fallen beast, knowing that he couldn't leave until he'd killed it. A good person wouldn't leave an animal to suffer a slow, agonizing death…even if that animal had tried to kill him first.

He unsheathed the Spatha Luna, then took a step toward the Ulfar, his heart pounding in his chest.

The Ulfar lifted its head immediately, a low growl rumbling in its throat. Blood-tinged drool dripped from its oversized fangs, forming a small pool under its jaws. It stared at him unblinkingly, making Kyle freeze in his tracks.

How did I get myself into this?

He took a deep breath in, clutching his sword tightly, and stepped forward again. The Ulfar's eyes locked on him, it's growling growing louder. It kicked its legs, then squealed, staying perfectly still on the ground.

Kyle held his sword out in front of him, taking another step forward, then another. He kept his eyes locked on the Ulfar's, continuing toward it. He'd never killed anything before…and had no desire to do it now.

Come on, he told himself. *Just do it.*

He inched forward, now only a few feet from where the Ulfar lay. It stared at him unblinkingly, its growl growing louder, more insistent.

Make it quick.

Taking a few rapid breaths to steel himself, Kyle raised his sword up over his head, his heart hammering in his chest. He cried out, lunging forward…and then stopped, lowering his sword. He stared at its dull blade, then backpedaled away from the beast. He'd almost forgotten to stream magic to the sword first! Without magic, the blade wouldn't have even cut the Ulfar. He'd almost tried to stab the deadly creature with an oversized butter knife.

Idiot!

He closed his eyes, sending a magic stream to the crystal on the sword's hilt. The crystal flared to life, a blue-white lining the sword's edges. He held it before him, taking a few deep breaths. Then he raised the sword over his head, and charged!

The Ulfar scrambled backward frantically, flailing its paws on the crushed grass beneath it. Kyle ran up to the beast, screaming at the top of his lungs. He swung the sword down as hard as he could, aiming for the beast's neck. He missed, the blade sinking into its upper back with startling ease.

The Ulfar howled.

Kyle raised the sword up again, bringing it down on the Ulfar's body. He heard a *yelp*, and closed his eyes, bringing the sword up and down again and again, until his arms were so exhausted that he couldn't lift the sword anymore. Then he opened his eyes, backpedaling rapidly, the sword dropping from his hands. He stumbled, falling onto his butt on the flattened grass, his eyes on the Ulfar.

Or rather, what was left of it.

A mangled heap of seared fur and flesh lay where the Ulfar had been, the smell of burnt hair and smoking grass making his nose and mouth burn. His stomach lurched, and he turned away from the gruesome sight, standing up and staggering away from the corpse. He stumbled through the tall grass, having no idea where he was going.

"Guys?" he called out. "Darius?"

There was no answer.

He felt lightheaded suddenly, and stopped in his tracks, his legs turning to rubber. He lowered himself to the ground, sitting there, waiting for the sensation to pass.

"Hey kid," a voice behind him said.

Kyle turned, seeing Darius appear through the tall grass. The bodyguard offered a gauntleted hand to Kyle, who hesitated, then grabbed it. He was hauled to his feet.

"You were only supposed to kill it once," Darius stated dryly.

Kyle's cheeks flushed, and he ignored the man, watching as the bodyguard strode toward the Ulfar, then returned moments later carrying Kyle's sword. He slid the sword back into its sheath at Kyle's hip.

"Let's go," Darius said, grabbing Kyle's arm and pulling him through the tall grass. The two caught up with Kalibar and Ariana quickly, and Darius motioned for Kyle to go to the back again with Ariana.

"You okay?" she asked. Kyle nodded.

"Yeah."

It wasn't long before the tall grass ended, revealing a narrow dirt road beyond...a road that looked awfully familiar.

"Is that...?" Kyle asked, glancing at Darius.

"Yup," he replied. "The side road we took to get to Crescent Lake."

"Excellent," Kalibar stated. "We'll continue west; it'll connect with the main road to Stridon soon enough."

"Maybe we can catch a ride back then," Kyle reasoned.

"Not a good idea," Kalibar countered. "We have to get back to the Great Tower to warn the Grand Weaver and Grand Runic without Orik knowing about it. He'll almost certainly try to have me killed if he finds out I'm coming...and in my state, he might succeed. If we hitch a ride, I'll risk being recognized."

"Oh."

"We should walk through the bordergrass flanking the road to avoid being seen," Kalibar suggested. "At least once we reach the main road."

"All right," Darius agreed.

"Let's go," Kalibar urged. "We need to get as far as we can before nightfall."

They continued forward then, following the narrow road as it twisted and turned through the wilderness. No one said much of anything, and Kyle fell into a sort of trance, barely even noticing the burning in his legs as he walked. The sun peaked overhead, then descended slowly before them, forcing Kyle to keep his eyes on the ground to avoid its glare.

In this way, one foot in front of the other, they pushed ever-forward, their shadows following close behind as they made their way to Stridon.

* * *

The sun had just begun to set by the time the narrow, winding road joined the main road leading to Stridon. As per Kalibar's instructions, Darius led them through the tall bordergrass a dozen feet off of the road to avoid being seen by any late-night travelers. They'd only taken a single break since that morning, to eat lunch. Now, Kyle's legs felt like lead weights, and his belly was complaining bitterly for dinner. In fact, his stomach growled so loudly that even Kalibar, walking a few steps ahead with Darius, could hear it.

"Let's make camp," the former Grand Weaver declared.

"I'll find a site," Darius replied. He turned away from the road, leading them through the tall grass. Eventually the grass gave way to forest, the trees having no doubt migrated as far as the bordergrass would let them. Darius found a small clearing, and ordered Ariana and Kyle to help him gather wood for a fire. With the three of them working, they soon had a large pile of wood in the center of the clearing. That done, Kalibar created a large gravity shield around the camp.

"Don't make the fire too large," Kalibar warned. "We don't want to risk drawing attention."

Darius complied, and soon the campfire was crackling gently, modest flames licking at the gathered wood. Dinner was made – the usual fare – and everyone huddled together before the fire. Kyle gazed at the smoke rising from the fire, watching as it reached the domed gravity shield above. To his surprise, he saw a small hole in the shield at the top, allowing the smoke to escape. Kalibar, as usual, had thought of everything.

"How is everyone doing?" Kalibar asked.

"Good," Kyle replied automatically.

"Tired," Ariana answered. Kalibar smiled at that.

"So am I," he admitted. "It's been a long two days, hasn't it?"

"Yes sir," Ariana replied.

"Please," Kalibar urged, "...call me Kalibar." He frowned. "I don't think I ever properly introduced myself, Ariana," he added. "I apologize."

"You were Grand Weaver," Ariana stated. "I saw you once when I was little."

"Ah, yes," Kalibar murmured. "That I was. So you were a prisoner of the Dead Man," he added. "I apologize if I came off a bit...harsh when we first met. I had trouble trusting that you weren't one of them."

"I know," Ariana replied. "Thanks for giving me a chance."

"Thank Kyle and Darius," Kalibar countered with a smile. "Tell me, where are you from, Ariana?"

"Mortown."

"Ah yes," Kalibar stated. "I've been there a few times. A beautiful village."

"Yeah," Ariana mumbled. She stared at the ground in front of her, laying her cup of soup on the ground beside her. Kalibar frowned.

"What's wrong?" he asked. Ariana shook her head, saying nothing. But Kyle saw tears welling up in her eyes. After a long, awkward pause, Kalibar's expression softened. "I'm sorry, did I say something to upset you?"

"It's okay," she replied, wiping her eyes with the back of her hand. She took a deep breath in, then let it out slowly. "It's just...there *is* no Mortown anymore."

Silence fell over the camp, the only sound the crackling of the fire. At length, Kalibar sighed.

"I see," he murmured. "May I ask what happened?"

"It was a little over a year ago," Ariana replied, her voice quiet, almost a whisper. "It was late, and I'd just gone to bed. I remember my mom putting me to sleep." She smiled a little, hugging her arms to her chest. "She tucked me in, and told me she loved me."

Kalibar said nothing, facing Ariana attentively.

"After she'd left, I fell asleep," Ariana continued. She paused, taking a deep breath in, then continuing. "I woke up sometime in the middle of the night. My room was filled with this gray fog. It was so thick that I could barely see. Then I heard someone scream. It...it was my mom. She ran into my room, I saw her come through the fog. She was...her hands were covered with blood."

Ariana swallowed, her lower lip trembling.

"Ariana..." Kalibar began.

"It wasn't her blood," Ariana interjected. "It was my father's."

She stared off into space, her damp cheeks glistening in the flickering light of the fire. The shadows it threw across her pale face gave her a haunted look.

"She almost reached me," Ariana whispered. "She was so close. And then the Dead Man was there behind her." She shook her head. "My mother didn't even see him. He just..."

Ariana said nothing for a long moment, staring down at the ground in front of her. When she lifted her head, fresh tears were streaming down her cheeks.

"The Dead Man took me outside and lined me up with the rest of the kids in town," she continued. "Then he walked up to the first boy in line...he must have been eight or nine. The Dead Man stood there for a moment, then shook his head. A Death Weaver took the boy away. I never saw him again."

"Monstrous," Kalibar muttered.

"He went up to the next boy, and shook his head. They took the boy away. Then a little girl, one of my friends. They took her away too. He shook his head at *everyone*. And they were all taken away." Ariana sniffled, wiping tears from her eyes. "Then he stepped in front of me." She turned to look at Kyle then, and gave a bitter smile. "I thought I was going to be taken away too. I was ready to die." She shook her head. "But the Dead Man, he just smiled, and patted me on the head. And then he brought me into one of his black carriages. I remember staring out of the back, before they closed the doors. The whole town was on fire. Everything was burning...there was nothing left."

With that, she fell silent. Kyle scooted over next to her, and she rested her head on his shoulder. Kyle glanced up at Kalibar; the former Grand Weaver's head was downcast, his hands clasped in front of him. And Darius...Darius was staring at Ariana, his expression as unreadable as ever.

At length, Ariana recovered, wiping her eyes with her sleeve.

"I spent every day in the Arena," she said, her voice angry now, "dreaming of escaping, of killing the Dead Man, of being free. And now I am." She shook her head. "But I don't have a home to go to. I don't have a family anymore." She gave a bitter smile. "Before I was trapped and now I'm just...lost."

They sat in silence then, everyone lost in their own thoughts. Kyle thought about his family back home. He had more in common with Ariana than he'd imagined...but she had lived through far worse. At least his parents and friends were still alive.

Kalibar lifted his head, rubbing his hands together slowly. Then he stopped, clasping his hands in front of himself.

"I'm so sorry, Ariana," he murmured. "Believe me, if I could have done something..." Ariana shook her head, putting a hand on Kalibar's.

"Thank you for saving me," she replied. Then she smiled. "I remember visiting Stridon once, when I was younger," she said. "My parents wanted me to see the city. I saw you there, a few years after you'd stopped being Grand Weaver," she added. "I only saw you from afar, but you were so intimidating. Everyone worshiped you...even my parents. I never thought you'd end up being such a nice man."

Kalibar smiled, putting Ariana's hand in his own, and patting it gently. "I suppose I'm not so intimidating now," he replied ruefully. Ariana shook her head.

"You were so brave, when…" she said, then stopped suddenly. "I'm sorry," she murmured.

"Don't be," Kalibar replied. "To be honest, I was terrified," he confessed. "I knew what the Dead Man was going to do, but when it happened…" he paused, shaking his head. "I had nothing left but my dignity. I wasn't about to let the Dead Man take that from me."

"Where are you from, Kalibar?" Ariana asked, changing the subject. Kyle was thankful for that; no matter what Kalibar said about that terrible night in the Arena, Kyle would always feel at least a little responsible for what had happened.

"I was born in Stridon," Kalibar replied. "My father owned a large fishing company, and was quite wealthy. My mother had graduated from the Secula Magna…she was a Weaver. They'd been childhood friends, and when she finished her schooling, my father married her. I was their only son."

"Did you ever have kids?" Ariana asked. Kalibar paused for a long moment, then sighed.

"That," he muttered, "…is a long story." Ariana blanched. "I'm sorry."

"Don't be," the former Grand Weaver replied. "You were brave enough to share your demons," he added. "It's time I did the same."

Kalibar sat there for a long moment, as if choosing his words.

"I…before I became Grand Weaver," he began, "well, before I even got elected to the Council, I met a woman. I'd just graduated from the Secula Magna, having more than inherited my mother's magical talents. I'd graduated top in my class, but I was sick of school at the time, and although I eventually wanted to become a Battle-Weaver, I decided to take some time off. I wasted a lot of time doing what young men do…which is to say I drank wine and chased women."

Kyle glanced at Darius, catching the bodyguard smiling ever-so-faintly.

"Then I found a woman unlike any other," Kalibar continued, a wistful expression on his face. "She was absolutely stunning…she took my breath away the first time I saw her. She wasn't a Weaver, or a Runic. She couldn't do any magic at all, really." Then Kalibar smiled. "But she was magical to me." He shook his head. "She was *too* good for me, really," he admitted. "And I knew it, let me tell you!

So I married her before she figured that out."

Darius chuckled, and Kalibar joined him. Kyle stared at the bodyguard, realizing that he'd never heard the man laugh before.

"With my stipend from the Secula Magna," Kalibar continued, "I was able to afford a house just outside of Stridon, on a small lake. It was a small home – barely larger than my living room now – but it was the only place in my adult life that had ever felt like *home*."

Ariana smiled at Kalibar. Kyle smiled too; they both understood how important having a home was. Kalibar said nothing for a long time, until Kyle began to wonder if that was the end of Kalibar's story.

"It didn't take very long for my wife to get pregnant," Kalibar said with a wry smile. Kyle caught Darius smirking from the other side of the campfire. "She wanted it to be a boy, so she could name him after me." Kalibar shook his head. "That's how she was, always thinking of me. I was always feeling guilty, because I could never be as good to her as she was to me."

Suddenly he stopped, taking a deep breath in, then slowly releasing it. He cleared his throat.

"It was hard to tell when she was going to give birth," he continued. "She kept having contractions, and then they'd go away. We'd called the family doctor to our home so many times, he must have been sick of us!" He chuckled at the thought, then sighed. "When it was time for her to give birth, we called in the doctor one last time, and he stayed with us for…oh, I don't know…it was a long time. And then she started pushing, and we knew that this was it…the baby was coming."

"She pushed, and pushed. She never yelled out, never complained. I held her hand, and put cold towels on her head. She pushed for hours. The doctor was afraid she would tire out, but she didn't." Kalibar smiled at the memory, clasping his hands together so tightly that his knuckles turned white.

"When I saw the top of my son's head…" He paused, then smiled. "He had so much hair! It was the same color as mine. She pushed and pushed, and his head came out a little more each time. Then it came out…" Kalibar held his hands close together in front of him, as if cradling a baby's head.

"His face was all smooshed up," Kalibar explained. "But it was just…just perfect. The most perfect thing I'd ever seen." Kalibar lips trembled, and he paused for a long moment. Ariana put her hand on his shoulder. Kalibar looked startled for a moment, then relaxed.

"She kept pushing," Kalibar continued, his eyebrows furrowing. "But then everything stopped. He wouldn't come any further. She pushed and pushed, but he kept rocking back and forth, and he wouldn't come. The doctor pushed on her belly, pushed so hard, but he still wouldn't come. We tried to pull him out, but he wouldn't move."

Kalibar turned his head to the sky, his blindfold damp with tears. "By the time we managed to get him out, it was already too late. He was gone."

Ariana rubbed Kalibar's back, wiping tears from her own cheeks. Kyle stared at his hands, feeling like he didn't deserve to be sitting here. He'd never seen a grown-up cry, not like this. And no adult, not even his mom and dad, had ever confided something so personal to him before. He didn't feel worthy of it.

"We gave him to my wife," Kalibar continued. "She knew right away. Oh, how she cried. I'd never seen her cry like that before." Kalibar shook his head. "And there was nothing I could do to help her. I was her husband, I was supposed to protect her, I was supposed to protect my son, but I couldn't."

Darius, who hadn't moved since they'd started talking, put a hand on Kalibar's other shoulder.

"Afterward, she was so angry," Kalibar said, his voice almost a whisper. "She said I should have been able to save him...I should have used my magic to save him." His jawline rippled. "She asked me...she said, what good was it that I was at the top of my class, the best Weaver of my generation, if I couldn't even save my own son?"

Kalibar lowered his head, staring at the ground. He sat there for a long time, saying nothing. Kyle and Ariana glanced at each other, unsure of what to say. Kyle glanced at Darius, but the warrior seemed lost in thought, his blue eyes focusing on nothing in particular. Then Kalibar stirred, raising his head. His red bandanna was soaked.

"And then she left me too," Kalibar said, his lower lip trembling. "She left me so that she could be with our son."

Silence came over the camp. Ariana sat by Kalibar, taking his hand in hers. Kyle and Darius stared at the ground. The wind blew through the forest around them beyond the shield, but the air inside the camp's shield was still.

Finally, Kalibar stirred.

"I hated her for that," he confessed. "For leaving me. And I hated myself for hating her. I...shut down. At first I thought about joining my wife and son, but I...couldn't. I blamed myself for my son's death. I vowed to learn everything I could about magic, so that I would never feel that helpless again."

"I threw myself into studying magic, and returned to the Secula Magna to start my specialization as a Battle-Weaver. I graduated first in my class there, too. Then I joined the military. I fought in the wars against the tribes...fought like a wild man, taking chances no one else would." He paused, then smiled bitterly.

"Of course, everyone else thought I was something quite extraordinary," he continued. "I won accolades and awards, got promoted, and eventually my superiors felt I was too valuable to waste on impossible missions anymore. They promoted me, and promoted me some more, and eventually I got promoted right out of the military. I was nominated for the Council, and won. Then I ran for Grand Weaver, and won that, too."

Kalibar paused, running a hand through his short white hair.

"I threw myself into that job, as before," he continued. "And most believed that I was the best of men, that I was the greatest leader in the history of the new Secula Magna. Even Erasmus fed into that deceit...and still does." He paused, then withdrew his hand from Ariana's.

"But I knew better," he continued. "Any time I felt my ego getting the better of me, I only had to remember my wife's words to me. Humility was always just a memory away. When my term was over, I decided to retire to Bellingham, to enjoy a quieter, simpler life in the countryside. I'd spent most of my life filling my days with work...when I finally had free time, I ended up spending it in my own head. I wondered where the last forty years had gone...how they'd gone by so fast. I often wondered what life would have been like had things...turned out differently so long ago."

He paused, then sighed.

"I never did get to have the family I'd always wanted," he said, not without a trace of bitterness. "I never remarried, never had children. I'd always wanted a son..." He paused, then chuckled. "I've been trying to figure out why I'm so fond of you, Kyle, and I think I know now," he added. "When you came around, lost and alone, so far from your family, I think that I felt I'd gotten a second chance...a chance to raise the son I'd never had. To...protect him, no matter what." He sighed, and Ariana grabbed his hand again. This time, he let her do so without a fuss.

"I know you feel responsible for what the Dead Man did to me," Kalibar continued, speaking to Kyle. "But for me, I felt like I finally had the chance to do what I wish I could have done for my son." He smiled warmly. "And if I had to do it again, I would."

Kyle nodded silently. Despite Kalibar's words, he couldn't help but feel a familiar guilt come over him.

"What I'm trying to say is," the old man continued, "well, neither you or Ariana have a home anymore, and I haven't had a family since my wife passed away. It would..." he paused, taking a deep breath in and letting it out slowly. "...it would be my honor to have you in my house, both of you, with me as your guardian. I know I'll never be your real father, but I'd like to try to be the next best thing."

Kyle's jaw dropped, and he glanced over at Ariana. She too looked stunned. Then a big smile lit up her face, and she gave a very surprised Kalibar a big hug.

"Thank you," she said tearfully, squeezing the old man so hard his face turned red. He laughed, then turned to Kyle.

"And you Kyle?" he asked tentatively. Kyle grinned.

"Yes," he answered. Then a horrible thought came to him. "Wait," he blurted out. Ariana and Kalibar frowned at him quizzically. "I mean, this won't, uh..." he stammered, blushing fiercely.

"Won't what?" Kalibar asked.

"This won't make us brother and sister, will it?" he asked, his cheeks burning terribly. If they became brother and sister, it would ruin any chances of...stuff. Darius, of course, rolled his eyes at them both. Kalibar smiled kindly, and shook his head.

"No, it won't," he answered. Kyle breathed a sigh of relief. That matter settled, all eyes – or rather, eye sockets – turned to Darius. The dour bodyguard frowned at the sudden attention.

"What?" he asked, his tone wary.

"So what's your story, Darius?" Kalibar asked. Darius stood up.

"Too long for tonight," he replied, walking over to one end of the camp, and laying down on the ground. With that, he fell fast asleep...or at least he seemed to. Ariana and Kyle exchanged befuddled glances.

"Well," Kalibar stated, raising his eyebrows. "I guess that's that. Good night, everyone."

"Good night," Kyle and Ariana said in unison. Ariana got up, grabbing levitating sleeping bags for them all, and setting them next to each other. Kalibar laid down in the middle, with Kyle and Ariana snuggling up to him on either side. The former Grand Weaver tensed up at first, clearly not expecting nor being accustomed to such affection, but then relaxed, a contented smile on his lips.

Kyle lay there next to his new guardian, feeling a sense of peace for the first time since the attack on Crescent Lake. He glanced at Kalibar, already asleep in his sleeping bag, and thought back to what Erasmus had said days ago. The former Grand Runic had been right all along; Kyle and Kalibar both had something the other needed. And now they had Ariana.

And so, with bellies full of food and hearts filled with happiness, they all fell asleep.

Chapter 21

Ampir passes through the illusory cliff wall, carrying Vera into the cave beyond. The illusion blocks all light from getting into the cave, leaving it pitch black. He hears Junior whimper, feels the boy's arms tighten around his neck.

"It's okay," Ampir reassures. With a thought, his armor begins to glow, white light illuminating some of the runes on his chest and back. He finds himself in a small cave. Opposite the cave entrance is a large door.

"Stand here," he orders, kneeling down to let Junior slide off of his back. The boy does so, looking up at his father with wide eyes, his small face terribly pale. Ampir turns, leaning over to kiss the boy's forehead. Then he turns to Vera. "Can you stand?" he asks.

"I think so," she answers. He sets her down beside Junior, then turns to the door at the far end of the cave, walking up to it. Sealed by incredibly sophisticated magic that recognized an individual's unique magical radiation, it can only be opened by the Grand Runic and Grand Weaver, or a member of the Council.

Ampir peels off one gauntlet, placing his bare palm on the door, and waits.

The door *clicks*, then swings outward.

Ampir turns around...just in time to see Vera stumble to the side. She slumps against the cave wall, sliding down to her butt on the floor.

"Mommy!" Junior cries, rushing to her side. Vera's eyes roll back, and she tips to the side.

"Vera!" Ampir shouts, sprinting to her and grabbing before she hits her head on the stone floor. "Vera," he repeats, gently slapping her cheek. "Come on Vera, stay with me."

Vera's eyes flutter open, and she stares at Ampir blankly for a moment.

"You okay?" he asks.

"What happened?"

"You passed out," he answers. He scoops her up in his arms, lifting her off of the floor and holding her close. "Get on my back, Junior," he orders, kneeling down again. Junior climbs on his back wordlessly. So quiet now, his son. So unlike his usual jubilant self. The poor boy had seen Grandpa – his best friend – murdered in cold blood. Had seen his home destroyed. Ampir wondered if Junior was old enough to remember these things…and hoped that he wasn't.

"I'm cold," Vera mumbles, shivering now.

"It's the cave," he replies. But he sees her sweat-slicked forehead, the terrible paleness of her lips. Fear grips him.

Stay with me baby, he prays, pulling his gauntlet back on and stepping through the doorway, Junior clinging to his back. *We're almost there.*

* * *

"Good morning, Kyle," Kalibar stated jovially from where he sat cross-legged by the burnt-out campfire. Kyle yawned, stretching his arms over his head, then rolling out of his sleeping bag. Despite his exhaustion last night, he hadn't slept well at all. He'd woken up over and over again, plagued by his dreams.

"Morning," Kyle replied. Then he frowned. "How'd you know it was me?"

"Everyone else is awake," Kalibar answered. And it was true; Ariana was sitting at the edge of her sleeping bag, sipping on a cup of hot soup, while Darius sat on the ground, sharpening his sword with a whetstone.

"Good morning," Kyle, nodding at Ariana. She turned to him, flashing him a smile, then hopped down from her sleeping bag, grabbing a cup of soup and a wrapped-up piece of bread that were lying on the ground there. She handed both to Kyle. "Thanks," he mumbled. He ate in silence then, watching Darius hone his blade.

"We should get going soon," Kalibar stated, standing up. "If we move quickly, we'll reach Stridon by mid-afternoon."

"What's the plan?" Darius asked.

"Well, if Orik finds out we're coming, we're dead men," Kalibar answered. "He has to assume that we've learned the truth about him, after all. And since he has a lot of friends on the Council, we can't go to them for help."

"So?"

"We need to go straight to the top," Kalibar replied. "The Grand Weaver and Grand Runic are friends of mine...and more importantly, they're not fans of Orik."

"What about Erasmus?" Kyle piped in.

"I can't risk going to him first," Kalibar answered. "His office is in the middle of the Tower...I'd be spotted going in. But I can get to the Grand Weaver's suite without attracting attention."

"How?"

"There's a series of tunnels that run under the city," Kalibar answered. "...that connect to the Tower. They were built as escape tunnels in case of an attack on the Ancient Secula Magna. Most of them are still functional." He smiled. "And they lead directly to the top floor of the Great Tower...where the Grand Weaver and Grand Runic live."

"Ohhh," Kyle breathed.

"There's an entrance to the tunnels just outside of Stridon," Kalibar continued. "We'll follow the main road until we reach the outskirts of the city, then take the tunnels to the Tower. Once we alert the authorities, we can meet up with Erasmus and get Kyle's ring back."

"Alright," Darius stated. "Let's clean up." Kyle and Ariana gathered the cups, rinsing them out with magical streams of water and placing them back in the pack. Then Darius lifted the pack up over his shoulder, carrying the considerable weight as if it were as light as a feather. They made their way back into the bordergrass, walking a dozen feet from the road to avoid being spotted. Ariana fell into step beside Kyle, walking so close that their hands brushed occasionally as they walked.

"Hey," Ariana almost whispered, glancing at Kyle.

"Yeah?"

"What's with Darius?" she asked.

"What do you mean?"

"Why'd they call him a traitor?" Ariana pressed. Kyle hesitated, glancing forward. Darius and Kalibar were too far ahead to overhear their conversation...he hoped.

"The soldiers that attacked us before we were kidnapped seemed to know him," Kyle answered. "They said he was a traitor."

"That doesn't make sense," Ariana whispered. "Why would he kill them and run if he was a traitor? And then help us escape?"

"I know."

"He saved all of us from the Dire Lurker," Ariana continued. "And the Dead Man."

Kyle nodded. There was no doubt that the bodyguard was on their side now…regardless of whether he had been before.

"What do you think?" Ariana asked.

"I don't know," Kyle admitted, his eyes on Darius's golden back. "I don't think I've ever fully trusted him."

"Well, we *have* to trust him now," Ariana replied.

"Why's that?"

"We don't have any other choice."

* * *

Hours passed, the sun rising up from behind them until it peaked over their heads, the full force of the noon sun shining on their scalps and shoulders as they walked. Suddenly, Ariana tapped Kyle on the shoulder.

"Look!" she gasped. He glanced up, realizing that the ground had begun to slope downward…revealing a view that made his jaw drop.

There, miles away in the distance, a vast river flowed. And beyond it stood a huge, sprawling city, hundreds of buildings forming a magnificent skyline reflected in the river's silvery waters. Standing head and shoulders above the other buildings was a lone, majestic tower, its pyramidal top glittering in the sunlight like an enormous jewel.

Kyle's heart soared, and he clapped his hands, laughing joyously. Ariana grabbed his hand, and he squeezed it tight.

"We made it!" Kyle blurted out. "Look!"

Kalibar paused, then grinned, leaning on Darius's shoulder.

"You see the city?" he asked.

"Yeah!" Kyle exclaimed.

They all stood facing the panorama in front of them for a few moments. That is, until Darius starting walking back the way they'd come.

"Hey, where are you going?" Kyle asked. Darius didn't even turn around.

"Remember the plan," he grumbled. "Which way?" he asked Kalibar.

"We're facing the great River, to the right of the road?" Kalibar asked.

"Yup."

"Then we turn right. The entrance to the tunnels is through a cave. We'll have to hike through the forest to get there."

"Wait," Kyle interjected. "The tunnels go under the river into the city?"

"Correct," Kalibar confirmed. "The forest should be about two miles from here."

"Let's go," Darius grumbled. He led them rightward, until they were moving parallel to the shore of the Great River, still far in the distance. They pushed through the tall bordergrass, emerging into a shallow valley beyond. Ahead, Kyle could see the tree line of the forest Kalibar had described.

"When we reach the forest," Kalibar told Darius, "…we should keep to the left. There's a cliff wall that rises up thirty feet or so a mile into the forest. The cave is there."

Darius nodded, and they continued forward in silence, until the first trees of the forest stood before them. The trees looked strikingly different than the ones Kyle had become accustomed to. They were tall, with thick, knobby trunks and innumerable twisted branches that extended outward, tangling with the branches of the trees surrounding them. These branches grew so densely that they blocked out most of the sun, leaving the forest floor dark and gloomy. Some had what looked like huge, dull gray spider webs on them, extending from branch to branch…and even from tree to tree.

"What are those?" Kyle asked, pointing to a particularly large web.

"Dreamweaver webs," Darius answered. Kalibar frowned at this.

"There are dreamweaver spiders here?" he asked. "We should be cautious."

"Why?" Kyle asked. "Are they dangerous?"

"Oh yes," Kalibar replied. "The fully-grown ones especially. But even hatchlings can be lethal in large enough numbers."

"How big do they get?" Kyle pressed, his hackles rising. He

glanced at a nearby tree, spotting a small web there, and gave it wide berth.

"Big enough," Kalibar answered. "Their silk is sticky, and has magic that makes prey sleepy…hence their name. Their venom has the same magic, but much more potent. One bite from a grown spider will put a man in a coma for days."

"Great," Kyle muttered. Kalibar smirked.

"Fully grown spiders are rare," he informed. "Most hatchlings die before reaching full size."

Kyle nodded absently, glancing from tree to tree, spotting more silvery webs. Suddenly he didn't feel so bad about hating spiders. In fact, he vowed to stomp on the next reasonably-sized one that he saw.

The four pressed onward carefully, avoiding the wispy silk as they passed. Some of the webs were truly enormous, spanning over twenty feet high, and even longer across. Looking carefully, Kyle noticed a few dozen dark shapes lying on the surface of one particularly large web. He couldn't make out what the shapes were, but he could tell that some were still breathing.

"We use dreamweaver silk to make pillows and beds," Kalibar explained. "A small amount of silk makes people tired, but won't make them sleep forever. My own pillow has dreamweaver silk in it."

"How do people get the silk without falling asleep?" Kyle asked.

"Dreamweaver silk harvesters must never harvest alone, and one person must carry small amounts of silk while another observes them," Kalibar explained. "The process is very slow, and exceedingly dangerous. That's why dreamweaver silk products are so expensive."

"Careful," Kyle heard Ariana say, and he turned to her. She pointed at his left shoulder. He saw a few wispy strands of silk sticking to his shirt there, and flinched.

"Jesus!" he swore, brushing off the webbing hastily. It fell lazily to the forest floor. He glanced up at Ariana. "Thanks."

"You're welcome," she replied with a pretty smile.

He felt a sudden, sharp pain in the back of his neck.

"Ow!" he exclaimed, reaching back and swatting at his neck. He felt something soft and prickly strike his hand. "What was…"

"Kyle!" Ariana shouted, pointing down. Kyle followed her hand, spotting something black climbing up the side of his leg. A furry spider with long, thin legs, nearly as big as a tarantula.

"Whoa!" Kyle shouted, jumping back. He kicked his leg, but the spider clung to his pants, climbing up his thigh and onto his belly. He swatted it away, sending it flying through the air.

"What's wrong?" Kalibar demanded.

"There were spiders on me," Kyle replied. He rubbed his neck, glancing nervously around himself. "I think I got bit."

"Watch out," Ariana cried, pointing straight up. Kyle jerked his gaze upward, spotting several more spiders descending through the air toward them, hanging by silver lines of webbing from the tree branches above. One of them dropped from their web, landing on Ariana's shoulder. She yelped, brushing it off.

"They're coming from above!" Kyle warned.

"Activate your armor, *now!*" Kalibar shouted. He grabbed onto Darius's shoulder, and a gravity shield appeared around both of them, spiders falling onto the spherical surface and bouncing off. Kyle backpedaled until his back hit a tree trunk behind him. Two spiders fell through the air, landing on his head. He jerked away from the trunk, batting at his head with his hands.

"Kyle, your armor!" Ariana cried.

Kyle *pulled* magic from his mind, sending it out to the crystal on his breastplate. He felt a vibration, and suddenly the spiders on his head flew off, careening through the air. More spiders landed on his shoulders, ricocheting off of the magical field protecting him.

"Everyone's armor activated?" Kalibar asked.

"Yes," Darius replied.

"Good."

A shockwave ripped outward from Kalibar, blasting through the trees. Branches snapped off of their trunks, hurtling outward in all directions. Spiders flew through the air away from them, their silvery webs snapping.

"Go," Darius ordered. He strode forward, Kalibar following at his side, the gravity shield protecting them both. Kyle felt a hand on his shoulder, and turned, but saw nothing but forest around him.

"I'm here," he heard Ariana say. He nodded, and sprinted forward to catch up with Darius. They continued through the dark forest at a rapid pace, dodging tree trunks and fallen logs as they went. The forest floor dipped downward at a gentle angle, the trees growing even taller. Darkness swallowed them, making it impossible to see anything more than ten feet away.

"Keep to the left," Kalibar ordered. "We should reach the cliff wall soon."

They angled leftward, trudging through fallen leaves, small twigs crunching underfoot. Kyle glanced upward nervously, searching for more spiders on the branches above, but could see nothing in the darkness. He stifled a yawn, concentrating on keeping pace with the others. Onward they went, until at last Kyle spotted a sheer rock wall to their left, rising some twenty to thirty feet above the ground. Vines grew in thick tangles over the rock, their leaves fluttering in the breeze. Darius led them to the wall, walking alongside it.

"We're at the wall," Darius informed Kalibar.

"Is it safe to drop the shield?" Kalibar asked.

"Seems so," Darius confirmed. The shield surrounding them vanished, and Kalibar walked alongside the wall, his left hand trailing over the rock.

"There are hidden wards near the entrance," he explained. "I should be able to sense them. Only the highest-ranking government officials can unlock them without triggering the defensive wards."

Their paced slowed as Kalibar ran his fingers over the stone of the wall, his head bowed. Kyle yawned a second time, feeling suddenly spent. He fought the urge to stop and lean against the cliff wall.

Keep your armor up, he reminded himself.

After a few minutes, Kalibar stopped.

"Here," he proclaimed. "Hold on while I deactivate the wards."

Kyle frowned, staring at the rock wall Kalibar had stopped at. Dense sheets of vines hung down from the stone, swaying a bit in the breeze. He leaned against the cliff-side, closing his eyes for a moment. He felt himself falling asleep, and jerked himself awake, pulling himself away from the wall.

Kalibar and Darius were gone.

Kyle froze, staring at the wall, then turning around. There were no trees, no forest...only a vast plain extending to a wide river miles away. And in the distance, Stridon rose over that river, flames engulfing its shattered skyline.

What the...

"Kyle? Are you alright?"

Kyle jerked his head up, opening his eyes. He found himself leaning against the rock wall...and Kalibar, Ariana, and Darius were staring at him.

"What?"

"You fell asleep," Ariana explained. "You weren't responding to us."

"I did?" Kyle exclaimed. "Sorry."

"Are you feeling okay?" Ariana pressed. "Let me see your neck." She turned him around, and he felt her fingers on the nape of his neck. He felt a sudden stinging sensation.

"Ow," he exclaimed, flinching away from her touch.

"You *did* get bitten," Ariana proclaimed. She turned to Darius and Kalibar. "He got bitten by a spider."

"How big was it?" Kalibar asked.

"I don't know," Kyle admitted, rubbing his neck gingerly. "I didn't see it."

"How far apart are the bite marks?" Kalibar pressed.

"Maybe a half-inch?" Ariana answered.

"You're going to get very sleepy," Kalibar warned. "Darius, you may need to carry him."

"Nothing new there," Darius muttered.

"I deactivated the wards," Kalibar stated. "Let's get going."

With that, Kalibar parted the vines, then stepped through them, vanishing from sight. Darius did the same, as did Ariana. Kyle hesitated, then followed behind her, finding himself surrounded by darkness. The air was cool and moist, and smelled faintly of earth. A bright light flared to life a few feet above him. Darius, Kalibar, and Ariana were standing around him, the magical light above them illuminating a small cave.

"This cave will bring us to the tunnels," Kalibar explained. "Most of them survived the Great War. Our architects repaired the damaged sections a few generations ago, restoring the original network of tunnels and rooms."

Kyle nodded, leaning against the cave wall. His eyelids grew heavy, and he forced them open, glancing back at the sheet of vines covering the entrance.

They were gone...and he was surrounded by utter blackness.

Kyle froze, his heart racing. He wove magic quickly, creating a light above his head...and saw the small cave around him. Except the cave was empty...everyone was gone. He looked down, seeing black gauntlets covering his hands, tiny runes etched into their metallic surface glowing faint blue.

"Kyle!" a voice hissed. "Wake up!"

Kyle opened his eyes, realizing that he had fallen asleep while leaning against the cave wall…and that Darius was standing before him, glaring down at him.

"What?" Kyle asked. He glanced over his shoulder, seeing the vines hanging down before the cave entrance…completely intact. "Uh, sorry…I fell asleep again."

"Come on," Darius urged.

Kyle took a deep breath in, then followed the bodyguard further into the cave. Kalibar's light led the way, floating a few feet above the former Grand Weaver's head. He glanced at Ariana, realizing that she was staring at him. She looked concerned.

"You okay?" she asked.

"Sleepy," Kyle admitted.

"You want Darius to carry you in his arms?" she asked, her eyes twinkling mischievously.

"No thanks," Kyle grumbled. Ariana laughed, grabbing his hand in her own. Her skin was very warm, and soft.

"It's going to be okay," she reassured.

Darius gestured for them to follow, and they went deeper into the cave. The dark rock formed an irregular tunnel, winding left, then right, then dipping downward. The ceiling became so low that Kalibar and Darius had to duck down to avoid hitting their heads. Kyle and Ariana, being shorter, were able to stand up straight without difficulty.

Kyle yawned, then glanced back the way he'd come. He could see nothing but darkness beyond the few feet of cave illuminated by Kalibar's magical light. He felt his eyes drifting closed, then felt Ariana's hand slip away from his. He opened his eyes, looking forward.

Everyone was gone.

Kyle froze, his heart skipping a beat. He turned in a circle, seeing nothing but blackness all around him. Kalibar's light was nowhere to be seen.

"Ariana?" he called out. "Kalibar?"

Nobody answered.

He closed his eyes, fighting down a surge of panic.

Make some light, he told himself.

He wove the light pattern, tossing it into the air above his head. A soft light appeared, bathing the cave in a gentle glow. Looking around, he found himself alone in the irregular tunnel. Where had the others gone?

He started walking down the tunnel, his footsteps echoing hollowly off of the stone walls. A thought came unbidden to his mind, a voice at once strange and familiar.

Stay with me.

The soft white light from above faded, replaced by a much paler blue light. He felt a heavy weight pulling downward on his arms, and he looked down at them. They were covered in black metal, countless intricate runes carved into its surface, glowing a soft blue. He started to run down the tunnel, moving forward with incredible ease, his metallic boots *clunking* on the rock underfoot with each step. He felt a weight shift on his back, felt small arms encircling his neck.

We're almost there.

He looked down, seeing a woman in his arms. Auburn hair spilled down the front of her white nightgown, strands of it falling in front of her deathly pale face. She stared up at him, sweat beading on her forehead, her hand on his chest.

"I'm so thirsty," she mumbled, closing her eyes.

A hand grabbed his shoulder from behind, spinning him around.

"Kyle!"

He opened his eyes, finding himself slumped against the wall again, a pair of blue eyes staring down at him.

"Wake up," Darius hissed. Kyle saw Ariana staring at him, Kalibar at her side. They all looked worried...except for Darius, who was clearly annoyed.

"Sorry," Kyle mumbled. "I can't help it." Darius turned to Ariana.

"Keep him awake," he commanded, then turned away, moving forward through the cavern. Ariana grabbed Kyle's hand, pulling him along. Kyle sighed, then glanced down at his arms. They were covered in the armor that Kalibar had given him...and not the black armor he'd been wearing only seconds ago. *Ampir's* armor.

"Come on," Ariana urged, her tone gentle. Kyle nodded at her, following her as she continued down the tunnel. Eventually the irregular rock walls gave way to smooth stone, the floor transitioning from rock to tiles. These, Kyle realized, must be the tunnels Kalibar mentioned earlier. They soon came to a fork in the tunnel, with one tunnel going left, the other right.

"There's a fork," Darius stated, turning to Kalibar. "Which way?"

"Left," Kalibar answered.

They followed Darius down the left tunnel, soon coming to another fork. This time Kalibar had them go right. Kyle and Ariana followed behind the two men, Ariana clutching his hand tightly, and glancing at him occasionally. Kyle smiled weakly at her, continuing down the long hallway. Eventually this ended, a closed door barring the way.

"There's a door," Darius warned Kalibar. The former Grand Weaver nodded, walking up to the door carefully, using his staff as a walking stick. Then he placed one palm on the door, lowering his head. Kyle saw runes flash on the surface of the door, and then it swung inward, revealing darkness beyond. Kalibar and Darius walked through the doorway; Ariana followed close behind, the doorway being too narrow for her and Kyle to go in side-by-side. Her hand slipped away from his, and he felt something *shift*.

He looked down, seeing the woman lying in his arms again. Blood stained the side of her nightgown. Fresh, wet blood.

Almost there baby.

He stepped up to the doorway, then through it, entering the darkness that lay below. The door closed behind him, leaving him in pitch blackness.

Here.

His visor adjusted to the darkness, making the room appear brighter almost instantly. He was standing in a massive chamber, so large that a house could have easily fit inside of it. Far above his head, he saw a majestic domed ceiling, huge pillars at the four corners of the room supporting its considerable weight. Fine cracks ran across the ceiling.

He felt a vibration in the stone beneath his feet. Fine dust fell from the cracks in the ceiling.

The Behemoth, he realized. It must be nearby, near the Tower above ground.

He turned his gaze toward the center of the room, where a small circular dais stood, made of plain gray stone. A brilliant red crystal lay embedded in its center, refracting and reflecting the dozen magical lights shining down from above. He paused, then walked up to the dais, standing in front of it. He stared down at the crystal, marveling at it. It was perhaps three feet in diameter, with innumerable tiny runes etched on its surface…and countless more deeper within.

Renval's greatest invention.

It was much, much larger, this crystal, than the one Renval had been working on nearly two decades ago. Larger even than it had been last year, when Ampir had used it last. And far more complex. He studied its runes, tracing the faint blue glow identifying each of them. There was something very different about the destination coordinates; he couldn't make sense of them.

"I need to set you down," he said, gently lowering Vera to the floor. He propped her against the dais, feeling Junior slide off of his back. He turned his attention to the dais, trying to figure out the coordinates.

Damn it Renval, he swore silently. *Why did you have to change things?*

A deafening boom echoed throughout the chamber, and the ceiling groaned again, small rocks falling through the widening cracks in the dome. He wove a gravity shield around the dais, and a few rocks bounced off of the shield harmlessly.

"What's that, Daddy?" Junior asked, looking upward.

"I don't know," Ampir lied. The Behemoth must be right above them. The chamber rumbled again, more dust falling from the ceiling. The ceiling was falling apart under the Behemoth's incredible weight.

It can't know I'm here, he told himself. But he only half-believed it. Either way, he – and Vera – were running out of time. He hesitated, rapidly weighing the possibilities. The coordinates in the crystal were different…and he had no time to change them. But Renval was a careful man; he would never leave the coordinates to an unsafe location. Wherever it would send them, it was better than here.

"Ampir," Vera called out. He turned to her, feeling his heart sink. Her nightgown was soaked with sweat, clinging to her body. She looked at him with those beautiful eyes. "Hold me."

Ampir hesitated, then reached out to her, carrying her in his arms once again.

"Hold on baby," he urged. "Just a little while longer."

The ceiling shook again, more dust and rocks falling from the ever-widening cracks there. He focused on the dais, sending a stream of magic to it. The teleporter came to life, its runes glowing faint blue.

Nothing else happened.

What the…

He stared at the dais, realizing that there wasn't enough magic to power it. The runes were supposed to be bright blue, but they were barely glowing.

The Behemoth drained part of it, he realized. *When it drained the Tower.* There was some magic left, but not enough.

"Shit," he swore.

"What baby?" Vera asked.

"There isn't enough magic," he answered. "Shit!"

"Your armor," Vera suggested. "Use it."

Ampir nodded, realizing that she was right. His armor was filled to the brim with magic, even if his body had been drained of it earlier. He focused on his armor, pulling its magic into himself, then redirecting it at the dais. The runes glowed slightly brighter.

"It needs a lot," he said with a frown. "Way more than it should."

Vera said nothing, closing her eyes again.

Ampir cursed, draining more magic from his armor and sending it to the dais. Still, the dais did nothing. He pulled even more magic, draining parts of his armor completely, pouring the magic into the crystal on the dais.

Maybe it's broken, he realized, terror gripping him. *Maybe it won't work.*

The runes in the crystal glowed brighter as he poured more magic into them. He felt the air in the chamber stir, saw a faint blue light appear in the air above the dais.

Yes!

Another deafening boom rocked the ceiling, huge slabs of stone falling down and crashing to the floor below. Beyond the widening holes in the ceiling, he spotted a massive black, metallic foot.

The Behemoth!

He drained his armor frantically, sucking every last bit into his mind, then redirecting it to the teleporter.

Come on, come on!

Suddenly the air ten feet above the dais *tore*, a black circular portal appearing there. Barely over a foot in diameter, it was far too small for him or Vera to fit through…and he was almost completely out of magic.

He stared at the rift, his mouth agape, unable to believe his eyes.

"It's too small," he exclaimed, dumbfounded. He'd put an enormous amount of magic into it. The rift shouldn't be that small!

Vera opened her eyes, looking at the rift.

"We'll go one at a time," she offered. But he shook his head angrily.

"We can't fit through there," he retorted. "It's too damn small!"

Vera stared at the rift, then looks at Junior.

"He can."

Ampir turned to Junior, realizing that she was right. The rift was just big enough for him to fit through.

The ceiling quaked above, and the dome sank suddenly, huge fragments of the ceiling breaking away, falling toward them both. One huge piece struck the shield protecting them, and cracked in two, each half falling to the floor on either side.

"Send him," Vera urged, putting a hand on his cheek. "Save him."

"I need to save *you*," he countered.

"Do it," she said, her tone harder now. He looked up at the rift, realizing it was slowly starting to shrink. His heart leapt in his throat, and he turned to Junior.

"Get on the dais," he ordered. Junior hesitated, then climbed up onto it. Ampir reached forward, kissing his son on the forehead, then pulling away. Then he reached for the ring hanging on the necklace around his own neck…the engagement ring Vera had proposed to him with.

He tore it from the necklace, staring at it. The band was shiny and silver-colored, with a large yellow gemstone set on top. Intricate symbols were carved in the band, with tiny crystals dotting the sides.

He closed his eyes, struggling to weave strands of magic with his remaining power. He threw the pattern at the ring.

This way, I'll never lose you.

He handed the ring to Junior.

"I love you, son."

Then he wove again, and Junior rose upward in the air toward the rift. It was shrinking rapidly now; Ampir thrust as much magic as he could at his son, lifting him through the rift.

Then, just as his son's left foot was vanishing into the rift, it snapped shut. Something small fell from where the rift had been, bouncing off of the dais and falling onto the floor. Ampir stared at it, taking a moment to realize what it was.

A toe.

He stared up at where his son had been, feeling a terrible emptiness come over him. Then he looked down at Vera, finding her looking back at him with those painfully beautiful eyes. She smiled at him.

"See something you like?" she inquired.

He smiled back at her, swallowing past a sudden lump in his throat.

"I do now," he replied.

She closed her eyes then, resting her head against his shoulder. Her breaths came more slowly now, her skin terribly pale.

"Kiss me," she murmured.

He leaned down, kissing her soft lips. He smelled her perfume, that intoxicating scent she'd worn the day they'd met. Tears spilled down his cheeks, and he choked back a sob, pulling away. He looked down at her, taking a deep breath in, then letting it out.

It took him a moment to realize she wasn't breathing.

"Baby," he called out, shaking her a little. She didn't move.

Oh god no. Please, no.

A massive *boom* echoed through the chamber. Ampir looked up; the ceiling above them was disintegrating, a huge, metallic foot smashing through it.

The Behemoth!

The single foot descended through the ceiling, filling the entire room with its obscene mass. The Behemoth fell downward, its single green eye locked on him from far above. The killing machine fell rapidly toward him.

He didn't even have time to run.

He looked down at his wife, running his hand through her hair.

"I love you baby," he whispered.

And then the darkness claimed them.

Chapter 22

Kyle opened his eyes, squinting against the sudden brightness. He waited for his eyes to adjust, then opened his eyes further, seeing a plain white ceiling above. He looked down, seeing a light blue sheet covering his body. He was laying on a bed.

What the...

He sat up slowly, feeling none of the usual pain he'd felt in his back from the healing wound there. He frowned, rubbing the sleep from his eyes, and took a look around.

Where am I?

The room around him was small, the walls painted off-white. Light streamed in from a large window behind his head. He turned to his left, spotted an alarm clock sitting on the nightstand beside the bed. Big red blocky numbers on its screen said "7:30." And to his left sat a dark cherry wooden dresser, a pair of jeans spilling out of the bottom drawer.

He sat up straighter, his heart pounding in his chest. He looked around the room, hardly believing what he was seeing. He knew this room.

This was *his* room.

He looked back at his alarm clock, and saw it turn to "7:31." He rubbed his eyes, half-expecting to see the room disappear, for Darius and Kalibar and Ariana to be standing around him back in the tunnels leading to Stridon. But the clock remained, as did his room.

I'm home, he realized.

A strange numbness came over him, not of his flesh, but of his soul. He swung his legs over the edge of his bed, rubbing his eyes again. Still, the room remained. He stood up, feeling none of the customary soreness and stiffness in his limbs, and walked across the room to the door at the far end, pulling it open. He peeked out into the hallway beyond. It was instantly familiar, the same hallway he'd seen a thousand times, at his dad's house.

How...?

He heard footsteps coming up the stairs, and took a step back. He pushed the door until it was nearly shut.

"Kyle?" he heard a familiar voice call out. Kyle's heart skipped a beat.

Dad?

He heard the footsteps reach the top of the stairway, then come down the hall, growing louder. He saw the doorknob turn, the door swinging open. And there, standing in the doorway, was his father.

"Dad!" Kyle cried, rushing forward and throwing his arms around his father. He closed his eyes, burying his face in his dad's shoulder.

"Hey buddy," Dad replied, hesitating for a second, then hugging Kyle back. Then he pushed Kyle away gently, frowning at him. "Something wrong?"

"No," Kyle replied automatically. He looked up, finding himself grinning stupidly at his father. He tried to control his expression, with little success. "Just...really happy to see you," he added rather lamely. Dad smiled back.

"Happy to see you too, kiddo," he said, tousling Kyle's hair. "I fell asleep on the couch. Almost had a heart attack when I saw the time," he added. "Didn't want to waste my day with you snoozing."

"Yeah," Kyle mumbled, staring at his father. He couldn't believe that he was actually *here*, standing with his father, in his own room again. He thought he'd never see his dad again...or his mom.

"You get any sleep?" Dad asked. Kyle nodded.

"Yeah," Kyle answered. He turned, glancing at his bed, with the sheets strewn haphazardly over it.

It was a dream, he realized, hardly able to believe it. He couldn't help but feel disappointed.

"You hungry?" Dad asked. Kyle nodded absently, still staring at his bed. "Let's go downstairs and get some grub."

"Okay," Kyle replied. He followed Dad out of the bedroom and into the hallway, trotting downstairs and making his way into the kitchen. Dad opened the freezer, grabbing a frozen pizza box.

"Pizza okay?"

"Sure."

Dad turned on the oven to preheat it, then gestured for Kyle to follow him to the living room. They both sat on the couch there, facing the blank TV screen. Kyle sighed, rubbing the sleep from his eyes, then staring at his feet.

I can't believe it was all just a dream.

He thought of Kalibar, and of Ariana. Of Darius. Of magic. He closed his eyes, willing cords of magic to *pull* into the center of his mind's eye...but nothing happened. Then he opened his eyes, staring at his left thumb. His ring – his father's ring – was there, right where it'd been before he'd fallen asleep.

Everyone he'd met, everything he'd been through, had been pure fantasy. A figment of his overactive imagination. He shook his head, clenching his teeth against a sudden wave of sadness, and took a deep breath in, letting it out shakily.

"You alright buddy?" Dad asked, putting a hand on Kyle's shoulder. Kyle cleared his throat, and nodded.

"Yeah, uh," he mumbled. "Just had another dream, that's all."

"Another nightmare?"

"Sort of," Kyle replied.

"Want to talk about it?"

"Not really," Kyle muttered. The thought of trying to explain what he'd experienced – of the incredible things he'd seen and gone through – was overwhelming. There was no way anyone could ever truly understand what he'd been through.

"Come on, talk to me," Dad pressed. Kyle shook his head.

"It's not that important."

"It is to me," Dad insisted. He grabbed Kyle's shoulders with both hands. "Come on," he said, his tone harsher this time.

"No," Kyle replied, trying to push Dad's hands from his shoulders. But his father gripped him harder, shaking him.

"Wake up," he nearly shouted, shaking Kyle again, harder this time. Kyle shrank back, grabbing his dad's arms and trying to pry them off, without success. He had a sudden pang of fear.

"Dad, stop it."

"Come on, Kyle," Dad growled, his voice getting louder. He gripped Kyle's shoulders hard, his fingers digging painfully into Kyle's flesh. "Wake up!"

"What are you talking about?" Kyle exclaimed. "Stop it!"

"Wake *up*!" Dad screamed.

Kyle opened his eyes, taking a deep, gasping breath in. He felt powerful hands gripping his shoulders, felt them shake him again. Something cold and hard pressed into his back, sending a burning pain through the middle of his spine.

"Stop it!" he screamed.

A pair of blue eyes stared at him, mere inches from his face. The hands gripping him let go suddenly.

"Took you long enough," the man standing over him grumbled. Kyle blinked, the man's face coming into focus. His heart skipped a beat.

"Darius!" he cried.

* * *

Darius reached out with one hand, grabbing Kyle's arm and hauling him up into a sitting position. Kyle stared at the bodyguard in disbelief, then looked around, realizing that Kalibar and Ariana were standing over him as well. He was sitting on the cold stone floor of a huge room, a few of Kalibar's magical lights illuminating the chamber. It was, Kyle realized, nearly identical to the room he'd been in...that *Ampir* had been in...when he'd used the teleportation device. He looked up, seeing the same arched ceiling the Behemoth had smashed through earlier.

What the...

He turned back to Kalibar and Ariana, staring at them. Then – seized with a sudden panic – he grabbed his arm with his finger and thumb, pinching it hard. He felt immediate pain. He pinched his other arm, with the same result.

I'm not dreaming, he realized.

"Kyle, are you okay?" Ariana asked, kneeling down and putting a hand on his shoulder. He found himself staring into her big brown eyes, and turned away, his cheeks flushing.

"I had the weirdest dream," he admitted. Then he frowned, looking around. "Wait, where are we?"

"Darius had to carry you through the tunnels," Ariana explained. "You were in and out of consciousness at first, and then you wouldn't wake up."

"Oh," Kyle mumbled. He looked around the room again. "This place...it looks almost exactly like the room Ampir was in." He described himself as Ampir, finding the teleportation device, and using it to send his son to safety. And the Behemoth's violent descent toward Ampir…and then the nothingness. He considered telling them about his dream about being back home, but decided against it. Nobody interrupted him while he told his tale, and when he was done, Kalibar looked perturbed. Ariana slipped her hand off of his shoulder, reaching for his hand and squeezing it gently. Her flesh was warm, soft…and very real. He smiled at her, and she smiled back, looking absolutely radiant.

"You say that a rift appeared above Ampir," Kalibar asked, "…and his son went through?"

"Yes," Kyle confirmed.

"And Ampir gave the ring to his son before sending him?" Kalibar pressed.

"Right."

"Unbelievable," Kalibar breathed. "Do you know what this means?" he added excitedly. "It means we were right about Ampir," he exclaimed. "He helped Renval create a teleportation device, and Renval discovered a way to travel to your world!" He began to pace, his chin in one hand. "And Ampir's ring was sent with his son to your planet," he continued. "Which explains how a magical device came to be in a world where magic doesn't exist."

"Right," Kyle breathed. It *did* explain everything.

"And it means teleportation is possible," Kalibar continued, "…and that…" He frowned then, stopping in his tracks.

"What?" Kyle asked.

"Ampir gave his son his ring at the last minute," Kalibar stated, resuming his pacing. "If your dream is correct, he wouldn't have had time to give your ring the power to teleport you anywhere, much less here. Which means…"

"My ring didn't send me here," Kyle finished, his eyes widening.

"Precisely."

"But if my ring didn't, then what did?" he asked.

"Good question," Kalibar replied. "And how have you been reliving Ampir's memories when you're not even wearing the ring?" he asked. "I should have thought of that earlier."

"Maybe it gave me all the memories at once," Kyle hypothesized, "…but I relived them over time."

"Possible," Kalibar admitted. "Still, if your ring didn't bring you to Doma, then something else did…or some*one* else."

"It protected me from the Ulfar and the killerpillar," Kyle stated.

"And the rip-vines."

"True," Kalibar agreed. "Given the circumstances, I think we should make getting your ring from Erasmus a priority. Especially if we run into trouble in the Tower."

"Wait," Ariana interjected, looking confused. "What ring?"

"It's…complicated," Kalibar replied.

"I'll tell you about it later," Kyle promised. He stood up then, stretching his back.

"To think that *this* is the same room that Ampir stood in over two thousand years ago," Kalibar murmured, rubbing his bearded chin thoughtfully. "Coming here must have triggered Ampir's memories, the ones that were already inside of you from the ring," he added. "You were living his memories, if only for a time…experiencing everything as if it were happening to you. Imagine if we could reverse-engineer that technology…we could record history so future generations could *live* it. We could pass down knowledge and experience, teaching a lifetime of lessons in a fraction of the time. This could revolutionize society!"

"Let's not die first," Darius replied dryly. The bodyguard put a hand on Kalibar's shoulder, turning him about gently. "We should go," he added. Kalibar nodded, following alongside Darius, who led them across the giant room, reaching a door at the other end. Beyond this door was another long tunnel. They walked through it for nearly ten minutes before reaching a second door. This opened up into a wide spiral staircase going up as high as the eye could see. Softly glowing magical lanterns were bolted to the walls at regular intervals.

"Pace yourselves," Kalibar advised, going up the steps, his hand on the railing. "This is going to take a while." Darius followed behind Kalibar, and Kyle went next, followed by Ariana. Upward they went, the stairs spiraling endlessly upward. It wasn't long before Kyle's legs began to burn. Sweat trickled down the backs of his legs, his breath coming in short gasps. He found himself lagging behind Darius, and had to force himself to keep up. He glanced back, seeing a sheen of sweat on Ariana's forehead.

"You," Kyle asked, "…okay?" Ariana nodded, but said nothing.

Eventually Kyle saw a door, the staircase continuing upward past it. Darius stopped before it, and Kyle stopped as well, leaning over and bracing his hands on his knees.

"Are we there?" he asked.

"Is this the first door?" Kalibar asked.

"Yeah."

"We're at the 20th floor," Kalibar explained. "The next door up will be the 40th floor, then the 41st and the 42nd."

"Which door do we take?" he asked.

"We want to bypass the Council, and go directly to the top. But we have to get Kyle's ring, too."

"Where is the ring?" Darius asked.

"Probably still in Erasmus's study," Kalibar answered. "Erasmus usually works well into the night, so he's probably still there, or in the Archives." He shook his head. "But we can't afford you being seen by Orik or his supporters. It's unlikely, but…"

"Which room is his study?" Darius interrupted. Kalibar paused, then sighed.

"3110."

"I'll get the ring," Darius stated, putting a hand on Kalibar's shoulder. "Where do I meet you?"

"Room 4209," Kalibar replied. "Grand Weaver Rivin's suite."

"Got it."

Darius opened the door, stepping through. The door closed behind him, and with that, he was gone. Kyle stared at the door, feeling strangely vulnerable without the bodyguard at his side.

"Let's go," Kalibar prompted. He continued up the stairs, his hand still on the railing. Kyle and Ariana followed, continuing upward for what seemed like an eternity. Eventually they reached another door – for the 40th floor. Ariana notified Kalibar, who nodded, passing by the door and continuing upward. They passed a second door shortly thereafter, and kept going. The next set of stairs went up quite a ways…probably to accommodate the high ceilings of Kalibar's room – until the spiral staircase ended at last, a single door facing them at the top.

Kyle rested on the guardrail for a moment, trying to catch his breath. Glancing down over the rail, he saw the staircase spiraling ever downward.

Next time, he vowed, *I'm taking the riser!*

"We're at the top," Ariana notified Kalibar, who reached for the door, touching it lightly with his fingers.

"The doors all have one-way locks on them," he explained. "They're meant to be opened from the other side, to escape the Tower…and to keep anyone from the outside from coming in."

"Can we unlock it?" Kyle asked.

"Hold on a minute," Kalibar replied. He stood there for a long moment, his head bowed. Something *clicked*, and the door swung outward toward them. Kyle pulled Kalibar backward to prevent the old man from being struck by the door, then led him through the doorway, with Ariana following. He found himself in a long hallway, the stone walls on either side adorned with brilliantly colored carvings of grave-looking men and women engaged in various acts of heroism. The floor was made of granite that had been polished to a mirror shine. Doors lined the walls on either side, spaced far apart.

"Where are we going again?" Kyle asked.

"Room 4209," Kalibar replied. "That's the Grand Weaver's room. His name is Rivin." Kalibar paused. "You should address him as "Grand Weaver Rivin," he advised.

Kyle led Kalibar and Ariana down the hallway, glancing at the numbers on the doors as he passed by. He couldn't understand the symbols, of course. How was he going to know which door to open? His confusion must've showed, because Ariana gave him a curious look.

"You can't read?" she whispered. Kyle blushed.

"I can read English," he retorted defensively. Ariana ignored him, grabbing Kalibar's hand, and leading him down the hallway until stopping at one of the doors.

"Here," she half-whispered. "This is it." Kalibar nodded, then reached out one hand, feeling for the door. When he'd found it, he gave the door three hard knocks, then stepped backward. They waited for a long moment, but the door remained closed. Kalibar paused, then knocked again. Seconds later, the surface of the door shimmered, then became translucent. A tall man stared back at them from the other side of the door. He appeared similar to the guards Kyle had seen in the guard shack the first time he'd been to the Secula Magna, resplendent in his black metallic armor and his helmet. The guard's eyes were barely visible behind his translucent visor. He lifted this, his eyes shifting from Kalibar to Kyle, then to Ariana. He did not look happy in the least.

"Who are you?" the guard demanded, his voice cold. "How did you get here?" Kyle froze, taken aback. Then he realized how they must look; an old, dirt-caked man with a bandanna over his eyes accompanied by two children wearing strange armor.

"My…" Kalibar began, but the guard cut him off.

"How did you get past the other guards?" the guard snapped.

"My name is Kalibar," Kalibar proclaimed. "And I *will* see Grand Weaver Rivin." The guard's eyes went from Kalibar's red bandanna to his scruffy, unkempt beard, then dropped to his dusty, hole-riddled clothing.

"Right," he sneered.

"If you don't open the door, I *will*," Kalibar threatened. He reached up, pulling away the cloth covering his empty eye sockets. The guard gasped, his eyes widening. "And then you will answer to *two* Grand Weavers."

The guard sank to one knee on the floor, bowing before Kalibar. Then he rose to his feet, pressing something on the wall. The door became opaque once more, the guard vanishing from sight.

Seconds passed, and nothing happened.

Kyle glanced at Kalibar and Ariana, feeling a growing sense of unease. If the guard didn't believe them, he might alert more guards…and the resulting commotion could alert Orik or his allies on the Council.

The door shimmered, becoming translucent once again. This time, a tall, elderly man in a long black robe stood behind it, facing Kalibar. He had white hair, was clean-shaven, and had dark circles under his eyes. He stared at Kalibar's empty eye sockets for a long time, then his tattered clothes. He glanced down at Kyle and Ariana, then back at Kalibar, peering at the former Grand Weaver's face.

"Evening, Rivin," Kalibar greeted, somehow sensing the man's presence. "Sorry for waking you, but as you can see, I have news that can't wait for the morning."

* * *

Grand Weaver Rivin's face paled, and the door to his suite became opaque once more. A few moments later, it swung inward, and Grand Weaver Rivin stood just beyond, gesturing hurriedly for Kalibar, Kyle, and Ariana to come in. Kyle spotted the guard standing behind Rivin, his gaze downcast. The three walked into the room, the door swinging shut behind them.

"Good god Kalibar, what happened to your eyes?" Rivin exclaimed. "You need a doctor!"

"No doctors," Kalibar retorted. "Not yet."

"But your eyes!" Rivin protested.

"I'm afraid those are many miles away," Kalibar stated grimly. He placed the bandanna back over his empty sockets. "We need to talk...and quickly."

"Yes, of course," Rivin agreed. "Come in, come in." He placed a hand on Kalibar's shoulder, ushering him in. Kyle and Ariana followed close behind. The hallway opened up into a truly enormous room, even larger and more opulent than Kalibar's suite had been. The exterior walls and ceiling were made entirely of huge glass panels, giving a panoramic view of the city far below, and of the stars twinkling in the night sky above. The ceiling, Kyle realized, was actually the glittering glass pyramid he'd seen at the top of the Tower, tapering to a peak dozens of feet above their heads. The floor was polished granite, and numerous plush couches, chairs, and other furniture were arranged tastefully throughout the large living area. Large marble columns rose from the floor, supporting the glass ceiling far above.

"Sit, sit," Rivin urged, guiding Kalibar to one of the high-backed white couches nearby. Kalibar sat, and Kyle and Ariana sat on either side of him. Rivin sat down on a couch opposite them. He stared at Kalibar's clothes; having been splattered with flesh-eating acid, stained with blood, and coated with a thin film of cave gunk, dust, and body odor, they were certainly a sight – and a smell – to behold.

"What happened to you, old friend?" Rivin asked. Kalibar sighed.

"That," he replied, "...is a long story."

"I'm listening."

Kalibar told Rivin the entire tale, starting with the first attempt on his life back at his estate in Bellingham. He spoke of meeting Kyle, who he introduced as his grand-nephew, and their harrowing journey to the Tower. Rivin's eyes widened when Kalibar revealed Orik's treachery.

"That *bastard*," Rivin swore, standing up and beginning to pace. "I can't believe it!" He strode the length of the room, then came back. "I *can* believe it," he corrected. "The..."

"Rivin, please," Kalibar interrupted. "It gets much, much worse."

Rivin nodded, sitting back down on the couch.

Kalibar told Rivin of their travels to Crescent Lake, and of Kyle's rapid progress learning magic. Then he relived the Death Weaver attack, and their first meeting with the Dead Man.

"You have no idea how powerful this man was," Kalibar stated, shaking his head. "He had runic technology that put ours to shame. He defeated me in combat, and took us prisoner."

"I'm sorry," Rivin stated. "If I had only known, I would..."

"You would have sent your best men to their deaths," Kalibar interjected grimly. "It is only through the remarkable resourcefulness of my bodyguard, and no small amount of luck, that we managed to kill the Dead Man, and escape in one piece."

"I will meet your bodyguard and give him every reward," Rivin stated resolutely.

"He should be here shortly," Kalibar replied.

"Good. I'm going to fetch Bartholos," Rivin added. "He needs to hear this." He leaned over, putting a hand on a glass orb laying on a side-table. The orb glowed faintly when touched.

"Thank you Rivin," Kalibar stated. "I can't tell you what a relief it is to be here."

"I can only imagine," Rivin replied. He turned to Kyle then. "So you're Kalibar's grand-nephew?"

"Yes sir," Kyle replied. "Grand Weaver," he added sheepishly. Rivin smiled.

"A pleasure to meet such a remarkable young Weaver," he stated.

"He's a remarkable young man indeed," Kalibar agreed. "Even without his magical talents."

"And what was your name again?" Rivin asked, turning to Ariana.

"Ariana," she answered.

"Good to meet you," Rivin stated. Ariana bowed deeply, and for the first time, Kyle saw her blush. Kyle couldn't blame her; he could only imagine that meeting Rivin must, to her, feel like meeting the President of the United States.

Rivin's front door opened, and soon after Rivin's guard escorted a tall, portly man in a white robe into the room. The man stopped dead in his tracks when he saw Kalibar, his jaw dropping.

"Good god, Kalibar!" he exclaimed in a deep, booming voice. He rushed up to where Kalibar sat, leaning over him. Kalibar broke into a grin.

"I'd recognize that voice anywhere," he replied. "Good to hear you, Bartholos." Bartholos grinned back at Kalibar, putting a meaty hand on Kalibar's dusty shoulder.

"Don't you use formalities with me, old friend!" Bartholos bellowed. Then his grin faded. "Why are you wearing that filthy rag over your eyes?

"Because he has no eyes," Rivin replied darkly. Bartholos stared at Rivin blankly.

"What?"

"I'm afraid he's correct," Kalibar sighed. He pulled off his bandana, revealing his sunken eye sockets. Bartholos jerked backward, drawing in a sharp breath.

"My god!" he exclaimed. "Who did this to you?" he demanded. "I'll have them hanged!"

"That would prove difficult," Kalibar replied with a wry smirk. He told Bartholos the same story he'd told Rivin. Bartholos remained silent throughout, but was clearly becoming more agitated with every revelation. When Kalibar finished, Bartholos sat down next to Rivin on the couch, shaking his head.

"Orik, a traitor?" he exclaimed in disbelief. "That is a very serious allegation, Kalibar...as I'm sure you're aware. He's as good as elected as the next Grand Weaver of the Secula Magna. The Council has...and this stays between us...they've already reached a majority vote."

"I guessed as much," Kalibar admitted. "This makes it all the more critical that we stop him now, before he wins the office."

"What proof do you have?" Bartholos pressed. "It's not that I don't believe you," he added hastily. "It's just that we can't prosecute him without sufficient evidence." Kalibar sighed heavily.

"Nothing but hearsay, I'm afraid."

"We must have evidence to convict him," the Grand Runic reasoned. "Remember what happened the last time you accused him?"

Kalibar stood there, his jaw clenched, saying nothing. Bartholos put a hand on Kalibar's shoulder.

"I'm sorry," he apologized. "What do you suggest we do?"

"We must have a formal investigation, of course," Kalibar replied. "We need time to gather evidence. We'll have to postpone the elections until Orik's innocence or guilt is proven; if he is confirmed as an agent of the Death Weavers, he'll be executed."

"You do understand that Orik will claim this to be a politically motivated move," Bartholos replied. "He'll accuse you of starting a smear campaign against him...and you know how persuasive he can be. If you end up not being able to find any hard evidence of his guilt, he'll ruin you...and end up winning anyway."

"I know," Kalibar replied with a sigh. "And that's why I didn't want to confront him at first." He shook his head then. "But now I'm willing to sacrifice my reputation to nail him, if that's what it takes."

"You've suffered enough," Rivin countered.

"There's a small army of Death Weavers near Crescent Lake," Bartholos reasoned. "Rivin, if you sent a contingent of Battle-Weavers there, you could round them up. If Orik grew up with them, they'll be able to confirm Kalibar's story."

"They're cultists," Kalibar retorted. "They're unlikely to betray their own."

"Well we have to do *something*," Bartholos complained. "We can't have a damned cult take over the Empire!"

"Agreed," Rivin stated. "The sanctity of the Secula Magna takes precedence over the political machine. It is our duty to protect the Empire from all enemies, foreign or domestic...or in Orik's case, both."

"What are you suggesting?" Kalibar asked.

"A traitor has subverted the democracy," Rivin stated. "If we go by the usual legal channels, Orik will almost certainly triumph."

"Are you suggesting we act outside of the law?" Bartholos asked. Rivin shrugged.

"What else can we do?" he replied. "I suggest we use our considerable influence to arrest Orik and...build evidence against him."

"Ah," Bartholos murmured. "I see."

"Whatever you do, you'll have to do it discreetly," Kalibar warned. "Spectacle will only hurt the Secula Magna. If the public finds out a traitor nearly achieved the highest office in the land, the government will lose credibility."

"One of us should call Orik to our office tomorrow," Grand Weaver Rivin stated. "For some unrelated purpose, of course. Perhaps under the pretense of congratulating him on his inevitable victory..."

"Yes," Bartholos replied. "And we can both confront him there, with a few trusted guards present, of course." He leaned back in the couch, patting his impressive belly with one hand. "After he is neutralized, we'll have his properties searched...and ensure that incriminating evidence is found. We should also send scouts to this 'Crescent Lake' to gather intelligence for a strike against these Death Weavers," he added. "We'll collect witnesses, and...*convince* them to testify against Orik."

"I can't say that I'm comfortable with subverting the law," Kalibar admitted. "But it may be our only way to stop Orik." He smiled then. "Thank you both," he added. "I can't tell you how relieved I am. A few days ago, I was alone in a cell, my eyes torn out, with no hope of ever escaping. I never would have dreamed that I'd be home today, surrounded by my good friends."

Grand Weaver Rivin smiled, putting a hand on Kalibar's shoulder.

"Kalibar, I've spent my life and career hoping to be like you one day," he confessed. "We both have," he added. Bartholos nodded in agreement. "We trust you completely...and we'll do everything we can to counter any threat to our Empire."

"But first," Bartholos interjected, "...so you don't pose any further threat to our noses, take a bath!"

Everyone burst out into laughter, and even Kyle found himself joining in. He felt as if a massive weight had been lifted off of his shoulders. Despite impossible odds, they'd made it back home, and alerted the authorities. Orik would be defeated, and Kalibar would finally be safe!

"Rivin, do you have any clean clothes for our esteemed colleague?" Bartholos asked. "I doubt he'll fit into mine," he added, patting his generous belly.

"Of course," Rivin replied. With that, the Grand Weaver led Kalibar through the door on the marble wall to their right. Kalibar disappeared beyond this, and the door closed. Soon Kyle heard the muffled sound of running water. Kyle couldn't help but be jealous of Kalibar; he'd been wearing the same clothes for days now, and they were getting awfully funky. A nice, warm bath would be heavenly about now. He glanced at Ariana, who was also staring at the door to the bathroom. By the longing expression on her face, she must have felt the same way.

Rivin came back to the couch, sitting next to Bartholos. He sighed, rubbing his eyes wearily.

"Now, what was your name again, son?" Bartholos asked, turning his eyes on Kyle.

"Kyle, sir," he replied. "Uh, I mean, Grand Runic Bartholos." His cheeks turned their customary red color, but Bartholos only chuckled.

"And you're...Ariana?" he pressed, turning to Ariana. She nodded.

"Yes Grand Runic Bartholos."

Bartholos leaned forward, peering at Kyle. Then his eyes widened.

"My goodness, boy!" he exclaimed. "You're a literal fountain of magic, aren't you? I didn't notice with Kalibar sitting next to you." He regarded Kyle hopefully. "Kalibar hasn't convinced you to waste your considerable talents as a Weaver, has he?"

"Uh..." Kyle started to answer, then stopped. How exactly to proceed? But Bartholos just laughed.

"He has, hasn't he? Ah, well..."

Kyle's obvious discomfort earned a good-natured laugh from Bartholos, whose ample belly shook with each guffaw. Kyle smiled in spite of himself; the Grand Runic's laughter was infectious, and pretty soon Kyle was chuckling too. Then a marble bust sitting on a pedestal behind Rivin flew forward, slamming into the back of the Grand Weaver's head, throwing the man bodily onto the floor. His arms and legs spasmed twice, and then he lay still.

A pool of blood appeared around his head, expanding rapidly.

"Rivin!" Bartholos cried, leaping up from the couch. He ran to Rivin's side, scanning the room with his eyes. A gravity shield appeared around him. "Guards! *Help!*" he bellowed.

Terror gripped Kyle, and he shot up from the couch, backing away from Rivin's motionless body. Ariana did the same. The one guard Kyle had seen earlier ran up to them, halting in his tracks when he spotted Grand Weaver Rivin lying on the floor. He stared at the body mutely, his eyes wide with shock.

"Activate the alarm!" Bartholos ordered. The guard just stood there, staring at Rivin. Bartholos swore under his breath, closing his eyes for a moment. A high-pitched, wailing alarm sounded throughout the room, forcing Kyle to cover his ears with his hands. Bartholos's gaze shifted to Rivin, and a shimmering globe sprang to life around the two men. Bartholos knelt before Rivin, picking the man's head up off of the floor. Blood streamed from a large dent in the back of his skull. Bloody gray-yellow goop oozed from the wound, dribbling over Bartholos's hand. Bartholos jerked his hand away, his face turning deathly pale.

The door to the bathroom burst open, and out rushed Kalibar, a black robe tied about his waist. His hair was still wet from the shower, water dripping onto the granite floor.

"What's happening?" he demanded.

"We're under attack!" Bartholos cried. "Rivin is dead. Protect yourself!"

Kalibar froze, a few layers of gravity shields appearing around him.

"Kyle, Ariana," he shouted, "...activate your armor!"

Kyle complied, streaming magic to the crystal on his breastplate. Ariana did the same, vanishing as her armor activated. Bartholos stood up, turning to the guard, who was still standing a dozen feet from them. He pointed right at the man.

"You, open the door for the rest of the guards!" The Grand Runic yelled. "Be careful, the assassin must be around here somewhere!" The guard stood there, unmoving, a blank expression on his face. "I said *go!*" Bartholos barked.

Still, the guard didn't move.

"I am your Grand Runic!" Bartholos shouted. The guard's eyes rose to meet Bartholos's.

"True," the guard replied. The corner of his lips curled into a smirk. "But not for long." He lifted one hand, and Rivin's body rose up from the floor, levitating in the air. Without warning, Bartholos's shield vanished, and Rivin's body flew into the portly Grand Runic, knocking him backward. Bartholos fell to the floor, Rivin's body splayed on top of him.

"Kalibar!" Kyle cried. "It's the guard...he's hurting Bartholos!" He ran toward Kalibar, vaulting over one of the white couches and skidding to a halt beside the former Grand Weaver. Kalibar stepped forward, drawing himself to his full height. Even with his empty eye sockets and his bathrobe, he looked imposing.

"Stop," he ordered, "...or die."

"Ah, the great Kalibar," the guard sneered, striding toward Bartholos. The fallen Grand Runic grunted, pushing Rivin's body off of himself. A gravity shield appeared around him, but a few runes on the guard's armor flashed, and Bartholos's shield quickly vanished. The guard reached into the recesses of his armor, withdrawing a small dagger. He walked right up to Bartholos, shoving the Grand Runic's chest down with his boot.

"No!" Kyle heard Ariana cry. He heard footsteps running toward the guard. The guard's head jerked toward the sound, and suddenly Ariana appeared out of thin air a few feet from the guard. The guard smirked at her, the air between them rippling. She flew backward into one of the couches, knocking it over, and landed on the floor with a loud *thump.*

"Ariana!" Kyle cried, rushing toward her. He skidded to a halt by her side, kneeling before her. The guard stood over Bartholos, grinding the heel on his boot into the man's chest. Another gravity shield appeared around the Grand Runic, but again, it vanished.

"Traitor!" Bartholos gasped, clutching at the assassin's boot. The guard said nothing, reaching down and drawing the wicked blade of the dagger across Bartholos's neck. His flesh gaped open, blood spurting from the wound.

"No!" Kyle cried.

The guard stood then, moving away from Bartholos, circling around Kalibar. Bartholos clutched at his own neck with both hands, his eyes wide, blood spurting from between his fingers. He rose to his knees, blood pouring from his mouth. He coughed, then gagged, vomiting bright red liquid onto the granite floor.

"Tell me," the guard stated casually, continuing to circle around Kalibar. "How are you going to kill me if you can't even *see* me?" He lobbed the dagger toward Kalibar, and it landed on the granite floor, sliding to a halt a foot in front of the former Grand Weaver. Kalibar tensed, his jawline rippling.

Suddenly the front door burst open, and a dozen guards in black swarmed in. The assassin stopped circling, and pointed right at Kalibar.

"He assassinated the Grand Weaver and Grand Runic!" he declared, gesturing at the dagger lying at Kalibar's feet.

The crowd of guards glanced at Kalibar, then at the bodies of the Grand Runic and Grand Weaver. Kyle stayed where he was behind one of the couches, shaking Ariana's limp shoulder frantically. She moaned, her eyes fluttering open, then closing again. Kyle felt a wave of relief...she was still alive! He glanced up, spotting a tall, well-built man with short black hair and a black goatee stride into the room, his black cloak rippling behind him. Kyle felt his guts twist in fear.

Orik!

The guards parted to let Orik through, and Orik stopped before the guard, staring at the bodies of the Grand Weaver and Grand Runic, then at Kalibar.

"Assassin!" he cried, pointing at Kalibar. "Guards, kill him!" Immediately, the guards ran toward Kalibar, magical shields flashing into existence around each of them. Kalibar drew himself up to his full height, facing the guards defiantly.

"You would kill Kalibar?" he bellowed, his voice resonating throughout the massive room. The guards slowed, then stopped, staring at the blind man before them. Recognition dawned...and the guards, to a man, took a step backward. Kalibar raised his right hand, pulling the red bandana off of his head and throwing it to the ground.

"You would accuse a cripple of being an assassin?" he cried.

A gasp went through the room, as everyone stared at Kalibar's sunken, empty eye sockets. Orik, however, stepped forward, unswayed.

"No doubt Bartholos and Rivin would have taken more than your eyes if you'd given them the chance," he retorted. "Here you stand," he added, pointing at the bloody dagger at Kalibar's feet, "...with the murder weapon at your feet, and you claim innocence?" He glared at the guards around him. "I said *kill* the man, damn it!"

"Stop!" came a loud shout. An elderly man in a white cloak ran into the room, followed by a few more men and women, each dressed in either a white or black cloak. The elderly man stormed past Orik, taking in the scene. When he turned his gaze to Kalibar, the old man's eyes widened.

"Dear god, Kalibar," he gasped. "What happened to you?"

"He murdered Rivin and Bartholos," Orik retorted. But the old man ignored Orik.

"Explain yourself Kalibar, and quickly," he ordered. Orik stepped back, his jawline rippling. But he held his tongue.

"Good evening, Councilman Jax," Kalibar greeted. "Orik claims that Rivin and Bartholos took my eyes when I tried to kill them," he added. "Anyone with half a brain would realize my wounds were days old."

"Granted," the old man – Jax – agreed.

"Rivin's guard assassinated Rivin and Bartholos," Kalibar

accused. "And would have tried to kill me if you hadn't intervened."

"That's a lie," the assassin retorted. Jax turned to him, arching one eyebrow.

"Is it now?" he asked. Kyle stood up, facing the guard.

"Kalibar's telling the truth," he declared, pointing at the assassin. "*He* killed Rivin and Bartholos!"

Everyone turned to face him, and Kyle swallowed in a suddenly dry throat, uneasy with the sudden attention. But he stood where he was, staring at the assassin defiantly.

"The boy is Kalibar's relative," Orik countered. "His testimony is useless."

"You seem eager to prosecute our former Grand Weaver," Jax declared, turning a cold glare on Orik. "And eager to have him killed without so much as a trial." His eyes narrowed. "One wonders why."

"I'll tell you why," a voice shouted from behind. A bald, heavyset man with a long white beard strode up the hallway into Rivin's suite, pointing a finger at Orik. Kyle's heart soared.

Erasmus!

"This bastard," Erasmus spat, "...tried to assassinate Kalibar to win the election...*twice*. He failed...and now he's trying to finish the job."

"That's a lie!" Orik shot back.

"Bullshit," Erasmus retorted. "Kalibar told me about your little scheme over a week ago."

"This is absurd," Orik stated, turning to Jax. "He..."

"Shut up," Jax interrupted.

"But..."

"I said *shut up*," Jax repeated, "...or I'll have you arrested." He stared Orik down. "You're not Grand Weaver yet, Councilman. And until you are, *I'm* in charge."

Orik said nothing, his fists clenched at his sides.

"My god Kalibar," Erasmus gasped in horror, hurrying to Kalibar's side. "What happened to your eyes?" Kalibar reached out, putting a hand on Erasmus's shoulder.

"We were attacked at Crescent Lake," Kalibar replied. "By members of a cult. They called themselves 'Death Weavers,' and their leader called himself 'the Dead Man.' The Dead Man defeated me, and tore out my eyes with his bare hands."

"My god," Erasmus gasped.

"We only barely managed to escape," Kalibar continued. "But during my imprisonment, the Dead Man made it quite clear that his greatest pupil – and the man who just seconds ago ordered my execution without trial – is Orik himself."

A gasp rose from the crowd, and all eyes turned to Orik.

"This is madness," Orik complained. "They're claiming I'm a member of a damned cult!" He turned back to Jax. "I ordered the death of the only man in the room present when our great leaders were murdered in cold blood!" He turned back to Kalibar and Erasmus. "Unless they want to pin that on me, too."

Kyle heard Ariana groan, saw her eyes flutter open again. She sat up slowly, rubbing the side of her head. She glanced at Kyle, then turned to the men and women filling the room…and froze.

"I was *not* the only man present," Kalibar retorted. "Rivin's guard is the assassin. Orik must have known that we'd escaped from his master's prison, and that we were returning here to tell Rivin and Bartholos. I suspect *he* is behind their assassination, as he was behind mine."

"This is absurd," Orik spat. He turned back to the other members of the Council. "There isn't a single shred of evidence to support his claims. Do you honestly believe I did all of this?"

"I do," a gruff voice replied from behind the Council members. A man walked through the door then, clad in pitted, light-gold armor, his piercing blue eyes locked onto Orik's.

"Darius!" Kyle cried.

"You must be the dead man," Darius murmured, stopping before Orik. Orik stood his ground, glaring contemptuously at the bodyguard.

"Are you suggesting that I'm the leader of these 'Death Weavers' Kalibar invented?" he asked. Darius smirked.

"Nope, killed him," the bodyguard replied.

Ariana stood up then, facing the guard who'd assassinated Rivin and Bartholos.

"He's the murderer," she declared, pointing at the assassin while clutching her bloodied left temple. "I saw it all." Everyone turned to her, including Jax.

"And you are?" he asked.

"Ariana," she answered. "I was a prisoner of the Death Weavers for over a year, until they saved me," she added, gesturing at Kyle, Kalibar, and Darius.

"I see," Jax murmured. He turned to face the assassin. "Guards, arrest this man," he ordered.

The guards rushed toward the assassin, gravity shields appearing around each of them. The assassin spun toward the nearest guard, the runes on his armor flashing. The guard's shield vanished, and the assassin slammed his gauntleted fist into the guard's chest. The guard flew backward, slamming into the gravity shield of the guard behind him and bouncing off. A flash of light burst outward from the assassin, searing Kyle's eyes. He cried out, turning away and throwing his hands up in front of his face. The light vanished as quickly as it had come, and Kyle opened his eyes.

The assassin was gone.

"Get him!" Jax ordered, a gravity shield appearing around him. "There!"

Kyle turned, spotting the assassin standing over Rivin's body, a long green crystal clutched in his hand. The assassin held the sharp point of the tapered crystal above the dead man's forehead, then plunged it downward. The tip of the crystal pierced the skin of Rivin's forehead, then sank deeper into the flesh. The assassin stood, backing away from the corpse. Jax's guards swarmed around the assassin, surrounding him. This time, he didn't resist, allowing them to restrain him and shove him chest-first into the floor.

Kyle stared at Rivin's forehead. To his horror, the crystal continued to slide deeper into Rivin's skull, sinking slowly until only the glimmering facets of the crystal's diamond-shaped base were visible. He felt a hand grab his wrist, and turned to see Ariana standing next to him, her eyes locked on Rivin's forehead. She was as pale as a ghost.

"So it's true," Jax stated, his tone grim as he stared down at the assassin. "You *are* the murderer."

The assassin said nothing, the smirk still on his lips.

"Kalibar was right," Jax declared. The elder Councilman turned to face Orik. He glared at the man, then faced the other men and women in the room. "Ladies and gentlemen of the Council, I hereby enact the emergency powers vested in me by our deceased leaders, and assume temporary leadership of the Empire. Are there any objections?"

The room was silent.

Jax turned to face Orik. "As my first act, I hereby sentence you to solitary confinement while we investigate the accusations leveled against you."

"But…" Orik began.

"And as you are accused of treason, I will use my emergency powers to veto any majority vote for your candidacy," Jax continued.

Orik stood there silently, staring at Jax, his fists clenching and unclenching. Then he gave a tight smile.

"Oh, I think not."

"Excuse me?" Jax replied, his eyebrows rising. "Guards…"

"In fact," Orik interrupted, his voice growing louder, "…as *my* first act as Grand Weaver, I think I'll have you hanged. If my Master lets you live that long, that is." His smile broadened. "I think you should turn around now."

Jax hesitated, then turned around…and drew in a sharp breath. For there, standing in the middle of the room, was Grand Weaver Rivin.

"My god!" Jax exclaimed, taking a step backward.

Rivin stared at Jax, then at the guards and Councilmen around him. He raised his hand to the back of his head, then jerked it away, staring at the blood on his palm. His face was dreadfully pale, the green diamond-shaped gem in his forehead glittering in the light.

"What's…" Rivin began, then stopped, turning back to Jax. "What are you doing here?" He looked back down at his bloody hand. "What happened to me?"

Everyone stared at Rivin, their mouths agape.

"Grand Weaver Rivin…" Jax stated. He took another step backward.

"What's happening?" Kalibar demanded.

"Rivin's…alive," Jax breathed.

"No," Kyle countered. All eyes turned to him. "He's not alive," Kyle insisted. "He's been turned into a Chosen, like the Dead Man."

"What?"

"The boy's right," the assassin declared, breaking into a smug smile. "And now you're all gonna die."

"Shut up," Jax growled, glaring at the assassin.

Without warning, the gem embedded into Rivin's forehead flashed bright green, shining like a miniature green sun.

Kyle's heart leapt into his throat, and he felt Ariana's fingers digging into his arm. He stumbled backward, his heel striking an end table, and nearly fell over it.

Rivin's posture *shifted*, his back straightening, his confused expression relaxing. He glanced down at himself, then turned his gaze to Jax and the other Councilmen.

"Good evening," he greeted, nodding slightly. His voice was deeper than it had been moments before, booming throughout the huge suite. Goosebumps rose on Kyle's arms.

"Rivin?" Jax asked. Rivin paused for a few seconds, then shook his head.

"Rivin is dead," he replied. "You now stand before Xanos incarnate." He straightened his shirt, smoothing out the wrinkles, then glanced up at Jax and the other members of the Council.

"Kneeling would be appropriate," he murmured.

An invisible force *slammed* into Kyle from above, forcing him down onto his knees on the granite below. Every last person in the room fell to their knees as well, their heads craning down in a bowing position. Kyle struggled against the power holding him down, but it was pointless. He couldn't move.

"Release us!" Kyle heard Jax bellow.

"As you wish," Xanos replied.

Kyle felt the force pinning him down vanish, and he grunted, pulling himself to his feet. He grabbed Ariana's hand, helping her up.

"I regret having to use such a disturbing vessel to meet you all," Xanos stated. "My true form is...indisposed."

"Who the hell do you think you are?" Erasmus demanded, rising unsteadily to his feet. Xanos paused, then turned to the former Grand Runic.

"I understand your animosity," Xanos replied evenly. "I had hoped to accomplish all of this far more...delicately." He turned to Kalibar then. "A shame that everything I've created has been threatened by the actions of one man."

"Agreed," Orik stated, crossing his arms over his chest and glaring at Kalibar. Xanos paused, then turned to Orik, his expression stony.

"I was referring," he murmured, "...to you."

Orik's eyes widened, and his mouth dropped open. He took a step backward, shaking his head.

"But Master..."

"Your ambition is admirable," Xanos interrupted. "Had you

succeeded, it would have been forgivable." He turned back to Kalibar. "You, Kalibar," he continued, "...are a difficult man to kill."

Kalibar said nothing.

"My Chosen who attacked your carriage on your way to Stridon...defeated," Xanos stated. "My Chosen you call the Dead Man...defeated." He stared at Kalibar unblinkingly, his pale lips tightening. "The two Chosen I sent after you to intercept you before you reached Stridon...defeated."

"What are you talking about?" Kalibar retorted. Xanos stared at him for a moment longer, then frowned.

"You don't know," he murmured. "Interesting."

"Master..." Orik pleaded, but Xanos ignored him.

"Someone," Xanos interrupted, "...has been killing my Chosen." He swept his gaze across the room, at the guards, the Council, and Jax. He stared at Darius, then at Ariana and Kyle. "I'd like to know who."

Jax scowled at Xanos, crossing his arms in front of his chest.

"Give me one reason why I shouldn't have you killed right now," the elder Councilman demanded. "You dare threaten us?" he added. "We're..."

"I do," Xanos interjected firmly, turning toward Jax.

Jax stood up tall, facing Xanos defiantly.

"You are facing the finest Weavers and Runics in the Empire!" he proclaimed.

"Unfortunately so," Xanos agreed. "A tragedy, really. Two thousand years ago, any one of the 'Ancient' Councilmen could have beaten you. All of you. At once." He smiled sadly. "I am the last of My kind," he lamented. "And I alone can bring the Empire back to its former glory...and beyond."

"What are you talking about?" Jax demanded. "Who *are* you?"

"I am the past," Xanos answered. "And I am the future." He smiled. "I am your shepherd," he continued, gesturing at the Councilmen before him. "And you are My wayward flock."

"You're speaking in riddles," Jax protested.

"Yes, well," Xanos replied. "Please understand this is all just a formality," he added, spreading his arms wide. "There's no point in my answering your questions."

"What do you mean?" Jax demanded.

"Well, you see, you're all about to die."

The huge glass windows behind Xanos burst inward, thousands of razor-sharp shards flying past the self-proclaimed god toward the Council. The pyramidal ceiling collapsed, hunks of glass raining downward toward them.

"Shields!" Jax screamed.

Gravity shields came to life around the guards and the Councilmen, glass shards bouncing off of them and flying in all directions. Ariana ducked low to the ground, pulling Kyle down with her, and scrambled on her hands and knees until she was behind the couch she'd knocked over earlier. Kyle followed, pieces of glass whizzing by inches above his head.

"Stay down!"

Kyle felt something slam into his back, pressing him and Ariana belly-first onto the floor. He cried out, struggling to get out from under the massive weight.

"I said *stay down*," a gruff voice shouted. Kyle turned his head to the side, and saw a pair of blue eyes glaring back at him.

"Darius!" he gasped. Darius was impossibly heavy, his armored body crushing Kyle's chest against the floor. Glass shards flew in a whirling hurricane above them, the razor-sharp projectiles slamming into the couch next to them, cutting large holes in the fabric. Shards slammed into Darius's back, bouncing off of his armor with loud clanging sounds.

"Stay here," Darius ordered. He got up from Kyle and Ariana's backs, grabbing the wooden frame of the upended couch. A large hunk of glass slammed into the bodyguard's shoulder, but the bodyguard didn't so much as flinch. He got in between Kyle and Ariana, pulling the couch forward and down, rotating it over Kyle and Ariana's heads until it laid upside-down above them, forming a triangular roof over their heads. Glass shards slammed into the couch with a terrible clatter, but none penetrated the makeshift barrier. Kyle spotted Jax ahead in the distance, shielding himself from the deadly whirlwind of glass, his jaw set in a firm grimace. His face was beet red, the veins popping out on his forehead. One guard's shield failed, and he was thrown violently backward, glass pelting his body mercilessly. Then another guard's shield vanished, and he too was cut down.

Kyle saw a white-robed Runic lurch forward, the amulet around his neck snapping at the chain and flying toward Xanos. The amulet shattered, scattering across the floor in front of the self-proclaimed god. Soon amulets, bracers, and rings were all flying from each Councilman, shattering before Xanos's gaze. Then, one by one, the shields around each Councilman failed. One by one they fell before the onslaught of razor-sharp glass, collapsing to the ground, glass whizzing over their fallen bodies.

Holy...

Something bumped Kyle from behind, and he yelped, twisting around. He saw Darius behind him, with Ariana close behind at the other end of the couch; the bodyguard said nothing, reaching one hand inside the recesses of his armor and pulling out a small object. He took Kyle's right hand in his own, placing the object in Kyle's palm. It was a small silver ring with a yellow gemstone on top, tiny crystals on the sides.

My ring!

"Put it on," the bodyguard commanded, shouting over the deafening clatter of glass raining against the couch. A large piece suddenly pierced *through* the wooden base on Kyle's left, lodging itself in the wood, its razor edge stopping an inch from his head. He flinched backward, lowering his belly to the ground.

"Put it on!" Darius urged.

Kyle hastily slid the ring over his left thumb, where he'd worn it so long ago. It felt strangely warm, and he felt a vibration coming from it. He heard someone shouting from beyond the couch, and immediately recognized the voice.

Kalibar!

Kyle crawled forward to the edge of the overturned couch, peering out at the room beyond. Half of the guards had fallen, the remaining men forming a barrier between Xanos and the Council. Jax stood directly behind them, and Kalibar was at his side, multiple layers of shields surrounding them both. As Kyle watched, two of the guards' shields vanished, glass pelting their armor mercilessly. They cried out, falling to their bellies on the ground and covering their heads with their gauntleted hands.

Xanos stood before them, a dozen layered gravity shields protecting him from the hurricane of broken glass, his dead eyes turning to Kalibar and Jax. The outermost gravity shields protecting the two men winked out. Kalibar grimaced, turning to Jax and saying something into the elder Councilman's ear. Jax nodded, and Kalibar lowered his head slightly, his jawline rippling.

Suddenly, the spinning vortex of glass pulled inward, each shard hurtling toward Xanos!

Xanos's gravity shields began to vanish, one-by-one, glass shards slamming into the remaining shields from all directions. Xanos regarded the two men, his lips curling into a slight smirk.

The whirlwind of glass surrounding him *exploded*.

Shards flew outward, slamming into Kalibar and Jax's shields. A large piece of glass struck the wooden armrest of the couch just to Kyle's left, embedding itself deep within it. Darius grabbed the waistline of Kyle's pants, yanking him backward to relative safety.

"Your armor," Darius yelled in Kyle's ear. "Use it!"

Kyle nodded, closing his eyes and *pulling* magic into his mind's eye, then streaming it to the crystal on his breastplate. He felt the immediate *hum* of it activating.

He heard a blood-curdling scream, and opened his eyes, seeing the last of the shields surrounding Jax and Kalibar vanish. A hunk of glass slammed into Jax's chest, throwing the old man backward and onto the floor, blood rapidly spreading across the front of his white cloak. Another piece struck Kalibar in the left shoulder, blood spraying from the wound. Kalibar cried out in pain, jerking backward and losing his balance. He fell to the floor next to Jax.

"Kalibar!" Kyle shouted, terror seizing him.

Multi-layered gravity shields appeared around the former Grand Weaver, the storm of glass bouncing harmlessly off. Kalibar grunted, rising unsteadily to his feet, his left shoulder wet with blood.

"Someone has been protecting you," Xanos's voice boomed, rising above the clatter of whirling glass. His dead eyes scanned the room, then settled on Kalibar. "Someone *here*."

Kalibar grit his teeth, holding his wounded shoulder.

"Stop this!" he shouted.

Xanos stared at Kalibar, then gestured with one hand.

"Tell me who killed five of my Chosen," he replied, "…and I will spare your life." Kalibar shook his head.

"I don't know what you're talking about!"

The whirlwind of glass pulled backward then, forming a spinning vortex around Xanos. Kyle heard Darius grunt, and turned to see Ariana squeezing past the bodyguard. She crawled up to Kyle.

"I'll help Kalibar," she stated, talking directly into his ear so that he could hear her over the clattering of glass. "You stay here."

"If you go out there, he'll kill you!" Kyle protested. Ariana gave him a weak smile, leaning in close and kissing him softly on the lips. Then she slid past him, turning around to stare at him with her big brown eyes.

"Thank you," she murmured, laying one hand gently on his cheek.

Then she vanished into thin air.

"Ariana, no!" Kyle cried, bolting forward. Darius grabbed him, yanking him backward. Kyle struggled against the bodyguard's grip. "No!"

Kalibar's shields winked out, one by one, until none remained.

"So be it," Xanos muttered.

The vortex of broken glass flew forward from Xanos, slamming into the former Grand Weaver, throwing him backward violently. He fell to the floor, razor-sharp shards flying into him and past him. Kyle watched in mute horror.

Kalibar!

The beam of glass ended, pieces bouncing off of the wall behind Kalibar and scattering to the floor. Kyle turned away from the gruesome sight.

"Interesting," he heard Xanos say.

Kyle hesitated, then turned forward, his gaze drawn to Kalibar's body. He stared at the former Grand Weaver, hardly believing his eyes. There was hardly a scratch on him...he was alive!

How...?

Xanos stared down at Kalibar, then smirked. A loud *crack* echoed through the suite...and then Ariana appeared, lying on top on Kalibar. She must have shielded him with her body, protected by her Ancient armor!

She got up from him, helping him to his feet, then turned around to face Xanos, unsheathing her dagger and holding it before her. Xanos stared at her for a moment.

Then the crystal in the center of her armor shattered.

"How interesting," Xanos murmured. He strode toward her, and Ariana backed up, her boots crunching on pieces of glass underfoot. Xanos closed the distance between them with frightening speed, reaching out with one pale hand and slapping her dagger away. It fell to the floor with a loud clatter, and Xanos grabbed Ariana by the throat, lifting her upward until her feet were dangling inches above the granite floor.

Ariana stared down at Xanos, her eyes wide, the veins in her forehead bulging.

"I seem to remember burning you alive," Xanos stated. He turned toward the shattered windows at the edge of Rivin's suite. "Strange that you still live."

Ariana opened her mouth, making garbled choking sounds. Kyle's heart leapt in his throat.

"Stop!" he cried, scrambling forward, emerging from the protection of the overturned couch. He rose to his feet, sprinting toward them. Xanos turned to face Kyle, his dead eyes regarding him for a moment. Then he turned back to Ariana.

"So delicate," Xanos murmured. "Like a little bird." He walked toward the shattered windows, stopping some twenty feet before the edge of the suite, the cool breeze from the open air beyond whipping through his black cloak. "I wonder if you can fly?"

Ariana burst backward, careening through the air toward the precipice!

Kyle pumped his legs frantically, changing direction to intercept her. Ariana slammed into the floor, sliding rapidly toward the edge. She screamed, clutching desperately at the slick granite, but it was useless. Kyle leaped forward onto his belly, reaching out with his hand, and grabbed her by the ankle as she slid by. Then they *both* slid, carried by Ariana's momentum…right over the edge.

No!

Kyle reached back with his free left hand, desperately grabbing for something, *anything*. His fingers closed around a metallic groove at the very edge, and he jerked to a halt, hanging over the edge. He cried out, his other hand slipping further down Ariana's ankle. He tightened his grip, looking down.

Ariana stared up at him, her eyes wide with terror, dangling upside-down in mid-air, hundreds of feet above the huge lawn of the Secula Magna.

"Kyle!" she screamed.

"Hang on!" Kyle shouted back. He grimaced, trying to pull himself up with his left arm. It was useless; Ariana was too heavy. He grit his teeth, feeling his fingers slipping from the ledge above, his forearms starting to burn. Ariana looked down, then back up at Kyle, her lovely face pale in the starlight.

"Let go," she ordered.

"What?"

"Kyle, let go, or we'll both die."

"Are you crazy?" Kyle exclaimed. "No!"

Ariana reached up, grabbing Kyle's hand, and started to pry his fingers from her ankle.

"What are you *doing?*" Kyle shouted, his voice rising in panic. She gripped his fingers and thumb, forcing them apart.

"Ariana!" Kyle cried.

Her hand slipped away from his, and she fell, plummeting through the night air.

Chapter 23

"*Ariana!*" Kyle screamed, watching in horror as Ariana fell away from him. He heard her scream, saw her flailing as she plummeted downward. He turned away from the awful sight, tears streaming down his cheeks.

No Ariana, no...

He heard a *thump*, and Ariana's screams stopped abruptly. Then there was silence.

Kyle grit his teeth, a tortured sob bursting from his throat, hot tears blurring his vision.

I'm sorry Ariana, I'm so sorry.

He felt his fingers starting to slip from the groove above, his forearm feeling as if it were on fire. He grunted, swinging his free hand up, grabbing onto the groove. He gathered himself, then pulled upward...but his elbows barely bent with the effort. His sweat-slicked hands slipped further from the metal groove.

No!

Kyle struggled, placing his boots on the wall of the Tower and bending his knees. Then he pushed upward with his legs, pulling with his arms at the same time. This time he managed to pull himself upward a little. But then his arms gave out, and he nearly fell, his hands slipping until only his fingertips were left clinging to the shallow groove.

He held himself there, his heart pounding in his chest.

And then his fingers slipped free from the ledge, and he fell.

Kyle's gut lurched as he entered into free fall, cold air rushing upward around him, tearing at his clothes. He tipped backward through the air, spinning until he was upside-down, the cobblestone road surrounding the base of the Tower accelerating toward him at a horrifying rate.

He heard someone screaming, and realized that it was *him*.

The windows marking each level of the Tower zipped by faster and faster, the wind screaming by his ears now. He continued to somersault, flailing his arms and legs helplessly. Then a bright light flashed in the periphery of his vision.

Kyle jerked his head toward the light, realizing it was coming from his left hand…from his thumb.

His *ring*.

He stared at the ring, at the yellow crystal glowing bright white, and then looked down again, seeing the ground, not even a hundred feet below, rushing up to meet him. He closed his eyes, throwing his arms in front of his face, and screamed one last time.

Suddenly something slammed into Kyle's back. He opened his eyes, seeing a pair of black, metallic arms wrapping around his torso, intricately carved symbols glowing a faint blue on the armor's surface. A powerful vibration filled his consciousness, pulsing through every particle of his being.

He felt the arms around him pull upward, felt his descent begin to slow. Still, he was falling far too fast…the ground was rushing toward him with lethal speed. Strangely, he felt no fear. The font of power surrounding him only allowed one sensation.

Awe.

And then the cobblestone road rose up to meet him.

Kyle's feet struck the ground – or rather, the ground caved in underneath him before his feet even touched the road. Kyle fell even as the ground dropped below him, forming an ever-deepening crater in the earth. A plume of dust shot upward and outward all around him, surrounding him in a dense, choking fog.

His descent slowed, then stopped, his feet touching down gently on the shattered ground below.

What the…

The black metal gauntlets released Kyle, and he felt his legs wobble underneath him. He fell onto his hands and knees on the cold dirt of the crater, his breath coming in short gasps, dust choking his lungs and stinging his eyes.

The wellspring of power vanished.

Kyle rose shakily to his feet. His legs gave out again, and he fell onto his butt, pain shooting up his back. He sat there for a moment, his entire body feeling numb. Dust swirled in the air around him, tickling his nose. He sneezed, then looked up, realizing that he was in a crater over ten feet deep, not a dozen feet from the base of the Great Tower.

He felt something heavy on his shoulder, and turned his head see a black gauntleted hand there, tiny blue runes etched into its surface, each pulsing with blue light. He tried to stand a third time, and this time his legs obeyed him. He tried to turn around, to face whoever was behind him, but the hand on his shoulder stopped him.

"Who are you?" Kyle asked.

He sensed a *presence* in his mind then, a powerful voice that echoed through his brain.

I've shown you who I am.

The hand on Kyle's shoulder lifted, freeing him from its powerful grasp.

Now you've shown me who you are.

Kyle hesitated, then turned around.

A tall man stood before him, his body covered in black, metallic armor. Countless tiny runes glowed blue across the surface of the armor, fading in and out slowly in random patterns. The man wore a silver reflective visor that hid his eyes, so that only his nose and mouth were visible. A tuft of short brown hair rippled in the cool night breeze above his visor.

Kyle stared mutely at the man before him, a being plucked out of time, out of his very dreams.

"*You!*" he gasped.

The man said nothing.

"But you're dead!" Kyle protested.

Come.

Suddenly Kyle lifted up off of the ground, pulled by an invisible force. He felt himself rising upward from the crater, the black-armored man rising with him. They exited the crater, landing a few feet from the edge. Kyle stared at the man before him, still unable to believe his eyes. Then he caught a glimpse of something in the periphery of his vision.

A body lying on the road.

Kyle's heart leaped into his throat, and he ran toward it, skidding to a halt before it. It *was* a body...a girl with long dark hair curled up in the fetal position on the ground.

"Ariana!" Kyle cried, reaching for her shoulder. He stared at her, seeing her chest rise and fall gently. "She's *alive!*" He fell to his hands and knees before her. "Thank you," he blurted, grabbing Ariana's soft, warm hand. Tears of joy streamed down his face.

He felt the hand on his shoulder again, and turned, facing his savior.

"Why?" he asked. He meant to ask much more – he had so many questions – but that one word was all he could muster.

The armored man did not reply, but he knelt down until his head was level with Kyle's, his visor shimmering in the starlight. Kyle stared into that perfect, curved mirror, seeing his own face reflected back at him.

Then he heard a scream from far above, in the Tower.

"Kalibar!" he cried, looking up at the massive Tower standing beside him. "And Darius...they're still up there. We have to save them!"

The armored man remained silent, the runes on his armor pulsing blue in random patterns. Kyle felt himself rise up from the ground then, pulled upward by an unseen force. Faster and faster he rose, his guts plummeting to his feet, the ground – and his savior – falling away beneath him. Within seconds, he was nearly at the top of the Tower; his ascent slowed, then stopped, and he flew forward and downward in a gentle arc toward the glass-strewn granite floor of Rivin's suite. His feet touched down, shards of glass crunching under his boots.

He stood there, seeing the motionless bodies of the Council and their guards sprawled across the floor, blood spattering the granite around them. And in the center of the suite stood Xanos. The dark Weaver had one hand around Kalibar's throat, and lifted the former Grand Weaver up until his feet were kicking a few inches above the floor. Kalibar's face turned purple, the veins on his forehead bulging.

"Stop!" Kyle yelled, taking a step forward.

Xanos turned to look at Kyle. His eyes narrowed, and he let go of Kalibar. The former Grand Weaver fell onto his hands and knees, gasping for air.

"Well well," Xanos murmured. "Isn't this unexpected." He stepped away from Kalibar, cocking his head to the side. He stared at Kyle with those dead eyes, the gemstone in his forehead glowing a bright, eerie green. "You're supposed to be dead."

Kyle stared back at Xanos, swallowing in a suddenly dry throat.

He glanced at Kalibar, who was struggling to rise to his feet.

"Who saved you?" Xanos inquired, taking one step toward Kyle, then another. Kyle glanced backward, seeing the edge of the suite not ten feet from where he stood.

Suddenly an overturned couch to Kyle's left rolled over, and Darius came out from underneath it. The golden warrior stepped in front of Xanos, blocking the dread Weaver's path.

"Darius!" Kyle cried.

The bodyguard ignored Kyle, facing Xanos defiantly. He drew his sword from its scabbard, pointing the tip directly at Xanos's chest.

"Step aside, insect," Xanos ordered, stepping forward until Darius's sword collided with his multi-layered gravity shields. The blade jerked backward.

"I'm gonna shove this through your heart," Darius shot back, standing his ground defiantly.

Xanos stared at the bodyguard for a moment, then rolled his eyes.

Darius's sword jerked up out of his hands, flying upward over his head, then arcing backward. The tip of the weapon slammed into his back, piercing through his armor, burying itself to the hilt.

Darius stumbled forward, twisting around. The tip of his sword jutted through his chest. Blood poured down his armor, his eyes wide, his mouth agape.

"No!" Kyle screamed, rushing forward. He grabbed Darius's upper arm, staring in horror at the bloodied blade impaling him. Darius fell to his knees, his armor striking the granite with a dull *clang*. He clutched at the hilt at his back with one hand, blood pouring from the corner of his mouth. Then he collapsed onto the ground, laying on his right side, his breath coming in short gasps. Xanos gazed down at the bodyguard, a smirk curling the corner of his mouth.

"Me first," he murmured. He turned to Kyle, stepping forward and grabbing Kyle's breastplate, lifting him up into the air. Then he let go...but Kyle remained levitating a foot above the ground, facing his undead tormentor.

"You killed him!" Kyle shouted, rage building within him. "You bastard!"

"I asked you a question," Xanos stated calmly. "How did you survive that fall?"

"Go to hell," Kyle spat.

"Answer me," Xanos ordered, reaching up with one hand and squeezing Kyle's cheeks together painfully. The man's dead eyes searched Kyle's face. "Tell me how, Kyle."

Kyle said nothing.

Xanos smirked, his grip on Kyle's face tightening. Kyle's cheeks mashed up against his teeth. He felt a sharp pain, then the metallic taste of blood in his mouth.

"Leave him alone!" a voice cried from behind.

Xanos let go of Kyle's face, turning around. Kalibar limped toward them, surrounded by a shimmering gravity shield. A bolt of energy shot outward from Kalibar toward Xanos, striking the self-proclaimed god's shields harmlessly.

Xanos smirked.

Kalibar's shields vanished immediately, and the former Grand Weaver fell to his knees, shoved downward by an unseen force. He cried out in pain as his knees slammed onto the hard granite.

"No!" Kyle yelled. "Don't hurt him, please!" He looked down at Kalibar, his anger vanishing instantly, terror seizing him. "Please, don't hurt him!"

"Tell me how you survived," Xanos commanded, gesturing toward the broken windows, "...and I'll let him live."

"I..." Kyle paused, feeling his mouth go dry.

Kalibar fell to his hands and knees, his palms shredded by shards of glass lying on the ground. Blood oozed between the old man's fingers.

"Stop it!" Kyle screamed.

"Tell Me and I will," Xanos replied. His gaze flicked to Darius, and the sword impaling him drew backward out of his body with a loud screeching sound, whipping around until the point of the blade was touching Kalibar's back. The bodyguard moaned once, then lay silently on the floor, gasping for air.

"No, don't!"

"Answer me," Xanos ordered.

Kyle glanced down at his left hand, at the ring on his thumb.

"It was my ring," he lied, staring back at Xanos. "It protects me."

"Kyle, no!" Kalibar cried.

Xanos paused, then grabbed Kyle's left wrist, peering at the ring.

"My, my..." he murmured. The sword hovering over Kalibar

dropped out of the air, falling to the ground beside the old man with a loud clatter. Xanos glanced up at Kyle. "This is a marvelous antique," he stated. "Where did you get it?"

Kyle stared at Xanos mutely.

"I said, where did you get this?" Xanos repeated. Darius's sword rose up from the floor, hovering with its point at Kalibar's back once again. Terror gripped Kyle.

"You promised!" he protested. Xanos frowned.

"I suppose I did," he admitted ruefully. Then Darius's sword flew through the air, sailing over Kyle's head. A moment later, something cold and sharp pressed against the back of Kyle's neck, and he yelped in surprise. Xanos raised one eyebrow.

"Better?"

Kyle swallowed hard, then winced as the cold blade pressed harder against his skin. He felt a sharp pain, and then something hot and wet trickled down the nape of his neck.

"It's a marvelous piece," Xanos murmured, staring down at the ring again. Then he sighed. "But it's just a glorified transmitter...extraordinary range, but nothing more." He let go of Kyle's wrist, staring into Kyle's eyes again. "You lied to me."

Kyle felt the blade behind him move forward a fraction of an inch, sending a deep, agonizing pain through him. More hot fluid poured down his neck. He moaned, the tip of the sword pressing forward another fraction of an inch. He felt it hit something hard, and knew it had struck bone. The pain became excruciating.

"The Dead Man was quite impressed with your potential," Xanos stated, eyeing Kyle coldly. "He imagined great things for you."

Kyle grit his teeth against the pain, his breath coming in short gasps. He felt the tip of the sword press hard against his spine, and groaned.

"The Empire needs Me," Xanos continued. "With My guidance, it will surpass the Ancients, and bring a new era for Mankind." He smiled then. "You can be a part of it, Kyle."

Kyle heard a crunch, agony lancing through his spine as the blade sank into his vertebra. He screamed, feeling suddenly woozy. Black spots floated in his vision.

"I am willing to forgive your disloyalty, Kyle," Xanos stated. "You have a great deal to offer." He extended one hand. "Swear your loyalty to Me, and I will let you live."

Sweat poured down Kyle's forehead, stinging his eyes. He moaned, trembling in mid-air.

"Swear your loyalty to Me," Xanos continued, his hand still outstretched, "...and I will even let Kalibar live."

Kyle glanced at Kalibar, who had risen to his feet on the glass-strewn floor. Blood stained the old man's palms.

"You said you'd..." Kyle began, swallowing back a wave of nausea as another burst of pain shot through his spine. "You said you wouldn't kill him!"

"I did," Xanos agreed. "If you hadn't lied to me, I would have honored that promise." He stared at Kyle, his cold eyes unblinking. "Join Me, Kyle."

Kyle glanced at Kalibar again, seeing the old man's head raise up. Kalibar shook his head.

"Don't do it," he urged. Then he slid backward on the ground, struck by an invisible force.

"Your friends are misguided," Xanos stated. "We both want the same thing, Kyle. Together, we can bring the Empire to heights the Ancients could only have dreamed of!"

Kyle felt the sword sink a fraction of an inch deeper, and he howled in pain, reaching up for the back of his neck with both hands and trying in vain to grab onto the blade. He felt a thin metal chain around his neck, and froze.

The amulet!

He slid his hands down the chain to his upper chest, where Darius's amulet still lay, under his armor. There was barely any magic in it, he knew. But what if...

"Swear your loyalty to Me," Xanos commanded.

Kyle glanced at Kalibar again. Then he turned his gaze back to Xanos, gritting his teeth. He felt a sudden calm come over him.

"No."

Xanos frowned, lowering his hand.

"This is your last chance," he warned.

"I won't do it," Kyle declared. He gave a grim smile. "And you can't make me."

Xanos stared at Kyle for a long moment, then sighed, shaking his head.

"Very well," he replied.

Kyle *shoved* as much magic as he could toward the amulet, just as the sword at his neck jerked forward. He screamed, agony coursing through his spine.

The green gem in Xanos's forehead went dark.

Kyle felt a tugging at his neck, felt the blade pull away from his flesh, falling to the ground with a clatter. The invisible force holding him in midair vanished, and he dropped onto the floor, stumbling backward and landing on his butt. Xanos's eyes widened, his gravity shields disappearing.

"What…" he began.

"Kalibar, kill him *now!*" Kyle cried.

Xanos jerked forward suddenly, his mouth hanging open in a silent "O." A white-hot blade jutted out of the center of his chest, smoke billowing from where it contacted his flesh. A golden arm wrapped around Xanos's neck from behind, pulling backward as the blade was shoved a few inches further through his heart.

"Surprise," Darius growled from behind.

The bodyguard yanked the blade out of Xanos's chest, then held the glowing blade – Kyle's magical sword – out to the side, swinging it full-force against Xanos's neck. The blade sliced through the dark god's skin, passing through his flesh and out the other side. Smoke rose from the black fissure created by its passage.

Xanos slumped to his knees, shards of glass crunching underneath. Then his body fell forward, slamming onto the floor with a dull thud, his head separating from his neck and rolling across the floor.

Darius stood over the fallen body, one hand over the wound on his chest, his blue eyes coldly surveying his work. Then he looked up at Kyle.

"About time you remembered that damn amulet," he grumbled.

Then he lurched to the side, falling onto his shoulder on the hard granite floor. He rolled onto his back, staring up at the ceiling, blood seeping from between his fingers over his chest.

"Darius!" Kyle cried, sprinting forward and leaping over Xanos's headless corpse, then sliding to Darius's side. "Darius, are you okay?" The bodyguard stared at Kyle as if he had three heads.

"Seriously?"

He coughed then, and turned his head, spitting blood onto the floor. His chest rose and fell in rapid, shallow breaths, his face terribly pale.

"Kalibar!" Kyle yelled, turning to the former Grand Weaver. Kalibar was climbing slowly to his feet.

"What's happening?" Kalibar asked.

"Xanos is dead," Kyle answered. "But Darius...he's been hurt really bad!"

"Wait, Xanos is dead? How?"

"The amulet I gave Kyle," Darius answered, exploding into another fit of coughing. "It...dropped his shields long enough for...me to kill him."

"Well done," Kalibar exclaimed, not without a bit of awe in his voice. "Darius, I think I'll retain your services indefinitely, if that's alright with you."

"Good luck," Darius gasped, "...with that."

"Xanos stabbed him through the chest," Kyle stated, his voice rising in panic. "He's dying!"

"Someone, get a doctor!" Kalibar shouted. But of course, no one answered; the room was filled with the corpses of the Councilman and their guards. And all of the communication orbs had been destroyed, along with most of the furniture.

"We have to get help!" Kyle exclaimed.

"Don't bother, kid," Darius mumbled. The warrior gripped Kyle's arm with one hand, squeezing tightly. His blue eyes stared into Kyle's. "It's too late."

"No," Kyle protested. "No, Darius, don't." He shook his head, tears dripping down his cheeks. "You can't die!"

Darius said nothing, his eyes unfocusing, his breathing slowing. His eyes rolled into the back of his head, his hand falling from Kyle's arm and striking the ground.

"No, no, no," Kyle whimpered. He glanced at his ring, the crystal glittering dully. He closed his eyes.

Save him, he pleaded silently. *Please, Ampir, save him!*

Kyle heard Darius groan, and opened his eyes. The bodyguard took a single, deep breath in, then let it out, a rattling sound coming from his throat.

And then he laid perfectly still, his blue eyes staring lifelessly up at the ceiling.

Chapter 24

Kyle stared down at Darius, his heart leaping in his throat. He waited for the bodyguard to move, to breathe. To do *something*. But Darius just laid there on the glass-strewn floor, his eyes unseeing.

"Darius?" Kyle said.

There was no response.

"Darius!" Kyle cried. He reached down, grabbing Darius's armored shoulders and shaking them frantically. Darius's head rolled limply, his chest no longer rising and falling. His eyes stared lifelessly upward.

"Darius, no!"

Kyle straddled Darius, clasping his hands together over Darius's breastplate and locking his arms. He pressed hard into the bodyguard's chest, pumping fast and hard like his parents had taught him.

"Come on, Darius!" he yelled, pumping harder. His efforts were in vain; the golden breastplate covering Darius's chest didn't budge under his palms. He scrambled to find the latches holding Darius's armor together, but couldn't find any. "Damn it!" he swore, slamming his fists onto Darius's chest. "Damn it!"

"Kyle..." he heard Kalibar say from behind. He felt the older man's hand on his shoulder. Kyle shrugged Kalibar's hand off, pounding one fist, then the other, into Darius's chest.

"No!" Kyle shouted, beating on the bodyguard's breastplate. Tears blurred his vision. "You can't die!"

He saw Kalibar reach out to Darius, saw the former Grand Weaver's fingers slide up to Darius's throat, checking for a pulse. Kalibar shook his head.

"Kyle, he's gone."

Kyle turned to Kalibar, then back to Darius, his shoulders

heaving. He stared down at the puddle of blood on Darius's breastplate, and at his own hands, slick with blood, and got lightheaded. He fell forward, collapsing on top of his friend, feeling Darius's still-warm cheek on his own.

"Kyle, I'm sorry," he heard Kalibar murmur.

"He saved us," Kyle said. He felt a crushing guilt come over him. "I called him a traitor," he added miserably. "I didn't believe in him."

"Kyle…" Kalibar began.

"He died trying to save me," Kyle interrupted bitterly, closing his eyes and clinging to Darius. He felt a hand grab his shoulder, and pushed it away.

"Stop," he mumbled, clutching Darius tighter. The hand grabbed his shoulder again, firmly this time, and pulled him up off of Darius.

"Leave me alone!" Kyle cried out angrily.

"You hit like a girl," a voice grumbled back.

Kyle opened his eyes.

There, laying on the floor below him, blue eyes staring right back at him, was Darius…his face pink, his lips twisted into a smirk.

"Darius?" Kyle breathed, jerking upright. Darius broke into a big grin, and Kyle whooped with delight, reaching down and giving the bodyguard a big bear hug. Then he pushed himself away, staring at Darius incredulously.

"Wait, you're…?" He paused then, looking Darius over. The man's breathing was no longer shallow and rapid, the wound on his chest having stopped bleeding. "Darius, you're okay!"

"Seems that way," Darius replied. The golden warrior propped himself on one elbow, then reached up with his other hand. "Help me up," he ordered. Kyle grabbed the man's hand with two of his own. He heaved upward, and after a few moments, Darius got to his knees. Then, with the sheer force of his will, the warrior rose slowly to his feet.

"What's going on?" Kalibar asked. "What's happening?"

"It appears I'm alive," Darius answered, staring down at his blood-spattered body.

"But you were dead!" Kyle exclaimed in disbelief.

"Guess I was too dead to notice," he muttered. "What happened?"

"*I* don't know," he answered. He frowned then, glancing at his ring. To his surprise, it was glowing. The light faded even as he watched. Goosebumps rose on his arms.

Ampir!

Kyle glanced up at Darius, who was staring down at Kyle's ring. The bodyguard shook his head.

"Glad I got you that ring," he muttered.

Kyle closed his eyes, sending a silent prayer.

Thank you.

"Kyle's ring?" Kalibar asked, his eyebrows furrowing.

"I think it saved me," Darius said.

"My god," Kalibar breathed.

Suddenly Kyle heard footsteps, and turned to see an elderly man in bloodied white robes walking toward them.

"What's going on here?" the man asked. It was Jax...he was alive!

Kyle looked beyond Jax, seeing movement there, among the corpses on the floor. They weren't corpses at all, he realized...the bodies were moving, pushing themselves up off of the floor. Every Councilman, every guard. They all stared down at themselves in disbelief, brushing glass off of their clothes. Then they looked around the room, shell-shocked.

"Xanos is dead," Kalibar proclaimed.

"What?" Jax replied. He walked up to Kyle and Kalibar, staring down at Xanos's headless body. Gasps of amazement echoed throughout the suite.

"Kalibar!" Jax exclaimed, grabbing Kalibar's shoulders and grinning broadly. "How in blazes did you manage to kill that ungodly bastard?"

"I didn't," Kalibar admitted. "Darius did, with Kyle's help. And Kyle's ring saved all of you," he added.

"Kyle's ring?" Jax asked. "What ring?"

"It's a long story," Kalibar replied with a sigh. "But Kyle used a runic Darius had given him to take away Xanos's shields, so Darius here could finish the job."

Jax turned to Darius, who shrugged.

"All I did was stab him through the heart and cut off his head," the bodyguard stated humbly.

"Then we all owe you...the Empire owes you...a debt of gratitude it can never repay!" Jax exclaimed, walking up to Darius and shaking his hand vigorously. Darius raised an eyebrow.

"It's not even going to try?" he quipped. Jax smirked.

"Oh, don't you worry about that," he replied with a chuckle. Kalibar chuckled as well for a moment, then froze, looking suddenly panicked.

"Wait, where's Ariana?" the former Grand Weaver asked.

"She's okay," Kyle answered, fabricating a story about how his ring had somehow saved them both from certain death. Two of the guards in the room were immediately sent to retrieve Ariana. After the guards had left, all of the Councilmen migrated toward the body of the fallen Xanos, forming a ring around the headless corpse. Erasmus knelt over the decapitated head, prying the green crystal from Rivin's skull. A large crack ran down the center of it, and it looked dull, no longer translucent. The former Grand Runic stood up, inspecting the elongated gem. He looked up after a moment, shaking his head.

"Its runes are completely destroyed," he stated, offering the crystal to Jax. Jax took it, and stood over it for a moment. Then he nodded.

"Indeed," he said with a sigh. "There must have been a clause within its patterns, to self-destruct in case of its owner's death, to prevent reverse-engineering." He handed the crystal back to Erasmus, then frowned, scanning the room. "Wait…where's the assassin?" he asked. Everyone looked about, but the man who had murdered Rivin and Bartholos was nowhere to be seen. They did find Orik however, still lying unconscious on the floor.

"Take him," Jax ordered. "I want him sent to Stridon Penitentiary, to solitary," he added. The guards nodded, carrying Orik out of the suite.

Kyle sighed, walking over to one of the large marble columns rising from the floor, and leaned against it. He felt a heavy, metallic hand on his shoulder, and turned around. Darius stood beside him, nodding tersely at his young friend.

"You did good, kid," the taciturn bodyguard said. "I'm proud of you."

Chapter 25

The aftermath was extraordinarily efficient.

Jax called a few dozen guards to Rivin's former chambers, and they removed the damaged furniture, placing magical shields across the wide expanse of shattered windows to protect the room from the elements. Rivin's corpse was removed, to be studied by Erasmus and other high-level Runics at a later time. Kalibar, Ariana, and Kyle – as well as the entire Council and members of the elite guard – were taken by elevator to the medical ward, where they were treated for their wounds. This mostly involved getting them rinsed out with magically produced – and therefore perfectly sterile – water, then putting balm-tree sap in them. Despite everyone's insistence, Darius flatly refused to undergo any medical workup or treatment, saying that he was just fine, dammit.

Given the option to go to sleep or sit in on an emergency meeting the Council was having, Kyle and Ariana both decided that they were far too revved up to go right to bed. That was how, within a few hours, Kyle found himself on the 40th floor, in a large conference room with a big round table in the middle.

Every member of the Council was present – except of course for Orik, who was busy being unpleasantly interrogated. They all sat in a circle, facing each other. Kalibar got to sit in Rivin's chair. Kyle sat in a chair in the corner of the room, and Ariana sat next to him, looking lovely as usual. He'd told her everything that had happened, save for the details of her rescue after falling from the Tower. He let his ring take all of the credit for Ampir's heroics. Ariana, to *her* credit, took it all amazingly in stride.

The Council spent an inordinately long time discussing the attack, going through each moment in agonizing, sleep-inducing detail. They pondered the origin of Xanos, submitting pieces of the crystal that had been lodged in his skull as evidence. Unfortunately, Erasmus's initial analysis of the crystal had been correct; it was beyond repair, the secrets it held utterly destroyed.

"I believe Xanos is still very much alive," Kalibar was saying. "The Dead Man had a similar crystal lodged into his brain." He shook his head, his expression grim. "If Xanos can make more Dead Men so easily…" He stopped then, letting the sentence hang in the air. Everyone's expression was as grim as the former Grand Weaver's.

"I still can't believe that Rivin was actually brought back from the dead," a balding man in black added. "Not even the Ancients had such power! How can we fight a man who can resurrect the dead?" There were nods all around. Jax frowned, rapping the knuckles of one hand against the table.

"Agreed," he muttered. "And if there are more of these Dead Men, or if Xanos can simply make more through the power of these crystals, then we are in no less danger than before. What if Xanos decides to send a dozen Dead Men next time?" He regarded his fellow Councilmen, who sat back in their chairs, troubled looks on their faces. Kyle felt the giddy sensation he'd had for the last hour seep away. The thought of Xanos striking again, with an army of Chosen no less, was sobering indeed.

"What truly frightens me," a white-robed man to Kyle's left said, "…is that Orik nearly became Grand Weaver, and one of Xanos's men was able to infiltrate the elite guard unnoticed." There were nods all around at this; Grand Weaver Rivin himself had been unaware of his personal guard's deceit.

"We must investigate every man, woman, and child within our gates," a black-robed man with slicked-back black hair and a formidable beard said. "If Orik and this guard managed to infiltrate the upper ranks of the Secula Magna, there could be others." Most of the Councilmen nodded at this. Kalibar was not among them.

"I agree with scanning all citizens for these green crystals," he replied, "…but it will be all but impossible to root out the Death Weavers among us, if there are any besides Orik. We cannot rely on such investigations alone to ensure our security."

"Nevertheless, it is a start," Jax stated. "We'll clear a group of our most trusted men ourselves," he decided. "Then they will search everyone in the Tower. We'll expand outward from there."

"Agreed," Erasmus replied. He turned to Kalibar. "Any other ideas, Kalibar?"

"We must prepare for an inevitable assault on Stridon," Kalibar answered. "We'll have to recall the bulk of our military," he added. "We can hold most of our borders with a skeleton crew, and use the bulk of our army to defend our major cities."

"Won't that embolden our neighbors?" a younger Councilman asked politely. He clearly knew of Kalibar's extensive military background; the question had been asked reverently, for the purposes of enlightenment. Kalibar shook his head.

"Our Battle-Weavers can quite believably create the illusion of larger numbers. I employed such tactics with great success in the past when forced to retreat from enemy lines."

"What about this Death Weaver base near Crescent Lake?" Jax asked.

"We should send our Battle-Weavers there," Kalibar replied, drumming his fingertips on the table. "That was Grand Runic Bartholos's plan before he was murdered, and I agree with it. Our Battle-Weavers could fly there and make it by late morning, and strike while they remain leaderless. If Xanos sends another Dead Man before we attack, we'll suffer extraordinary losses."

"Agreed," Jax replied. Erasmus nodded as well. Kalibar frowned suddenly, then pushed his chair back from the table.

"I apologize," the former Grand Weaver said. "I am not a member of the Council. I should not be interfering." Jax looked at Kalibar with a puzzled expression on his face.

"Kalibar, you are our most decorated war hero, and a most honorable former Grand Weaver. I do think you've earned your place at this table."

"I don't mean to dominate the discussion," Kalibar continued apologetically. "You are of course the senior Councilman," he added, nodding deferentially at in Jax's general direction. The chief Runic snorted.

"Well you'd better damned well get used to it," Jax replied with a scowl. Kalibar frowned, his eyebrows knitting together.

"What do you mean?"

"I mean," Jax replied, "...you'd better get used to bossing us around again, because that's exactly what we'll be expecting you to do from now on."

Jax stood up from his chair then, facing the Council.

"I hereby submit to the Council," he declared, "...my nomination of Kalibar for Grand Weaver!"

Kalibar's mouth fell open.

Another Councilman stood. "I second that nomination," he exclaimed. Soon, every member of the Council – without exception – had risen to their feet, endorsing Kalibar.

"Please," Kalibar said, rising slowly to his feet. "I must respectfully decline your nominations." Jax frowned at Kalibar.

"And why is that?" the elder Runic inquired.

"I'm not fit for duty," Kalibar answered, pointing to the red bandanna covering his empty eye sockets. Jax snorted.

"Like hell you're not," he replied. "We need your brain, not your eyes. Besides, soon you'll have more eyes than you'll know what to do with," he added with a smile. Kalibar sat back down in his seat slowly, folding his arms in front of him on the tabletop. He lowered his head for a moment, then gave a wry smile, shaking his head.

"You know," he stated, "...a week ago, I would have told you all right where you could shove your nominations." There were chuckles across the room, and Kyle saw Erasmus winking at Jax. Kalibar's expression turned suddenly serious, and the chuckling died away.

"But now," Kalibar continued, "...after watching these terrorists torture my family and murder my friends, I can't imagine going back to my home in Bellingham. When I die, I want to do it knowing I did everything I could to protect the people that I love." He paused for a moment, then turned back to the Council, giving them a slight bow. "I accept your nominations."

"Excellent," Jax replied. Then he turned to Erasmus. "You're not going to put up a fight too, are you?" he asked. Erasmus chuckled.

"Not a chance," he replied. "If Kalibar is in, I'm in."

"Then it's decided," Jax declared. "The Council is unanimous. We vote for Kalibar and Erasmus for Grand Weaver and Grand Runic. The public will vote in one week!"

* * *

The Council adjourned, with most of the Councilmen leaving to carry out the various tasks assigned to them. Kalibar insisted on staying to discuss the details of the Tower's defenses, but Jax and

Erasmus would have nothing to do with it; they demanded that he have a good meal, and then go to sleep. When Kalibar resisted, Jax told him quite crossly that he wasn't Grand Weaver yet, and he was hereby ordered by the Council to get some shut-eye, damn it.

And so, Kyle found himself taking the elevator up a floor with Kalibar and Ariana, making their way to Kalibar's suite. Of course, Jax and Erasmus weren't about to risk the life of their future Grand Weaver; they sent an elite group of guards to escort them all. Kyle got to hold Kalibar's arm and guide the blind man to his room. When they walked through the front door, none other than Darius was sitting on one of the couches, gorging himself with a steaming hot plate of roasted meat. The minute Kyle smelled the delicious aroma of real, honest-to-goodness food, his stomach growled so loudly that everyone else – including the elite guards – could hear it.

The guards stood watch outside the room, closing the door. Kalibar ordered dinner for everyone, which of course was roast duck – the same meal they'd eaten that first night at the Tower. They all piled on the couch around Darius, waiting impatiently for their meals to arrive. Ariana even swiped a piece of meat from Darius's tray with her quick fingers, earning a murderous glare from the bodyguard. Luckily he'd already ordered his second plate, so he took the theft in stride.

At long last – really only a couple of minutes, but it seemed like an eternity to Kyle – none other than Jenkins arrived at the door, carrying a huge silver platter. Four big plates filled to the brim with roasted duck and other delicacies lay on the platter. It was fair to say that Jenkins had never before received a more delighted and boisterous greeting than when he placed that tray upon the table in front of them! Jenkins also brought four glasses of wine – and an additional bottle, no less – and distributed these to each of his charges. When Jenkins left, his cheeks were still glowing from the enormous praise Kalibar had bestowed upon him.

Everyone dug in furiously, dismembering their respective ducks with gleeful violence. All efforts at decorum were abandoned. Kalibar was the first to be done, which was particularly impressive given his inability to see what he was doing. When everyone else had finished, they all slouched back in their seats with their bellies protruding, sighing contently. Jenkins returned soon afterward, his eyes widening in horror at the colossal mess they'd made. He hurriedly disappeared, returning with two arms full of towels. After a considerable amount of cleaning up, and additional accolades tossed his way, Jenkins left them with some dessert and more wine. No one touched the former, having been stuffed to the gills already, but the same could not be said for the wine. Kalibar grabbed Darius's glass by accident – which was just as well, as Darius just took Kalibar's instead – and proposed a toast.

"To my three friends," he declared, raising his glass up. Everyone else grabbed their glasses and raised them as well. "Never before in my life have I shared such an adventure with more brave and worthy people. I love you all..." he paused, then smiled. "...even you, Darius," he added, and Darius had to chuckle. "...with all of my heart, and if we never part, I'll consider myself the luckiest man alive!"

They all clinked glasses, and drank their wine. Kyle managed a single throat-searing sip before feeling queasy, putting his glass down and pushing it away. Luckily Darius, in a fit of generosity, finished it for him. When Jenkins arrived a final time, he found the desserts untouched, and the bottle of wine completely emptied. These he took away, and bid the four goodnight.

At last, their bellies near to bursting and their heads swimming pleasantly with wine, the four friends got ready for bed. Luckily Kalibar's suite had plenty of guest rooms, and they each got a luxurious bed to sleep in. Having already taken a shower in the medical ward, Kyle flopped unceremoniously onto his bed, not even bothering to get undressed. He buried himself deep within his blankets, curling into a warm ball in the center of the bed. And within a minute of his head sinking into his pillow, he fell fast asleep.

Chapter 26

Almost a week had passed since the deaths of Grand Weaver Rivin and Grand Runic Bartholos, and representatives from all over the Empire had traveled to Stridon to take part in the funeral for the late Grand Weaver and Grand Runic. Their closed caskets were paraded through the main street in Stridon on a carriage for all to see, with tall, stately horses pulling the carriage along. The carriage was escorted by a ring of elite guards, and was followed by massive, ornate floats that magically levitated above the ground. The floats displayed actors playing out historically important parts of Rivin's and Bartholos's lives. One showed Rivin battling tribal warriors, setting them all on fire. At first Kyle thought they were real flames, but it was clearly a magical illusion; the "burning" actors survived unscathed, repeating the mock battle over and over again. It was the most elaborate parade Kyle had ever seen.

The parade ended with Rivin and Bartholos being brought to the Memorial Mall, a huge expanse of lawn just outside the Great Tower, with large, ornate gravestones marking each deceased Grand Weaver and Runic. The eleven remaining members of the Council, Kalibar, Erasmus, and the entire staff of the Secula Magna was present. Even high-ranking members of the military brass arrived, along with scores of soldiers standing solemnly in silent rows, facing the two ornate caskets. Kalibar himself presided over the funeral, giving a heartfelt eulogy for Rivin, then Bartholos. Bartholos's wife and two small boys were there, weeping quietly as his casket was lowered into the ground.

It was all terribly sad.

Even though Kyle had only met the two men for a few minutes, he found himself choking up after each eulogy. He pictured

Bartholos's big belly jiggling when he laughed, and his kindness to a strange boy waking him in the middle of the night. He remembered Rivin's clear love for Kalibar, and his shockingly quick death. He hated Xanos now even more than he had before; the self-proclaimed god had attacked everyone who'd mattered to Kyle, senselessly destroying the lives of good men for his own selfish ends.

Kyle stayed for the whole funeral, Ariana and Darius at his side. Darius was uncharacteristically glum during the whole funeral, his eyes downcast. More characteristically, he ignored everyone, not saying a word during the entire funeral. Ariana appeared equally somber, holding his hand quietly throughout. She'd worn a black dress for the occasion, looking quite lovely in a morose kind of way.

Soon both caskets had been lowered into the ground, and Kalibar stood at the head of Bartholos's grave, while Erasmus stood at the head of Rivin's. Both were given gold-plated shovels. Erasmus scooped up some dirt with his shovel, tossing it into the grave. Then Kalibar did the same, tossing dirt into Bartholos's grave. Then they both stepped back, and each Council member took turns doing the same. Then, members of the elite guard, those trusted with protecting their rulers, finished the somber task of burying them.

And that was that.

* * *

The next day was election day. As Erasmus had predicted, he and Kalibar won the popular vote by a landslide!

If Kyle had been impressed by the funeral, he was astounded by the coronation of Kalibar and Erasmus; the entire city celebrated in grand style, with citizens dressing in their finest clothes, hanging bright banners out of their windows congratulating their new leaders. Thousands of colorful shapes made of folded paper filled with feathergrass floated high above the rooftops all around Stridon like origami balloons. Parades of men, women, and children marched down the streets toward the Great Amphitheater, a Coliseum-like structure a few blocks away from gates of the Secula Magna. This was where the coronation was to take place.

Due to security concerns, there was a heavy military presence in and around the Amphitheater. People had to be searched before they could come in, which slowed things down quite a bit. No one seemed to mind, however; most of the city's businesses were closed for the event, save for the hotels and restaurants. Everything went without a hitch.

Kyle, being part of the "in" crowd for the first time in his life, got front-row seats inside the Amphitheater, right before the stage. Darius sat on his right, and Ariana to his left. Jax and the other Councilmen sat around them. It was quite an honor to sit among them, but a bit awkward as well; he felt out of place among the ruling elite of the Empire.

It took quite a while for the Amphitheater to fill. Unlike the Coliseum on Earth, the Great Amphitheater had a ceiling, and plush, comfortable seating. Like the Coliseum, the seats completely surrounded a central stage. It was all very rich and elegant, with luxurious red tapestries lining the walls and giant marble statues acting as support pillars. Magical lanterns hung from the ceiling, lighting the stage. A few minutes after the amphitheater had filled, these lights winked out, leaving the stage in near-complete darkness. Moments later, they flared back to life.

There, standing on the stage, was Jax and the other Councilmen. Kyle frowned, glancing from side-to-side, realizing that the Councilmen had left their seats without him knowing. He looked back to the stage, spotting Kalibar and Erasmus standing with the Councilman. He felt Ariana's warm hand grip his, and turned to see her smiling at him. He smiled back, squeezing her hand.

Jax stepped forward, raising his arms up to the crowd.

"Good afternoon, citizens of the Empire!" he shouted, turning in a slow circle to address the entire theater. The audience burst into applause, then hushed moments later when Jax raised one hand for silence. He lowered his hand.

"We are gathered here to witness the inauguration of the thirty-fourth Grand Weaver and Grand Runic of the New Empire, elected by a vote agreed upon between the people and their Council. Please rise to welcome the return of his Excellency Grand Weaver Kalibar and his Excellency Grand Runic Erasmus!" Jax stepped to the side, while Kalibar and Erasmus strode forward on the stage. The crowd rose to their feet, applause echoing throughout the theater. After a long moment, the applause died away. Kyle noticed that Kalibar was wearing dual golden eye-patches, looking quite regal despite his handicap.

Jax had Kalibar and Erasmus recant a rather long-winded and tedious oath, undoubtedly the product of centuries of pomp and tradition. He noticed that Ariana had stopped paying attention after a minute or two. When she saw Kyle looking at her, she smiled prettily. He blushed despite himself, turning his gaze back to the stage to hide his glowing cheeks. He was suddenly glad for the dim lighting over the crowd.

"...and now I pronounce you Grand Weaver Kalibar and Grand Runic Erasmus. May you guide the Empire to peace and prosperity!" Jax proclaimed. Everyone in the crowd stood up, and Kyle hastily stood as well. There was thunderous applause throughout the massive theater, with scattered cheers as Erasmus and Kalibar bowed before the crowd. The applause lasted for quite some time, fading gradually.

Kalibar stepped forward on the stage then, holding his head up high.

"I know that some of you fell asleep as we were reciting our oaths," Kalibar began, his voice echoing powerfully from the amphitheater walls. "Don't worry," he added with a wry grin, "I have no idea who you are." There was nervous laughter from the crowd at that.

"I wanted to take this unique opportunity to force you all to listen to me a little while longer," he continued. "...and entertain an old man's desire to give thanks for everything he's been given." Then he paused, lowering his head slightly. "I would hardly be standing here before you today, gifted with the responsibility of serving you all, if it weren't for three special people sitting among you." He paused, then raised his right hand to the side. "Ariana, please come forward."

Kyle blanched, glancing at Ariana. She glanced back at him, her face equally pale. But she stood up, walking up onto the stage. The crowd applauded politely as she mounted the steps and stood at Kalibar's right side. She touched Kalibar's hand to let the Grand Weaver know she was there, then faced the massive crowd, looking enormously ill at ease.

"Ariana," Kalibar intoned, "...for bravery in facing a Dire Lurker, for aiding in my escape from the enemy, and for risking your own life to save my life and the lives of your friends, I award you the Tempest Cloak!" Kalibar was handed a gray cloak by Jax.

Kalibar offered the cloak to Ariana, who took it, holding it out before herself. It shimmered in the light cast by the lanterns overhead, its edges glowing silver, like the lining of a cloud.

"This cloak was worn by elite soldiers in Ancient times," Kalibar stated, "...allowing them to draw lightning from the very heavens to attack their foes. It would also allow its wearer to fall from any height as lightly as a feather. It may be a hundred more years before we can ever hope to create such a masterpiece of runic technology. There are only a dozen left in existence; you will never need fear falling again."

The audience exploded into applause, rising to their feet enthusiastically. Ariana smiled weakly, her knuckles white as she gripped the cloak in front of her. Kalibar smiled, and motioned for Ariana to step to the side. Then he lifted his head once more, creating the illusion of staring out into the crowd.

"Kyle, please come forward."

Kyle blanched, feeling butterflies in his stomach. He stood up, a smile frozen on his lips, and forced himself to walk toward the steps leading up to the stage, as Ariana had done. He strode up to Kalibar's right side, then stared out at the crowd, feeling terror grip his throat. He hoped fervently that he didn't look as shell-shocked as he felt.

"Kyle," Kalibar exclaimed, "...for showing mercy and excellence of character, for your indomitable spirit in withstanding torture as a prisoner of the enemy, for aiding in my escape from imprisonment by the enemy, and for your willingness to sacrifice your life for your principles, I award you the Aegis of Athanasia!" He produced a gleaming silver breastplate, holding it before the crowd for a moment, then handing it to Kyle.

"The Aegis of Athanasia," Kalibar explained, "...was worn by the personal guards of the Ancient Grand Weavers and Runics. Whoever wears it will fear neither heat nor cold, or acid, or the claws of an Ulfar. May it serve you well!" There was thunderous applause, and Kyle bowed slightly before the crowd. Kalibar motioned for Kyle to stand to the side, and Kyle did so, shuffling over to Ariana and giving her a weak smile.

"Now," Kalibar stated, his voice suddenly grave, "...I highly recommend that you avoid nodding off during this final speech. Our last honoree *will* remember who you are, and you do *not* want to make him angry." He smiled then, and gestured with one hand.

"Darius, please come forward!"

Darius, wearing his usual golden armor, which was still pitted from his battle with the Dire Lurker, strode up the steps and onto the stage, halting with military precision at Kalibar's side. He faced the audience fearlessly, of course, staring calmly out into the crowd.

"Darius," Kalibar began, "...we are all heavily in your debt." He paused for a moment, putting a hand on his bodyguard's broad armored shoulder. "For saving my life, and the lives of every award recipient on this stage on countless occasions; for planning and executing our escape from imprisonment by the enemy; for risking your life and limb to slay a beast a thousand times your own size; for defeating the most powerful Weaver I've ever met; and for repeating that performance a few days later, saving the lives of every member of the Council, nearly at the sacrifice of your own, I award you the highest honor that I can bestow upon a citizen of the Empire: the Sword of the Ancients!"

A loud gasp came from the audience, and they all stood, thunderous applause rolling in from all sides. Kalibar smiled, retrieving a sword sheathed in a scabbard of the purest gold, with a shimmering diamond sparkling in the ornate gilded hilt. He held the sword – still in its scabbard – out before the crowd.

"This blade was crafted by the Ancients over two thousand years ago," he explained. "It was given to the greatest warriors of their generation, for unmatched prowess in battle. I leave it in its sheath because its blade can cut through any other substance with ease, and never grows dull." He paused for a moment, then handed the sword to Darius. "This is one of the last of its kind, one of the finest weapons in existence today. I leave it in your capable hands."

The audience exploded into another round of applause, giving the golden warrior a standing ovation. Darius bowed curtly before the crowd, then turned and bowed to Kalibar. Kyle beamed at Darius, feeling a sudden affection for the man who'd saved his skin so many times before. He'd never imagined that he'd end up even liking the man, much less considering him among his best of friends.

Kyle applauded, bursting with pride for his taciturn friend. The muscle-bound oaf was finally getting what he deserved!

* * *

That night, Kyle lay in his bed, staring up at the ceiling. He glanced at the ring on his thumb, twisting it around over and over, thinking about his parents. It seemed like a lifetime since he'd seen them last. He missed them terribly, a part of him hoping that he'd wake up tomorrow and find himself at his Dad's house again.

He sighed, leaving his ring alone at last, and rubbed his eyes sleepily. So much had happened to him in such a short amount of time, he'd spent the last few nights tossing and turning, trying to process it all.

Especially Ampir.

He rolled onto his side, staring at the wall. He still couldn't believe what he'd seen, that night when Xanos had nearly killed them all. A man in black armor, runes flashing a bright blue. Standing before him as if plucked from his dreams…dreams that were supposed to be memories from over two thousand years ago. It *had* to have been Ampir…there was no other explanation.

But that's impossible, he thought. *He'd be over two thousand years old by now!*

Kyle sighed, rolling onto his other side. It'd been Ampir protecting Kyle all along, not his ring…that much was clear. And if his ring was just a glorified transmitter – as Xanos had concluded – then that meant Ampir had been sending Kyle his dreams all along. Not to mention that, since Ampir was the only man alive who could possibly know how to teleport Kyle from Earth to this planet, it *had* to be the Ancient Battle-Weaver.

There was no other explanation.

But how had the man survived the attack of the Behemoth so many centuries ago? And why would he bring Kyle, of all people, to this planet in the first place, or want to protect him? He felt like Ampir had tried to tell him somehow, but no matter how hard he tried, he couldn't figure it out. He knew he had missed something, something terribly important.

Kyle stifled a yawn, his lids growing heavy. He rolled onto his back, closing his eyes.

If Ampir brought me here, he reasoned, *then he can send me home.*

And that idea – the mere possibility of being able to go home again – made things a little more bearable.

Kyle yawned, and this time he didn't try to suppress it. His mind, however, refused to stop working. There were so many other questions, after all. Who exactly was Xanos? Was he really a god?

Why did he want to destroy the Secula Magna? And when would he strike again? It was only a matter of time, after all. There had to be more Chosen out there like the Dead Man…and they would undoubtedly come for vengeance.

So many questions, and so few answers.

You're not going to answer any of them tonight, he reminded himself. *You need to get some sleep.*

Still, he found his thoughts turning to his friends. Of Kalibar, Darius, and Ariana…three strangers who had, in the course of a week or two, become the closest friends he'd ever had. They almost felt like a second family…no, they *were* a second family. Kalibar had signed papers to become his father, after all, as well as Ariana's. And Darius had agreed to serve as the royal bodyguard for Kalibar and his two newest family members. That meant the golden warrior wasn't about to leave anytime soon, for which Kyle was quite grateful. Being Kalibar's charge, Ariana would stay nearby as well. All of his new friends were together for the foreseeable future, sharing a bond that no one else would ever understand. It was a kind of love…not the romantic kind, but something deeper. The love between people who had risked their lives to protect each other, who had gone to hell and back for one another.

Kyle sighed, closing his eyes at last. He'd lived, and learned, more in the past week than he'd ever thought possible. Learning to sense magic, and then how to use it. Meeting and rescuing a beautiful, brave girl who'd nearly sacrificed her life to repay him. Suffering the cruelty of the Dead Man, and standing up to a self-proclaimed god, helping to defeat him and save an Empire. And last but not least, giving Kalibar a second chance at having a son, and a reason to resume his rightful place as the most powerful man in the Empire.

Kyle smiled then, picturing a man in black armor, tiny blue symbols glowing across the surface, kneeling down to face him, Kyle's own awe-struck face reflected in the man's silvery visor.

A perfect coincidence, indeed.

Chapter 27

The old man looked very sick.

He was tall, or at least he used to be. Age had bent his spine into a sharp hump, and long gangly arms hung from his shoulders. His teeth, what few remained, were rotted stumps that protruded at odd angles from his pale gums. He had a large scar running across his forehead, and smaller scars on his neck and arms. Countless warty bumps covered his body, from what little one could see of it. For he wore a thin beige cloak around his bony frame, the fabric torn and caked with mud. His odor was atrocious, making everyone around him – other than the flies – keep their distance.

The old man hobbled down the street, the worn wooden cane he held clicking on the brick sidewalk underfoot with each step. After a few minutes, he stopped in front of a massive stone building. Broad steps led up to the entrance to the building, a set of huge stone double-doors. Two guards stood at either side of this entrance, their eyes following the wretch as he shambled up the half-dozen steps to reach them.

"Move along old man," one of the guards commanded stepping forward to block his path. The guard took a step back as the wretch approached, wrinkling his nose at the foul stench. The old man stopped at the top of the steps, gazing at the guards with cataract-glazed eyes. His lips parted in a revolting smile.

"Morning gentlemen," he rasped, bowing his sparse head of dusty gray hair. "I have a bit of business here if you don't mind."

Both guards stood there, watching the old man silently. The old man smiled, bowing again.

"Much appreciated," he said, limping past the two guards. The double-doors to the building beyond opened before him seemingly by their own accord, and the old man shambled through, his cane clicking rhythmically on the stone below. The doors swung closed behind him.

The two guards stood perfectly still in the morning sun, their eyes unblinking, long after the strange old man had passed.

* * *

The old man hobbled slowly down the narrow hallways of Stridon Penitentiary, passing over a dozen guards as he went. No one moved to stop him. His path was met by countless barred doors, all of which opened themselves for him.

Down the maze-like corridors he went. There were bars on either side of the hallways now, small cells holding men in blue and orange uniforms. The prisoners stared at the wretch as he went by, choking on the stench he left as he passed. A few yelled after him, their comments less than kind.

He paid them no mind.

The old man made his way through the maze of hallways, stopping at last at a dead end, where a single, iron-wrought door blocked his path. He paused before it, then pulled on the handle. The door swung open easily, and he continued through it, allowing it to close behind him.

The wretch found himself in a small room. There were no windows, a small lantern providing the only illumination. A disheveled man sat in the center of the room on a small chair bolted into the floor. Chains bound the prisoner, wrapped around his neck on one end, and bolted to the floor at the other.

The prisoner looked up, staring at the old man standing before him. He had short black hair and a thin black mustache. A week's worth of scruffy beard graced his jawline.

"Who the hell are you?" the prisoner asked, his voice dripping with disdain. A waft of putrid air reached his nostrils, making him gag. The old man placed both hands on the head of his cane, leaning on it heavily.

"Now Orik," the wretch admonished, "show some respect for your elders."

Orik frowned, studying the old man.

"Who are you?" he asked. He glanced at the heavy metal door the old man had walked through. "And how did you get in here?"

The old man's sunken eyes regarded Orik silently for a moment. Then he smirked.

"I have a Dead Man's promise to keep," he replied at last, answering neither of Orik's questions. "A promise that is very important to *you*, I imagine."

"You know the Dead Man?" Orik asked. The old man nodded silently. "Thank god," Orik breathed, a relieved smile lighting up his face. He stood up from his chair awkwardly, the chains binding his wrists and ankles rattling. The old man smirked.

"Close enough."

"Get me out of here!" Orik commanded, leaning forward as far as he could, stopping a few feet from the wretch's face. The old man's breath smelled like a freshly exhumed corpse; Orik almost gagged again, but did not back away. He breathed through his mouth instead, his eyes locked on the old man's, his expression earnest. "Set me free!" he half-commanded, half-pleaded.

"Oh, I intend to," the old man replied, stepping up to Orik. He brought one hand up from his cane, patting Orik on the cheek. Orik shrank back despite himself; the old man's hands were ice cold, the skin dry and cracked. His fingernails were long, yellow, and chipped, with dirt caked underneath.

"I must say, I never understood the Dead Man's fondness for you," the old man mused. "Trading an eternity of power for being a puppet Emperor six years earlier...not your brightest move."

"I had it under control," Orik protested. "The Dead Man screwed up...he should have killed Kalibar when he had the chance, not imprison him!"

"Perhaps," the old man conceded. "But none of that would have been necessary if you hadn't disobeyed orders. Now if you'd been competent, you could have killed Kalibar the first time around, and I might have forgiven you. But you failed, and forced me to send a Chosen for your second attempt. Couldn't have Kalibar finding out about you, could we? But that Chosen was inexplicably killed. So we sent the Dead Man...one of our brightest, by the way...and he was also killed. Two more died trying to stop them from reaching Stridon. Now a fifth lies dead in the Tower, and after centuries of secrecy you have revealed my existence...all thanks to your pathetic ego."

"Who sent you, damn it?" Orik demanded.

"I sent me," he replied with an amused grin, tapping his cane on the floor once. "A shame you'll never understand what that means," he added, raising the butt of his cane and rapping it on Orik's forehead. Orik jerked backward, his expression darkening, but he held back his anger, his jaw clenching, then relaxing.

"Who are you?" Orik asked, as politely as he could muster. The old man sighed.

"There is value in having manners, Orik," he replied. "You can call me Sabin," he added, patting Orik on the cheek with one desiccated hand. "It's the closest to the truth, after all." He turned away from Orik then, walking slowly toward the door.

"Wait, where are you going?" Orik demanded, stretching his chains taught. "You're not leaving me here, are you?" The old man paused, turning around partway, his hunched profile half-hidden in shadow.

"Of course I am," he answered. Orik leaned forward, the chain around his neck going taught, his hands balled into fists.

"You can't!" he retorted angrily. "Xanos promised me he would make me into a Dead Man!"

The old man paused, then stepped forward, hobbling toward Orik slowly. His lips twisted into an awful smile.

"Ah, my boy," he said, patting Orik's cheek with one ancient hand, "…but that's *exactly* what you're about to become!"

* * *

The old man walked through the doorway of Orik's cell, closing the door behind him. His rotted clothes were spattered with fresh blood. Little crimson streams dribbled down his cane, the butt of it leaving bloody circles on the prison floor.

He ignored this, hobbling back the way he'd come.

He passed the men in blue and orange clothes standing in their cells, ignoring their stares. They said nothing this time, their jeers silenced by the blood on the old man's clothes. As he passed by, the bars to each cell twisted with a horrible screeching sound, popping out of their foundations and falling with a clattering noise onto the ground. The prisoners backed away from the falling metal, holding their hands over their ears.

The old man did not return their stares, ignoring them as he had before. He limped along, his cane clicking on the stone floor, the sound echoing off of the walls. The prisoners waited a long time after he'd passed before gathering the courage to step out of their cells, making their way over the fallen bars and into the hallway, far behind the old man. They watched in astonishment as their prison uniforms slowly turned from blue and orange to pure black. They followed behind from a distance, walking slowly to keep pace with their silent benefactor.

An hour later, when the old man finally stepped out of the front door into the morning sun, the two guards were still standing motionlessly at either side of the entrance. They did not turn to look at him as he passed between them.

He carefully maneuvered down the stone steps leading to the sidewalk, then turned left, walking back the way he'd come.

A long while later, long after the old man had left, the two guards fell limply to the ground, never to move again.

Epilogue

Kalibar stepped out of the shower, groping blindly for the towel he knew was hanging to his right. He felt its softness, and grabbed it, using it to wipe the water off of his body. He winced as it brushed against the innumerable tiny cuts on his face, but didn't stop. When he was done, he wrapped the towel around his waist, and searched in the blackness for the railing that had been installed on each of his walls. He found it, clutching the cool metal with one hand.

He stepped out of the bathroom, making his way slowly around the corner, turning right. After six years of living in this room during his previous tenure as Grand Weaver, he knew that his bed would be straight ahead. He let go of the railing, and walked forward carefully, sliding his feet forward across the floor with each small step. He put his hands out in front of him, waiting for his palms to touch soft bedsheets. He found himself tilting his chin up as he walked, and lowered his head. He would have to work on that.

At last he found the edge of the bed, and exhaled. He hadn't realized that he'd been holding his breath. It was going to take a while to get used to this.

He'd never told anybody, and he never would, but sometimes when he woke up – when he tried to open his eyes, and there was nothing but blackness – he would weep quietly into his pillow. He missed seeing the sky in the morning, a brilliant painting that was never the same as the one composed the day before. He missed colors, and textures. He missed being able to see people's faces. It was so hard to talk with people when he couldn't see their faces. So much communication was visual, more than he'd ever imagined.

Kalibar eased himself onto the bed, groaning as is aching

muscles complained with each movement. His recent adventure had taken more from him than just his sight. It'd already been a few days since his coronation as Grand Weaver, and even longer since he'd escaped the Dead Man's lair, but he still got awful headaches from time to time, and the side of his chest hurt if he breathed in too deeply. He was pretty sure he'd broken a few ribs. He knew that, at his age, he would never fully recover. Pain was now, and would forever be, an everyday fact of life.

He laid down on the bed, kicking the sheets down with his legs, then sitting up to pull them up over his body. He should have pulled the sheets down first, before he'd gotten into bed. If he'd been able to see, he wouldn't have made that mistake.

He sighed, trying to find a comfortable position on the bed. His doctors had mixed the extract of a narcotic-producing plant with some herbal tea…the same potion he'd given Kyle the day they'd met, for the boy's wounds. He knew that a glass of the pain-killing tea lay within his reach, on the nightstand to his left. Jenkins had, of course, seen to it. The man was brilliant, in his own way…anticipating every need. Even a half-glass would ensure him a pleasant night's sleep.

He left the glass on the nightstand.

Kalibar sighed again, bringing his hands up to his face. He ran his fingers over his lips, then up along either side of his nose. When he reached his lower eyelids, he paused, his heart skipping a beat. He'd promised himself he'd stop doing this, stop torturing himself. But he couldn't resist, running his fingertips lightly over his sunken lids, grimacing as they dipped inward. When his fingers reached his eyebrows, he stopped, dropping his hands to his sides.

He'd never considered himself a particularly vain man, but now he knew that he'd been deceiving himself. He wished he could see what he looked like, and at the same time, he was thankful that he could not.

Kalibar shifted his weight again, rolling onto his good ribs. It still hurt to take a breath in, but he ignored this as best as he could. He thought again of the glass of tea on his nightstand. He almost reached over to grab it, but stopped himself. If he drank that now, he would do it every night. Then he would do it just to get through the day. He would end up *needing* it.

He lay there, his mind starting to drift. He played with the images in his mind, the only images he had left. The last thing he'd ever seen was the Dead Man's fingers reaching toward his face again, after he'd pulled out the first eye. The manipulative bastard had been correct; Kalibar would never be able to forget his face. He shuddered at the memory.

It took a long time for his mind to wander again, swirls of color exploding in his mind's eye. Sleep came to him slowly, offering him shelter from his pain.

He jerked awake.

He waited, straining his ears. Had he heard something?

A soft *click* came from the distance, the sound of a door closing gently.

Kalibar's body went rigid, the hair on his neck standing on end. No one else was supposed to be in his room. His door locked automatically, protected by impossibly complex runic locks and wards.

Footsteps echoed off of the stone walls, getting louder with each step.

Kalibar scrambled to sit up in his bed, but his muscles did not obey him. He panicked, trying to lift his arms up off of the bed. He could feel them, but he could not move them. His heart pounded in his chest.

The footsteps grew louder as they came closer.

Kalibar tried to yell, but his lips did not move, and no sound came from his mouth. He lay in bed, a prisoner in his own body.

He was going to be murdered in his own bed, and there was nothing he could do about it!

He heard the footsteps enter his bedroom, then stop.

Kalibar gathered magic into his mind, weaving it into a tight pattern. His body was paralyzed, but his mind was still his own! He threw the lethal pattern out in the general direction the footsteps had stopped in.

Nothing happened.

Suddenly Kalibar felt *something* slam into his mind, stunning him. An immense power coursed over his body, a power unlike any he had felt before. He lost himself in that veritable ocean of power, feeling it overpower his senses.

The footsteps returned, coming right up to the side of Kalibar's bed. The power grew ever stronger, until it all but overwhelmed him.

He knew beyond a doubt that whoever was standing at his side was the source of this energy, this awesome, limitless source of magical power. If Kalibar could have trembled, if he could have fallen to his knees before this being, he would have.

He felt something heavy press down on the bed beside him. A warm hand touched his forehead. He wanted to turn his head away, but he could not. A voice whispered in his mind, soft yet firm.

You wanted to meet me.

Kalibar felt a chill run through him. He was still paralyzed, only able to breathe and swallow. He could not speak. He could not answer this being's statement. He could not ask any questions of his own.

Now you have.

Suddenly he was in rapture. The pain left his body, and ecstasy coursed through him. He felt a pressure on his face, over his empty orbits. The rapture intensified, and he cried out, his breathing fast and shallow. His lips tingled, the tips of his fingers going numb.

Then the rapture left him, and the weight lifted off of the bed. The wellspring of power vanished.

Kalibar lay there, unable to move. After what seemed like an eternity, his arms twitched, coming to life suddenly. His legs did the same, and he bent them, flexing his toes against the soft bedsheets. There was none of the usual pain in his joints, no aching in his ribs...no discomfort in his body whatsoever.

He paused, then sat up, placing his palms on the bed to brace himself.

Then, very slowly, he opened his eyes.

A pair of blue eyes stared back at him.